Change of Heart

JODI PICOULT

Change of Heart

HODDER &
STOUGHTON

LINCOLNSHIRE COUNTY COUNCIL

First published in Great Britain in 2008 by Hodder & Stoughton
An Hachette Livre UK company
First published in America in 2008 by Simon & Schuster, Inc.

1

A CIP catalogue record for this title is available from the British Library

Hardback ISBN 978 0 340 935811
Trade paperback ISBN 978 0 340 93582 8

Typeset in Berkeley Book by Palimpsest Book Production Limited, Grangemouth, Stirlingshire

Printed and bound by Mackays of Chatham Ltd, Chatham, Kent

Hodder & Stoughton policy is to use papers that are natural, renewable and
recyclable products and made from wood grown in sustainable forests. The
logging and manufacturing processes are expected to conform to the
environmental regulations of the country of origin.

Hodder & Stoughton Ltd
338 Euston Road
London NW1 3BH

www.hodder.co.uk

With love, and too much admiration to fit on these pages

*To my grandfather, Hal Friend, who has
always been brave enough to question what we believe . . .*

*And to my grandmother, Bess Friend,
who has never stopped believing in me.*

ACKNOWLEDGMENTS

Writing this book was its own form of miracle; it's very hard to write about religion responsibly, and that means taking the time to find the right people to answer your questions. For their time and their knowledge, I must thank Lori Thompson, Rabbi Lina Zerbarini, Father Peter Duganscik, Jon Saltzman, Katie Desmond, Claire Demarais, and Pastor Ted Brayman. Marjorie Rose and Joan Collison were willing to theorize about religion whenever I brought it up. Elaine Pagels is a brilliant author herself and one of the smartest women I've ever spoken with – I chased her down and begged her for a private tutorial on the Gnostic Gospels, one of her academic specialties, and would hang up the phone after each conversation with my mind buzzing and a thousand more questions to explore – surely something the Gnostics would have heartily endorsed.

Jennifer Sternick is still the attorney I'd want fighting for me, no matter what, Chris Keating provides legal information for me at blistering speed, and Chris Johnson's expertise on the appeals process for death penalty cases was invaluable.

Thanks to the medical team that didn't mind when I asked how to kill someone, instead of how to save them – among other things: Dr Paul Kispert, Dr Elizabeth Martin, Dr David Axelrod, Dr Vijay Thadani, Dr Jeffrey Parsonnet, Dr Mary Kay Wolfson, Barb Danson, James Belanger. Jacquelyn Mitchard isn't a doc, but a wonderful writer who gave me the nuts and bolts of LD kids. And a special thank-you to Dr Jenna Hirsch, who was so generous with her knowledge of cardiac surgery.

Thanks to Sindy Buzzell, and Kurt Feuer, for their individual expertise. Getting to death row was a significant challenge. My New Hampshire law enforcement contacts included Police Chief Nick Giaccone, Captain Frank Moran, Kim Lacasse, Unit Manager Tim Moquin, Lieutenant Chris Shaw, and Jeff Lyons, PIO of the New Hampshire State Prison. For finessing my trip to the Arizona State Prison Florence, thanks to Sergeant Janice Mallaburn, Deputy Warden Steve Gal, CO II Dwight Gaines, and Judy Frigo (former warden). Thanks also to Rachel Gross and Dale Baich. However, this book would not be what it was without the prisoners who opened up to me both in person and via mail: Robert Purtell, a former death row inmate; Samuel Randolph, currently on death row in Pennsylvania; and Robert Towery, currently on death row in Arizona.

Thanks to my dream team at Atria: Carolyn Reidy, Judith Curr, David Brown, Danielle Lynn, Mellony Torres, Kathleen Schmidt, Sarah Branham, Laura Stern, Gary Urda, Lisa Keim, Christine Duplessis, and everyone else who has worked so hard on my behalf. Thanks to Camille McDuffie – who was so determined to make people stop asking 'Jodi Who?' and who exceeded my expectations beyond my wildest dreams. To my favorite first reader, Jane Picoult, who I was fortunate enough to get as a mom. To Laura Gross, without whom I'd be completely adrift. To Emily Bestler, who is just so damn good at making me look brilliant.

And of course, thanks to Kyle, Jake, Sammy – who keep me asking the questions that might make the world a better place – and Tim, who makes it possible for me to do that. It just doesn't get better than all of you, all of this.

Alice laughed. 'There's no use trying,' she said. 'One can't believe impossible things.'
'I dare say you haven't had as much practice,' said the Queen. 'When I was your age I did it for half an hour a day. Why sometimes I've believed as many as six impossible things before breakfast.'

– Lewis Carroll, *Through the Looking-Glass*

PROLOGUE: 1996

June

In the beginning, I believed in second chances. How else could I account for the fact that years ago, right after the accident – when the smoke cleared and the car had stopped tumbling end over end to rest upside down in a ditch – I was still alive; I could hear Elizabeth, my little girl, crying? The police officer who had pulled me out of the car rode with me to the hospital to have my broken leg set, with Elizabeth – completely unhurt, a miracle – sitting on his lap the whole time. He'd held my hand when I was taken to identify my husband Jack's body. He came to the funeral. He showed up at my door to personally inform me when the drunk driver who ran us off the road was arrested.

The policeman's name was Kurt Nealon. Long after the trial and the conviction, he kept coming around just to make sure that Elizabeth and I were all right. He brought toys for her birthday and Christmas. He fixed the clogged drain in the upstairs bathroom. He came over after he was off duty to mow the savannah that had once been our lawn.

I had married Jack because he was the love of my life; I had planned to be with him forever. But that was before the definition of forever was changed by a man with a blood alcohol level of .22. I was surprised that Kurt seemed to understand that you might never love someone as hard as you had the first time you'd fallen; I was even more surprised to learn that maybe you *could*.

Five years later, when Kurt and I found out we were going to have a baby, I almost regretted it – the same way you stand beneath a perfect blue sky on the most glorious day of the summer and admit to yourself that all moments from here on in couldn't possibly measure up. Elizabeth had been two when Jack died; Kurt was the only father she'd ever known. They had a connection so special it sometimes made me feel I should turn away, that I was intruding. If Elizabeth was the princess, then Kurt was her knight.

The imminent arrival of this little sister (how strange is it that none of us ever imagined the new baby could be anything but a girl?) energized Kurt and Elizabeth to fever pitch. Elizabeth drew elaborate sketches of what the baby's room should look like. Kurt hired a contractor to build the addition. But then the builder's mother had a stroke and he had to move unexpectedly to Florida; none of the other crews had time to fit our job into their schedules before the baby's birth. We had a hole in our wall and rain leaking through the attic ceiling; mildew grew on the soles of our shoes.

When I was seven months pregnant, I came downstairs to find Elizabeth playing in a pile of leaves that had blown past the plastic sheeting into the living room. I was deciding between crying and raking my carpet when the doorbell rang.

He was holding a canvas roll that contained his tools, something that never left his possession, like another man might tote around his wallet. His hair brushed his shoulders and was knotted. His clothes were filthy and he smelled of snow – although it wasn't the right season. Shay Bourne arrived, unexpected, like a flyer from a summer carnival that blusters in on a winter wind, making you wonder just where it's been hiding all this time.

He had trouble speaking – the words tangled, and he had to stop and unravel them before he could say what he needed to say. 'I want to . . .' he began, and then started over: 'Do you, is there, because . . .' The effort made a fine sweat break out on his forehead. 'Is there anything I can do?' he finally managed, as Elizabeth came running toward the front door.

You can leave, I thought. I started to close the door, instinctively protecting my daughter. 'I don't think so . . .'

Elizabeth slipped her hand into mine and blinked up at him. 'There's a lot that needs to be fixed,' she said.

He got down to his knees then and spoke to my daughter easily – words that had been full of angles and edges for him a minute before now flowed like a waterfall. 'I can help,' he replied.

Kurt was always saying people are never who you think they are, that it was necessary to get a complete background check on a person before you made any promises. I'd tell him he was being too suspicious, too much the cop. After all, I had let Kurt himself into my life simply because he had kind eyes and a good heart, and even *he* couldn't argue with the results.

'What's your name?' I asked.

'Shay. Shay Bourne.'

'You're hired, Mr Bourne,' I said, the beginning of the end.

SEVEN MONTHS LATER

Michael

Shay Bourne was nothing like I expected.

I had prepared myself for a hulking brute of a man, one with hammy fists and no neck and eyes narrowed into slits. This was, after all, the crime of the century – a double murder that had captured the attention of people from Nashua to Dixville Notch; a crime that seemed all the worse because of its victims: a little girl, and a police officer who happened to be her stepfather. It was the kind of crime that made you wonder if you were safe in your own house, if the people you trusted could turn on you at any moment – and maybe because of this, New Hampshire prosecutors sought the death penalty for the first time in fifty-eight years.

Given the media blitz, there was talk of whether twelve jurors who hadn't formed a reaction to this crime could even be found, but they managed to locate us. They unearthed me in a study carrel at UNH, where I was writing a senior honors thesis in mathematics. I hadn't had a decent meal in a month, much less read a newspaper – and so I was the perfect candidate for Shay Bourne's capital murder case.

The first time we filed out of our holding pen – a small room in the superior courthouse that would begin to feel as familiar as my apartment – I thought maybe some bailiff had let us into the wrong courtroom. This defendant was small and delicately proportioned – the kind of guy who grew up being the punch line to high school jokes. He wore a tweed jacket that swallowed him whole, and the knot of his necktie squared away from him at the perpendicular, as if it were being magnetically repelled. His cuffed hands curled in his lap like small animals; his hair was shaved nearly to the skull. He stared down at his lap, even when the judge spoke his name and it hissed through the room like steam from a radiator.

The judge and the lawyers were taking care of housekeeping details when the fly came in. I noticed this for two reasons: in March, you don't see many flies in New Hampshire, and I wondered how you went about swatting one away from you when you were handcuffed and chained at the waist. Shay Bourne stared at the insect when it paused on the legal pad in front of him, and then in a jangle of metal, he raised his bound hands and crashed them down on the table to kill it.

Or so I thought, until he turned his palms upward, his fingers opened one petal at a time, and the insect went zipping off to bother someone else.

In that instant, he glanced at me, and I realized two things:

1.   He was terrified.
2.   He was approximately the same age that I was.

This double murderer, this *monster*, looked like the water polo team captain who had sat next to me in an economics seminar last semester. He resembled the deliveryman from the pizza place that had a thin crust, the kind I liked. He even reminded me of the boy I'd seen walking in the snow on my way to court, the one I'd rolled down my window for and asked if he wanted a ride. In other words, he didn't look the way I figured a killer would look, if I ever ran across one. He could have been any other kid in his twenties. He could have been me.

Except for the fact that he was ten feet away, chained at the wrists and ankles. And it was my job to decide whether or not he deserved to live.

A month later, I could tell you that serving on a jury is nothing like you see on TV. There was a lot of being paraded back and

forth between the courtroom and the jury room; there was bad
food from a local deli for lunch; there were lawyers who liked to
hear themselves talk, and trust me, the DAs were never as hot as
the girl on *Law & Order: SVU*. Even after four weeks, coming into
this courtroom felt like landing in a foreign country without a
guidebook . . . and yet, I couldn't plead ignorant just because I
was a tourist. I was expected to speak the language fluently.

Part one of the trial was finished: we had convicted Bourne.
The prosecution presented a mountain of evidence proving Kurt
Nealon had been shot in the line of duty, attempting to arrest
Shay Bourne after he'd found him with his stepdaughter, her
underwear in Bourne's pocket. June Nealon had come home from
her OB appointment to find her husband and daughter dead.
The feeble argument offered up by the defense – that Kurt had
misunderstood a verbally paralyzed Bourne; that the gun had
gone off by accident – didn't hold a candle to the overwhelming
evidence presented by the prosecution. Even worse, Bourne never
took the stand on his own behalf – which could have been
because of his poor language skills . . . or because he was not
only guilty as sin but such a wild card that his own attorneys
didn't trust him.

We were now nearly finished with part two of the trial – the
sentencing phase – or in other words, the part that separated this
trial from every other criminal murder trial for the past half century
in New Hampshire. Now that we knew Bourne had committed
the crime, did he deserve the death penalty?

This part was a little like a *Reader's Digest* condensed version
of the first one. The prosecution gave a recap of evidence presented
during the criminal trial; and then the defense got a chance to
garner sympathy for a murderer. We learned that Bourne had been
bounced around the foster care system. That when he was sixteen,
he set a fire in his foster home and spent two years in a juvenile
detention facility. He had untreated bipolar disorder, central audi-
tory processing disorder, an inability to deal with sensory over-
load, and difficulties with reading, writing, and language skills.

We heard all this from witnesses, though. Once again, Shay Bourne never took the stand to beg us for mercy.

Now, during closing arguments, I watched the prosecutor smooth down his striped tie and walk forward. One big difference between a regular trial and the sentencing phase of a capital punishment trial is who gets the last word in edgewise. I didn't know this myself, but Maureen – a really sweet older juror I was crushing on, in a wish-you-were-my-grandma kind of way – didn't miss a single *Law & Order* episode, and had practically earned her JD via Barcalounger as a result. In most trials, when it was time for closing arguments, the prosecution spoke last . . . so that whatever they said was still buzzing in your head when you went back to the jury room to deliberate. In a capital punishment sentencing phase, though, the prosecution went *first*, and then the defense got that final chance to change your mind.

Because, after all, it really *was* a matter of life or death.

He stopped in front of the jury box. 'It's been fifty-eight years in the history of the state of New Hampshire since a member of my office has had to ask a jury to make a decision as difficult and as serious as the one you twelve citizens are going to have to make. This is not a decision that any of us takes lightly, but it is a decision that the facts in this case merit, and it is a decision that must be made in order to do justice to the memories of Kurt Nealon and Elizabeth Nealon, whose lives were taken in such a tragic and despicable manner.'

He took a huge, eleven-by-fourteen photo of Elizabeth Nealon and held it up right in front of me. Elizabeth had been one of those little girls who seem to be made out of something lighter than flesh, with their filly legs and their moonlight hair; the ones you think would float off the jungle gym if not for the weight of their sneakers. But this photo had been taken after she was shot. Blood splattered her face and matted her hair; her eyes were still wide open. Her dress, hiked up when she had fallen, showed that she was naked from the waist down. 'Elizabeth Nealon will never learn how to do long division, or how to ride a horse, or do a back handspring. She'll never go to sleepaway camp or her junior prom or high school graduation. She'll never try on her first pair of high heels or experience her first kiss. She'll never bring a boy home to meet her mother; she'll never be walked down a wedding aisle by her stepfather; she'll never get to know her sister, Claire. She will miss all of these moments, and a thousand more – not because of a tragedy like a car accident or childhood leukemia – but because Shay Bourne made the decision that she didn't deserve any of these things.'

He then took another photo out from behind Elizabeth's and held it up. Kurt Nealon had been shot in the stomach. His blue uniform shirt was purpled with his blood, and Elizabeth's. During the trial we'd heard that when the paramedics reached him, he wouldn't let go of Elizabeth, even as he was bleeding out. 'Shay Bourne didn't stop at ending Elizabeth's life. He took Kurt Nealon's life, as well. And he didn't just take away Claire's father and June's husband – he took away Officer Kurt Nealon of the Lynley Police. He took away the coach of the Grafton County championship Little League team. He took away the founder of Bike Safety Day at Lynley Elementary School. Shay Bourne took away a public servant who, at the time of his death, was not just protecting his daughter . . . but protecting a citizen, and a community. A community that includes each and every one of you.'

The prosecutor placed the photos facedown on the table. 'There's a reason that New Hampshire hasn't used the death penalty for fifty-eight years, ladies and gentlemen. That's because, in spite of the many cases that come through our doors, we hadn't seen one that merited that sentence. However, by the same token, there's a reason why the good people of this state have reserved the option to use the death penalty . . . instead of overturning the capital punishment statute, as so many other states have done. And that reason is sitting in this courtroom today.'

My gaze followed the prosecutor's, coming to rest on Shay Bourne. 'If any case in the past fifty-eight years has ever cried out for the ultimate punishment to be imposed,' the attorney said, 'this is it.'

College is a bubble. You enter it for four years and forget there is a real world outside of your paper deadlines and midterm exams and beer-pong championships. You don't read the newspaper – you read textbooks. You don't watch the news – you watch Letterman. But even so, bits and snatches of the universe manage to leak in: a mother who locked her children in a car and let it roll into a lake to drown them; an estranged husband who shot his wife in front of their kids; a serial rapist who kept a teenager tied up in a basement for a month before he slit her throat. The murders of Kurt and Elizabeth Nealon were horrible, sure – but were the others any *less* horrible?

Shay Bourne's attorney stood up. 'You've found my client guilty of two counts of capital murder, and he's not contesting that. We accept your verdict; we respect your verdict. At this point in time, however, the state is asking you to wrap up this case – one that involves the death of two people – by taking the life of a third person.'

I felt a bead of sweat run down the valley between my shoulder blades.

'You're not going to make anyone safer by killing Shay Bourne. Even if you decide not to execute him, he's not going anywhere. He'll be serving two life sentences without parole.' He put his hand on Bourne's shoulder. 'You've heard about Shay Bourne's childhood. Where was he supposed to learn what all the rest of you had a chance to learn from your families? Where was he supposed to learn right from wrong, good from bad? For that matter, where was he even supposed to learn his colors and his numbers? Who was supposed to read him bedtime stories, like Elizabeth Nealon's parents had?'

The attorney walked toward us. 'You've heard that Shay Bourne has bipolar disorder, which was going untreated. You heard that he suffers from learning disabilities, so tasks that are simple for us become unbelievably frustrating for him. You've heard how hard it is for him to communicate his thoughts. These all contributed to Shay making poor choices – which you agreed with, beyond a reasonable doubt.' He looked at each of us in turn. 'Shay Bourne made poor choices,' the attorney said. 'But don't compound that by making one of your own.'

June

It was up to the jury. Again.

It's a strange thing, putting justice in the hands of twelve strangers. I had spent most of the sentencing phase of the trial watching their faces. There were a few mothers; I would catch their eye and smile at them when I could. A few men who looked like maybe they'd been in the military. And the boy, the one who barely looked old enough to shave, much less make the right decision.

I wanted to sit down with each and every one of them. I wanted to show them the note Kurt had written me after our first official date. I wanted them to touch the soft cotton cap that Elizabeth had worn home from the hospital as a newborn. I wanted to play them the answering machine message that still had their voices on it, the one I couldn't bear to erase, even though it felt like I was being cut to ribbons every time I heard it. I wanted to take them on a field trip to see Elizabeth's bedroom, with its Tinker Bell night-light and dress-up clothes; I wanted them to bury their faces in Kurt's pillow, breathe him in. I wanted them to live my life, because that was the only way they'd really know what had been lost.

That night after the closing arguments, I nursed Claire in the middle of the night and then fell asleep with her in my arms. But I dreamed that she was upstairs, distant, and crying. I climbed the stairs to the nursery, the one that still smelled of virgin wood and drying paint, and opened the door. 'I'm coming,' I said, and I crossed the threshold only to realize that the room had never been built, that I had no baby, that I was falling through the air.

Michael

Only certain people wind up on a jury for a trial like this.
Mothers who have kids to take care of, the accountants with
deadlines, doctors attending conferences – they all get excused.
What's left are retired folks, housewives, disabled folks, and
students like me, because none of us have to be any particular
place at any particular time.

Ted, our foreman, was an older man who reminded me of my
grandfather. Not in the way he looked or even the way he spoke,
but because of the gift he had of making us measure up to a task.
My grandfather had been like that, too – you wanted to be your
best around him, not because he demanded it, but because there
was nothing like that grin when you knew you'd impressed him.

My grandfather was the reason I'd been picked for this jury.
Even though I had no personal experience with murder, I knew
what it was like to lose someone you loved. You didn't get past
something like that, you got *through* it – and for that simple reason
alone, I understood more about June Nealon than she ever would
have guessed. This past winter, four years after my grandfather's
death, someone had broken into my dorm and stolen my computer,
my bike, and the only picture I had of my grandfather and me
together. The thief left behind the sterling silver frame, but when
I'd reported the theft to the cops, it was the loss of that photograph that hurt the most.

Ted waited for Maureen to reapply her lipstick, for Jack to go
to the bathroom, for everyone to take a moment for themselves
before we settled down to the task of acting as a unified body.

'Well,' he said, flattening his hands on the conference table. 'I suppose we should just get down to business.'

As it turned out, though, it was a lot easier to say that someone deserved to die for what they did than it was to take the responsibility to make that happen.

'I'm just gonna come right out and say it.' Vy sighed. 'I really have no idea what the judge told us we need to do.'

At the start of the testimony, the judge had given us nearly an hour's worth of verbal instructions. I figured there'd be a handout, too, but I'd figured wrong. 'I can explain it,' I said. 'It's kind of like a Chinese food menu. There's a whole check-list of things that make a crime punishable by death. Basically, we have to find one from column A, and one or more from column B . . . for each of the murders to qualify for the death penalty. If we check off one from column A, but none from column B . . . then the court automatically sentences him to life without parole.'

'I don't understand what's in column A or B,' Maureen said.

'I never liked Chinese food,' Mark added.

I stood up in front of the white board and picked up a dry-erase marker. COLUMN A, I wrote. PURPOSE. 'The first thing we have to decide is whether or not Bourne *meant* to kill each victim.' I turned to everyone else. 'I guess we've pretty much answered that already by convicting him of murder.'

COLUMN B. 'Here's where it gets trickier. There are a whole bunch of factors on this list.'

I began to read from the jumbled notes I'd taken during the judge's instructions:

Defendant has already been convicted of murder once before.

Defendant has been convicted of two or more different offenses for which he's served imprisonment for more than a year – a three-strikes rule.

Defendant has been convicted of two or more offenses involving distribution of drugs.

In the middle of the capital murder, the defendant risked the death of someone in addition to the victims.

The defendant committed the offense after planning and pre-meditation.

The victim was vulnerable due to old age, youth, infirmity.

The defendant committed the offense in a particularly heinous, cruel, or depraved manner that involved torture or physical abuse to the victim.

The murder was committed for the purpose of avoiding lawful arrest.

Ted stared at the board as I wrote down what I could remember. 'So if we find one from column A, and one from column B, we have to sentence him to death?'

'No,' I said. 'Because there's also a column C.'

MITIGATING FACTORS, I wrote. 'These are the reasons the defense gave as excuses.'

Defendant's capacity to appreciate what he was doing was wrong, or illegal, was impaired.

Defendant was under unusual and substantial duress.

Defendant is punishable as an accomplice in the offense which was committed by another.

Defendant was young, although not under the age of 18.

Defendant did not have a significant prior criminal record.

Defendant committed the offense under severe mental or emotional disturbance.

Another defendant equally culpable will not be punished by death.

Victim consented to the criminal conduct that resulted in death.

Other factors in the defendant's background mitigate against the death sentence.

Underneath the columns, I wrote, in large red letters: $(A + B) - C = $ SENTENCE.

Marilyn threw up her hands. 'I stopped helping my son with math homework in sixth grade.'

'No, it's easy,' I said. 'We need to agree that Bourne intended to kill each victim when he picked up that gun. That's column A. Then we need to see whether any other aggravating factor fits from column B. Like, the youth of the victim – that works for Elizabeth, right?'

Around the table, people nodded.

'If we've got A and B, then we take into account the foster care, the mental illness, stuff like that. It's just simple math. If A + B is greater than all the things the defense said, we sentence him to death. If A + B is less than all the things the defense said, then we don't.' I circled the equation. 'We just need to see how things add up.'

Put that way, it hardly had anything to do with us. It was just plugging in variables and seeing what answer we got. Put that way, it was a much easier task to perform.

1:12 P.M.

'Of course Bourne planned it,' Jack said. 'He got a job with them so that he'd be near the girl. He picked this family on purpose, and had access to the house.'

'He'd gone home for the day,' Jim said. 'Why else would he come back, if he didn't need to be there?'

'The tools,' Maureen answered. 'He left them behind, and they were his prized possessions. Remember what that shrink said? Bourne stole them out of other people's garages, and didn't understand why that was wrong, since he needed them, and they were pretty much just gathering dust otherwise.'

'Maybe he left them behind on purpose,' Ted suggested. 'If they were really so precious, wouldn't he have taken them with him?'

There was a general assent. 'Do we agree that there was substantial planning involved?' Ted asked. 'Let's see a show of hands.'

Half the room, myself included, raised our hands. Another few people slowly raised theirs, too. Maureen was the last, but the minute she did, I circled that factor on the white board.

'That's two from column B,' Ted said.

'Speaking of which . . . where's lunch?' Jack asked. 'Don't they usually bring it by now?'

Did he really want to eat? What did you order off a deli menu when you were in the process of deciding whether to end a man's life?

Marilyn sighed. 'I think we ought to talk about the fact that this poor girl was found without her underpants on.'

'I don't think we can,' Maureen said. 'Remember when we were deliberating over the verdict, and we asked the judge about Elizabeth being molested? He said then that since it wasn't being charged, we couldn't use it to find him guilty. If we couldn't bring it up then, how can we bring it up *now*?'

'This is different,' Vy said. 'He's *already* guilty.'

'The man was going to rape that little girl,' Marilyn said. 'That counts as cruel and heinous behavior to me.'

'You know, there wasn't any evidence that that's what was happening,' Mark said.

Marilyn raised an eyebrow. 'Hello?! The girl was found without her panties. Seven-year-olds don't go running around without their panties. Plus, Bourne had the underwear in his pocket . . . what else would he be doing with them?'

'Does it even matter? We already agree that Elizabeth was young when she was killed. We don't need any more from column B.' Maureen frowned. 'I think I'm confused.'

Alison, a doctor's wife who hadn't said much during the original deliberations, glanced at her. 'When I get confused, I think about that officer who testified, the one who said that he heard the little girl screaming when he was running up the stairs. *Don't shoot* – she was begging. She begged for her life.' Alison sighed. 'That sort of makes it simple again, doesn't it?'

As we all fell quiet, Ted asked for a show of hands in favor of the execution of Shay Bourne.

'No,' I said. 'We still have the rest of the equation to figure out.' I pointed to column C. 'We have to consider what the defense said.'

'The only thing I want to consider right now is where is my lunch,' Jack said.

The vote was 8–4, and I was in the minority.

3:06 P.M.

I looked around the room. This time, nine people had their hands in the air. Maureen, Vy, and I were the only ones who hadn't voted for execution.

'What is it that's keeping you from making this decision?' Ted asked.

'His age,' Vy said. 'My son's twenty-four,' she said. 'And all I can think is that he doesn't always make the best decisions. He's not done growing up yet.'

Jack turned toward me. 'You're the same age as Bourne. What are you doing with *your* life?'

I felt my face flame. 'I, um, probably I'll go to graduate school. I'm not really sure.'

'You haven't killed anyone, have you?'

Jack got to his feet. 'Let's take a bathroom break,' he suggested, and we all jumped at the chance to separate. I tossed the dry-erase marker on the table and walked to the window. Outside, there were courthouse employees eating their lunch on benches. There were clouds caught in the twisted fingers of the trees. And there were television vans with satellites on their roofs, waiting to hear what we'd say.

Jim sat down beside me, reading the Bible that seemed to be an extra appendage. 'You religious?'

'I went to parochial school a long time ago.' I faced him. 'Isn't there something in there about turning the other cheek?'

Jim pursed his lips and read aloud. '*If thy right eye offend thee, pluck it out, and cast it from thee; for it is profitable for thee that one of thy members should perish, and not that thy whole body should be cast into hell.* When one apple's gone bad, you don't let it ruin the whole bunch.' He passed the Bible to me. 'See for yourself.'

I looked at the quote, and then closed the book. I didn't know nearly as much as Jim did about religion, but it seemed to me that no matter what Jesus said in that passage, he might have taken it back after being sentenced to death himself. In fact, it seemed to me that if Jesus were here in this jury room, he'd be having just as hard a time doing what needed to be done as I was.

4:02 P.M.

Ted had me write Yes and No on the board, and then he polled us, one by one, as I wrote our names in each of the columns.

Jim?
Yes.
Alison?
Yes.
Marilyn?
Yes.
Vy?
No.

I hesitated, then wrote my own name beneath Vy's.

'You agreed to vote for death if you had to,' Mark said. 'They asked each of us before we got picked for the jury if we could do that.'

'I know.' I *had* agreed to vote for the death penalty if the case merited it. I just hadn't realized it was going to be this difficult to do.

Vy buried her face in her hands. 'When my son used to hit his little brother, I didn't smack him and say 'Don't hit.' It felt hypocritical then. And it feels hypocritical now.'

'Vy,' Marilyn said quietly, 'what if it had been *your* seven-year-old who was killed?' She reached onto the table, where we had piled up transcripts and evidence, and took the same picture of Elizabeth Nealon that the prosecutor had presented during his closing argument. She set it down in front of Vy, smoothed its glossy surface.

After a minute, Vy stood up heavily and took the marker out of my hand. She wiped her name off the No column and wrote it beneath Marilyn's, with the ten other jurors who'd voted Yes.

'Michael,' Ted said.

I swallowed.

'What do you need to see, to hear? We can help you find it.' He reached for the box that held the bullets from ballistics, the bloody clothing, the autopsy reports. He let photos from the crime scene spill through his hands like ribbons. On some of them, there was so much blood, you could barely see the victim lying beneath its sheen. 'Michael,' Ted said, 'do the math.'

I faced the white board, because I couldn't stand the heat of their eyes on me. Next to the list of names, mine standing alone, was the original equation I'd set up for us when we first came into this jury room: $(A + B) - C = \text{SENTENCE}$.

What I liked about math was that it was safe. There was always a right answer – even if it was imaginary.

This, though, was an equation where math did not hold up. Because $A + B$ – the factors that had led to the deaths of Kurt and Elizabeth Nealon – would always be greater than C. You couldn't bring them back, and there was no sob story in the world big enough to erase that truth.

In the space between yes and no, there's a lifetime. It's the difference between the path you walk and one you leave behind; it's the gap between who you thought you could be and who you really are; it's the legroom for the lies you'll tell yourself in the future.

I erased my name on the board. Then I took the pen and rewrote it, becoming the twelfth and final juror to sentence Shay Bourne to death.

'If God did not exist, it would be necessary to invent him.'

— *VOLTAIRE*, FOR AND AGAINST

ELEVEN YEARS LATER

Lucius

I have no idea where they were keeping Shay Bourne before they brought him to us. I knew he was an inmate here at the state prison in Concord – I can still remember watching the news the day his sentence was handed down and scrutinizing an outside world that was starting to fade in my mind: the rough stone of the prison exterior; the golden dome of the statehouse; even just the general shape of a door that wasn't made of metal and wire mesh. His conviction was the subject of great discussion on the pod all those years ago – where do you keep an inmate who's been sentenced to death when your state hasn't had a death row prisoner for ages?

Rumor had it that in fact, the prison did have a pair of death row cells – not too far from my own humble abode in the Secure Housing Unit on I-tier. Crash Vitale – who had something to say about everything, although no one usually bothered to listen – told us that the old death row cells were stacked with the thin, plastic slabs that pass for mattresses here. I wondered for a while what had happened to all those extra mattresses after Shay arrived. One thing's for sure, no one offered to give them to us.

Moving cells is routine in prison. They don't like you to become too attached to anything. In the fifteen years I've been here, I have been moved eight different times. The cells, of course, all look alike – what's different is who's next to you, which is why Shay's arrival on I-tier was of great interest to all of us.

This, in itself, was a rarity. The six inmates in I-tier were radically different from one another; for one man to spark curiosity in all of us was nothing short of a miracle. Cell 1 housed Joey Kunz, a pedophile who was at the bottom of the pecking order. In Cell 2 was Calloway Reece, a card-carrying member of the Aryan Brotherhood. Cell 3 was me, Lucius DuFresne. Four and five were empty, so we knew the new inmate would be put in one of them – the only question was whether he'd be closer to me, or to the guys in the last three cells: Texas Wridell, Pogie Simmons, and Crash, the self-appointed leader of I-tier.

As Shay Bourne was escorted in by a phalanx of six correctional officers wearing helmets and flak jackets and face shields, we all came forward in our cells. The COs passed by the shower stall, shuffled by Joey and Calloway, and then paused right in front of me, so I could get a good look. Bourne was small and slight, with close-cropped brown hair and eyes like the Caribbean Sea. I knew about the Caribbean, because it was the last vacation I'd taken with Adam. I was glad I didn't have eyes like that. I wouldn't want to look in the mirror every day and be reminded of a place I'd never see again.

Then Shay Bourne turned to me.

Maybe now would be a good time to tell you what I look like. My face was the reason the COs didn't look me in the eye; it was why I sometimes preferred to be hidden inside this cell. The sores were scarlet and purple and scaly. They spread from my forehead to my chin.

Most people winced. Even the polite ones, like the eighty-year-old missionary who brought us pamphlets once a month, always did a double take, as if I looked even worse than he remembered. But Shay just met my gaze and nodded at me, as if I were no different than anyone else.

I heard the door of the cell beside mine slide shut, the clink of chains as Shay stuck his hands through the trap to have his cuffs removed. The COs left the pod, and almost immediately Crash started in. 'Hey, Death Row,' he yelled.

There was no response from Shay Bourne's cell.

'Hey, when Crash talks, you answer.'

'Leave him alone, Crash,' I sighed. 'Give the poor guy five minutes to figure out what a moron you are.'

'Ooh, Death Row, better watch it,' Calloway said. 'Lucius is kissing up to you, and his last boyfriend's six feet under.'

There was the sound of a television being turned on, and then Shay must have plugged in the headphones that we were all required to have, so we didn't have a volume war with one another. I was a little surprised that a death row prisoner would have been able to purchase a television from the canteen, same as us. It would have been a thirteen-inch one, specially made for us wards of the state by Zenith, with a clear plastic shell around its guts and cathodes, so that the COs would be able to tell if you were extracting parts to make weapons.

While Calloway and Crash united (as they often did) to humiliate me, I pulled out my own set of headphones and turned on my television. It was five o'clock, and I didn't like to miss *Oprah*. But when I tried to change the channel, nothing happened. The screen flickered, as if it were resetting to channel 22, but channel 22 looked just like channel 3 and channel 5 and CNN and the Food Network.

'Hey.' Crash started to pound on his door. 'Yo, CO, the cable's down. We got rights, you know . . .'

Sometimes headphones don't work well enough.

I turned up the volume and watched a local news network's coverage of a fund-raiser for a nearby children's hospital up near Dartmouth College. There were clowns and balloons and even two Red Sox players signing autographs. The camera zeroed in on a girl with fairy-tale blond hair and blue half-moons beneath her eyes, just the kind of child they'd televise to get you to open up your wallet. 'Claire Nealon,' the reporter's voice-over said, 'is waiting for a heart.'

Boo-hoo, I thought. Everyone's got problems. I took off my headphones. If I couldn't listen to *Oprah*, I didn't want to listen at all.

Which is why I was able to hear Shay Bourne's very first word on I-tier. 'Yes,' he said, and just like that, the cable came back on.

*   *   *

You have probably noticed by now that I am a cut above most of the cretins on I-tier, and that's because I don't really belong here. It was a crime of passion – the only discrepancy is that I focused on the *passion* part and the courts focused on the *crime*. But I ask you, what would *you* have done, if the love of your life found a new love of *his* life – someone younger, thinner, better-looking?

The irony, of course, is that no sentence imposed by a court for homicide could trump the one that's ravaged me in prison. My last CD4+ was taken six months ago, and I was down to seventy-five cells per cubic millimeter of blood. Someone without HIV would have a normal T cell count of a thousand cells or more, but the virus becomes part of these white blood cells. When the white blood cells reproduce to fight infection, the virus reproduces, too. As the immune system gets weak, the more likely I am to get sick, or to develop an opportunistic infection like PCP, toxoplasmosis, or CMV. The doctors say I won't die from AIDS – I'll die from pneumonia or TB or a bacterial infection in the brain; but if you ask me, that's just semantics. Dead is dead.

I was an artist by vocation, and now by avocation – although it's been considerably more challenging to get my supplies in a place like this. Where I had once favored Winsor & Newton oils and red sable brushes, linen canvases I stretched myself and coated with gesso, I now used whatever I could get my hands on. I had my nephews draw me pictures on card stock in pencil that I erased so that I could use the paper over again. I hoarded the foods that produced pigment. Tonight I had been working on a portrait of Adam, drawn of course from memory, because that was all I had left. I had mixed some red ink gleaned from a Skittle with a dab of toothpaste in the lid of a juice bottle, and coffee with a bit of water in a second lid, and then I'd combined them to get just the right shade of his skin – a burnished, deep molasses.

I had already outlined his features in black – the broad brow, the strong chin, the hawk's nose. I'd used a shank to shave ebony curls from a picture of a coal mine in a *National Geographic* and added a dab of shampoo to make a chalky paint. With the broken tip of a pencil, I had transferred the color to my makeshift canvas.

God, he was beautiful.

It was after three a.m., but to be honest, I don't sleep much. When I do, I find myself getting up to go to the bathroom – as little as I eat these days, food passes through me at lightning speed. I get sick to my stomach; I get headaches. The thrush in my mouth and throat makes it hard to swallow. Instead, I use my insomnia to fuel my artwork.

Tonight, I'd had the sweats. I was soaked through by the time I woke up, and after I stripped off my sheets and my scrubs, I didn't want to lie down on the mattress again. Instead, I had pulled out my painting and started re-creating Adam. But I got side-tracked by the other portraits I'd finished of him, hanging on my cell wall: Adam standing in the same pose he'd first struck when he was modeling for the college art class I taught; Adam's face when he opened his eyes in the morning. Adam, looking over his shoulder, the way he'd been when I shot him.

'I need to do it,' Shay Bourne said. 'It's the only way.'

He had been utterly silent since this afternoon's arrival on I-tier; I wondered who he was having a conversation with at this hour of the night. But the pod was empty. Maybe he was having a nightmare. 'Bourne?' I whispered. 'Are you okay?'

'Who's . . . there?'

The words were hard for him – not quite a stutter; more like each syllable was a stone he had to bring forth. 'I'm Lucius. Lucius DuFresne,' I said. 'You talking to someone?'

He hesitated. 'I *think* I'm talking to you.'

'Can't sleep?'

'I can sleep,' Shay said. 'I just don't want to.'

'You're luckier than I am, then,' I replied.

It was a joke, but he didn't take it that way. 'You're no luckier than me, and I'm no unluckier than you,' he said.

Well, in a way, he was right. I may not have been handed down the same sentence as Shay Bourne, but like him, I would die within the walls of this prison – sooner rather than later.

'Lucius,' he said. 'What are *you* doing?'

'I'm painting.'

There was a beat of silence. 'Your cell?'

'No. A portrait.'

'Why?'

'Because I'm an artist.'

'Once, in school, an art teacher said I had classic lips,' Shay said. 'I still don't know what that means.'

'It's a reference to the ancient Greeks and Romans,' I explained. 'And the art that we see represented on—'

'Lucius? Did you see on TV today . . . the Red Sox . . .'

Everyone on I-tier had a team they followed, myself included. We each kept meticulous score of their league standings, and we debated the fairness of umpire and ref calls as if they were law and we were Supreme Court judges. Sometimes, like us, our teams had their hopes dashed; other times we got to share their World Series. But it was still preseason; there hadn't been any televised games today.

'Schilling was sitting at a table,' Shay added, still struggling to find the right words. 'And there was a little girl—'

'You mean the fund-raiser? The one up at the hospital?'

'That little girl,' Shay said. 'I'm going to give her my heart.'

Before I could respond, there was a loud crash and the thud of flesh smacking against the concrete floor. 'Shay?' I called. 'Shay?!'

I pressed my face up against the Plexiglas. I couldn't see Shay at all, but I heard something rhythmic smacking his cell door. 'Hey!' I yelled at the top of my lungs. 'Hey, we need help down here!'

The others started to wake up, cursing me out for disturbing their rest, and then falling silent with fascination. Two officers stormed into I-tier, still Velcroing their flak jackets. One of them, CO Kappaletti, was the kind of man who'd taken this job so that he'd always have someone to put down. The other, CO Smythe, had never been anything but professional toward me. Kappaletti stopped in front of my cell. 'DuFresne, if you're crying wolf—'

But Smythe was already kneeling in front of Shay's cell. 'I think Bourne's having a seizure.' He reached for his radio and the electronic door slid open so that other officers could enter.

'Is he breathing?' one said.

'Turn him over, on the count of three . . .'

The EMTs arrived and wheeled Shay past my cell on a gurney – a stretcher with restraints across the shoulders, belly, and legs that was used to transport inmates like Crash who were too much trouble even cuffed at the waist and ankles; or inmates who were too sick to walk to the infirmary. I always assumed I'd leave I-tier on one of those gurneys. But now I realized that it looked a lot like the table Shay would one day be strapped onto for his lethal injection.

The EMTs had pushed an oxygen mask over Shay's mouth that frosted with each breath he took. His eyes had rolled up in their sockets, white and blind. 'Do whatever it takes to bring him back,' CO Smythe instructed; and that was how I learned that the state will save a dying man just so that they can kill him later.

Michael

There was a great deal that I loved about the Church.

Like the feeling I got when two hundred voices rose to the rafters during Sunday Mass in prayer. Or the way my hand still shook when I offered the host to a parishioner. I loved the double take on the face of a troubled teenager when he drooled over the 1969 Triumph Trophy motorcycle I'd restored – and then found out I was a priest; that being cool and being Catholic were not mutually exclusive.

Even though I was clearly the junior priest at St Catherine's, we were one of only four parishes to serve all of Concord, New Hampshire. There never seemed to be enough hours in the day. Father Walter and I would alternate officiating at Mass or hearing confession; sometimes we'd be asked to drop in and teach a class at the parochial school one town over. There were always parishioners to visit who were ill or troubled or lonely; there were always rosaries to be said. But I looked forward to even the humblest act – sweeping the vestibule, or rinsing the vessels from the Eucharist in the sacrarium so that no drop of Precious Blood wound up in the Concord sewers.

I didn't have an office at St Catherine's. Father Walter did, but then he'd been at the parish so long that he seemed as much a part of it as the rosewood pews and the velveteen drapes at the altar. Although he kept telling me he'd get around to clearing out a spot for me in one of the old storage rooms, he tended to nap after lunch, and who was I to wake up a man in his seventies and tell him to get a move on? After a while, I gave up asking and instead set a small desk up inside a broom closet. Today, I was supposed to be writing a homily – if I could get it down to seven minutes, I knew the older members of the congregation wouldn't fall asleep – but instead, my mind kept straying to one of our youngest members. Hannah Smythe was the first baby I baptized at St Catherine's. Now, just one year later, the infant had been hospitalized repeatedly. Without warning, her throat would simply close, and her frantic parents would rush her to the ER for intubation, where the vicious cycle would start all over again. I offered up a quick prayer to God to lead the doctors to cure Hannah. I was just finishing up with the sign of the cross when a small, silver-haired lady approached my desk. 'Father Michael?'

'Mary Lou,' I said. 'How are you doing?'

'Could I maybe talk to you for a few minutes?'

Mary Lou Huckens could talk not only for a few minutes; she was likely to go on for nearly an hour. Father Walter and I had an unwritten policy to rescue each other from her effusive praise after Mass. 'What can I do for you?'

'Actually, I feel a little silly about this,' she admitted. 'I just wanted to know if you'd bless my bust.'

I smiled at her. Parishioners often asked us to offer a prayer over a devotional item. 'Sure. Have you got it with you?'

She gave me an odd look. 'Well, of course I do.'

'Great. Let's see it.'

She crossed her hands over her chest. 'I hardly think *that's* necessary!'

I felt heat flood my cheeks as I realized what she actually wanted me to bless. 'I-I'm sorry . . .' I stammered. 'I didn't mean . . .'

Her eyes filled with tears. 'They're doing a lumpectomy tomorrow, Father, and I'm terrified.'

I stood up and put my arm around her, walked her a few yards to the closest pew, offered her Kleenex. 'I'm sorry,' she said. 'I don't know who else to talk to. If I tell my husband I'm scared, he'll get scared, too.'

'You know who to talk to,' I said gently. 'And you know He's always listening.' I touched the crown of her head. 'Omnipotent and eternal God, the everlasting Salvation of those who believe, hear us on behalf of Thy servant Mary Lou, for whom we beg the aid of Thy pitying mercy, that with her bodily health restored, she may give thanks to Thee in Thy church. Through Christ our Lord, amen.'

'Amen,' Mary Lou whispered.

That's the other thing I love about the Church: you never know what to expect.

Lucius

When Shay Bourne returned to I-tier after three days in the hospital infirmary, he was a man with a mission. Every morning, when the officers came to poll us to see who wanted a shower or time in the yard, Shay would ask to speak to Warden Coyne. 'Fill out a request,' he was told, over and over, but it just didn't seem to sink in. When it was his turn in the little caged kennel that was our exercise yard, he'd stand in the far corner, looking toward the opposite side of the prison, where the administrative offices were housed, and he'd yell his request at the top of his lungs. When he was brought his dinner, he'd ask if the warden had agreed to talk to him.

'You know why he was moved to I-tier?' Calloway said one day when Shay was bellowing in the shower for an audience with the warden. 'Because he made everyone else on his last tier go deaf.'

'He's a retard,' Crash answered. 'Can't help how he acts. Kinda like our own diaper sniper. Right, Joey?'

'He's not mentally challenged,' I said. 'He's probably got double the IQ that you do, Crash.'

'Shut the fuck up, fruiter,' Calloway said. 'Shut up, all of you!' The urgency in his voice silenced us. Calloway knelt at the door of his cell, fishing with a braided string pulled out of his blanket and tied at one end to a rolled magazine. He cast into the center of the catwalk – risky behavior, since the COs would be back any minute. At first we couldn't figure out what he was doing – when we fished, it was with one another, tangling our lines to pass along anything from a paperback book to a Hershey's bar – but then we noticed the small, bright oval on the floor. God only knew why a bird would make a nest in a hellhole like this, but one had a few months back, after flying in through the exercise yard. One egg had fallen out and cracked; the baby robin lay on its side, unfinished, its thin, wrinkled chest working like a piston.

Calloway reeled the egg in, inch by inch. 'It ain't gonna live,' Crash said. 'Its mama won't want it now.'

'Well, *I* do,' Calloway said.

'Put it somewhere warm,' I suggested. 'Wrap it up in a towel or something.'

'Use your T-shirt,' Joey added.

'I don't take advice from a cho-mo,' Calloway said, but then, a moment later: 'You think a T-shirt will work?'

While Shay yelled for the warden, we all listened to Calloway's play-by-play: The robin was wrapped in a shirt. The robin was tucked inside his left tennis shoe. The robin was pinking up. The robin had opened its left eye for a half second.

We all had forgotten what it was like to care about something so much that you might not be able to stand losing it. The first year I was in here, I used to pretend that the full moon was my pet, that it came once a month just to me. And this past summer, Crash had taken to spreading jam on the louvers of his vent to cultivate a colony of bees, but that was less about husbandry than his misguided belief that he could train them to swarm Joey in his sleep.

'Cowboys comin' to lock 'em up,' Crash said, fair warning that the COs were getting ready to enter the pod again. A moment later the doors buzzed open; they stood in front of the shower cell waiting for Shay to stick his hands through the trap to be cuffed for the twenty-foot journey back to his own cell.

'They don't know what it could be,' CO Smythe said. 'They've ruled out pulmonary problems and asthma. They're saying maybe an allergy – but there's nothing in her room anymore, Rick, it's bare as a cell.'

Sometimes the COs talked to one another in front of us. They never spoke to inmates directly about their lives, and that actually was fine. We didn't want to know that the guy strip-searching us had a son who scored the winning goal in his soccer game last Thursday. Better to take the humanity out of it.

'They said,' Smythe continued, 'that her heart can't keep taking this kind of stress. And neither can I. You know what it's like to see your baby with all these bags and wires coming out of her?'

The second CO, Whitaker, was a Catholic who liked to include, on my dinner tray, handwritten scripture verses that denounced homosexuality. 'Father Walter led a prayer for Hannah on Sunday. He said he'd be happy to visit you at the hospital.'

'There's nothing a priest can say that I want to hear,' Smythe muttered. 'What kind of God would do this to a baby?'

Shay's hands slipped through the trap of the shower cell to be cuffed, and then the door was opened. 'Did the warden say he'd meet with me?'

'Yeah,' Smythe said, leading Shay toward his cell. 'He wants you to come for high friggin' tea.'

'I just need five minutes with him—'

'You're not the only one with problems,' Smythe snapped. 'Fill out a request.'

'I *can't*,' Shay replied.

I cleared my throat. 'Officer? Could I have a request form, too, please?'

He finished locking Shay up, then took one out of his pocket and stuffed it into the trap of my cell.

Just as the officers exited the tier, there was a small, feeble chirp.

'Shay?' I asked. 'Why not just fill out the request slip?'

'I can't get my words to come out right.'

'I'm sure the warden doesn't care about grammar.'

'No, it's when I write. When I start, the letters all get tangled.'

'Then tell me, and I'll write the note.'

There was a silence. 'You'd do that for me?'

'Will you two cut the soap opera?' Crash said. 'You're making me sick.'

'Tell the warden,' Shay dictated, 'that I want to donate my heart, after he kills me. I want to give it to a girl who needs it more than I do.'

I leaned the ticket up against the wall of the cell and wrote in pencil, signed Shay's name. I tied the note to the end of my own fishing line and swung it beneath the narrow opening of his cell door. 'Give this to the officer who makes rounds tomorrow morning.'

'You know, Bourne,' Crash mused, 'I don't know what to make of you. I mean, on the one hand, you're a child-killing piece of shit. You might as well be fungus growing on Joey, for what you done to that little girl. But on the other hand, you took down a cop, and I for one am truly grateful there's one less pig in the world. So how am I supposed to feel? Do I hate you, or do I give you my respect?'

'Neither,' Shay said. 'Both.'

'You know what I think? Baby killing beats anything good you might have done.' Crash stood up at the front of his cell and began to bang a metal coffee mug against the Plexiglas. 'Throw him out. Throw him out. *Throw him out!*'

Joey – unused to being even one notch above low-man-on-the-totem-pole – was the first to join in the singing. Then Texas and Pogie started in, because they did whatever Crash told them to do.

Throw him out.

Throw him out.

Whitaker's voice bled through the loudspeaker. 'You got a problem, Vitale?'

'I don't got a problem. This punk-ass child killer here's the one with the problem. I tell you what, Officer. You let me out for five minutes, and I'll save the good taxpayers of New Hampshire the trouble of getting rid of him—'

'Crash,' Shay said softly. 'Cool off.'

I was distracted by a whistling noise coming from my tiny sink. I had no sooner stood up to investigate than the water burst out of the spigot. This was remarkable on two counts – normally, the water pressure was no greater than a trickle, even in the showers. And the water that was splashing over the sides of the metal bowl was a deep, rich red.

'Fuck!' Crash yelled. 'I just got soaked!'

'Man, that looks like blood,' Pogie said, horrified. 'I'm not washing up in that.'

'It's in the toilets, too,' Texas added.

We all knew our pipes were connected. The bad news about this was that you literally could not get away from the shit brought down by the others around you. On the bright side, you could actually flush a note down the length of the pod; it would briefly appear in the next cell's bowl before heading through the sewage system. I turned and looked into my toilet. The water was as dark as rubies.

'Holy crap,' Crash said. 'It ain't blood. It's *wine*.' He started to crow like a madman. 'Taste it, ladies. Drinks are on the house.'

I waited. I did not drink the tap water in here. As it was, I had a feeling that my AIDS medications, which came on a punch card, might be some government experiment done on expendable inmates . . . I wasn't about to imbibe from a water treatment system run by the same administration. But then I heard Joey start laughing, and Calloway slurping from the faucet, and Texas and Pogie singing drinking songs. In fact, the entire mood of the tier changed so radically that CO Whitaker's voice boomed over the intercom, confused by the visions on the monitors. 'What's going on in there?' he asked. 'Is there a water main leak?'

'You could say that,' Crash replied. 'Or you could say we got us a powerful thirst.'

'Come on in, CO,' Pogie added. 'We'll buy the next round.'

Everyone seemed to find this hilarious, but then, they'd all downed nearly a half gallon of whatever this fluid was by now. I dipped my finger into the dark stream that was still running strong from my sink. It could have been iron or manganese, but it was true – this water smelled like sugar, and dried sticky. I bent my head to the tap and drank tentatively from the flow.

Adam and I had been closet sommeliers, taking trips to the California vineyards. To that end, for my birthday that last year, Adam had gotten me a 2001 Dominus Estate cabernet sauvignon. We were going to drink it on New Year's Eve. Weeks later, when I came in and found them, twisted together like jungle vines, that bottle was there, too – tipped off the nightstand and staining the bedroom carpet, like blood that had already been spilled.

If you've been in prison as long as I have, you've experienced a good many innovative highs. I've drunk hooch distilled from fruit juice and bread and Jolly Rancher candies; I've huffed spray deodorant; I've smoked dried banana peels rolled up in a page of the Bible. But this was like none of those. This was honest-to-God wine.

I laughed. But before long I began to sob, tears running down my face for what I had lost, for what was now literally coursing through my fingers. You can only miss something you remember having, and it had been so long since creature comforts had been part of my ordinary life. I filled a plastic mug with wine and drank it down; I did this over and over again until it became easier to forget the fact that all extraordinary things must come to an end – a lesson I could have lectured on, given my history.

By now, the COs realized that there had been some snafu with the plumbing. Two of them came onto the tier, fuming, and paused in front of my cell. 'You,' Whitaker commanded. 'Cuffs.'

I went through the rigmarole of having my wrists bound through the open trap so that when Whitaker had my door buzzed open I could be secured by Smythe while he investigated. I watched over my shoulder as Whitaker touched a pinky to the stream of wine and held it up to his tongue. 'Lucius,' he said, 'what is this?'

'At first I thought it was a cabernet, Officer,' I said. 'But now I'm leaning toward a cheap merlot.'

'The water comes from the town reservoir,' Smythe said. 'Inmates can't mess with that.'

'Maybe it's a miracle,' Crash sang. 'You know all about miracles, don't you, Officer Bible-thumper?'

My cell door was closed and my hands freed. Whitaker stood on the catwalk in front of our cells. 'Who did this?' he asked, but nobody was listening. 'Who's responsible?'

'Who cares?' Crash replied.

'So help me, if one of you doesn't fess up, I'll have maintenance turn off your water for the next week,' Whitaker threatened.

Crash laughed. 'The ACLU needs a poster child, Whit.'

As the COs stormed off the tier, we were all laughing. Things that weren't humorous became funny; I didn't even mind listening to Crash. At some point, the wine trickled and dried up, but by then, Pogie had already passed out cold, Texas and Joey were singing 'Danny Boy' in harmony, and I was fading fast. In fact, the last thing I remember is Shay asking Calloway what he was going to name his bird, and Calloway's answer: Batman the Robin. And Calloway challenging Shay to a chugging contest, but Shay saying he would sit that one out. That actually, he didn't drink.

For two days after the water on I-tier had turned into wine, a steady stream of plumbers, scientists, and prison administrators visited our cells. Apparently, we were the only unit within the prison where this had happened, and the only reason anyone in power even believed it was because when our cells were tossed, the COs confiscated the shampoo bottles and milk containers and even plastic bags that we had all innovatively used to store some extra wine before it had run dry; and because swabs taken in the pipes revealed a matching substance. Although nobody would officially give us the results of the lab testing, rumor had it that the liquid in question was definitely not tap water.

Our exercise and shower privileges were revoked for a week, as if this had been our fault in the first place, and forty-three hours passed before I was allowed a visit from the prison nurse, Alma, who smelled of lemons and linen; and who had a massive coiled tower of braided hair that, I imagined, required architectural intervention in order for her to sleep. Normally, she came twice a day to bring me a card full of pills as bright and big as dragon-flies. She also spread cream on inmates' fungal foot infections, checked teeth that had been rotted out by crystal meth, and did anything else that didn't require a visit to the infirmary. I admit to faking illness several times so that Alma would take my temper-ature or blood pressure. Sometimes, she was the only person who touched me for weeks.

'So,' she said, as she was let into my cell by CO Smythe. 'I hear things have been pretty exciting on I-tier. You gonna tell me what happened?'

'Would if I could,' I said, and then glanced at the officer accom-panying her. 'Or maybe I wouldn't.'

'I can only think of one person who ever turned water into wine,' she said, 'and my pastor will tell you it didn't happen in the state prison this Monday.'

'Maybe your pastor can suggest that next time, Jesus try a nice full-bodied Syrah.'

Alma laughed and stuck a thermometer into my mouth. Over her back, I stared at CO Smythe. His eyes were red, and instead of watching me to make sure I didn't do anything stupid, like take Alma hostage, he was staring at the wall behind my head, lost in thought.

The thermometer beeped. 'You're still running a fever.'

'Tell me something I don't know,' I replied. I felt blood pool under my tongue, courtesy of the sores that were part and parcel of this horrific disease.

'You taking those meds?'

I shrugged. 'You see me put them in my mouth every day, don't you?'

Alma knew there were as many different ways for a prisoner to kill himself as there were prisoners. 'Don't you check out on me, Jupiter,' she said, rubbing something viscous on the red spot on my forehead that had led to this nickname. 'Who else would tell me what I miss on *General Hospital*?'

'That's a pretty paltry reason to stick around.'

'I've heard worse.' Alma turned to CO Smythe. 'I'm all set here.'

She left, and the control booth slid the door home again, the sound of metallic teeth gnashing shut. 'Shay,' I called out. 'You awake?'

'I am now.'

'Might want to cover your ears,' I offered.

Before Shay could ask me why, Calloway let out the same explosive run of curses he always did when Alma tried to get within five feet of him. 'Get the fuck out, nigger,' he yelled. 'Swear to God, I'll fuck you up if you put your hand on me—'

CO Smythe pinned him against the side of his cell. 'For Christ's sake, Reece,' he said. 'Do we have to go through this every single day for a goddamn Band-Aid?'

'We do if that black bitch is the one putting it on.'

Calloway had been convicted of burning a synagogue to the ground seven years ago. He sustained head injuries and needed massive skin grafts on his arms, but he considered the mission a success because the terrified rabbi had fled town. The grafts still needed checking; he'd had three surgeries alone in the past year.

'You know what,' Alma said, 'I don't really care if his arms rot off.'

She didn't, that much was true. But she did care about being called a nigger. Every time Calloway hurled that word at her, she'd stiffen. And after she visited Calloway, she moved a little more slowly down the pod.

I knew exactly how she felt. When you're different, sometimes you don't see the millions of people who accept you for what you are. All you notice is the one person who doesn't.

'I got hep C because of you,' Calloway said, although he'd probably gotten it from the blade of the barber's razor, like the other inmates who'd contracted it in prison. 'You and your filthy nigger hands.'

Calloway was being particularly awful today, even for Calloway. At first I thought he was cranky like the rest of us, because our

meager privileges had been taken away. But then it hit me –
Calloway couldn't let Alma into his house, because she might find
the bird. And if she found the bird, CO Smythe would confiscate
it.

'What do you want to do?' Smythe asked Alma.

She sighed. 'I'm not going to fight him.'

'That's right,' Calloway crowed. 'You know who's boss. *Rahowa!*'

At his call, short for Racial Holy War, inmates from all over the
Secure Housing Unit began to holler. In a state as white as New
Hampshire, the Aryan Brotherhood ran the prison population.
They controlled drug deals done behind bars; they tattooed one
another with shamrocks and lightning bolts and swastikas. To be
jumped into the gang, you had to kill someone sanctioned by the
Brotherhood – a black man, a Jew, a homosexual, or anyone else
whose existence was considered an affront to your own.

The sound became deafening. Alma walked past my cell, Smythe
following. As they passed Shay, he called out to the officer, 'Look
inside.'

'I know what's inside Reece,' Smythe said. 'Two hundred and
twenty pounds of crap.'

As Alma and the CO left, Calloway was still yelling his head
off. 'For God's sake,' I hissed at Shay. 'If they find Calloway's stupid
bird they'll toss *all* our cells again! You want to lose the shower
for *two* weeks?'

'That's not what I meant,' Shay said.

I didn't answer. Instead I lay down on my bunk and stuffed
more wadded-up toilet paper into my ears. And still, I could hear
Calloway singing his white-pride anthems. Still, I could hear Shay
when he told me a second time that he hadn't been talking about
the bird.

That night when I woke up with the sweats, my heart drilling
through the spongy base of my throat, Shay was talking to himself
again. 'They pull up the sheet,' he said.

'Shay?'

I took a piece of metal I'd sawed off from the lip of the counter in the cell – it had taken months, carved with a string of elastic from my underwear and a dab of toothpaste with baking soda, my own diamond band saw. Ingeniously, the triangular result doubled as both a mirror and a shank. I slipped my hand beneath my door, angling the mirror so I could see into Shay's cell.

He was lying on his bunk with his eyes closed and his arms crossed over his heart. His breathing had gone so shallow that his chest barely rose and fell. I could have sworn I smelled the worms in freshly turned soil. I heard the ping of stones as they struck a grave digger's shovel.

Shay was practicing.

I had done that myself. Maybe not quite in the same way, but I'd pictured my funeral. Who would come. Who would be well dressed, and who would be wearing something outrageously hideous. Who would cry. Who wouldn't.

God bless those COs; they'd moved Shay Bourne right next door to someone else serving a death sentence.

Two weeks after Shay arrived on I-tier, six officers came to his cell early one morning and told him to strip. 'Bend over,' I heard Whitaker say. 'Spread 'em. Lift 'em. Cough.'

'Where are we going?'

'Infirmary. Routine checkup.'

I knew the drill: they would shake out his clothes to make sure there was no contraband hidden, then tell him to get dressed again. They'd march him out of I-tier and into the great beyond of the Secure Housing Unit.

An hour later, I woke up to the sound of Shay's cell door being opened again as he returned to his cell. 'I'll pray for your soul,' CO Whitaker said soberly before leaving the tier.

'So,' I said, my voice too light and false to fool even myself. 'Are you the picture of health?'

'They didn't take me to the infirmary. We went to the warden's office.'

I sat on my bunk, looking up at the vent through which Shay's voice carried. 'He finally agreed to meet with—'

'You know why they lie?' Shay interrupted. 'Because they're afraid you'll go ballistic if they tell you the truth.'

'About what?'

'It's all mind control. And we have no choice but to be obedient because what if this is the one time that really—'

'Shay,' I said, 'did you talk to the warden or not?'

'*He* talked to *me*. He told me my last appeal was denied by the Supreme Court,' Shay said. 'My execution date is May twenty-third.'

I knew that before he was moved to this tier, Shay had been on death row for eleven years; it wasn't like he hadn't seen this coming. And yet, that date was only two and a half months away.

'I guess they don't want to come in and say hey, we're taking you to get your death warrant read out loud. I mean, it's easier to just pretend you're going to the infirmary, so that I wouldn't freak out. I bet they talked about how they'd come and get me. I bet they had a *meeting*.'

I wondered what I would prefer, if it were my death that was being announced like a future train departing from a platform. Would I want the truth from an officer? Or would I consider it a kindness to be spared knowing the inevitable, even for those four minutes of transit?

I knew what the answer was for me.

I wondered why, considering that I'd only known Shay Bourne for two weeks, there was a lump in my throat at the thought of his execution. 'I'm really sorry.'

'Yeah,' he said. 'Yeah.'

'Po-lice,' Joey called out, and a moment later, CO Smythe walked in, followed by CO Whitaker. He helped Whitaker transport Crash to the shower cell – the investigation into our bacchanal tap water had yielded nothing conclusive, apparently, except some mold in the pipes, and we were now allowed personal hygiene hours again. But afterward, instead of leaving I-tier,

Smythe doubled back down the catwalk to stand in front of Shay's cell.

'Listen,' Smythe said. 'Last week, you said something to me.'

'Did I?'

'You told me to look inside.' He hesitated. 'My daughter's been sick. Really sick. Yesterday, the doctors told my wife and me to say good-bye. It made me want to explode. So I grabbed this stuffed bear in her crib, one we'd brought from home to make going to the hospital easier for her – and I ripped it wide open. It was filled with peanut shells, and we never thought to look there.' Smythe shook his head. 'My baby's not dying; she was never even sick. She's just allergic,' he said. 'How did you know?'

'I didn't—'

'It doesn't matter.' Smythe dug in his pocket for a small square of tinfoil, unwrapping it to reveal a thick brownie. 'I brought this in from home. My wife, she makes them. She wanted you to have it.'

'John, you can't give him contraband,' Whitaker said, glancing over his shoulder at the control booth.

'It's not contraband. It's just me . . . sharing a little bit of my lunch.'

My mouth started to water. Brownies were not on our canteen forms. The closest we came was chocolate cake, offered once a year as part of a Christmas package that also included a stocking full of candy and two oranges.

Smythe passed the brownie through the trap in the cell door. He met Shay's gaze and nodded, then left the tier with CO Whitaker.

'Hey, Death Row,' Calloway said, 'I'll give you three cigarettes for half of that.'

'I'll trade you a whole pack of coffee,' Joey countered.

'He ain't going to waste it on you,' Calloway said. 'I'll give you coffee and *four* cigarettes.'

Texas and Pogie joined in. They would trade Shay a CD player. A *Playboy* magazine. A roll of tape.

'A teener,' Calloway announced. 'Final offer.'

The Brotherhood made a killing on running the methamphet-amine trade at the New Hampshire state prison; for Calloway to solicit his own personal stash, he must have truly wanted that chocolate.

As far as I knew, Shay hadn't even had a cup of coffee since coming to I-tier. I had no idea if he smoked or got high. 'No,' Shay said. 'No to all of you.'

A few minutes passed.

'For God's sake, I can still smell it,' Calloway said.

Let me tell you, I am not exaggerating when I say that we were forced to inhale that scent – that glorious scent – for hours. At three in the morning, when I woke up as per my usual insomnia, the scent of chocolate was so strong that the brownie might as well have been sitting in my cell instead of Shay's. 'Why don't you just eat the damn thing,' I murmured.

'Because,' Shay replied, as wide awake as I, 'then there wouldn't be anything to look forward to.'

Maggie

There were many reasons I loved Oliver, but first and foremost was that my mother couldn't stand him. *He's a mess*, she said every time she came to visit. *He's destructive. Maggie*, she said, *if you got rid of him, you could find Someone.*

Someone was a doctor, like the anesthesiologist from Dartmouth-Hitchcock they'd set me up with once, who asked me if I thought laws against downloading child porn were an infringement on civil rights. Or the son of the cantor, who actually had been in a monogamous gay relationship for five years but hadn't told his parents yet. *Someone* was the younger partner in the accounting firm that did my father's taxes, who asked me on our first and only date if I'd always been a *big* girl.

On the other hand, Oliver knew just what I needed, and when I needed it. Which is why, the minute I stepped on the scale that morning, he hopped out from underneath the bed, where he was diligently severing the cord of my alarm clock with his teeth, and settled himself squarely on top of my feet so that I couldn't see the digital readout.

'Nicely done,' I said, stepping off, trying not to notice the numbers that flashed red before they disappeared. Surely the reason there was a seven in there was because Oliver had been on the scale, too. Besides, if I were going to be writing a formal complaint about any of this, I'd have said that (a) size fourteen isn't really all that big, (b) a size fourteen here was a size sixteen in London, so in a way I was thinner than I'd be if I had been born British, and (c) weight didn't really matter, as long as you were healthy.

All right, so maybe I didn't exercise all that much either. But I would, one day, or so I told my mother the fitness queen, as soon as all the people on whose behalf I worked tirelessly were absolutely, unequivocally rescued. I told her (and anyone else who'd listen) that the whole reason the ACLU existed was to help people take a stand. Unfortunately, the only stands my mother recognized were pigeon pose, warrior two, and all the other staples of yoga.

I pulled on my jeans, the ones that I admittedly didn't wash very often because the dryer shrank them just enough that I had to suffer half a day before the denim stretched to the point of comfort again. I picked a sweater that didn't show my bra roll and then turned to Oliver. 'What do you think?'

He lowered his left ear, which translated to, 'Why do you even care, since you're taking it all off to put on a spa robe?'

As usual, he was right. It's a little hard to hide your flaws when you're wearing, well, nothing.

He followed me into the kitchen, where I poured us both bowls of rabbit food (his literal, mine Special K). Then he hopped off to the litter box beside his cage, where he'd spend the day sleeping.

I'd named my rabbit after Oliver Wendell Holmes Jr, the famous Supreme Court Justice known as the Great Dissenter. He once said, 'Even a dog knows the difference between being kicked and being tripped over.' So did rabbits. And my clients, for that matter.

'Don't do anything I wouldn't do,' I warned Oliver. 'That includes chewing the legs of the kitchen stools.'

I grabbed my keys and headed out to my Prius. I had used nearly all my savings last year on the hybrid – to be honest, I didn't understand why car manufacturers charged a premium if you were a buyer with a modicum of social conscience. It didn't have all-wheel drive, which was a real pain in the neck during a New Hampshire winter, but I figured that saving the ozone layer was worth sliding off the road occasionally.

My parents had moved to Lynley – a town twenty-six miles east of Concord – seven years ago when my father took over as rabbi at Temple Beth Or. The catch was that there *was* no Temple Beth

Or: his reform congregation held Friday night services in the cafeteria of the middle school, because the original temple had burned to the ground. The expectation had been to raise funds for a new temple, but my father had overestimated the size of his rural New Hampshire congregation, and although he assured me that they were closing in on buying land somewhere, I didn't see it happening anytime soon. By now, anyway, his congregation had grown used to readings from the Torah that were routinely punctuated by the cheers of the crowd at the basketball game in the gymnasium down the hall.

The biggest single annual contributor to my father's temple fund was the ChutZpah, a wellness retreat for the mind, body, and soul in the heart of Lynley that was run by my mother. Although her clientele was nondenominational, she'd garnered a word-of-mouth reputation among temple sisterhoods, and patrons came from as far away as New York and Connecticut and even Maryland to relax and rejuvenate. My mother used salt from the Dead Sea for her scrubs. Her spa cuisine was kosher. She'd been written up in *Boston* magazine, the *New York Times,* and *Luxury SpaFinder.*

The first Saturday of every month, I drove to the spa for a free massage or facial or pedicure. The catch was that afterward, I had to suffer through lunch with my mother. We had it down to a routine. By the time we were served our passion fruit iced tea, we'd already covered 'Why Don't You Call.' The salad course was 'I'm Going to Be Dead Before You Make Me a Grandmother.' The entrée – fittingly – involved my weight. Needless to say, we never got around to dessert.

The ChutZpah was white. Not just white, but scary, I'm-afraid-to-breathe white: white carpets, white tiles, white robes, white slippers. I have no idea how my mother kept the place so clean, given that when I was growing up, the house was always comfortably cluttered.

My father says there's a God, although for me the jury is still out on that one. Which isn't to say that I didn't appreciate a miracle as much as the next person – such as when I went up to the front desk and the receptionist told me my mother was going to have to miss our lunch because of a last-minute meeting with a wholesale orchid salesman. 'But she said you should still have your treatment,' the receptionist said. 'DeeDee's going to be your aesthetician, and you've got locker number two twenty.'

I took the robe and slippers she handed me. Locker 220 was in a bank with fifty others, and several toned middle-aged women were stripping out of their yoga clothes. I breezed into another section of lockers, one that was blissfully empty, and changed into my robe. If someone complained because I was using locker 664 instead, I didn't think my mother would disown me. I punched in my key code – 2358, for ACLU – took a bracing breath, and tried not to glance in the mirror as I walked by.

There wasn't very much that I liked about the outside of me. I had curves, but to me, they were in all the wrong places. My hair was an explosion of dark curls, which could have been sexy if I didn't have to work so hard to keep them frizz-free. I'd read that stylists on the *Oprah* show would straighten the hair of guests with hair like mine, because curls added ten pounds to the camera – which meant that even my *hair* made objects like me look bigger than they appeared. My eyes were okay – they were mud-colored on an average day and green if I felt like embellishing – but most of all, they showed the part of me I *was* proud of: my intelligence. I might never be a cover girl, but I was a girl who could cover it all.

The problem was, you never heard anyone say, 'Wow, check out the brain on that babe.'

My father had always made me feel special, but I couldn't even look at my mother without wondering why I hadn't inherited her tiny waist and sleek hair. As a kid I had only wanted to be just like her; as an adult, I'd stopped trying.

Sighing, I entered the whirlpool area: a white oasis surrounded by white wicker benches where primarily white women waited for their white-coated therapists to call their name.

DeeDee appeared in her immaculate jacket, smiling. 'You must be Maggie,' she said. 'You look just like your mother described you.'

I wasn't about to take *that* bait. 'Nice to meet you.' I never quite figured out the protocol for this part of the experience – you said hello and then disrobed immediately so that a total stranger could lay their hands on you . . . and you *paid* for this privilege. Was it just me, or was there a great deal that spa treatments had in common with prostitution?

'You looking forward to your Song of Solomon Wrap?'

'I'd rather be getting a root canal.'

DeeDee grinned. 'Your mom told me you'd say something like that, too.'

If you haven't had a body wrap, it's a singular experience. You're lying on a cushy table covered by a giant piece of Saran Wrap and you're naked. Totally, completely naked. Sure, the aesthetician tosses a washcloth the size of a gauze square over your privates when she's scrubbing you down, and she's got a poker face that never belies whether she's calculating your body mass index under her palms – but still, you're painfully aware of your physique, if only because someone's experiencing it firsthand with you.

I forced myself to close my eyes and remember that being washed beneath a Vichy shower by someone else was supposed to make me feel like a queen and not a hospitalized invalid.

'So, DeeDee,' I said. 'How long have you been doing this?'

She unrolled a towel and held it like a screen as I rolled onto my back. 'I've been working at spas for six years, but I just got hired on here.'

'You must be good,' I said. 'My mother doesn't sweat amateurs.'

She shrugged. 'I like meeting new people.'

I like meeting new people, too, but when they're fully clothed.

'What do you do for work?' DeeDee asked.

'My mother didn't tell you?'

'No . . . she just said—' Suddenly she broke off, silent.

'She said *what*.'

'She, um, told me to treat you to an extra helping of seaweed scrub.'

'You mean she told you I'd need twice as much.'

'She didn't—'

'Did she use the word *zaftig*?' I asked. When DeeDee didn't answer – wisely – I blinked up at the hazy light in the ceiling, listened to Yanni's canned piano for a few beats, and then sighed. 'I'm an ACLU lawyer.'

'For real?' DeeDee's hands stilled on my feet. 'Do you ever take on cases, like, for free?'

'That's *all* I do.'

'Then you must know about the guy on death row . . . Shay Bourne? I've been writing to him for ten years, ever since I was in eighth grade and I started as part of an assignment for my social studies class. His last appeal just got rejected by the Supreme Court.'

'I know,' I said. 'I've filed briefs on his behalf.'

DeeDee's eyes widened. 'So you're his lawyer?'

'Well . . . no.' I hadn't even been living in New Hampshire when Bourne was convicted, but it was the job of the ACLU to file amicus briefs for death row prisoners. *Amicus* was Latin for *friend of the court*; when you had a position on a particular case but weren't directly a party involved in it, the court would let you legally spell out your feelings if it might be beneficial to the decision-making process. My amicus briefs illustrated how hideous the death penalty was; defined it as cruel and unusual punishment, as unconstitutional. I'm quite sure the judge looked at my hard work and promptly tossed it aside.

'Can't you do something else to help him?' DeeDee asked.

The truth was, if Bourne's last appeal had been rejected by the Supreme Court, there wasn't much *any* lawyer could do to save him now.

'Tell you what,' I promised. 'I'll look into it.'

DeeDee smiled and covered me with heated blankets until I was trussed tight as a burrito. Then she sat down behind me and wove her fingers into my hair. As she massaged my scalp, my eyes drifted shut.

'They say it's painless,' DeeDee murmured. 'Lethal injection.'

They: the establishment, the lawmakers, the ones assuaging their guilt over their own actions with rhetoric. 'That's because no one ever comes back to tell them otherwise,' I said. I thought of Shay Bourne being given the news of his own impending death. I thought of lying on a table like this one, being put to sleep.

Suddenly I couldn't breathe. The blankets were too hot, the cream on my skin too thick. I wanted out of the layers and began to fight my way free.

'Whoa,' DeeDee said. 'Hang on, let me help you.' She pulled and peeled and handed me a towel. 'Your mother didn't tell me you were claustrophobic.'

I sat up, drawing great gasps of air into my lungs. *Of course she didn't*, I thought. *Because she's the one who's suffocating me.*

Lucius

It was late afternoon, almost time for the shift change, and I-tier was relatively quiet. Me, I'd been sick all day, hazing in and out of sleep brought on by fever. Calloway, who usually played chess with me, was playing with Shay instead. 'Bishop takes a6,' Calloway called out. He was a racist bigot, but Calloway was also the best chess player I'd ever met.

During the day, Batman the Robin resided in his breast pocket, a small lump no bigger than a pack of Starburst candies. Sometimes it crawled onto his shoulder and pecked at the scars on his scalp. At other times, he kept Batman in a paperback copy of *The Stand* that had been doctored as a hiding place – starting on chapter six, a square had been cut out of the pages of the thick book with a pilfered razor blade, creating a little hollow that Calloway lined with tissues to make a bed. The robin ate mashed potatoes; Calloway traded precious masking tape and twine and even a homemade handcuff key for extra portions.

'Hey,' Calloway said. 'We haven't made a wager on this game.'

Crash laughed. 'Even Bourne ain't dumb enough to bet you when he's losing.'

'What have you got that I want?' Calloway mused.

'Intelligence?' I suggested. 'Common sense?'

'Keep out of this, homo.' Calloway thought for a moment. 'The brownie. I want the damn brownie.'

By now, the brownie was two days old. I doubted that Calloway would even be able to swallow it. What he'd enjoy, mostly, was the act of taking it away from Shay.

'Okay,' Shay said. 'Knight to g6.'

I sat up on my bunk. 'Okay? Shay, he's beating the pants off you.'

'How come you're too sick to play, DuFresne, but you don't mind sticking your two cents into every conversation?' Calloway said. 'This is between me and Bourne.'

'What if *I* win?' Shay asked. 'What do I get?'

Calloway laughed. 'It won't happen.'

'The bird.'

'I'm not giving you Batman—'

'Then I'm not giving you the brownie.' There was a beat of silence.

'Fine,' Calloway said. 'You win, you get the bird. But you're not going to win, because my bishop takes d3. Consider yourself officially screwed.'

'Queen to h7,' Shay replied. 'Checkmate.'

'What?' Calloway cried. I scrutinized the mental chessboard I'd been tracking – Shay's queen had come out of nowhere, screened by his knight. There was nowhere left for Calloway to go.

At that moment the door to I-tier opened, admitting a pair of officers in flak jackets and helmets. They marched to Calloway's cell and brought him onto the catwalk, securing his handcuffs to a metal railing along the far wall.

There was nothing worse than having your cell searched. In here, all we had were our belongings, and having them pored over was a gross invasion of privacy. Not to mention the fact that when it happened, you had an excellent chance of losing your best stash, be that drugs or hooch or chocolate or art supplies or the stinger rigged from paper clips to heat up your instant coffee.

They came in with flashlights and long-handled mirrors and worked systematically. They'd check the seams of the walls, the vents, the plumbing. They'd roll deodorant sticks all the way out to make sure nothing was hidden underneath. They'd shake containers of powder to hear what might be inside. They'd sniff shampoo bottles, open envelopes, and take out the letters inside.

They'd rip off your bedsheets and run their hands over the mattresses, looking for tears or ripped seams.

Meanwhile, you were forced to watch.

I could not see what was going on in Calloway's cell, but I had a pretty good idea based on his reactions. He rolled his eyes as his blanket was checked for unraveled threads; his jaw tensed when a postage stamp was peeled off an envelope, revealing the black tar heroin underneath. But when his bookshelf was inspected, Calloway flinched. I looked for the small bulge in his breast pocket that would have been the bird and realized that Batman the Robin was somewhere inside that cell.

One of the officers held up the copy of *The Stand*. The pages were riffled, the spine snapped, the book tossed against the cell wall. 'What's this?' an officer asked, focusing not on the bird that had been whipped across the cell but on the baby-blue tissues that fluttered down over his boots.

'Nothing,' Calloway said, but the officer wasn't about to take his word for it. He picked through the tissues, and when he didn't find anything, he confiscated the book with its carved hidey-hole.

Whitaker said something about a write-up, but Calloway wasn't listening. I could not remember ever seeing him quite so unraveled. As soon as he was released back into his cell, he ran to the rear corner where the bird had been flung.

The sound that Calloway Reece made was primordial; but then maybe that was always the case when a grown man with no heart started to cry.

There was a crash, and a sickening crunch. A whirlwind of destruction as Calloway fought back against what couldn't be fixed. Finally spent, Calloway sank down to the floor of his cell, cradling the dead bird. 'Motherfucker. Mother*fucker*.'

'Reece,' Shay interrupted, 'I want my prize.'

My head snapped around. Surely Shay wasn't stupid enough to antagonize Calloway.

'What?' Calloway breathed. 'What did you say?'

'My prize. I won the chess game.'

'Not *now*,' I hissed.

'Yes, now,' Shay said. 'A deal's a deal.'

In here, you were only as good as your word, and Calloway – with his Aryan Brotherhood sensibilities – would have known that better than anyone else. 'You better make sure you're always behind those bars,' Calloway vowed, 'because the next time I get the chance, I'm going to mess you up so bad your own mama wouldn't know you.' But even as he threatened Shay, Calloway gently wrapped the dead bird in a tissue and attached the small, slight bundle to the end of his fishing line.

When the robin reached me, I drew it under the three-inch gap beneath the door of my cell. It still looked half cooked, its closed eye translucent blue. One wing was bent at a severe backward angle; its neck lolled sideways.

Shay sent out his own line of string, with a weight made of a regulation comb on one end. I saw his hands gently slide the robin, wrapped in tissue, into his cell. The lights on the catwalk flickered.

I've often imagined what happened next. With an artist's eye, I like to picture Shay sitting on his bunk, cupping his palms around the tiny bird. I imagine the touch of someone who loves you so much, he cannot bear to watch you sleep; and so you wake up with his hand on your heart. In the long run, though, it hardly matters how Shay did it. What matters is the result: that we all heard the piccolo trill of that robin; that Shay pushed the risen bird beneath his cell door onto the catwalk, where it hopped, like broken punctuation, toward Calloway's outstretched hand.

June

If you're a mother, you can look into the face of your grown child and see, instead, the one that peeked up at you from the folds of a baby blanket. You can watch your eleven-year-old daughter painting her nails with glitter polish and remember how she used to reach for you when she wanted to cross the street. You can hear the doctor say that the real danger is adolescence, because you don't know how the heart will respond to growth spurts – and you can pretend that's ages away.

'Best two out of three,' Claire said, and from the folds of her hospital johnny she raised her fist again.

I lifted my hand, too. *Rock, paper, scissors, shoot.*

'Paper.' Claire grinned. 'I win.'

'You totally do not,' I said. 'Hello? Scissors?'

'What I forgot to tell you is that it's raining, and the scissors got rusty, and so you slip the paper underneath them and carry them away.'

I laughed. Claire shifted slightly, careful not to dislodge all the tubes and the wires. 'Who'll feed Dudley?' she asked.

Dudley was our dog – a thirteen-year-old springer spaniel who, along with me, was one of the only pieces of continuity between Claire and her late sister. Claire may never have met Elizabeth, but they had both grown up draping faux pearls around Dudley's neck, dressing him up like the sibling they never had. 'Don't worry about Dudley,' I said. 'I'll call Mrs Morrissey if I have to.'

Claire nodded and glanced at the clock. 'I thought they'd be back already.'

'I know, baby.'

'What do you think's taking so long?'

There were a hundred answers to that, but the one that floated to the top of my mind was that in some other hospital, two counties away, another mother had to say good-bye to her child so that I would have a chance to keep mine.

The technical name for Claire's illness was pediatric dilated cardiomyopathy. It affected twelve million kids a year, and it meant that her heart cavity was enlarged and stretched, that her heart couldn't pump blood out efficiently. You couldn't fix it or reverse it; if you were lucky you could live with it. If you weren't, you died of congestive heart failure. In kids, 79 percent of the cases came from an unknown origin. There was a camp that attributed its onset to myocarditis and other viral infections during infancy; and another that claimed it was inherited through a parent who was a carrier of the defective gene. I had always assumed the latter was the case with Claire. After all, surely a child who grew out of grief would be born with a heavy heart.

At first, I didn't know she had it. She got tired more easily than other infants, but I was still moving in slow motion myself and did not notice. It wasn't until she was five, hospitalized with a flu she could not shake, that she was diagnosed. Dr Wu said that Claire had a slight arrhythmia that might improve and might not; he put her on Captopril, Lasix, Lanoxin. He said that we'd have to wait and see.

On the first day of fifth grade, Claire told me it felt like she had swallowed a hummingbird. I assumed it was nerves about starting classes, but hours later – when she stood up to solve a math problem at the chalkboard – she passed out cold. Progressive arrhythmias made the heart beat like a bag of worms – it wouldn't eject any blood. Those basketball players who seemed so healthy and then dropped dead on the court? That was ventricular fibrillation, and it was happening to Claire. She had surgery to implant an AICD – an automatic implantable cardioverter-defibrillator, or, in simpler terms, a tiny, internal ER resting right on her heart, which would fix future arrhythmias by administering an electric shock. She was put on the list for a transplant.

The transplant game was a tricky one – once you received a heart, the clock started ticking, and it wasn't the happy ending everyone thought it was. You didn't want to wait so long for a transplant that the rest of the bodily systems began to shut down. But even a transplant wasn't a miracle: most recipients could only tolerate a heart for ten or fifteen years before complications ensued, or there was outright rejection. Still, as Dr Wu said, fifteen years from now, we might be able to buy a heart off a shelf and have it installed at Best Buy . . . the idea was to keep Claire alive long enough to let medical innovation catch up to her.

This morning, the beeper we carried at all times had gone off. *We have a heart*, Dr Wu had said when I called. *I'll meet you at the hospital.*

For the past six hours, Claire had been poked, pricked, scrubbed, and prepped so that the minute the miracle organ arrived in its little Igloo cooler, she could go straight into surgery. This was the moment I'd waited for, and dreaded, her whole life.

What if . . . I could not even let myself say the words.

Instead, I reached for Claire's hand and threaded our fingers together. *Paper and scissors*, I thought. *We are between a rock and a hard place.* I looked at the fan of her angel hair on the pillow, the faint blue cast of her skin, the fairy-light bones of a girl whose body was still too much for her to handle. Sometimes, when I looked at her, I didn't see her at all; instead, I pretended that she was—

'What do you think she's like?'

I blinked, startled. 'Who?'

'The girl. The one who died.'

'Claire,' I said. 'Let's not talk about this.'

'Why not? Don't you think we should know all about her if she's going to be a part of me?'

I touched my hand to her head. 'We don't even know it's a girl.'

'Of course it's a girl,' Claire said. 'It would be totally gross to have a boy's heart.'

'I don't think that's a qualification for a match.'

She shuddered. 'It *should* be.' Claire struggled to push herself upright so that she was sitting higher in the hospital bed. 'Do you think I'll be different?'

I leaned down and kissed her. 'You,' I pronounced, 'will wake up and still be the same kid who cannot be bothered to clean her room or walk Dudley or turn out the lights when she goes down-stairs.'

That's what I said to Claire, anyway. But all I heard were the first four words: *You will wake up.*

A nurse came into the room. 'We just got word that the harvest's begun,' she said. 'We should have more information shortly; Dr Wu's on the phone with the team that's on-site.'

After she left, Claire and I sat in silence. Suddenly, this was real – the surgeons were going to open up Claire's chest, stop her heart, and sew in a new one. We had both heard numerous doctors explain the risks and the rewards; we knew how infrequently pedi-atric donors came about. Claire shrank down in the bed, her covers sliding up to her nose. 'If I die,' Claire said, 'do you think I'll get to be a saint?'

'You won't die.'

'Yeah, I will. And so will you. I just might do it a little sooner.'

I couldn't help it; I felt tears welling up in my eyes. I wiped them on the edge of the hospital sheets. Claire fisted her hand in my hair, the way she used to when she was little. 'I bet I'd like it,' Claire said. 'Being a saint.'

Claire had her nose in a book constantly, and recently, her Joan of Arc fascination had bloomed into all things martyred.

'You aren't going to be a saint.'

'You don't know that for sure,' Claire said.

'You're not Catholic, for one thing. And besides, they all died horrible deaths.'

'That's not always true. You can be killed while you're being good, and that counts. St Maria Goretti was my age when she fought off a guy who was raping her and was killed and *she* got to be one.'

'That's atrocious,' I said.

'St Barbara had her eyeballs cut out. And did you know there's a patron saint of heart patients? John of God?'

'The question is, why do *you* know there's a patron saint of heart patients?'

'Duh,' Claire said. 'I *read* about it. It's all you let me do.' She settled back against the pillows. 'I bet a saint can play softball.'

'So can a girl with a heart transplant.'

But Claire wasn't listening; she knew that hope was just smoke and mirrors; she'd learned by watching me. She looked up at the clock. 'I think I'll be a saint,' she said, as if it were entirely up to her. 'That way no one forgets you when you're gone.'

The funeral of a police officer is a breathtaking thing. Officers and firemen and public officials will come from every town in the state and some even farther away. There is a procession of police cruisers that precedes the hearse; they blanket the highway like snow.

It took me a long time to remember Kurt's funeral, because I was working so hard at the time to pretend it wasn't happening. The police chief, Irv, rode with me to the graveside service. There were townspeople lining the streets of Lynley, with handmade signs that read PROTECT AND SERVE, and THE ULTIMATE SACRIFICE. It was summertime, and the asphalt sank beneath the heels of my shoes where I stood. I was surrounded by other policemen who'd worked with Kurt, and hundreds who didn't, a sea of dress blue. My back hurt, and my feet were swollen. I found myself concentrating on a lilac tree that shuddered in the breeze, petals falling like rain.

The police chief had arranged for a twenty-one-gun salute, and as it finished, five fighter jets rose over the distant violet mountains. They sliced the sky in parallel lines, and then, just as they flew overhead, the plane on the far right broke off like a splinter, soaring east.

When the priest stopped speaking – I didn't listen to a word of it; what could he tell me about Kurt that I didn't already know? – Robbie and Vic stepped forward. They were Kurt's closest friends in the department. Like the rest of the Lynley force, they had covered their badges with black fabric. They reached for the flag that draped Kurt's coffin and began to fold it. Their gloved hands moved so fast – I thought of Mickey Mouse, of Donald Duck, with their oversized white fists. Robbie was the one who put the triangle into my arms, something to hold on to, something to take Kurt's place.

Through the radios of the other policemen came the voice of the dispatcher: *All units stand by for a broadcast.*

Final call for Officer Kurt Nealon, number 144.

144, report to 360 West Main for one last assignment.

It was the address of the cemetery.

You will be in the best of hands. You will be deeply missed.

144, 10-7. The radio code for end of shift.

I have been told that afterward, I walked up to Kurt's coffin. It was so highly polished I could see my own reflection, pinched and unfamiliar. It had been specially made, wider than normal, to accommodate Elizabeth, too.

She was, at seven, still afraid of the dark. Kurt would lie down beside her, an elephant perched among pink pillows and satin blankets, until she fell asleep; then he'd creep out of the room and turn off the light. Sometimes, she woke up at midnight shrieking. *You turned it off*, she'd sob into my shoulder, as if I had broken her heart.

The funeral director had let me see them. Kurt's arms were wrapped tight around my daughter; Elizabeth rested her head on his chest. They looked the way they looked on nights when Kurt fell asleep waiting for Elizabeth to do that very thing. They looked the way I wished I could: smooth and clear and peaceful, a pond with a stone unthrown. It was supposed to be comforting that they would be together. It was supposed to make up for the fact that I couldn't go with them.

'Take care of her,' I whispered to Kurt, my breath blowing a kiss against the gleaming wood. 'Take care of my baby.'

As if I'd summoned her, Claire moved inside me then: a slow tumble of butterfly limbs, a memory of why I had to stay behind.

There was a time when I prayed to saints. What I liked about them were their humble beginnings: they were human, once, and so you knew that they just *got* it in a way Jesus never would. They understood what it meant to have your hopes dashed or your promises broken or your feelings hurt. St Therese was my favorite – the one who believed you could be perfectly ordinary, but that great love could somehow transport you. However, this was all a long time ago. Life has a way of pointing out, with great sweeping signs, that you are looking at the wrong things, doesn't it? It was when I started to admit to myself that I'd rather be dead that I was given a child who had to fight to stay alive.

In the past month, Claire's arrhythmias had worsened. Her AICD was going off six times a day. I'd been told that when it fired, it felt like an electric current running through the body. It restarted your heart, but it hurt like hell. Once a month would be devastating; once a day would be debilitating. And then there was Claire's frequency.

There were support groups for adults who had to live with AICDs; there were stories of those who preferred the risk of dying from an arrhythmia to the sure knowledge that they would be shocked by the device sooner or later. Last week, I had found Claire in her room reading the *Guinness Book of World Records*. 'Roy Sullivan was struck by lightning seven times over thirty-six years,' she'd said. 'Finally, he killed himself.' She lifted her shirt, staring down at the scar on her chest. 'Mom,' she begged, 'please make them turn it off.'

I did not know how long I would be able to convince Claire to stay with me, if this was the way she had to do it.

Claire and I both turned immediately when the hospital door opened. We were expecting the nurse, but it was Dr Wu. He sat down on the edge of the bed and spoke directly to Claire, as if she were my age instead of eleven. 'The heart we had in mind for you had something wrong with it. The team didn't know until they got inside . . . but the right ventricle is dilated. If it isn't functioning now, chances are it will only get worse by the time the heart's transplanted.'

'So . . . I can't have it?' Claire asked.

'No. When I give you a new heart, I want it to be the healthiest heart possible,' the doctor explained.

My body felt stiff. 'I don't – I don't understand.'

Dr Wu turned. 'I'm sorry, June. Today's not going to be the day.'

'But it could take years to find another donor,' I said. I didn't add the rest of my sentence, because I knew Wu could hear it anyway: *Claire can't last that long.*

'We'll just hope for the best,' he said.

After he left, we sat in stunned silence for a few moments. Had I done this? Had the fear I'd tried to quash – the one that Claire wouldn't survive this operation – somehow bled into reality?

Claire began to pull the cardiac monitors off her chest. 'Well,' she said, but I could hear the hitch in her voice as she struggled not to cry. 'What a total waste of a Saturday.'

'You know,' I said, forcing the words to unroll evenly, 'you were *named* for a saint.'

'For real?'

I nodded. 'She founded a group of nuns called the Poor Clares.'

She glanced at me. 'Why did you pick her?'

Because, on the day you were born, the nurse who handed you to me shook her head and said, 'Now there's a sight for sore eyes.' And you were. And she is the patron saint of that very thing. And I wanted you protected, from the very first moment I spoke your name.

'I liked the way it sounded,' I lied, and I held up Claire's shirt so that she could shimmy into it.

We would leave this hospital, maybe go get chocolate Fribbles at Friendly's and rent a movie with a happy ending. We'd take Dudley for a walk and feed him. We'd act like this was an ordinary day. And after she went to sleep, I would bury my face in my pillow and let myself feel everything I wasn't letting myself feel right now: shame over knowing that I've had five more years in Claire's company than I did with Elizabeth, guilt over being relieved this transplant did not happen, since it might just as easily kill Claire as save her.

Claire stuffed her feet into her pink Converse high-tops. 'Maybe I'll join the Poor Clares.'

'You still can't be a saint,' I said. And added silently, *Because I will not let you die.*

Lucius

Shortly after Shay brought Batman the Robin back to life, Crash Vitale lit himself on fire.

He'd created a makeshift match the way we all do – by pulling the fluorescent bulb out of its cradle and holding the metal tines just far enough away from the socket to have the electricity arc to meet it. Stick a piece of paper in the gap, and it becomes a torch. Crash had crumpled up pages of a magazine and set them around himself in a circle. By the time Texas started screaming for help, smoke was filling the pod. The COs held the fire hose at full spray as they opened his cell door; we could hear Crash being knocked against the far wall by the stream. Dripping wet, he was strapped onto a gurney to be transported, his hair a matted mess, his eyes wild. 'Hey, Green Mile,' he yelled as he was wheeled off the tier, 'how come you didn't save *me*?'

'Because I *like* the bird,' Shay murmured.

I was the first one to laugh, then Texas snickered. Joey, too – but only because Crash wasn't present to shut him up.

'Bourne,' Calloway said, the first words any of us had heard from him since the bird had hopped back to his cell. 'Thanks.'

There was a beat of silence. 'It deserved another chance,' Shay said.

The pod door buzzed open, and this time CO Smythe walked in with the nurse, doing her evening rounds. Alma came to my cell first, holding out my card of pills. 'Smells like someone had a barbecue in here and forgot to invite me,' she said. She waited for me to put the pills in my mouth, take a swallow of water. 'You sleep well, Lucius.'

As she left, I walked to the front of the cell. Rivulets of water ran down the cement catwalk. But instead of leaving the tier, Alma stopped in front of Calloway's cell. 'Inmate Reece, are you going to let me take a look at that arm?'

Calloway hunched over, protecting the bird he held in his hand. We all knew he was holding Batman; we all held our collective breath. What if Alma saw the bird? Would she rat him out?

I should have known Calloway would never let that happen – he'd be offensive enough to scare her off before she got too close. But before he could speak, we heard a fluted chirp – not from Calloway's cell but from Shay's. There was an answering call – the robin looking for its own kind. 'What the hell's that?' CO Smythe asked, looking around. 'Where's it coming from?'

Suddenly, a twitter rose from Joey's cell, and then a higher cheep from Pogie's. To my surprise, I even heard a tweet come from the vicinity of my own bunk. I wheeled around, tracing it to the louvers of the vent. Was there a whole colony of robins in here? Or was it Shay, a ventriloquist in addition to a magician, this time throwing his voice?

Smythe moved down the tier, hands covering his ears as he peered at the skylight and into the shower cell to find the source of the noise. 'Smythe?' an officer said over the control booth intercom. 'What the hell's going on?'

A place like this wears down everything, and tolerance is no exception. In here, coexistence passes for forgiveness. You do not learn to like something you abhor; you come to live with it. It's why we submit when we are told to strip; it's why we deign to play chess with a child molester; it's why we quit crying ourselves to sleep. You live and let live, and eventually that becomes enough.

Which maybe explains why Calloway's muscled arm snaked through the open trap of his door, his 'Anita Bryant' patch shadowing his biceps. Alma blinked, surprised.

'I won't hurt you,' she murmured, peering at the new skin

growing where it had been grafted, still pink and evolving. She took a pair of latex gloves out of her pocket and snapped them on, making her hands just as lily-white as Calloway's. And wouldn't you know it – the moment Alma touched him, all of that crazy noise fell dead silent.

Michael

A priest has to say Mass every day, even if no one shows up, although this was rarely the case. In a city as large as Concord there were usually at least a handful of parishioners, already praying the rosary by the time I came out in my vestments.

I was just at the part of the Mass where miracles occurred. 'For this is my body, which will be given up for you,' I said aloud, then genuflected and lifted the host.

Next to 'How the heck is one God also a Holy Trinity?' the most common question I got asked as a priest by non-Catholics was about transubstantiation: the belief that at consecration, the elements of bread and wine truly became the Body and Blood of Christ. I could see why people were baffled – if this was true, wasn't Holy Communion cannibalistic? And if a change really occurred, why couldn't you see it?

When I went to church as a kid, long before I came back to it, I received Holy Communion like everyone else, but I didn't really give much thought to what I received. It looked, to me, like a cracker and a cup of wine . . . before *and* after the priest consecrated it. I can tell you now that it still looks like a cracker and a cup of wine. The miracle part comes down to philosophy. It isn't the accidents of an object that make it what it is . . . it's the essential parts. We'd still be human even if we didn't have limbs or teeth or hair; but if we suddenly stopped being mammals, that wouldn't be the case. When I consecrated the host and the wine at Mass, the very substance of the elements changed; it was the other properties – the shape, the taste, the size – that remained the same. Just like John the Baptist saw a man and knew, right away, that he was looking at God; just like the wise men came upon a baby and knew He was our Savior . . . every day I held what looked like crackers and wine but actually *was* Jesus.

For this very reason, from this point on in the Mass, my fingers and thumb would be kept pinched together until washed after the Sacrament of the Eucharist. Not even the tiniest particle of the consecrated host could be lost; we went to great pains to make sure of this when disposing of the leftovers from Holy Communion. But just as I was thinking this, the wafer slipped out of my hand.

I felt the way I had when, in third grade, during the Little League play-offs, I'd watched a pop fly come into my corner of left field too fast and too high – knotted with the need to catch it, sick with the knowledge that I wouldn't. Frozen, I watched the host tumble, safely, into the belly of the chalice of wine.

'Five-second rule,' I murmured, and I reached into the chalice and snagged it.

The wine had already begun to soak into the wafer. I watched, amazed, as a jaw took shape, an ear, an eyebrow.

Father Walter had visions. He said that the reason he became a priest in the first place was because, as an altar boy, a statue of Jesus had reached for his robe and tugged, telling him to stay the course. More recently, Mary had appeared to him in the rectory kitchen when he was frying trout, and suddenly they began leaping in the pan. *Don't let a single one fall to the floor,* she'd warned, and then disappeared.

There were hundreds of priests who excelled at their calling but never received this sort of divine intercession – and yet, I didn't want to fall among their ranks. Like the teens I worked with, I understood the need for miracles – they kept reality from paralyzing you. So I stared at the wafer, hoping the wine-sketched features would solidify into a portrait of Jesus . . . and instead I found myself looking at something else entirely. The shaggy dark hair that looked more like a grunge-band drummer than a priest, the nose broken while wrestling in junior high, the razor stubble.

Engraved onto the surface of the host, with a printmaker's delicacy, was a picture of me.

What is my *head doing on the body of Christ?* I thought as I placed the host on the paten, plum-stained and dissolving already. I lifted the chalice. 'This is my blood,' I said.

June

When Shay Bourne was working at our house as a carpenter, he gave Elizabeth a birthday present. Made of scrap wood and crafted after hours wherever he went when he left our house, it was a small, hinged chest. He had carved it intricately, so that each face portrayed a different fairy, dressed in the trappings of the seasons. Summer had bright peony wings, and a crown made of the sun. Spring was covered in climbing vines, and a bridal train of flowers swept beneath her. Autumn wore the jewel tones of sugar maples and aspen trees, the cap of an acorn balanced on her head. And Winter skated across a frozen lake, leaving a trail of silver frost in her wake. The cover was a painted picture of the moon, rising through a field of stars with its arms outstretched toward a sun that was just out of reach.

Elizabeth loved that box. The night that Shay gave it to her, she lined it with blankets and slept inside. When Kurt and I told her she couldn't do that again – what if the top fell on her while she was sleeping? – she turned it into a cradle for her dolls, then a toy chest. She named the fairies. Sometimes I heard her talking to them.

After Elizabeth died, I took the box out to the yard, planning to destroy it. There I was, eight months pregnant and grieving, swinging Kurt's axe, and at the last minute, I could not do it. It was what Elizabeth had treasured; how could I stand to lose that, too? I put the box in the attic, where it remained for years.

I could tell you I forgot about the box, but I would be lying. I knew it was there, buried behind our luggage and old toddler clothes and paintings with broken frames. When Claire was about ten, I found her trying to lug the box downstairs. 'It's so pretty,' she said, winded with the effort. 'And no one's using it.' I snapped at her and told her to go lie down and rest.

But Claire kept asking about it, and eventually I brought the box to her room, where it sat at the end of her bed, just like it had for Elizabeth. I never told her who'd carved it. And yet sometimes, when Claire was at school, I found myself peeking inside. I wondered if Pandora, too, wished she had scrutinized the contents first – heartache, cleverly disguised as a gift.

Lucius

It had been said, among those on I-tier, that I had achieved Bassmaster status when it came to fishing. My equipment was a sturdy line made from yarn I'd stored up over the years, tempered by weight – a comb, or a deck of cards, depending on what I was angling for. I was known for my ability to fish from my cell into Crash's, at the far end of the tier; and then down to the shower cell at the other end. I suppose this was why, when Shay cast out his own line, I found myself watching out of curiosity.

It was after *One Life to Live* but before *Oprah*, the time of day when most of the guys napped. I myself was not feeling so well. The sores in my mouth made it difficult to speak; I had to keep using the toilet. The skin around my eyes, stained by Kaposi's sarcoma, had swollen to the point where I could barely see. Then suddenly, Shay's fishing line whizzed into the narrow space beneath my cell door. 'Want some?' he asked.

When we fish, it's to get something. We trade magazines; we barter food; we pay for drugs. But Shay didn't want anything, except to give. Wired to the end of his line was a piece of Bazooka bubble gum.

It's contraband. Gum can be used as putty to build all sorts of things, and to tamper with locks. God only knew where Shay had come across this bounty – and, even more astounding, why he wouldn't just hoard it.

I swallowed, and my throat nearly split along a fault line. 'No thanks,' I rasped.

I sat up on my bunk and peeled the sheet off the plastic mattress.

One of the seams had been carefully doctored by me. The thread, laced like a football, could be loosened enough for me to rummage around inside the foam padding. I jammed my forefinger inside, scooping out my stash.

There were the 3TC pills – Epivir – and the Sustiva. Retrovir. Lomotil for my diarrhea. All the medications that, for weeks, Alma had watched me place on my tongue and apparently swallow – when in fact they were tucked up high in the purse of my cheek.

I had not yet made up my mind whether I would use these to kill myself . . . or if I'd just continue to save them instead of ingest them: a slower but still sure suicide.

It's funny how when you are dying, you still fight for the upper hand. You want to pick the terms; you want to choose the date. You'll tell yourself anything you have to, to pretend that you're still the one in control.

'Joey,' Shay said. 'Want some?' He cast again, his line arcing over the catwalk.

'For real?' Joey asked. Most of us just pretended Joey wasn't around; it was safer for him. No one went out of their way to acknowledge him, much less offer him something as precious as a piece of gum.

'I want some,' Calloway demanded. He must have seen the bounty going by, since his cell was between Shay's and Joey's.

'Me, too,' Crash said.

Shay waited for Joey to take the gum, and then pulled his line gently closer, until it was within reach of Calloway. 'There's plenty.'

'How many pieces you got?' Crash asked.

'Just the one.'

Now, you've seen a piece of Bazooka gum. *Maybe* you can split it with a friend. But to divvy up one single piece among seven greedy men?

Shay's fishing line whipped to the left, past my cell en route to Crash's. 'Take some and pass it on,' Shay said.

'Maybe I want the whole thing.'

'Maybe you do.'

'Fuck,' Crash said. 'I'm taking it all.'

'If that's what you need,' Shay replied.

I stood up, unsteady, and crouched down as Shay's fishing line reached Pogie's cell. 'Have some,' Shay offered.

'But Crash took the whole piece—'

'Have some.'

I could hear paper being unwrapped, the fullness of Pogie speaking around the bounty softening in his mouth. 'I ain't had chewing gum since 2001.'

By now, I could smell it. The pinkness, the sugar. I began to salivate.

'Oh, man,' Texas breathed, and then everyone chewed in silence, except for me.

Shay's fishing line swung between my own feet. 'Try it,' he urged.

I reached for the packet on the end of the line. Since six other men had already done the same, I expected to see only a fragment remaining, a smidgen of gum, if anything at all – yet, to my surprise, the piece of Bazooka was intact. I ripped the gum in half and put a piece into my mouth. The rest I wrapped up, and then I tugged on Shay's line. I watched it zip away, back to his own cell.

At first I could barely stand it – the sweetness against the sores in my mouth, the sharp edges of the gum before it softened. It brought tears to my eyes to so badly want something that I knew would cause great pain. I held up my hand, ready to spit the gum out, when the most remarkable thing happened: my mouth, my throat, they stopped aching, as if there were an anesthetic in the gum, as if I were no longer an AIDS patient but an ordinary man who'd picked up this treat at the gas station counter after filling his tank in preparation for driving far, far away. My jaw moved, rhythmic. I sat down on the floor of my cell, crying as I chewed – not because it hurt, but because it didn't.

We were silent for so long that CO Whitaker came in to see what we were up to; and what he found, of course, was not what he had expected. Seven men, imagining childhoods that we all wished we'd had. Seven men, blowing bubbles as bright as the moon.

For the first time in nearly six months, I slept through the night. I woke up rested and relaxed, without any of the stomach knotting that usually consumed me for the first two hours of every day. I walked to the basin, squeezed toothpaste onto the stubby brush they gave us, and glanced up at the wavy sheet of metal that passed for a mirror.

Something was different.

The sores, the Kaposi's sarcoma that had spotted my cheeks and inflamed my eyelids for a year now, were gone. My skin was clear as a river.

I leaned forward for a better look. I opened up my mouth, tugged my lower lip, searching in vain for the blisters and cankers that had kept me from eating.

'Lucius,' I heard, a voice spilling from the vent over my head. 'Good morning.'

I glanced up. 'It is, Shay. God, yes, it is.'

In the end, I didn't have to call for a medical consult. Officer Whitaker was shocked enough at my improved appearance to call Alma himself. I was taken into the attorney-client cell so that she could draw my blood, and an hour later, she came back to my own cell to tell me what I already knew.

'Your CD4+ is 1250,' Alma said. 'And your viral load's undetectable.'

'That's good, right?'

'It's normal. It's what someone who doesn't have AIDS would look like if we drew his blood.' She shook her head. 'Looks to me like your drug regimen's kicked in in a big way—'

'Alma,' I said, and I glanced behind her at Officer Whitaker before peeling the sheet off my mattress and ripping open my hiding place for pills. I brought them to her, spilled several dozen into her hand. 'I haven't been taking my meds for months.'

Color rose in her cheeks. 'Then this isn't possible.'

'It's not probable,' I corrected. '*Anything's* possible.'

She stuffed the pills into her pocket. 'I'm sure there's a medical explanation—'

'It's Shay.'

'Inmate Bourne?'

'He *did* this,' I said, well aware of how insane it sounded, and yet desperate to make her understand. 'I saw him bring a dead bird back to life. And take one piece of gum and turn it into enough for all of us. He made wine come out of our faucets the first night he was here . . .'

'Okey-dokey. Officer Whitaker, let me see if we can get a psych consult for—'

'I'm not crazy, Alma; I'm – well, I'm healed.' I reached for her hand. 'Haven't you ever seen something with your own eyes that you never imagined possible?'

She darted a glance at Calloway Reece, who had submitted to her ministrations now for seven days straight. 'He did that, too,' I whispered. 'I know it.'

Alma walked out of my cell and stood in front of Shay's. He was listening to his television, wearing headphones. 'Bourne,' Whitaker barked. 'Cuffs.'

After his wrists were secured, the door to his cell was opened. Alma stood in the gap with her arms crossed. 'What do you know about Inmate DuFresne's condition?'

Shay didn't respond.

'Inmate Bourne?'

'He can't sleep much,' Shay said quietly. 'It hurts him to eat.'

'He's got AIDS. But suddenly, this morning, that's all changed,' Alma said. 'And for some reason, Inmate DuFresne thinks you had something to do with it.'

'I didn't do anything.'

Alma turned to the CO. 'Did *you* see any of this?'

'Traces of alcohol were found in the plumbing on I-tier,' Whitaker admitted. 'And believe me, it was combed for a leak, but nothing conclusive was found. And yeah, I saw them all chewing gum. But Bourne's cell's been tossed religiously – and we've never found any contraband.'

'I didn't do anything,' Shay repeated. 'It was them.' Suddenly, he stepped toward Alma, animated. 'Are you here for my heart?'

'What?'

'My heart. I want to donate it, after I die.' I heard him rummaging around in his box of possessions. 'Here,' he said, giving Alma a piece of paper. 'This is the girl who needs it. Lucius wrote her name down for me.'

'I don't know anything about that . . .'

'But you can find out, right? You can talk to the right people?'

Alma hesitated, and then her voice went soft, the flannel-bound way she used to speak to me when the pain was so great that I could not see past it. 'I can talk,' she said.

It is an odd thing to be watching television and know that in reality, it is happening right outside your door. Crowds had flooded the parking lot of the prison. Camping out on the stairs of the parole office entrance were folks in wheelchairs, elderly women with walkers, mothers clutching sick infants to their chests. There were gay couples, mostly one man supporting another frail, ill partner; and crackpots holding up signs with scriptural references about the end of the world. Lining the street that led past the cemetery and downtown were the news vans – local affiliates, and even a crew from FOX in Boston.

Right now, a reporter from ABC 22 was interviewing a young mother whose son had been born with severe neurological damage. She stood beside the boy, in his motorized wheelchair, one hand resting on his forehead. 'What would I like?' she said, repeating the reporter's question. 'I'd like to know that he knows me.' She smiled faintly. 'That's not too greedy, is it?'

The reporter faced the camera. 'Bob, so far there's been no confirmation or denial from the administration that any miraculous behavior has in fact taken place within the Concord state prison.

We have been told, however, by an unnamed source, that these occurrences stemmed from the desire of New Hampshire's sole death row inmate, Shay Bourne, to donate his organs post-execution.'

I yanked my headphones down to my neck. 'Shay,' I called out. 'Are you listening to this?'

'We got us our own celebrity,' Crash said.

The brouhaha began to upset Shay. 'I'm who I've always been,' he said, his voice escalating. 'I'm who I'll always be.'

Just then two officers arrived, escorting someone we rarely saw: Warden Coyne. A burly man with a flattop on which you could have served dinner, he stood beside the cell while Officer Whitaker told Shay to strip. His scrubs were shaken out, and then he was allowed to dress again before he was shackled to the wall across from our cells.

The officers started to toss Shay's house – upending the meal he hadn't finished, yanking his headphones out of the television, overturning his small box of property. They ripped his mattress, balled up his sheets. They ran their hands along the edges of his sink, his toilet, his bunk.

'You got any idea, Bourne, what's going on outside?' the warden said, but Shay just stood with his head tucked into his shoulder, like Calloway's robin did when he slept. 'You care to tell me what you're trying to prove?'

At Shay's pronounced silence, the warden began to walk the length of our tier. 'What about you?' he called out to the rest of us. 'And I will inform you that those who cooperate with me will not be punished. I can't promise anything for the rest of you.'

Nobody spoke.

Warden Coyne turned to Shay. 'Where did you get the gum?'

'There was only one piece,' Joey Kunz blurted, the snitch. 'But it was enough for all of us.'

'You some kind of magician, son?' the warden said, his face inches away from Shay's. 'Or did you hypnotize them into believing they were getting something they weren't? I know about mind control, Bourne.'

'I didn't do anything,' Shay murmured.

Officer Whitaker stepped closer. 'Warden Coyne, there's nothing in his cell. Not even in his mattress. His blanket's intact – if he's been fishing with it, then he managed to weave the strings back together when he was done.'

I stared at Shay. Of course he'd fished with his blanket; I'd seen the line he'd made with my own eyes. I'd untied the bubble gum from the braided blue strand.

'I'm watching you, Bourne,' the warden hissed. 'I know what you're up to. You know damn well your heart isn't going to be worth anything once it's pumped full of potassium chloride in a death chamber. You're doing this because you've got no appeals left, but even if you get Barbara freaking Walters to do an interview with you, the sympathy vote's not going to change your execution date.'

The warden stalked off I-tier. Officer Whitaker released Shay's handcuffs from the bar where he was tethered and led him back to his cell. 'Listen, Bourne. I'm Catholic.'

'Good for you,' Shay replied.

'I thought Catholics were against the death penalty,' Crash said.

'Yeah, don't do him any favors,' Texas added.

Whitaker glanced down the tier, where the warden stood outside the soundproof glass, talking to another officer. 'The thing is . . . if you want . . . I could ask one of the priests from St Catherine's to visit.' He paused. 'Maybe he can help with the whole heart thing.'

Shay stared at him. 'Why would you do that for me?'

The officer fished inside the neck of his shirt, pulling out a length of chain and the crucifix that was attached to the end of it. He brought it to his lips, then let it fall beneath his uniform again. 'He that believeth on me,' Whitaker murmured, 'believeth not on me, but on him that sent me.'

I did not know the New Testament, but I recognized a biblical passage when I heard one – and it didn't take a rocket scientist to realize that he was suggesting Shay's antics, or whatever you wanted to call them, were heaven-sent. I realized then that even though Shay was a prisoner, he had a certain power over Whitaker. He had a certain power over *all* of us. Shay Bourne had done what no brute force or power play or gang threat had been able to do all the years I'd been on I-tier: he'd brought us together.

Next door, Shay was slowly putting his cell to rights. The news program was wrapping up with another bird's-eye view of the state prison. From the helicopter footage, you could see how many people had gathered, how many more were heading this way.

I sat down on my bunk. It wasn't possible, was it?

My own words to Alma came back to me: *It's not probable. Anything's possible.*

I pulled my art supplies out of my hiding spot in the mattress, riffling through my sketches for the one I'd done of Shay being wheeled off the tier after his seizure. I'd drawn him on the gurney, arms spread and tied down, legs banded together, eyes raised to the ceiling. I turned the paper ninety degrees. This way, it didn't look like Shay was lying down. It looked like he was being crucified.

People were always 'finding' Jesus in jail. What if he was already here?

'I don't want to achieve immortality through my work;
I want to achieve immortality through not dying.'

— WOODY ALLEN, QUOTED IN WOODY ALLEN AND
HIS COMEDY, BY ERIC LAX

Maggie

There were many things I was grateful for, including the fact that I was no longer in high school. Let's just say it wasn't a walk in the park for a girl who didn't fit into the smorgasbord of clothing at the Gap, and who tried to become invisible so she wouldn't be noticed for her size. Today, I was in a different school and it was ten years later, but I was still suffering from a flashback anxiety attack. It didn't matter that I was wearing my Jones New York I'm-going-to-court suit; it didn't matter that I was old enough to be mistaken for a teacher instead of a student – I still expected a football jock to turn the corner, at any moment, and make a fat joke.

Topher Renfrew, the boy who was sitting beside me in the lobby of the high school, was dressed in black jeans and a frayed T-shirt with an anarchy symbol, a guitar pick strung around his neck on a leather lanyard. Cut him, and he'd bleed antiestablishment. His iPod earphones hung down the front of his shirt like a doctor's stethoscope; and as he read the decision handed down by the court just an hour before, his lips mouthed the words. 'So, what does all this bullshit mean?' he asked.

'That you won,' I explained. 'If you don't want to say the Pledge of Allegiance, you don't have to.'

'What about Karshank?'

His homeroom teacher, a Korean War veteran, had sent Topher to detention every time he refused to say the Pledge. It had led to a letter-writing campaign by my office (well, me) and then we'd gone to court to protect his civil liberties.

Topher handed me back the decision. 'Sweet,' he said. 'Any chance you can get pot legalized?'

'Uh, not my area of expertise. Sorry.' I shook Topher's hand, congratulated him, and headed out of the school.

It was a day for celebration – I unrolled the windows of the Prius, even though it was cold outside, and turned up Aretha on the CD player. Mostly, my cases got shot down by the courts; I spent more time fighting than I did getting a response. As one of three ACLU attorneys in New Hampshire, I was a champion of the First Amendment – freedom of speech, freedom of religion, freedom to organize. In other words, I looked really great on paper, but in reality, it meant I had become an expert letter writer. I wrote on behalf of the teenagers who wanted to wear their Hooters shirts to school, or the gay kid who wanted to bring his boyfriend to the prom; I wrote to take the cops to task for enforcing DWB – driving while black – when statistics showed they corralled more minorities than whites for routine traffic stops. I spent countless hours at community meetings, negotiating with local agencies, the AG's office, the police departments, the schools. I was the splinter they couldn't get rid of, the thorn in their side, their conscience.

I took out my cell phone and dialed my mother's number at the spa. 'Guess what,' I said when she picked up. 'I won.'

'Maggie, that's fantastic. I'm so proud of you.' There was the slightest beat. 'What did you win?'

'My case! The one I was telling you about last weekend at dinner?'

'The one against the community college whose mascot is an Indian?'

'Native American. And no,' I said. 'I lost that one, actually. I was talking about the Pledge case. And' – I pulled out my trump card – 'I think I'm going to be on the news tonight. There were cameras all over the courthouse.'

I listened to my mother drop the phone, yelling to her staff about her famous daughter. Grinning, I hung up, only to have the cell ring against my palm again. 'What were you wearing?' my mother asked.

'My Jones New York suit.'

My mother hesitated. 'Not the pin-striped one?'

'What's that supposed to mean?'

'I'm just asking.'

'Yes, the pin-striped one,' I said. 'What's wrong with it?'

'Did I *say* there was anything wrong with it?'

'You didn't have to.' I swerved to avoid a slowing car. 'I have to go,' I said, and I hung up, tears stinging.

It rang again. 'Your mother's crying,' my father said.

'Well, that makes two of us. Why can't she just be happy for me?'

'She is, honey. She thinks you're too critical.'

'*I'm* too critical? Are you kidding?'

'I bet Marcia Clark's mother asked her what she was wearing to the O.J. trial,' my father said.

'I bet Marcia Clark's mother doesn't get her daughter exercise videos for Chanukah.'

'I bet Marcia Clark's mother doesn't get her *anything* for Chanukah,' my father said, laughing. 'Her Christmas stocking, though . . . I hear it's full of *The Firm* DVDs.'

A smile twitched at the corners of my mouth. In the background, I could hear the rising strains of a crying baby. 'Where *are* you?'

'At a bris,' my father said. 'And I'd better go, because the mohel's giving me dirty looks, and believe me, I don't want to upset him before he does a circumcision. Call me later and tell me every last detail. Your mother's going to TiVo the news for us.'

I hung up and tossed my phone into the passenger seat. My father, who had made a living out of studying Jewish law, was always good at seeing the gray areas between the black-and-white letters. My mother, on the other hand, had a remarkable talent for taking a celebratory day and ruining it. I pulled into my driveway and headed into my house, where Oliver met me at the front door. 'I need a drink,' I told him, and he cocked an ear, because after all it was only 11:45 a.m. I went straight to the refrigerator – in spite of what my mother likely imagined, the only food inside of it was ketchup, a jar of pimientos, Ollie's carrots, and yogurt with an expiration date from Bill Clinton's administration – and poured myself a glass of Yellow Tail chardonnay. I wanted to be pleasantly buzzed before I turned on the television set, where no doubt my fifteen minutes of fame was now going to be marred by a suit with stripes that made my already plus-size butt look positively planetary.

Oliver and I settled onto the couch just as the theme song for the midday news spilled into my living room. The anchor, a woman with a blond helmet head, smiled into the camera. Behind her was a graphic of an American flag with a line through it, and the caption NO PLEDGE? 'In today's top story, a winning decision was handed down in the case of the high school student who refused to say the Pledge of Allegiance.' The screen filled with a video of the courthouse steps, where you could see my face with a bouquet of microphones thrust under my nose.

Dammit, I *did* look fat in this suit.

'In a stunning victory for individual civil liberties,' I began onscreen, and then a bright blue BREAKING NEWS banner obliterated my face. The picture switched to a live feed in front of the state prison, where there were squatters with tents and people holding placards and . . . was that a chorus line of wheelchairs?

The reporter's hair was being whipped into a frenzy by the wind. 'I'm Janice Lee, reporting live from the New Hampshire State Prison for Men in Concord, which houses the man other inmates are calling the Death Row Messiah.'

I picked up Oliver and sat down, cross-legged, in front of the television. Behind the reporter were dozens of people – I couldn't tell if they were picketing or protesting. Some stuck out from the crowd: the man with the sandwich board that read JOHN 3:16, the mother clutching a limp child, the small knot of nuns praying the rosary.

'This is a follow-up to our initial report,' the reporter said, 'in which we chronicled the inexplicable events that have occurred since inmate Shay Bourne – New Hampshire's only death row inhabitant – expressed his desire to donate his organs post-execution. Today there might be scientific proof that these incidents aren't magic . . . but something more.'

The screen filled with a uniformed officer's face – Correctional Officer Rick Whitaker, according to the caption beneath him. 'The first one was the tap water,' he said. 'One night, when I was on duty, the inmates got intoxicated, and sure enough the pipes tested positive for alcohol residue one day, although the water source tested perfectly normal. Some of the inmates have mentioned a bird being brought back to life, although I didn't witness that myself. But I'd have to say the most dramatic change involved Inmate DuFresne.'

The reporter again: 'According to sources, inmate Lucius DuFresne – an AIDS patient in the final stages of the disease – has been miraculously cured. On tonight's six o'clock report, we'll talk to physicians at Dartmouth-Hitchcock Medical Center about whether this can be explained medically . . . but for the newly converted followers of this Death Row Messiah,' the reporter said, gesturing to the crowds behind her, 'anything's possible. This is Janice Lee, reporting from Concord.'

Then I saw a familiar face in the crowd behind the reporter – DeeDee, the spa technician who'd given me my body wrap. I remembered telling her that I'd look into Shay Bourne's case.

I picked up the phone and dialed my boss at the office. 'Are you watching the news?'

Rufus Urqhart, the head of the ACLU in New Hampshire, had two televisions on his desk that he kept tuned to different channels so that he didn't miss a thing. 'Yeah,' he said. 'I thought you were supposed to be on.'

'I got preempted by the Death Row Messiah.'

'Can't beat divinity,' Rufus said.

'Exactly,' I replied. 'Rufus, I want to work on his behalf.'

'Wake up, sweetheart, you already *are*. At least, you were *supposed* to be filing amicus briefs,' Rufus said.

'No – I mean, I want to take him on as a client. Give me a week,' I begged.

'Listen, Maggie, this guy's already been through the state court, the first circuit of the federal court, and the Supreme Court. If I remember correctly, they punted last year and denied cert. Bourne's exhausted all his appeals . . . I don't really see how we can reopen the door.'

'If he thinks he's the Messiah,' I said, 'he just gave us a crowbar.'

The Religious Land Use and Institutionalized Persons Act of 2000 didn't actually come into play until five years later, when the Supreme Court upheld the decision in the case of *Cutter v. Wilkinson*, where a bunch of Ohio prisoners who were Satanists sued the state for not accommodating their religious needs. As long as a prison guaranteed the right to practice religion – without *forcing* religion on those who didn't want to practice it – the law was constitutional.

'Satanists?' my mother said, putting down her knife and fork. 'That's what this guy is?'

I was at their house, having dinner, like I did every Friday night before they went to Shabbat services. My mother would invite me on Monday, and I'd tell her I'd have to wait and see whether anything came up – like a date, or Armageddon, both of which had the same likelihood of occurring in my life. And then, of course, by Friday, I'd find myself passing the roasted potatoes and listening to my father say the kiddush over the wine.

'I have no idea,' I told her. 'I haven't met with him.'

'Do Satanists have messiahs?' my father asked.

'You're missing the point, both of you. Legally, there's a statute that says that even prisoners have a right to practice their religion as long as it doesn't interfere with the running of the prison.' I shrugged. 'Besides, what if he *is* the Messiah? Aren't we morally obligated to save his life if he's here to save the world?'

My father cut a slice of his brisket. 'He's not the Messiah.'

'And you know this because . . . ?'

'He isn't a warrior. He hasn't maintained the sovereign state of Israel. He hasn't ushered in world peace. And okay, so maybe he's brought something dead back to life, but if he was the Messiah he would have resurrected everyone. And if that was the case, your grandparents would be here right now asking if there was more gravy.'

'There's a difference between a Jewish messiah, Dad, and . . . well . . . the other one.'

'What makes you think that there might be more than one?' he asked.

'What makes you think there might not?' I shot back.

My mother threw her napkin down. 'I'm getting a Tylenol,' she said, and left the table.

My father grinned at me. 'You would have made such a good rabbi, Mags.'

'Yeah, if only that pesky religion thing didn't keep getting in the way.'

I had, of course, been raised Jewish. I would sit through Friday night services and listen to the soaring, rich voice of the cantor; I would watch my father reverently carry the Torah and it would remind me of how he looked in my baby pictures when he held me. But I'd also grow so bored that I'd find myself memorizing the names of who begat whom in Numbers. The more I learned about Jewish law the more I felt that, as a girl, I was bound to be considered unclean or limited or lacking. I had my bat mitzvah, like my parents wanted; and the day after I read from the Torah and celebrated my transition into adulthood, I told my parents I was never going to temple again.

Why? my father had asked when I told him.

Because I don't think God really cares whether or not I'm sitting there every Friday night. Because I don't buy into a religion that's based on what thou shalt not do, instead of what thou ought to be doing for the greater good. Because I don't know what I believe.

I didn't have the heart to tell him the truth: that I was much closer to an atheist than an agnostic, that I doubted there was a God at all. In my line of work, I'd seen too much injustice in the world to buy into the belief that a merciful, all-powerful deity would continue to allow such atrocities to exist; and I downright detested the party line that there was some divine grand plan for humanity's bumbling existence. It was a little like a parent watching her children playing with fire and thinking, *Well, let them burn. That'll teach 'em.*

Once, when I was in high school, I asked my father about religions that were, with the passage of time, considered to be false. The Greeks and Romans, with all their gods, thought they were making sacrifices and praying at temples in order to receive favor from their deities; but today, pious people would scoff. How do you know, I'd asked my father, that five hundred years from now, some alien master race won't be picking over the artifacts of your Torah and their crucifix and wondering how you could be so naive?

My father, who was the first to take a controversial situation and say 'Let's think about that,' had been speechless. Because, he'd said finally, a religion doesn't last two thousand years if it's based on a lie.

Here's my take on it: I don't think religions are based on lies, but I don't think they're based on truths, either. I think they come about because of what people need at the time that they need them. Like the World Series player who won't take off his lucky socks, or the mother of the sick child who believes that her baby can sleep only if she's sitting by the crib – believers need, by definition, something to believe *in*.

'So what's your plan?' my father asked, bringing my attention back.

I glanced up. 'I'm going to save him.'

'Maybe *you're* the Messiah,' he mused.

My mother sat down again, popped two pills into her mouth, and swallowed them dry. 'What if he's creating this whole to-do so that somebody like you will come out of the woodwork and keep him from being executed?'

Well, I'd already considered that. 'It doesn't matter if it's all a big ruse,' I said. 'As long as I can get the court to buy it, it's still a blow against the death penalty.' I imagined myself being interviewed by Stone Phillips. Who, when the cameras cut, would ask me out to dinner.

'Promise me you won't be one of these lawyers who falls for the criminal and marries him in the prison . . .'

'Mom!'

'Well, it happens, Maggie. Felons are very persuasive people.'

'And you know this because you've personally spent so much time in prison?'

She held up her hands. 'I'm just saying.'

'Rachel, I think Maggie's got this under control,' my father said. 'Why don't we get ready to go?'

My mother started clearing the dishes, and I followed her into the kitchen. We fell into a familiar routine: I'd load the dishwasher and rinse off the big platters; she'd dry. 'I can finish,' I said, like I did every week. 'You don't want to be late for temple.'

She shrugged. 'They can't start without your father.' I passed her a dripping serving bowl, but she set it on the counter and examined my hand instead. 'Look at your nails, Maggie.'

I pulled away. 'I've got more important things to do than make sure my cuticles are trimmed, Ma.'

'It's not about the manicure,' she said. 'It's about taking forty-five minutes where the most important thing in the world is not someone else . . . but *you*.'

That was the thing about my mother: just when I thought I was ready to kill her, she'd say something that made me want to cry. I tried to curl my hands into fists, but she threaded our fingers together. 'Come to the spa next week. We'll have a nice afternoon, just the two of us.'

A dozen comments sprang to the back of my tongue: *Some of us have to work for a living. It won't be a nice afternoon if it's just the two of us. I may be a glutton, but not for punishment.* Instead, I nodded, even though we both knew I had no intention of showing up.

When I was tiny, my mother would have spa days in the kitchen, just for me. She'd concoct hair conditioners out of papaya and banana; she'd rub coconut oil into the skin of my shoulders and arms; she'd lay slices of cucumber on my eyes and sing Sonny & Cher songs to me. Afterward, she would hold a hand mirror up to my face. *Look at my beautiful girl*, she would say, and for the longest time, I believed her.

'Come to temple,' my mother said. 'Just tonight. It would make your father so happy.'

'Maybe next time,' I answered.

I walked them out to their car. My father turned the ignition and unrolled his window. 'You know,' he said. 'When I was in college, there was a homeless guy who used to hang out near the subway. He had a pet mouse that used to sit on his shoulder and nibble at the collar of his coat, and he never took that coat off, not even when it was ninety-five degrees out. He knew the entire first chapter of *Moby-Dick* by heart. I always gave him a quarter when I passed by.'

A neighbor's car zoomed past – someone from my father's congregation, who honked a hello.

My father smiled. 'The word *Messiah* isn't in the Old Testament . . . just the Hebrew word for *anointed*. He's not a savior; he's a king or a priest with a special purpose. But the Midrash – well, it mentions the *moshiach* a lot, and he looks different every time. Sometimes he's a soldier, sometimes he's a politician, sometimes he's got supernatural powers. And sometimes he's dressed like a vagrant. The reason I gave that bum a quarter,' he said, 'is because you never know.'

Then he put the car in reverse and pulled out of the driveway. I stood there until I couldn't see them anymore, until there was nothing left to do but go home.

Michael

Before you can go into a prison, you're stripped of the trappings that make you *you*. Take off your shoes, your belt.
Remove your wallet, your watch, your saint's medal. Loose change
in your pockets, cell phone, even the crucifix pin on your lapel.
Hand over your driver's license to the uniformed officer, and in
return, you become one of the faceless people who has entered a
place the residents aren't allowed to leave.

'Father?' an officer said. 'Are you okay?'

I tried to smile and nod, imagining what he saw: a big tough
guy who was shaking at the thought of entering this prison. Sure,
I rode a Triumph Trophy, volunteered to work with gang youth,
and broke the stereotype of a priest any chance I got – but inside
here was the man whose life I had voted to end.

And yet.

Ever since I had taken my vows and asked God to help me
offset what I had done to one man with what I might yet be able
to do for others – I knew this would happen one day. I knew I'd
wind up face-to-face with Shay Bourne.

Would he recognize me?

Would I recognize *him*?

I walked through the metal detector, holding my breath, as if I
had something to hide. And I suppose I did, but my secrets wouldn't
set off those alarms. I started to weave my belt into the loops of
my trousers again, to tie the laces of my Converse sneakers. My
hands were still trembling. 'Father Michael?' I glanced up to find
another officer waiting for me. 'Warden Coyne's expecting you.'

'Right.' I followed the officer through dull gray hallways. When we passed inmates, the officer pivoted his body so that he stood between us – a shield.

I was delivered to an administrative office that overlooked the interior courtyard of the state prison. A conga line of prisoners was walking from one building to another. Behind them was a double line of fencing, capped with razor wire.

'Father.'

The warden was a stocky man with silver hair who offered a handshake and a grimace that was supposed to pass for a smile. 'Warden Coyne. Nice to meet you.'

He led me into his private office, a surprisingly modern, airy space with no desk – just a long, spare steel table with files and notes spread across it. As soon as he sat down, he unwrapped a piece of gum. 'Nicorette,' he explained. 'My wife's making me quit smoking and to be honest, I'd rather cut off my left arm.' He opened a file with a number on its side – Shay Bourne had been stripped of his name in here as well. 'I do appreciate you coming. We're a little short on chaplains right now.'

The prison had one full-time chaplain, an Episcopal priest who had flown to Australia to be with his dying father. Which meant that if an inmate requested to speak to a clergyman, one of the locals would be called in.

'It's my pleasure,' I lied, and mentally marked the rosary I'd say later as penance.

He pushed the file toward me. 'Shay Bourne. You know him?'

I hesitated. 'Who doesn't?'

'Yeah, the news coverage is a bitch, pardon my French. I could do without all the attention. Bottom line is the inmate wants to donate his organs after execution.'

'Catholics support organ donation, as long as the patient is brain-dead and no longer breathing by himself,' I said.

Apparently, it was the wrong answer. Coyne lifted up a tissue, frowned, and spit his gum into it. 'Yeah, great, I get it. That's the party line. But the reality of the situation is that this guy's at the twenty-third hour. He's a convicted murderer, two times over. You think he's suddenly developed a humanitarian streak . . . or is it more likely that he's trying to gain public sympathy and stop his execution?'

'Maybe he just wants something good to come out of his death . . .'

'Lethal injection is designed to stop the inmate's heart,' Coyne said flatly.

I had helped a parishioner earlier this year when she made the decision to donate her son's organs after a motorcycle accident that had left him brain-dead. Brain death, the doctor had explained, was different from cardiac death. Her son was still irrevocably gone – he would not eventually recover, like people in a coma – but thanks to the respirator, his heart was still beating. If cardiac death had occurred, the organs wouldn't be viable for transplant.

I sat back in the chair. 'Warden Coyne, I was under the impression that Inmate Bourne had requested a spiritual advisor . . .'

'He did. And we'd like you to advise him against this crazy idea.' The warden sighed. 'Look, I know what this must sound like to you. But Bourne's going to be executed by the state. That's a fact. Either it can become a sideshow . . . or it can be done with discretion.' He stared at me. 'Are we clear on what you need to do?'

'Crystal,' I said quietly.

I had once before let myself be led by others, because I assumed they knew more than me. Jim, another juror, had used the 'eye for an eye' line from Jesus's Sermon on the Mount to convince me that repaying a death with a death was just. But now, I understood that Jesus had actually been saying the opposite – criticizing those who let the punishment compound the crime.

No way was I going to let Warden Coyne tell me how to advise Shay Bourne.

In that instant, I realized that if Bourne didn't recognize me, I wasn't going to tell him I'd met him before. This wasn't about *my* salvation; it was about *his*. And even if I'd been instrumental in ruining his life, now – as a priest – it was my job to redeem him.

'I'd like to meet Mr Bourne,' I said.

The warden nodded. 'I figured.' He stood up and led me back through the administrative offices. We took a turn and came to a control booth, a set of double-barred doors. The warden raised his hand and the officer inside unlocked the first steel door with a buzz and a sound of metal scraping metal. We stepped into the midchamber, and that same door automatically sealed.

So this was what it felt like to be locked in.

Before I could begin to panic, the interior door buzzed open, and we walked along another corridor. 'You ever been in here?' the warden asked.

'No.'

'You get used to it.'

I looked around at the cinder-block walls, the rusting catwalks. 'I doubt that.'

We stepped through a fire door marked I-TIER. 'This is where we keep the most hard-core inmates,' Coyne said. 'I can't promise they'll be on their best behavior.'

In the center of the room was a control tower. A young officer sat there, watching a television monitor that seemed to have a bird's-eye view of the inside of the pod. It was quiet, or maybe the door that led inside was soundproof.

I walked up to the door and peered inside. There was an empty shower stall closest to me, then eight cells. I could not see the faces of the men and wasn't sure which one was Bourne. 'This is Father Michael,' the warden said. 'He's come to speak with Inmate Bourne.' He reached into a bin and handed me a flak jacket and protective goggles, as if I were going to war instead of death row.

'You can't go in unless you've got the right equipment,' the warden said.

'Go *in*?'

'Well, where'd you think you were going to meet Inmate Bourne, Father? Starbucks?'

I had thought there would be some kind of . . . room, I guess. Or the chapel. 'I'll be alone with him? In a cell?'

'Hell, no,' Warden Coyne said. 'You stand out on the catwalk and talk through the door.'

Taking a deep breath, I slipped the jacket on over my clothes and fitted the goggles to my face. Then I winged a quick prayer and nodded.

'Open up,' Warden Coyne said to the young officer.

'Yes, sir,' the kid said, clearly flustered to be under Coyne's regard. He glanced down at the control panel before him, a myriad display of buttons and lights, and pushed one near his left hand, only to realize at the last minute it was the wrong choice. The doors of all eight cells opened at once.

'Ohmygod,' the boy said, his eyes wide as saucers, as the warden shoved me out of the way and began punching a series of levers and buttons on the control panel.

'Get him out of here,' the warden yelled, jerking his head in my direction. Over the loudspeaker came his radio call: *Multiple inmates released on I-tier; need officer assistance immediately.*

I stood, riveted, as the inmates spilled out of their respective cells like poison. And then . . . well . . . all hell broke loose.

Lucius

When the doors released in unison, like all the strings tuning up in an orchestra and magically hitting the right note the first time the bow was raised, I didn't run out of the cell like the others. I stopped for a beat, paralyzed by freedom.

I quickly tucked my painting beneath the mattress of the bunk and stashed my ink in a roll of dirty laundry. I could hear Warden Coyne's voice on the loudspeakers, calling over the radio for the SWAT team. This had happened only once before when I was in prison; a new officer screwed up and two cells were opened simultaneously. The inmate who'd been accidentally freed rushed into the other's cell and cracked his skull open against the sink, a gang hit that had been waiting for years to come to pass.

Crash was the first one out of his cell. He ran past mine with his fist curled around a shank, making a beeline for Joey Kunz – a child molester was fair game for anyone. Pogie and Texas followed him like the dogs they were. 'Grab him, boys,' Crash hollered. 'Let's just cut it right off.'

Joey's voice escalated as he was cornered. 'For God's sake, someone help!'

There was the sound of a fist hitting flesh, of Calloway swearing. By now, he was in Joey's cell, too.

'Lucius?' I heard, a slow ribbon of a voice, as if it had come from underwater, and I remembered that Joey wasn't the only one on the tier who'd hurt a child. If Joey was Crash's first victim, Shay could very well be the second.

There were people outside the prison praying to Shay; there were religious pundits on TV who promised hell and damnation to those who worshipped a false messiah. I didn't know what Shay was or wasn't, but I credited him for my health one hundred percent. And there was something about him that just didn't fit in here, that made you stop and look twice, as if you'd come across an orchid growing in a ghetto.

'Stay where you are,' I called out. 'Shay, you hear me?'

But he didn't answer. I stood at the threshold of my cell, trembling. I stared at that invisible line between here and now, no and yes, if and when. With one deep breath, I stepped outside.

Shay was not in his cell; he was moving slowly toward Joey's. Through the door of I-tier, I could see the officers suiting up in flak jackets and shields and masks. There was someone else, too – a priest I'd never seen before.

I reached for Shay's arm to stop him. That's all, just that small heat, and it nearly brought me to my knees. Here in prison we did not touch; we were not touched. I could have held on to Shay, at the innocent crook of his elbow, forever.

But Shay turned, and I remembered the first unwritten rule of being in prison: you did not invade someone's space. I let go. 'It's okay,' Shay said softly, and he took another step toward Joey's cell.

Joey was spread-eagled on the floor, sobbing, his pants pulled down. His head was twisted away, and blood streamed from his nose. Pogie had one of his arms, Texas the other; Calloway sat on his fighting feet. From this angle, they were obscured from the view of the officers who were mobilizing to subdue everyone. 'You heard of Save the Children?' Crash said, brandishing his homemade blade. 'I'm here to make a donation.'

Just then, Shay sneezed.

'God bless,' Crash said automatically.

Shay wiped his nose on his sleeve. 'Thanks.'

The interruption made Crash lose some of his momentum. He glanced out at the army on the other side of the door, screaming commands we couldn't hear. He rocked back on his heels and surveyed Joey, shivering against the cement floor.

'Let him go,' Crash said.

'Let him . . . ?' Calloway echoed.

'You heard me. All of you. Go back.'

Pogie and Texas listened; they always did what Crash said. Calloway was slower to leave. 'We ain't done here,' he said to Joey, but then he left.

'What the fuck are you waiting for?' Crash said to me, and I hurried back to my own cell, forgetting entirely anyone else's welfare except my own.

I do not know what it was that led to Crash's change of plan – if it was knowing that the officers would storm the tier and punish him; if it was Shay's well-timed sneeze; if it was a prayer – *God bless* – on the lips of a sinner like Crash. But by the time the SWAT team entered seconds later, all seven of us were sitting in our cells even though the doors were still wide open, as if we were angels, as if we had nothing to hide.

There's a flower I can see from the exercise yard. Well, I can't really see it – I have to sort of hook my fingers on the ledge of the only window and spider-walk up the cement wall, but I can glimpse it then before I fall back down. It's a dandelion, which you might think is a weed, but it can be put into salads or soups. The root can be ground up and used as a coffee substitute. The juices can get rid of warts or be used as an insect repellent. I learned all this from a *Mother Earth News* magazine piece that I keep wrapped around my treasures – my shank, my Q-tips, the tiny Visine bottles where I keep the ink I manufacture. I read the article every time I take my supplies out for inventory, which is daily. I keep my cache behind a loosened cinder block beneath my cot, refilling the mortar with Metamucil and toothpaste, mixed, so that the officers don't get suspicious when they toss the cell.

I never gave it much thought before I came in here, but I wish I knew more about horticulture. I wish I'd taken the time to learn what makes things grow. Hell, if I had, maybe I could have started a watermelon plant from a seedling. Maybe I'd have vines hanging all over the place by now.

Adam had the green thumb in our household. I used to find him outside at the crack of dawn, rooting around in the dirt between our daylilies and sedums. *The weeds shall inherit the earth,* he had said.

Meek, I'd corrected. *The meek shall inherit it.*

No way, Adam had said, and laughed. *The weeds will blow right by them.*

He used to say that if you picked a dandelion, two would grow back in its place. I guess they are the botanical equivalent of the men in this prison. Take one of us off the street, and more will sprout up in his wake.

With Crash back in solitary, and Joey in the infirmary, I-tier was oddly quiet. In the wake of Joey's beating, our privileges had been suspended, so all showers and exercise yard visits were canceled for the day. Shay was pacing. Earlier, he'd been complaining that his teeth were vibrating with the air-conditioning unit; sometimes sounds got to be too much for him – usually when he was agitated. 'Lucius,' he said. 'Did you see that priest today?'

'Yeah.'

'Do you think he came for me?'

I didn't want to give him false hope. 'I don't know, Shay. Maybe someone was dying on another tier and needed last rites.'

'The dead aren't alive, and the living don't die.'

I laughed. 'Thanks for that, Yoda.'

'Who's Yoda?'

He was talking crazy, the way Crash had a year ago when he'd started to peel the lead paint from the cinder blocks and eat it, hoping it would serve as a hallucinogen. 'Well, if there *is* a heaven, I bet it's full of dandelions.' (Actually, I think heaven's full of guys who look like Wentworth Miller from *Prison Break*, but for right now, I was only talking landscaping.)

'Heaven's not a *place*.'

'I didn't say it had map coordinates . . .'

'If it was in the sky, then birds would get there before you. If it was under the sea, fish would be first.'

'Then where is it?' I asked.

'It's inside you,' Shay said, 'and outside, too.'

If he wasn't eating the lead paint, then he'd been making hooch I didn't know about. 'If this is heaven, I'll take a rain check.'

'You can't wait for it, because it's already here.'

'Well, you're the only one of us who got rose-colored glasses when he was booked, I guess.'

Shay was silent for a while. 'Lucius,' he asked finally. 'Why did Crash go after Joey instead of me?'

I didn't know. Crash was a convicted murderer; I had no doubt he could and would kill again if given the opportunity. Technically, both Joey and Shay had sinned equally in Crash's code of justice; they had harmed children. Maybe Crash figured Joey would be easier to kill. Maybe Shay had gained a modicum of respect through his miracles. Maybe he'd just gotten lucky.

Maybe even Crash thought there was something special about Shay.

'He's not any different than Joey . . .' Shay said.

'Teensy suggestion? Don't let Crash hear you say that.'

'. . . and we're not any different than Crash,' he finished. 'You don't know what would make you do what Crash did, just like you didn't know what would make you kill Adam, until it happened.'

I drew in my breath. No one in prison talked about another person's crime, even if you secretly believed they were guilty. But I *had* killed Adam. It was my hand holding the gun; it was his blood on my clothes. It wasn't what had been done that was at issue for me in court; it was why.

'It's okay to not know something,' Shay said. 'That's what makes us human.'

No matter what Mr Philosopher Next Door thought, there were

things I knew for sure: That I had been loved, once, and had loved back. That a person could find hope in the way a weed grew. That the sum of a man's life was not where he wound up but in the details that brought him there.

That we made mistakes.

I closed my eyes, sick of the riddles, and to my surprise all I could see were dandelions – as if they had been painted on the fields of my imagination, a hundred thousand suns. And I remembered something else that makes us human: faith, the only weapon in our arsenal to battle doubt.

June

They say God won't give you any more than you can handle, but that begs a more important question: why would God let you suffer in the first place?

'No comment,' I said into the phone, and I slammed down the receiver loud enough that Claire – on the couch with her iPod on – sat up and took notice. I reached beneath the table and yanked out the cord completely so that I would not have to hear the phone ring.

They had been calling all morning; they had set up camp outside my home. *How does it feel to know that there are protesters outside the prison, hoping to free the man who murdered your child and your husband?*

Do you think Shay Bourne's request to be an organ donor is a way to make up for what he's done?

What I thought was that nothing Shay Bourne could do or say would ever make up for the lives of Elizabeth and Kurt. I knew firsthand how well he could lie and what might come of it – this was nothing more than some publicity stunt to make everyone feel badly for him, because after a decade, who even remembered feeling badly for that police officer, that little girl?

I did.

There are people who say that the death penalty isn't just because it takes so long to execute a man. That it's inhumane to have to wait eleven years or more for punishment. That at least for Elizabeth and Kurt, death came quickly.

Let me tell you what's wrong with that line of reasoning: it assumes that Elizabeth and Kurt were the only victims. It leaves out me; it leaves out Claire. And I can promise you that every day for the last eleven years I've thought of what I lost at the hands of Shay Bourne. I've been anticipating his death just as long as he has.

I heard voices coming from the living room and realized that Claire had turned on the television. A grainy photograph of Shay Bourne filled the screen. It was the same photo that had been used in the newspapers, although Claire would not have seen those, since I'd thrown them out immediately. Bourne's hair was cut short now, and there were parenthetical lines around his mouth and fanning from the corners of his eyes, but he otherwise did not look any different.

'That's him, isn't it?' Claire asked.

God, Complex? read the caption beneath the photograph.

'Yes.' I walked toward the television, intentionally blocking her view, and turned it off.

Claire looked up at me. 'I remember him,' she said.

I sighed. 'Honey, you weren't even born yet.'

She unfolded the afghan that sat on the couch and wrapped it around her shoulders, as if she'd suddenly taken a chill. 'I remember him,' Claire repeated.

Michael

I would have had to be living under a rock to not know what I was being said about Shay Bourne, but I was the last person in the world who would ever have believed him to be messianic. As far as I was concerned, there was one Son of God, and I knew who He was. As for Bourne's showmanship – well, I'd seen David Blaine make an elephant disappear on Fifth Avenue in New York City, but that wasn't a miracle, either. Plain and simple: my job here wasn't to feed into Shay Bourne's delusional beliefs . . . only to help him accept Jesus Christ as his Lord and Savior before his execution so that he'd wind up in the Kingdom of Heaven.

And if I could help him donate his heart somewhere along the way, so be it.

Two days after the incident at I-tier had occurred, I parked my Trophy outside the prison. My mind kept tripping over a verse from Matthew where Jesus spoke to his disciples: *I was a stranger, and you took me in; naked, and you clothed me; I was sick, and you visited me; I was in prison, and you came unto me.* The disciples – who were, to be brutally honest, a thick bunch – were confused. They couldn't remember Jesus being lost or naked or sick or imprisoned. And Jesus told them: *Inasmuch as you have done it unto one of the least of my brethren, you have done it unto me.*

Inside, I was handed a flak jacket and goggles again. The door to I-tier opened, and I was led down the hallway to Shay Bourne's cell.

It wasn't all that different from being in the confessional. The same Swiss-cheese holes perforated the metal door of the cell, so I could get a glimpse of Shay. Although we were the same age, he looked like he'd aged a lifetime. Now gray at the temples, he still was slight and wiry. I hesitated, silent, waiting to see if his eyes would go wide with recognition, if he would start banging on the door and demand to get away from the person who'd set the wheels of his execution in motion.

But a funny thing happens when you're in clerical dress: you aren't a man. You're somehow more than one, and also less. I've had secrets whispered in front of me; I've had women hike up their skirts to fix their panty hose. Like a physician, a priest is supposed to be unflappable, an observer, a fly on the wall. Ask ten people who meet me what I look like, and eight of them won't be able to tell you the color of my eyes. They simply don't look past the collar.

Shay walked directly up to the door of the cell and started to grin. 'You came,' he said.

I swallowed. 'Shay, I'm Father Michael.'

He flattened his palms against the door of the cell. I remembered a photograph from the crime evidence, those fingers dark with a little girl's blood. I had changed so much in the past eleven years, but what about Shay Bourne? Was he remorseful? Had he matured? Did he wish, like me, that he could erase his mistakes?

'Hey, Father,' a voice yelled out – I would later learn it was Calloway Reece – 'you got any of those wafers? I'm near starving.'

I ignored him and focused on Shay. 'So . . . I understand you're Catholic?'

'A foster mother had me baptized,' Shay said. 'A thousand years ago.' He glanced at me. 'They could put you in the conference room, the one they use for lawyers.'

'The warden said we'd have to talk here, at your cell.'

Shay shrugged. 'I don't have anything to hide.'

Do you? I heard, although he hadn't said it.

'Anyway, that's where they give us hep C,' Shay said.

'Give you hep C?'

'On haircut day. Every other Wednesday. We go to the conference room and they buzz us. Number two blade, even if you want
it longer for winter. They don't make it this hot in here in the
winter. It's freezing from November on.' He turned to me. 'How
come they can't make it hot in November and freezing now?'

'I don't know.'

'It's on the blades.'

'Pardon?'

'Blood,' Shay said. 'On the razor blades. Someone gets nicked,
someone else gets hep C.'

Following his conversation was like watching a SuperBall
bounce. 'Did that happen to you?'

'It happened to other people, so sure, it happened to me.'

*Inasmuch as you have done it unto one of the least of my brethren,
you have done it unto me.*

My head was swimming; I hoped it was Shay's nonlinear speech,
and not a panic attack coming on. I'd been suffering those for
eleven years now, ever since the day we'd sentenced Shay. 'But for
the most part, you're all right?'

After I said it, I wanted to kick myself. You didn't ask a dying
man how he was feeling. *Other than that, Mrs Lincoln*, I thought,
how was the play?

'I get lonely,' Shay answered.

Automatically, I replied, 'God's with you.'

'Well,' Shay said, 'he's lousy at checkers.'

'Do you believe in God?'

'Why do *you* believe in God?' He leaned forward, suddenly
intense. 'Did they tell you I want to donate my heart?'

'That's what I came to talk about, Shay.'

'Good. No one else wants to help.'

'What about your lawyer?'

'I fired him.' Shay shrugged. 'He lost all the appeals, and then
he started talking about going to the governor. The governor's not
even from New Hampshire, did you know that? He was born in
Mississippi. I always wanted to see that river, take one of those

gambling boats down it like some kind of cardsharp. Or maybe that's *shark*. Do they have those in rivers?'

'Your lawyer . . .'

'He wanted the governor to commute my sentence to life, but that's just another death sentence. So I fired him.'

I thought about Warden Coyne, how sure he was that this was all just a ploy to get Shay Bourne's execution called off. Could he have been wrong? 'Are you saying that you *want* to die, Shay?'

'I *want* to live,' he said. 'So I *have* to die.'

Finally, something I could latch onto. 'You *will* live,' I said. 'In the Kingdom of the Father. No matter what happens here, Shay. And no matter whether or not you can donate your organs.'

Suddenly his face went dark. 'What do you mean, whether or not?'

'Well, it's complicated . . .'

'I have to give her my heart. I have to.'

'Who?'

'Claire Nealon.'

My jaw dropped. This specific part of Shay's request had not made it to the broadcast news. '*Nealon?* Is she related to Elizabeth?' Too late I realized that the average person – one who hadn't been on Shay's jury – might not recognize that name and identify it as quickly. But Shay was too agitated to notice.

'She's the sister of the girl who was killed. She has a heart problem; I saw it on TV. What's inside me is going to save me,' Shay said. 'If I don't bring it forward, it's going to kill me.'

We were making the same mistake, Shay and I. We both believed that you could right a former wrong by doing a good deed later on. But giving Claire Nealon his heart wasn't going to bring her sister back to life. And being Shay Bourne's spiritual advisor wasn't going to erase the fact that I was part of the reason he was here.

'You can't get salvation by donating your organs, Shay. The only way to find salvation is to admit your guilt and seek absolution through Jesus.'

'What happened then doesn't matter now.'

'You don't have to be afraid to take responsibility; God loves us, even when we screw up.'

'I couldn't stop it,' Shay said. 'But this time, I can fix it.'

'Leave that to God,' I suggested. 'Tell Him you're sorry for what you did, and He'll forgive you.'

'No matter what?'

'No matter what.'

'Then why do you have to say you're sorry first?'

I hesitated, trying to find a better way to explain sin and salvation to Shay. It was a bargain: you made an admission, you got redemption in return. In Shay's economy of salvation, you gave away a piece of yourself – and somehow found yourself whole again.

Were the two ideas really so different?

I shook my head to clear it.

'Lucius is an atheist,' Shay said. 'Right, Lucius?'

From next door, Lucius mumbled, 'Mm-hmm.'

'And he didn't die. He was sick, and he got better.'

The AIDS patient; I'd heard about him on the news. 'Did you have something to do with it?'

'I didn't do anything.'

'Lucius, do you believe that, too?'

I leaned back so that I could make eye contact with this other inmate, a slim man with a shock of white hair. 'I think Shay had *everything* to do with it,' he said.

'Lucius should believe whatever he needs to,' Shay said.

'What about the miracles?' Lucius added.

'What miracles?' Shay said.

Two facts struck me: Shay Bourne was not claiming to be the Messiah, or Jesus, or anyone but himself. And through some misguided belief, he truly felt that he wouldn't rest in peace unless he could donate his heart to Claire Nealon.

'Look,' Lucius said. 'Are you or are you not going to help him?'

Maybe none of us could compensate for what we'd done wrong in the past, but that didn't mean we couldn't make our futures matter more. I closed my eyes and imagined being the last person Shay Bourne spoke with before he was executed by the State of New Hampshire. I imagined picking a section of the Bible that would resonate with him, a balm of prayer during those last few minutes. I could do this for him. I could be who he needed me to be now, because I hadn't been who he needed me to be back then. 'Shay,' I said, 'knowing that your heart is beating in some other person isn't salvation. It's altruism. Salvation is coming home. It's understanding that you don't have to prove yourself to God.'

'Oh, for Christ's sake,' Lucius snorted. 'Don't listen to him, Shay.'

I turned to him. 'Do you *mind*?' Then I shifted position, so that I blocked Lucius from my sight, focusing on Shay. 'God loves you – whether or not you give up your organs, whether or not you've made mistakes in the past. And the day of your execution, he'll be waiting for you. Christ can save you, Shay.'

'Christ can't give Claire Nealon a heart.' Suddenly Shay's gaze was piercing and lucid. 'I don't need to find God. I don't want catechism,' he said. 'All I want to know is whether, after I'm killed, I can save a little girl.'

'No,' I said bluntly. 'Not if you're given a lethal injection. The drugs are meant specifically to stop your heart, and after that, it's worthless for donation.'

The light in his eyes dimmed, and I drew in my breath. 'I'm sorry, Shay. I know you were hoping to hear something different, and your intentions are good . . . but you need to channel those good intentions to make peace with God another way. And that is something I can make happen.'

Just then a young woman burst onto I-tier. She had a cascade of black curls tumbling down her back, and peeking out from her flak jacket was the ugliest striped suit I'd ever seen. 'Shay Bourne?' she said. 'I know a way you can donate your organs.'

Maggie

Some people may find it tough to break out of prison, but for me, it was equally as hard to get in. Okay, so I wasn't officially Shay Bourne's attorney – but the prison officials didn't know that. I could argue the technicality with Bourne himself, if and when I reached him.

I hadn't counted on how difficult it would be to get through the throng outside the prison. It's one thing to shove your way past a group of college kids smoking pot in a tent, their MAKE PEACE NOT MIRACLES signs littering the muddy ground; it's another thing entirely to explain to a mother and her smooth-scalped, cancer-stricken toddler why you deserved to cut their place in line. In the end, the only way I could edge forward was by explaining to those who'd been waiting (in some cases, for *days*) that I was Shay Bourne's legal advisor and that I would pass along their pleas: from the elderly couple with knotted hands, whose twin diagnoses – breast cancer and lymphatic cancer – came within a week of each other; to the father who carried pictures of the eight children he couldn't support since losing his job; to the daughter pushing her mother's wheelchair, wishing for just one more lucid moment in the fog of Alzheimer's so that she could say she was sorry for a transgression that had happened years earlier. *There is so much pain in this world,* I thought, *how do any of us manage to get up in the morning?*

When I reached the front gate, I announced that I had come to see Shay Bourne, and the officer laughed at me. 'You and the rest of the free world.'

'I'm his lawyer.'

He looked at me for a long moment, and then spoke into his radio. A moment later, a second officer arrived and escorted me past the blockade. As I left, a cheer went up from the crowd.

Stunned, I turned around, waved hesitantly, and then hurried to catch up.

I had never been to the state prison. It was a large, old brick building; its courtyard stretched out behind the razor-wire fencing. I was told to sign in on a clipboard and to take off my jacket before I went through the metal detector.

'Wait here,' the officer said, and he left me sitting in a small anteroom. There was an inmate mopping the floor who did not make eye contact with me. He was wearing white tennis shoes that squelched every time he stepped forward. I watched his hands on the mop and wondered if they'd been part of a murder, a rape, a robbery.

There was a reason I didn't become a criminal defense attorney: this setting freaked me out. I had been to the county jail to meet with clients, but those were small-potatoes crimes: picketing outside a rally for a political candidate, flag burning, civil disobedience. None of my clients had ever killed anyone before, much less a child and a police officer. I found myself considering what it would be like to be locked in here forever. What if my dress clothes and day clothes and pajamas were all the same orange scrubs? What if I was told when to shower, when to eat, when to go to bed? Given that my career was about maintaining personal freedoms, it was hard to imagine a world where they'd all been stripped away.

As I watched the inmate mop beneath a bank of seats, I wondered what would be the hardest luxury to leave behind. There were the trivial things: losing chocolate practically qualified as cruel and unusual punishment; I couldn't sacrifice my contact lenses; I'd sooner die than relinquish the Ouidad Climate Control gel that kept my hair from becoming a frizzy rat's nest. But what about the rest – missing the dizzying choice of all the cereals in the grocery store aisle, for example? Not being able to receive a phone call? Granted, it had been so long since I was intimate with a man that I had spiderwebs between my legs, but what would it be like to give up being touched casually, even a handshake?

I bet I'd even miss fighting with my mother.

Suddenly a pair of boots appeared on the floor before me. 'You're out of luck. He's got his spiritual advisor with him,' the officer said. 'Bourne's pretty popular today.'

'That's fine,' I bluffed. 'The spiritual advisor can join us during our meeting.' I saw the slightest flicker of uncertainty on the face of the officer. Not allowing an inmate to see his attorney was a big no-no, and I was planning to capitalize on that.

The officer shrugged and led me down a hallway. He nodded to a man in a control booth, and a door scraped open. We stepped into a small metal midroom, and I sucked in my breath as the steel door slid home. 'I'm a little claustrophobic,' I said.

The officer smiled. 'Too bad.'

The inner door buzzed, and we entered the prison. 'It's quiet in here,' I remarked.

'That's because it's a good day.' He handed me a flak jacket and goggles and waited for me to put them on. For one brief moment, I panicked – what if a man's jacket like this didn't zip shut on me? How embarrassing would *that* be? But there were Velcro straps and it wasn't an issue, and as soon as I was outfitted, the door to a long tier opened. 'Have fun,' the officer said, and that was when I realized I was supposed to go in alone.

Well. I wasn't going to convince Shay Bourne I was brave enough to save his life if I couldn't muster the courage to walk through that door.

There were whoops and catcalls. Leave it to me to find my only appreciative audience in the maximum-security tier of the state prison. 'Baby, you here for me?' one guy said, and another pulled down his scrubs so that I could see his boxer shorts, as if I'd been waiting for that kind of peep show all my life. I kept my eyes focused on the priest who was standing outside one of the cells.

I should have introduced myself. I should have explained why I had lied my way into this prison. But I was so flustered that nothing came out the way it should have. 'Shay Bourne?' I said. 'I know a way that you can donate your organs.'

The priest frowned at me. 'Who are you?'

'His lawyer.'

He turned to Shay. 'I thought you said you didn't have a lawyer.'

Shay tilted his head. He looked at me as if he were sifting through the grains of my thoughts, separating the wheat from the chaff. 'Let her talk,' he said.

My streak of bravery widened after that: leaving the priest with Shay, I went back to the officers and demanded a private attorney-client conference room. I explained that legally, they had to provide one and that due to the nature of our conversation, the priest should be allowed into the meeting. Then the priest and I were taken into a small cubicle from one side, while Shay was escorted through a different entrance by two officers. When the door was closed, he backed up to it, slipping his hands through the trap to have his handcuffs removed.

'All right,' the priest said. 'What's going on?'

I ignored him and faced Shay. 'My name is Maggie Bloom. I'm an attorney for the ACLU, and I think I know a way to save you from being executed.'

'Thanks,' he said, 'but that's not what I'm looking for.'

I stared at him. 'What?'

'I don't need you to save all of me. Only my heart.'

'I . . . I don't understand,' I said slowly.

'What Shay means,' the priest said, 'is that he's resigned to his execution. He just wants to be an organ donor, afterward.'

'Who are you, exactly?' I asked.

'Father Michael Wright.'

'And you're his spiritual advisor?'

'Yes.'

'Since when?'

'Since ten minutes before you became his lawyer,' the priest said.

I turned back to Shay. 'Tell me what you want.'

'To give my heart to Claire Nealon.'

Who the hell was Claire Nealon? 'Does she *want* your heart?'

I looked at Shay, and then I looked at Michael, and I realized that I had just asked the one question no one had considered up till this point.

'I don't know if she wants it,' Shay said, 'but she needs it.'

'Well, has anyone talked to her?' I turned to Father Michael. 'Isn't that *your* job?'

'Look,' the priest said, 'the state has to execute him by lethal injection. And if that happens, organ donation isn't viable.'

'Not necessarily,' I said slowly.

A lawyer can't care more about the case than the client does. If I couldn't convince Shay to enter a courtroom hoping for his life to be spared, then it would be foolish for me to take this on. However, if his mission to donate his heart dovetailed with mine – to strike down the death penalty – then why not use the same loophole law to get what we both wanted? I could fight for him to die on his own terms – donate his organs – and in the process, raise enough awareness about the death penalty to make more people take a stand against it.

I glanced up at my new client and smiled.

Michael

The crazy woman who'd barged in on our little pastoral counseling session was now promising Shay Bourne happy endings she could not deliver. 'I need to do a little research,' she explained. 'I'm going to come back to see you in a few days.'

Shay, for what it was worth, was staring at her as if she had just handed him the moon. 'But you think . . . you think I'll be able to donate my heart to her?'

'Yes,' she said. 'Maybe.'

Yes. Maybe. Mixed signals, that's what she was giving him. As opposed to my message: *God. Jesus. One true course.*

She knocked on the window, in just as big a hurry to get out of the conference room as she'd been to enter it. As an officer buzzed open the door, I grasped her upper arm. 'Don't get his hopes up,' I whispered.

She raised a brow. 'Don't cut them down.'

The door closed behind Maggie Bloom, and I watched her walk away through the oblong window in the conference room. In the faint reflection, I could see Shay watching, too. 'I like her,' he announced.

'Well,' I sighed. 'Good.'

'Did you ever notice how sometimes it's a mirror, and sometimes it's glass?'

It took me a moment to realize that he was talking about the reflection. 'It's the way the light hits,' I explained.

'There's light inside a man of light,' Shay murmured. 'It can light up the whole world.' He met my gaze. 'So, what were you saying is impossible?'

My grandmother had been so fervently Catholic that she was on the committee of women who would come to scrub down the church, sometimes taking me along. I'd sit in the back, setting up a traffic jam of Matchbox cars on the kneeler. I'd watch her rub Murphy Oil Soap into the scarred wooden pews and sweep down the aisle with a broom; and on Sunday when we went to Mass she'd look around – from the entryway to the arched ceilings to the flickering candles – and nod with satisfaction. On the other hand, my grandfather never went to church. Instead, on Sundays, he fished. In the summer, he went out fly-fishing for bass; in the winter, he cut a hole in the ice and waited, drinking from his thermos of coffee, with steam wreathing his head like a halo.

It wasn't until I was twelve that I was allowed to skip a Sunday Mass to tag along with my grandfather. My grandmother sent me off with a bag lunch and an old baseball hat to keep the sun off my face. 'Maybe you can talk some sense into him,' she said. I had heard enough sermons to understand what happened to those who didn't truly believe, so I climbed into his little aluminum boat and waited until we had stopped underneath the reaching arm of a willow tree along the shoreline. He took out a fly rod and handed it to me, and then started casting with his own ancient bamboo rod.

One two three, one two three. There was a rhythm to fly-fishing, like a ballroom dance. I waited until we had both unspooled the long tongue of line over the lake, until the flies that my grandfather laboriously tied in his basement had lightly come to rest on the surface. 'Grandpa,' I asked, 'you don't want to go to hell, do you?'

'Aw, Christ,' he had answered. 'Did your grandmother put you up to this?'

'No,' I lied. 'I just don't understand why you never go to Mass with us.'

'I have my own Mass,' he had said. 'I don't need some guy in a collar and a dress telling me what I should and shouldn't believe.'

Maybe if I'd been older, or smarter, I would have left it alone at that. Instead, I squinted into the sun, up at my grandfather. 'But you got married by a priest.'

He sighed. 'Yeah, and I even went to parochial school, like you.'

'What made you stop?'

Before he could answer, I felt that tug on my line that always felt like Christmas, the moment before you opened the biggest box under the tree. I reeled in, fighting the whistle and snap of the fish on the other end, certain that I'd never caught anything quite like this before. Finally, it burst out of the water, as if it were being born again.

'A salmon!' my grandfather crowed. 'Ten pounds, easy . . . imagine all the ladders it had to climb to make its way back here from the ocean to spawn.' He held the fish aloft, grinning. 'I haven't seen one in this lake since the sixties!'

I looked down at the fish, still on my line, thrashing in splendor. It was silver and gold and crimson all at once.

My grandfather held the salmon, stilling it enough to unhook the fly, and set the fish back into the lake. We watched the flag of its tail, the ruddy back as it swam away. 'Who says that if you want to find God on a Sunday morning, you ought to be looking in church?' my grandfather murmured.

For a long time after that, I believed my grandfather had it right: God was in the details. But that was before I learned that the requirements of a true believer included Mass every Sunday and holy day of obligation, receiving the Eucharist, reconciliation once a year, giving money to the poor, observing Lent. Or in other words – just because you say you're Catholic, if you don't walk the walk, you're not.

Back when I was at seminary, I imagined I heard my grandfather's voice: *I thought God was supposed to love you unconditionally. Those sure sound like a lot of conditions to me.*

The truth is, I stopped listening.

* * *

By the time I left the prison, the crowd outside had doubled in size. There were the ill, the feeble, the old and the hungry, but there was also a small cadre of nuns from a convent up in Maine, and a choir singing 'Holy Holy Holy.' I was surprised at how hearsay about a so-called miracle could produce so many converts, so quickly.

'You see?' I heard a woman say, pointing to me. 'Even Father Michael's here.'

She was a parishioner, and her son had cystic fibrosis. He was here, too, in a wheelchair being pushed by his father.

'Is it true, then?' the man asked. 'Can this guy really work miracles?'

'*God* can,' I said, heading that question off at the pass. I put my hand on the boy's forehead. 'Dear St John of God, patron saint of those who are ill, I ask for your intercession that the Lord will have mercy on this child and return him to health. I ask this in Jesus's name.'

Not Shay Bourne's, I thought.

'Amen,' the parents murmured.

'If you'll excuse me,' I said, turning away.

The chances of Shay Bourne being Jesus were about as likely as me being God. These people, these falsely faithful, didn't know Shay Bourne – they'd never *met* Shay Bourne. They were imposing the face of our Savior on a man with a tendency to talk to himself; a man whose hands had been covered with the blood of two innocent people. They were confusing showmanship and inexplicable events with divinity. A miracle was a miracle only until it could be proved otherwise.

I started pushing through the mob, moving in the opposite direction, away from the prison gates, a man on a mission. Maggie Bloom wasn't the only one who could do research.

Maggie

In retrospect, it would have been much simpler to place a phone call to a medical professional who might lecture me on the ins and outs of organ donation. But it could take a week for a busy doctor to call me back, and my route home from the prison skirted the grounds of the Concord hospital, and I was still buzzing with righteous legal fervor. These are the only grounds I can offer for why I decided to stop in the emergency room. The faster I could speak to an expert, the faster I could start building Shay's case.

However, the triage nurse – a large graying woman who looked like a battleship – compressed her mouth into a flat line when I asked to talk to a doctor. 'What's the problem?' she asked.

'I've got a few questions—'

'So does everyone else in that waiting room, but you'll still have to explain the nature of the illness to me.'

'Oh, I'm not sick . . .'

She glanced around me. 'Then where's the patient?'

'At the state prison.'

The nurse shook her head. 'The patient has to be present for registration.'

I found that hard to believe. Surely someone knocked unconscious in a car accident wasn't left waiting in the hall until he came to and could recite his Blue Cross group number.

'We're busy,' the nurse said. 'When the patient arrives, sign in again.'

'But I'm a lawyer—'

'Then sue me,' the nurse replied.

I walked back to the waiting room and sat down next to a college-age boy with a bloody washcloth wrapped around his hand. 'I did that once,' I said. 'Cutting a bagel.'

He turned to me. 'I put my hand through a plate-glass window because my girlfriend was screwing my roommate.'

A nurse appeared. 'Whit Romano?' she said, and the boy stood up.

'Good luck with that,' I called after him, and I speared my fingers through my hair, thinking hard. Leaving a message with the nurse didn't guarantee a doctor would see it anytime in the next millennium – I had to find another way in.

Five minutes later I was standing in front of the battleship again. 'The patient's arrived?' she asked.

'Well. Yes. It's me.'

She put down her pen. 'You're sick now. You weren't sick before.'

I shrugged. 'I'm thinking appendicitis . . .'

The nurse pursed her lips. 'You know you'll be charged a hundred and fifty dollars for an emergency room visit, even a fabricated one.'

'You mean insurance doesn't—'

'Nope.'

I thought of Shay, of the sound the steel doors made when they scraped shut in prison. 'It's my abdomen. Sharp pains.'

'Which side?'

'My left . . . ?' The nurse narrowed her eyes. 'I meant my *other* left.'

'Take a seat,' she said.

I settled in the waiting room again and read two issues of *People* nearly as old as I was before being called into an exam room. A nurse – younger, wearing pink scrubs – took my blood pressure and temperature. She wrote down my health history, while I mentally reviewed whether you could be brought up on criminal charges for falsifying your own medical records.

I was lying on the exam table, staring at a Where's Waldo? poster on the ceiling, when the doctor came in.

'Ms Bloom?' he said.

Okay, I'm just going to come out and say it – he was stunning. He had black hair and eyes the color of the blueberries that grew in my parents' garden – almost purple in a certain light, and translucent the next moment. He could have sliced me wide open with his smile. He was wearing a white coat and a denim collared shirt with a tie that had Barbie dolls all over it.

He probably had a real live one of those at home, too – a 38-22-36 fiancée who had double-majored in law and medicine, or astrophysics and political science.

Our whole relationship was over, and I hadn't even said a word to him.

'You *are* Ms Bloom?'

How had I not noticed that British accent? 'Yes,' I said, wishing I was anyone *but*.

'I'm Dr Gallagher,' he said, sitting down on a stool. 'Why don't you tell me what's been going on?'

'Well,' I began. 'Actually, I'm fine.'

'For the record, appendicitis rates as pretty ill.'

Ill. I loved that. I bet he said things like *flat* and *loo* and *lift*, too.

'Let's just check you out,' he said. He stood and hooked his stethoscope into his ears, then settled it under my shirt. I couldn't remember the last time a guy had slipped his hand under my shirt. 'Just breathe,' he said.

Yeah, right.

'Really,' I said. 'I'm not sick.'

'If you could just lie back . . . ?'

That was enough to bring me crashing down to reality. Not only would he realize, the moment he palpated my stomach, that I didn't have appendicitis . . . he'd also probably be able to tell that I had the two-donut combo at Dunkin' Donuts for breakfast, when everyone knows they take three days – *each* – to digest.

'I don't have appendicitis,' I blurted out. 'I just told the nurse I did because I wanted to talk to a doctor for a few minutes—'

'All right,' he said gently. 'I'm just going to call in Dr Tawasaka. I'm sure she'll talk to you all you like . . .' He stuck his head out the door. 'Sue? Page psych . . .'

Oh, excellent, now he thought I had a mental health problem. 'I don't need a psychiatrist,' I said. 'I'm an attorney and I need a medical consultation about a client.'

I hesitated, expecting him to call in security, but instead he sat down and folded his arms. 'Go on.'

'Do you know anything about heart transplants?'

'A bit. But I can tell you right now that if your client requires one, he'll have to register with UNOS and get in line like everyone else . . .'

'He doesn't need a heart. He wants to *donate* one.'

I watched his face transform as he realized that my client had to be the death row inmate. There just weren't a lot of prisoners in New Hampshire clamoring to be organ donors these days. 'He's going to be executed,' Dr Gallagher said.

'Yes. By lethal injection.'

'Then he won't be able to donate his heart. A heart donor has to be brain-dead; lethal injection causes cardiac death. In other words, once your client's heart stops beating during that execution, it's not going to work in someone else.'

I knew this; Father Michael had *told* me this, but I hadn't wanted to believe it.

'You know what's interesting?' the doctor said. 'I believe it's potassium that's used in lethal injection – the chemical that stops the heart. That's the same chemical we use in cardioplegia solution, which is perfused into the donor heart just prior to sewing it into the patient. It keeps the heart arrested while it's not receiving a normal blood flow, until all the suturing's finished.' He looked up at me. 'I don't suppose the prison would agree to a surgical cardiectomy – a heart removal – as a method of execution?'

I shook my head. 'The execution has to happen within the walls of the prison.'

He shrugged. 'I cannot believe I'm saying this, but it's too bad that they don't use a firing squad anymore. A well-placed shot could leave an inmate a perfect organ donor. Even hanging would work, if one could hook up a respirator after brain death was confirmed.' He shuddered. 'Pardon me. I'm used to saving patients, not theoretically killing them.'

'I understand.'

'Then again, even if he *could* donate his heart, chances are it would be too large for a child's body. Has anyone addressed that yet?'

I shook my head, feeling even worse about Shay's odds.

The doctor glanced up. 'The bad news, I'm afraid, is that your client is out of luck.'

'Is there any good news?'

'Of course.' Dr Gallagher grinned. 'You don't have appendicitis, Ms Bloom.'

'Here's the thing,' I said to Oliver when I had gotten us enough Chinese takeout to feed a family of four (you could keep the leftovers, and Oliver really did like vegetable moo shu, even if my mother said that rabbits didn't eat real food). 'It's been sixty-nine years since anyone's been executed in the state of New Hampshire. We're assuming that lethal injection is the only method, but that doesn't mean we're right.'

I picked up the carton of lo mein and spooled the noodles into my mouth. 'I know it's here somewhere,' I muttered as the rabbit hopped across another stack of legal texts scattered on the floor of the living room. I was not in the habit of reading the New Hampshire Criminal Code; going through the sections and subsections was like navigating through molasses. I'd turn back a page, and the spot I'd been reading a moment before would disappear in the run of text.

Death.
Death penalty.
Capital murder.

Injection, lethal.
630:5 (XXIII). When the penalty of death is imposed, the sentence
shall be that the defendant is imprisoned in the state prison at
Concord until the day appointed for his execution, which shall not be
within one year from the day sentence is passed.

Or in Shay's case, *eleven* years.

The punishment of death shall be inflicted by continuous, intravenous
administration of a lethal quantity of an ultra-short-acting barbiturate
in combination with a chemical paralytic agent until death is
pronounced by a licensed physician according to accepted standards of
medical practice.

Everything I knew about the death penalty I had learned at the ACLU. Prior to working there, I hadn't given the death penalty much thought, beyond when someone was executed and the media made a huge story out of it. Now I knew the names of those who were killed. I heard about their last-minute appeals. I knew that, after death, some inmates were found to be innocent.

Lethal injection was supposed to be like putting a dog to sleep – a drowsiness overcame you, and then you just never woke up. No pain, no stress. It was a cocktail of three drugs: Sodium Pentothal, a sedative to put the inmate to sleep; Pavulon, to paralyze the muscular system and stop breathing; and potassium chloride, to stop the heart. The Sodium Pentothal was ultra-short-acting – which meant that you could recover quickly from its effects. It also meant that a subject might have feeling in his nerves, yet be just sedated enough to be unable to communicate or move.

The British medical journal the *Lancet* published a 2005 study of the toxicology reports of forty-nine executed inmates in four U.S. states; forty-three of the inmates had a level of anesthesia lower than required for surgery, and twenty-one had levels that would indicate awareness. Anesthesiologists say that if a person were conscious at the time potassium chloride is administered, it would feel like boiling oil in the veins. An inmate might feel as if he were being burned alive from the inside, but be unable to move or speak because of the muscle paralysis and minimal sedation caused by the other two drugs. The Supreme Court had even had its doubts: although they still ruled that capital punishment was constitutional, they'd halted executions of two inmates on a narrower issue: whether the excessive pain caused by lethal injection was a civil rights infraction that could be argued in a lower court.

Or – to put it simply – lethal injection might not be as humane as everyone wanted to believe.

> 630:5 (XIV). The commissioner of corrections or his designee shall determine the substance or substances to be used and the procedures to be used in any execution, provided, however, that if for any reason the commissioner finds it to be impractical to carry out the punishment of death by administration of the required lethal substance or substances, the sentence of death may be carried out by hanging under the provisions of law for the death penalty by hanging in effect on December 31, 1986.

Oliver settled on my lap as I read the words again.

Shay didn't have to be executed by lethal injection, if I could make the commissioner – or a court – find it impractical. If you coupled that with the RLUIPA – the law that said a prisoner's religious freedoms had to be protected in prison – and if I could prove that part of Shay's belief system for redemption included organ donation, then lethal injection *was* impractical.

In which case, Shay would be hanged.

And – here was the *real* miracle – according to Dr Gallagher, that meant Shay Bourne *could* donate his heart.

Lucius

The day the priest returned, I was working on pigments. My favorite substance was tea – it made a stain you could vary in intensity from an almost white to a yellowish brown. M&M's were vibrant, but they were the hardest to work with – you had to moisten a Q-tip and rub it over the surface of the M&M, you couldn't just soak off the pigment like I was doing this morning with Skittles.

I set my jar lid on the table and added about fifteen drops of warm water. The green Skittle went in next, and I rolled it around with my finger, watching the food dye coating come off. The trick here was to pull the candy out just as I started to see the white sugar beneath the coating – if the sugar melted into the paint, it wouldn't work as well.

I popped the bleached button of candy into my mouth – I could do that these days, now that the thrush was gone. As I sucked on it, I poured the contents of the lid (green, like the grass I had not walked on with my bare feet in years; like the color of a jungle; like Adam's eyes) into an aspirin bottle for safekeeping. Later, I could vary the pigment with a dab of white toothpaste, diluted with water to make the right hue.

It was a laborious process, but then again . . . I had time.

I was just about to repeat the endeavor with a yellow jawbreaker – the yield of paint was four times as much as a Skittle – when Shay's priest walked up to my cell door in his flak jacket. I had, of course, seen the priest briefly the day he first visited Shay, but only at a distance. Now, with him directly in front of my cell door, I could see that he was younger than I would have expected, with hair that seemed decidedly un-priestlike and eyes as soft as gray flannel. 'Shay's getting his hair cut,' I said, because it was barber day, and that's where he had been taken about ten minutes before.

'I know, Lucius,' the priest said. 'That's why I was hoping to talk to you.'

Let me tell you, the last thing I wanted to do was chat with a priest. I hadn't asked for one, certainly, and in my previous experience, the clergy only wanted to give a lecture on how being gay was a choice, and how God loved me (but not my pesky habit of falling in love with other men). Just because Shay had come back to his cell convinced that his new team – some lawyer girl and this priest – were going to move mountains for him didn't mean that I shared his enthusiasm. In spite of the fact that he'd been incarcerated for eleven years, Shay was still the most naive inmate I'd ever met. Just last night, for example, he'd had a fight with the correctional officers because it was laundry day and they'd brought new sheets, which Shay refused to put on the bed. He said he could feel the bleach, and instead insisted on sleeping on the floor of the cell.

'I appreciate you seeing me, Lucius,' the priest said. 'I'm happy to hear you're feeling better these days.'

I stared at him, wary.

'How long have you known Shay?'

I shrugged. 'Since he was put in the cell next to me a few weeks ago.'

'Was he talking about organ donation then?'

'Not at first,' I said. 'Then he had a seizure and got transferred to the infirmary. When he came back, donating his heart was all he could talk about.'

'He had a seizure?' the priest repeated, and I could tell this was news to him. 'Has he had any more since then?'

'Why don't you just ask Shay these questions?'

'I wanted to hear what you had to say.'

'What you want,' I corrected, 'is for me to tell you whether or not he's really performing miracles.'

The priest nodded slowly. 'I guess that's true.'

Some had already been leaked to the press; I imagined the rest would be brought to light sooner or later. I told him what I'd seen with my own eyes, and by the time I was finished, Father Michael was frowning slightly. 'Does he go around saying he's God?'

'No,' I joked. 'That would be Crash.'

'Lucius,' the priest asked, 'do *you* believe Shay is God?'

'You need to back up, Father, because I don't believe in God. I quit around the same time one of your esteemed colleagues told me that AIDS was my punishment for sinning.' To be honest, I had split religion along the seam of secular and nonsecular; choosing to concentrate on the beauty of a Caravaggio without noticing the Madonna and child; or finding the best lamb recipe for a lavish Easter dinner, without thinking about the Passion. Religion gave hope to people who knew the end wasn't going to be pretty. It was why inmates started praying in prison and why patients started praying when the doctors said *terminal*. Religion was supposed to be a blanket drawn up to your chin to keep you warm, a promise that when it came to the end, you wouldn't die alone – but it could just as easily leave you shivering out in the cold, if *what* you believed became more important than the fact *that* you believed.

I stared at him. 'I don't believe in God. But I do believe in Shay.'

'Thank you for your time, Lucius,' the priest said softly, and he walked down the tier.

He may have been a priest, but he was looking for his miracles in the wrong place. That day with the gum, for example. I had seen the coverage on the news – it was reported that Shay had somehow taken one tiny rectangle of Bazooka gum and multiplied it. But ask someone who'd been there – like me, or Crash, or Texas – and you'd know there weren't suddenly seven pieces of bubble gum. It was more like this: when the piece was fished underneath our cell doors, instead of taking as much as we could, we made do with less instead.

The gum was magically replicated. But we – the blatantly greedy – balanced the needs of the other seven guys and in that instant found them just as worthy as our own.

Which, if you asked me, was an even greater miracle.

Michael

The Holy Father has an entire office at the Vatican devoted to analyzing alleged miracles and passing judgment on their authenticity. They scrutinize statues and busts, scrape Crisco out of the corners of supposedly bleeding eyes, track scented oil on walls that emit the smell of roses. I was nowhere as experienced as those priests, but then again, there was a crowd of nearly five hundred people outside the state prison calling Shay Bourne a savior – and I wasn't going to let people give up on Jesus that easily.

To that end, I was now ensconced in a lab on the Dartmouth campus, with a graduate student named Ahmed who was trying to explain to me the results of the test he'd run on the soil sample taken from the vicinity of the pipes that ran into I-tier. 'The reason the prison couldn't get a conclusive explanation is because they were looking *in* the pipes, not *outside* them,' Ahmed said. 'So the water tested positive for something that looked like alcohol, but only in certain pipes. And you'll never guess what's growing near those pipes: rye.'

'Rye? Like the grain?'

'Yeah,' Ahmed said. 'Which accounts for the concentration of ergot into the water. It's a fungal disease of rye. I'm not sure what brings it on – I'm not a botanist – but I bet it had something to do with the amount of rain we've had, and there was a hairline crack in the piping they found when they first investigated, which accounts for the transmission in the first place. Ergot was the first kind of chemical warfare. The Assyrians used it in the seventh century B.C. to poison water supplies.' He smiled. 'I double-majored in chemistry and ancient history.'

'It's deadly?'

Ahmed shrugged. 'In repeated doses. But at first, it's a hallu-cinogen that's related to LSD.'

'So, the prisoners on I-tier might not have been drunk . . .' I said carefully.

'Right,' Ahmed replied. 'Just tripping.'

I turned over the vial with the soil sample. 'You think the water got contaminated?'

'That would be my bet.'

But Shay Bourne, in prison, would not have been able to know that there was a fungus growing near the pipes that led into I-tier, would he?

I suddenly remembered something else: the following morning, those same inmates on I-tier had ingested the same water and had not acted out of the ordinary. 'So how did it get uncontaminated?'

'Now that,' Ahmed said, 'I haven't quite figured out.'

'There are a number of reasons that an advanced AIDS patient with a particularly low CD4 count and high viral load might suddenly appear to get better,' Dr Perego said. An autoimmune disease specialist at Dartmouth-Hitchcock Medical Center, he also served as the doctor for HIV/AIDS patients at the state prison and knew all about Lucius and his recovery. He didn't have time for a formal talk, but was perfectly willing to chat if I wanted to walk with him from his office to a meeting at the other end of the hospital – as long as I realized that he couldn't violate doctor-patient confidentiality. 'If a patient is hoarding meds, for example, and suddenly decides to start taking them, sores will disappear and health will improve. Although we draw blood every three months from AIDS patients, sometimes we'll get a guy who refuses to have his blood drawn – and again, what looks like sudden improvement is actually a slow turn for the better.'

'Alma, the nurse at the prison, told me Lucius hasn't had his blood drawn in over six months,' I said.

'Which means we can't be quite sure what his recent viral count was.' We had reached the conference room. Doctors in white coats milled into the room, taking their seats. 'I'm not sure what you wanted to hear,' Dr Perego said, smiling ruefully. 'That he's special . . . or that he's not.'

'I'm not sure either,' I admitted, and I shook his hand. 'Thanks for your time.'

The doctor slipped into the meeting, and I started back down the hall toward the parking garage. I was waiting at the elevator, grinning down at a baby in a stroller with a patch over her right eye, when I felt a hand on my shoulder. Dr Perego was standing there. 'I'm glad I caught you,' he said. 'Have you got a moment?'

I watched the baby's mother push the stroller onto the yawning elevator. 'Sure.'

'This is what I didn't tell you,' Dr Perego said. 'And you didn't hear it from me.'

I nodded, understanding.

'HIV causes cognitive impairment – a permanent loss of memory and concentration. We can literally see this on an MRI, and DuFresne's brain scan showed irreparable damage when he first entered the state prison. However, another MRI brain scan was done on him yesterday – and it shows a reversal of that atrophy.' He looked at me, waiting for this to sink in. 'There's no physical evidence of dementia anymore.'

'What could cause that?'

Dr Perego shook his head. 'Absolutely nothing,' he admitted.

The second time I went to meet with Shay Bourne, he was lying on his bunk, asleep. Not wanting to disturb him, I started to back away, but he spoke to me without opening his eyes. 'I'm awake,' he said. 'Are you?'

'Last time I checked,' I answered.

He sat up, swinging his legs over the side of his bunk. 'Wow.

I dreamed that I was struck by lightning, and all of a sudden I had the power to locate anyone in the world, anytime. So the government cut a deal with me – find bin Laden, and you're free.'

'I used to dream that I had a watch, and turning the hands could take you backward in time,' I said. 'I always wanted to be a pirate, or a Viking.'

'Sounds pretty bloodthirsty for a priest.'

'Well, I wasn't born with a collar on.'

He looked me in the eye. 'If I could turn back time, I'd go out fly-fishing with my grandfather.'

I glanced up. 'I used to do that with my grandfather, too.'

I wondered how two boys – like Shay and me – could begin our lives at the same point and somehow take turns that would lead us to be such different men. 'My grandfather's been gone a long time, and I still miss him,' I admitted.

'I never met mine,' Shay said. 'But I must have had one, right?'

I looked at him quizzically. What kind of life had he suffered, to have to craft memories from his imagination? 'Where did you grow up, Shay?' I asked.

'The light,' Shay replied, ignoring my question. 'How does a fish know where it is? I mean, things shift around on the floor of the ocean, right? So if you come back and everything's changed, how can it really be the place you were before?'

The door to the tier buzzed, and one of the officers came down the catwalk, carrying a metal stool. 'Here you go, Father,' he said, settling it in front of Shay's cell door. 'Just in case you want to stay awhile.'

I recognized him as the man who had sought me out the last time I'd been here, talking to Lucius. His baby daughter had been critically ill; he credited Shay with her recovery. I thanked him, but waited until he'd left to talk to Shay again.

'Did you ever feel like that fish?'

Shay looked at me as if I were the one who couldn't follow a linear conversation. 'What fish?' he said.

'Like you can't find your way back home?'

I knew where I was heading with this topic – straight to true salvation – but Shay took us off course. 'I had a bunch of houses, but only one home.'

He'd been in the foster care system; I remembered that much from the trial. 'Which place was that?'

'The one where my sister was with me. I haven't seen her since I was sixteen. Since I got sent to prison.'

I remembered he'd been sent to a juvenile detention center for arson, but I hadn't remembered anything about a sister.

'Why didn't she come to your trial?' I asked, and realized too late that I had made a grave mistake – that there was no reason for me to know that, unless I had been there.

But Shay didn't notice. 'I told her to stay away. I didn't want her to tell anyone what I'd done.' He hesitated. 'I want to talk to her.'

'Your sister?'

'No. She won't listen. The other one. She'll hear me, after I die. Every time her daughter speaks.' Shay looked up at me. 'You know how you said you'd ask her if she wants the heart? What if I asked her myself?'

Getting June Nealon to come visit Shay in prison would be like moving Mt. Everest to Columbus, Ohio. 'I don't know if it will work . . .'

But then again, maybe seeing June face-to-face would make Shay see the difference between personal forgiveness and divine forgiveness. Maybe putting the heart of a killer into the chest of a child would show – literally – how good might blossom from bad. And the beat of Claire's pulse would bring June more peace than any prayer I could offer.

Maybe Shay *did* know more about redemption than I.

He was standing in front of the cinder-block wall now, trailing his fingertips over the cement, as if he could read the history of the men who'd lived there before him.

'I'll try,' I said.

*   *   *

There was a part of me that knew I should tell Maggie Bloom that I had been on the jury that convicted Shay Bourne. It was one thing to keep the truth from Shay; it was another to compromise whatever legal case Maggie was weaving together. On the other hand, it was up to me to make sure that Shay found peace with God before his death. The minute I told Maggie about my past involvement with Shay, I knew she'd tell me to get lost, and would find him another spiritual advisor the judge couldn't find fault with. I had prayed long and hard about this, and for now, I was keeping my secret. God wanted me to help Shay, or so I told myself, because it kept me from admitting that *I* wanted to help Shay, too, after failing him the first time.

The ACLU office was above a printing shop and smelled like fresh ink and toner. It was filled with plants in various stages of dying, and filing cabinets took up most of the floor space. A paralegal sat at a reception desk, typing so furiously that I almost expected her computer screen to detonate. 'How can I help,' she said, not bothering to look up.

'I'm here to see Maggie Bloom.'

The paralegal lifted her right hand, still typing with her left, and hooked a thumb overhead and to the left. I wound down the hallway, stepping over boxes of files and stacks of newspapers, and found Maggie sitting at her desk, scribbling on a legal pad. When she saw me, she smiled. 'Listen,' she said, as if we were old friends. 'I have some fantastic news. I think Shay can be hanged.' Then she blanched. 'I didn't mean fantastic news, really. I meant . . . well, you know what I meant.'

'Why would he want to do that?'

'Because then he can donate his heart.' Maggie frowned. 'But first we need to get the prison to agree to send him for tests, to make sure it's not too big for a kid—'

I drew in my breath. 'Look. We need to talk.'

'It's not often I get a priest who wants to confess.'

She didn't know the half of it. *This is not about you*, I reminded myself, and firmly settled Shay in the front of my mind. 'Shay wants to be the one to ask June Nealon if she'll take his heart. Unfortunately, visiting him is not on her top-ten list of things to do. I want to know if there's some kind of court-ordered mediation we can ask for.'

Maggie raised a brow. 'Do you really think he's the best person to relay this information to her? I don't see how that will help our case . . .'

'Look, I know you're doing your job,' I said, 'but I'm doing mine, too. And saving Shay's soul may not be important to you, but it's critical to me. Right now, Shay thinks that donating his heart is the only way to save himself – but there's a big difference between mercy and salvation.'

Maggie folded her hands on her desk. 'Which is?'

'Well, June can forgive Shay. But only God can redeem him – and it has nothing to do with giving up his heart. Yes, organ donation would be a beautiful, selfless final act on earth – but it's not going to cancel out his debt with the victim's family, and it's not necessary to get him special brownie points with God. Salvation's not a personal responsibility. You don't have to *get* salvation. You're *given* it, by Jesus.'

'So,' she said. 'I guess you don't think he's the Messiah.'

'No, I think that's a pretty rash judgment.'

'You're preaching to the choir. I was raised Jewish.'

My cheeks flamed. 'I didn't mean to suggest—'

'But now I'm an atheist.'

I opened my mouth, snapped it shut.

'Believe me,' Maggie said, 'I'm the last person in the world to buy into the belief that Shay Bourne is Jesus incarnate—'

'Well, of *course* not—'

'— but not because a messiah wouldn't inhabit a criminal,' she qualified. 'I can tell you right now that there are plenty of innocent people on death row in this country.'

I wasn't about to tell her that I knew Shay Bourne was guilty. I had studied the evidence; I had heard the testimony; I had convicted him. 'It's not that.'

'Then how can you be so sure he's not who everyone thinks he is?' Maggie asked.

'Because,' I replied, 'God only had one son to give us.'

'Right. And – correct me if I'm wrong – he was a thirty-three-year-old carpenter with a death sentence on his head, who was performing miracles left and right. Nah, you're right. That's *nothing* like Shay Bourne.'

I thought of what I'd heard from Ahmed and Dr Perego and the correctional officers. Shay Bourne's so-called miracles were nothing like Jesus's . . . or were they? Water into wine. Feeding many with virtually nothing. Healing the sick. Making the blind – or in Calloway's case, the prejudiced – see.

Like Shay, Jesus didn't take credit for his miracles. Like Shay, Jesus had known he was going to die. And the Bible even said Jesus *was* supposed to be returning. But although the New Testament is very clear about this coming to pass, it is a bit muddier on the details: the when, the why, the how.

'He's not Jesus.'

'Okey-dokey.'

'He's *not*,' I pressed.

Maggie held up her hands. 'Got it.'

'If he was Jesus . . . if this was the Second Coming . . . well, there'd be rapture and destruction and resurrections and we wouldn't be sitting here having a normal conversation.'

Then again, there was nothing in the Bible that said *before* the Second Coming, Jesus wouldn't pop in to see how things were going here on earth.

I suppose in that case, it would make sense to be incognito – to pose as the least likely person anyone would ever assume to be the Messiah.

For the love of God, what was I *thinking*? I shook my head, clearing it. 'Let him meet with June Nealon once before you petition for organ donation, that's all I'm asking. I want the same things you do – Shay's voice to be heard, a little girl to be saved, and capital punishment to be put in the hot seat. I just also want to make sure that if and when Shay does donate his heart, he does it for all the right reasons. And that means untangling Shay's spiritual health from the whole legal component of this mess.'

'I can't do that,' Maggie said. 'It's the crux of my case. Look, it doesn't matter to me whether you think Shay is Jesus or Shay thinks Shay is Jesus or if he's just plain off his rocker. What does matter is that Shay's rights don't get shuffled aside in the grand mechanism of capital punishment – and if I have to use the fact that other people seem to think he's God to do it, I will.'

I raised a brow. 'You're using Shay to spotlight an issue you find reprehensible, in the hopes that you can change it.'

'Well,' Maggie said, coloring, 'I guess that's true.'

'Then how can you criticize me for having an agenda because of what *I* believe in?'

Maggie raised her gaze and sighed. 'There's something called restorative justice,' she said. 'I don't know if the prison will even allow it, much less Shay or the Nealons. But it would let Shay sit down in a room with the family of his victims and ask for forgiveness.'

I exhaled the breath I had not even realized I was holding. 'Thank you,' I said.

Maggie picked up her pen and began to write on the legal pad again. 'Don't thank me. Thank June Nealon – if you get her to agree to it.'

Motivated, I started out of the ACLU office, then paused. 'It's the right thing to do.'

Maggie didn't look up. 'If June won't meet with him,' she said, 'I'm still filing the suit.'

June

At first, when the victim's assistance advocate asked me if I'd attend a restorative justice meeting with Shay Bourne, I started to laugh. 'Yeah,' I said. 'And maybe after that, I could get dunked in boiling oil or drawn and quartered.'

But she was serious, and I was just as serious when I refused. The last thing in the world I wanted to do was sit down with that monster to make him feel better about himself so that he could die at peace.

Kurt didn't. Elizabeth didn't. Why should he?

I thought that was that, until one morning when there was a knock on the door. Claire was lying on the couch with Dudley curled over her feet, watching the Game Show Network. Our days were spent waiting for a heart with the shades drawn, both of us pretending there was nowhere we wanted to go, when in reality, neither of us could stand seeing how even the smallest trips exhausted Claire. 'I'll get it,' she called out, although we both knew she couldn't and wouldn't. I put down the knife I was using to chop celery in the kitchen and wiped my hands on my jeans.

'I bet it's that creepy guy who was selling magazines,' Claire said as I passed her.

'I bet it's not.' He'd been a corn-fed Utah boy, pitching subscriptions to benefit the Church of Jesus Christ of Latter-Day Saints. I'd been upstairs in the shower; Claire had been talking to him through the screen door – for which I'd read her the riot act. It was that word *Saints* that had intrigued her; she didn't know it was a fancy word for Mormon. I had suggested that he try a town where there hadn't been a double murder committed by a young man who'd come around door to door looking for work, and after he left, I'd called the police.

No, I was sure it wasn't the same guy.

To my surprise, though, a priest was standing on my porch. His motorcycle was parked in my driveway. I opened the door and tried to smile politely. 'I think you have the wrong house.'

'I'm sure I don't, Ms Nealon,' he replied. 'I'm Father Michael, from St Catherine's. I was hoping I could speak to you for a few minutes.'

'I'm sorry . . . do I know you?'

He hesitated. 'No,' he said. 'But I was hoping to change that.'

My natural inclination was to slam the door. (Was that a mortal sin? Did it matter, if you didn't even believe in mortal sins?) I could tell you the exact moment I had given up on religion. Kurt and I had been raised Catholic. We'd had Elizabeth baptized, and a priest presided over their burials. After that, I had promised myself I would never set foot in a church again, that there was nothing God could do for me that would make up for what I'd lost. However, this priest was a stranger. For all I knew, though, this was not about saving my soul but about saving Claire's life. What if this priest knew of a heart that UNOS didn't?

'The house is a mess,' I said, but I opened the door so that he could walk inside. He stopped as we passed the living room, where Claire was still watching television. She turned, her thin, pale face rising like a moon over the back of the sofa. 'This is my daughter,' I said as I turned to him, and faltered – he was looking at Claire as if she were already a ghost.

I was just about to throw him out when Claire said hello and propped her elbows on the back of the sofa. 'Do you know anything about saints?'

'Claire!'

She rolled her eyes. 'I'm just *asking*, Mom.'

'I do,' the priest said. 'I've always sort of liked St Ulric. He's the patron saint who keeps moles away.'

'Get *out*.'

'Have you ever had a mole in here?'

'No.'

'Then I guess he's doing his job,' he said, and grinned.

Because he'd made Claire smile, I decided to let him in and give him the benefit of the doubt. He followed me into the kitchen, where I knew we could talk without Claire overhearing. 'Sorry about the third degree,' I said. 'Claire reads a lot. Saints are her latest obsession. Six months ago, it was blacksmithing.' I gestured to the table, offering him a seat.

'About Claire,' he said. 'I know she's sick. That's why I'm here.'

Although I'd hoped for this, my own heart still leapfrogged. 'Can you help her?'

'Possibly,' the priest said. 'But I need you to agree to something first.'

I would have become a nun; I would have walked over burning coals. 'Anything,' I vowed.

'I know the prosecutor's office already asked you about restorative justice—'

'Get out of my house,' I said abruptly, but Father Michael didn't move.

My face flamed – with anger, and with shame that I had not connected the dots: Shay Bourne wanted to donate his organs; I was actively searching for a heart for Claire. In spite of all the news coverage from the prison, I had never linked them. I wondered whether I had been naive, or whether, even subconsciously, I'd been trying to protect my daughter.

It took all my strength to lift my gaze to the priest's. 'What makes you think I would want a part of that man still walking around on this earth, much less inside my child?'

'June – please, just listen to me. I'm Shay's spiritual advisor. I talk to him. And I think you should talk to him, too.'

'Why? Because it rubs your conscience the wrong way to give sympathy to a murderer? Because you can't sleep at night?'

'Because I think a good person can do bad things. Because God forgives, and I can't do any less.'

Do you know how, when you are on the verge of a breakdown, the world pounds in your ears – a rush of blood, of consequence? Do you know how it feels when the truth cuts your tongue to ribbons, and still you have to speak it? 'Nothing he says to me could make any difference.'

'You're absolutely right,' Father Michael said. 'But what *you* say to *him* might.'

There was one variable that the priest had left out of this equation: I owed Shay Bourne nothing. It already felt like a second, searing death to watch the broadcasts each night, to hear the voices of supporters camping out near the prison, who brought their sick children and their dying partners along to be healed. *You fools*, I wanted to shout to them. *Don't you know he's conned you, just like he conned me? Don't you know that he killed my love, my little girl?* 'Name one person John Wayne Gacy killed,' I demanded.

'I . . . I don't know,' Father Michael said.

'Jeffrey Dahmer?'

He shook his head.

'But you remember *their* names, don't you?'

He got out of his chair and walked toward me slowly. 'June, people can change.'

My mouth twisted. 'Yeah. Like a mild-mannered, homeless carpenter who becomes a psychopath?'

Or a silver-haired fairy of a girl whose chest, in a heartbeat, blooms with a peony of blood. Or a mother who turns into a woman she never imagined being: bitter, empty, broken.

I knew why this priest wanted me to meet with Shay Bourne. I knew what Jesus had said: *Don't pay back in kind, pay back in kindness. If someone does wrong to you, do right by them.*

I'll tell you this: Jesus never buried his own child.

I turned away, because I didn't want to give him the satisfaction of seeing me cry, but he put his arm around me and led me to a chair. He handed me a tissue. And then his voice, a murmur, clotted into individual words.

'Dear St Felicity, patron saint of those who've suffered the death of a child, I ask for your intercession that the Lord will help this woman find peace . . .'

With more strength than I knew I had, I shoved him away. 'Don't you dare,' I said, my voice trembling. 'Don't you pray for me. Because *if* God's listening now, he's about eleven years too late.' I walked toward the refrigerator, where the only decoration was a picture of Kurt and Elizabeth, held up by a magnet Claire had made in kindergarten. I had fingered the photo so often that the edges had rounded; the color had bled onto my hands. 'When it happened, everyone said that Kurt and Elizabeth were at peace. That they'd gone *someplace better*. But you know what? They didn't *go* anywhere. They were *taken*. I was *robbed*.'

'Don't blame God for that, June,' Father Michael said. 'He didn't take your husband and your daughter.'

'No,' I said flatly. 'That was Shay Bourne.' I stared up at him coldly. 'I'd like you to leave now.'

I walked him to the door, because I didn't want him saying another word to Claire – who twisted around on the couch to see what was going on but must have picked up enough nonverbal cues from my stiff spine to know better than to make a peep. At the threshold, Father Michael paused. 'It may not be *when* we want, or *how* we want, but eventually God evens the score,' he said. 'You don't have to be the one to seek revenge.'

I stared at him. 'It's not revenge,' I said. 'It's justice.'

After the priest left, I was so cold that I could not stop shivering. I put on a sweater and then another, and wrapped a blanket around myself, but there's no way of warming up a body whose insides have turned to stone.

Shay Bourne wanted to donate his heart to Claire so that she'd live.

What kind of mother would I be if I let that happen?

And what kind of mother would I be if I turned him down?

Father Michael said Shay Bourne wanted to balance the scales: give me one daughter's life because he had taken another's. But

Claire wouldn't replace Elizabeth; I should have had them both. And yet, this was the simplest of equations: *You can have one, or you can have neither. What do you choose?*

I was the one who hated Bourne – Claire had never met him. If I did not take the heart, was I making that choice because of what I thought was best for Claire . . . or what I could withstand myself?

I imagined Dr Wu removing Bourne's heart from an Igloo cooler. There it was, a withered nut, a crystal black as coal. Put one drop of poison into the purest water, and what happens to the rest?

If I didn't take Bourne's heart, Claire would most likely die.

If I did, it would be like saying I could somehow be compensated for the death of my husband and daughter. And I couldn't – not ever.

I believe a good person can do bad things, Father Michael had said. Like make the wrong decision for the right reasons. Sign your daughter's life away, because she can't have a murderer's heart.

Forgive me, Claire, I thought, and suddenly I wasn't cold anymore. I was burning, seared by the tears on my cheeks.

I couldn't trust Shay Bourne's sudden altruistic turnaround; and maybe that meant he had won: I had gone just as bitter and rotten as he was. But that only made me more certain that I had the stamina to tell him, face-to-face, what balancing the scales really meant. It wasn't giving me a heart for Claire; it wasn't offering a future that might ease the weight of the past. It was knowing that Shay Bourne badly wanted something, and that this time, I'd be the one to take *his* dream away.

Maggie

Stunned, I hung up the phone and stared at the receiver again. I was tempted to *69 the call, just to make sure it hadn't been some kind of prank.

Well, maybe miracles *did* happen.

But before I could mull over this change of events, I heard footsteps heading toward my desk. Father Michael turned the corner, looking like he'd just been through Dante's Inferno. 'June Nealon wants nothing to do with Shay.'

'That's interesting,' I said, 'since June Nealon just got off the phone with me, agreeing to a restorative justice meeting.'

Father Michael blanched. 'You've got to call her back. This isn't a good idea.'

'*You're* the one who came up with it.'

'That was before I spoke to her. If she goes to that meeting, it's not because she wants to hear what Shay has to say. It's because she wants to run him through before the state finishes him off.'

'Did you really think that whatever Shay has to say to her is going to be any less painful than what she says to him?'

'I don't know . . . I thought that maybe if they saw each other . . .' He sank down into a chair in front of my desk. 'I don't know what I'm doing. I guess there are just some things you can't make amends for.'

I sighed. 'You're trying. That's the best any of us can do. Look, it's not like I fight death penalty cases all the time — but my boss used to. He worked down in Virginia before he came up north. They're emotional minefields — you get to know the inmate, and you excuse some heinous crime with a lousy childhood or alcoholism or an emotional upheaval or drugs, until you see the victim's family and a whole different level of suffering. And suddenly you start to feel a little ashamed of being in the defendant's camp.'

I walked to a small cooler next to a file cabinet and took out a bottle of water for the priest. 'Shay's guilty, Father. A court already told us that. June knows it. I know it. Everyone knows that it's wrong to execute an innocent man. The real question is whether it's still wrong to execute someone who's guilty.'

'But you're trying to get him hanged,' Father Michael said.

'I'm not trying to get him hanged,' I corrected. 'I want to champion his civil liberties, and at the same time, bring front and center what's wrong with the death penalty in this country. The only way to do both is to find a way for him to die the way *he* wants to. That's the difference between you and me. You're trying to find a way for him to die the way *you* want him to.'

'You're the one who said Shay's heart might not be a viable match. And even if it is, June Nealon will never agree to taking it,' the priest said.

That was, of course, entirely possible. What Father Michael had conveniently put out of his mind when he dreamed up a meeting between June and Shay was that in order to forgive, you have to remember how you were hurt in the first place. And that in order to forget, you had to accept your role in what had happened.

'If we don't want Shay to lose hope,' I said, 'then we'd better not lose it either.'

Michael

Every day when I wasn't running the noon Mass, I went to visit Shay. Sometimes we talked about television shows we'd seen – we were both pretty upset with Meredith on *Grey's Anatomy*, and thought the girls on *The Bachelor* were hot but dumb as bricks. Sometimes we talked about carpentry, how a piece of wood would tell him what it needed to be, how I could say the same of a parishioner in need. Sometimes we talked about his case – the appeals he'd lost, the lawyers he'd had over the years. And sometimes, he was less lucid. He'd run around his cell like a caged animal; he'd rock back and forth; he'd swing from topic to topic as if it was the only way to cross the jungle of his thoughts.

One day, Shay asked me what was being said about him outside.

'You know,' I told him. 'You watch the news.'

'They think I can save them,' Shay said.

'Well. Yeah.'

'That's pretty fucking selfish, isn't it? Or is it selfish of me if I don't try?'

'I can't answer that for you, Shay,' I said.

He sighed. 'I'm tired of waiting to die,' he said. 'Eleven years is a long time.'

I pressed my stool up close to the cell door; it was more private that way. It had taken me a week, but I had managed to separate out the way I felt about Shay's case from the way that he felt. I had been stunned to learn that Shay believed he was innocent – although Warden Coyne told me that everyone in prison believed they were innocent, regardless of the conviction. I wondered if his memory of the events, over time, had blurred – me, I could still remember that awful evidence as if it had been presented to me yesterday. When I pushed a bit – encouraged him to tell me more about his wrongful conviction, suggested that Maggie might be able to use the information in court, asked him why he was willing to go along with an execution so passively if he wasn't guilty – he shut down. He'd say, over and over, that what had happened then didn't matter now. I began to understand that proclaiming his innocence had a lot less to do with the reality of his case and more to do with the fragile connection between us. I was becoming his confidant – and he wanted me to think the best of him.

'What do you think is easier?' Shay asked. 'Knowing you're going to die on a certain date and time, or knowing it might happen any moment when you least expect it?'

A thought swam through my mind like a minnow: *Did you ask Elizabeth that?* 'I'd rather not know,' I said. 'Live every day like it's your last, and all that. But I think if you *do* know you're going to die, Christ showed the way to do it with grace.'

Shay smirked. 'Just think. It took you a whole forty-two minutes to bring up good ol' Jesus today.'

'Sorry. Professional hazard,' I said. 'When He says, in Gethsemane, '*O my Father, if it be possible, let this cup pass from me* . . .' He's wrestling with destiny . . . but ultimately, He accepts God's will.'

'Sucks for him,' Shay said.

'Well, sure. I bet His legs felt like Jell-O when He was carrying the Cross. He was human, after all. You can be brave, but that doesn't keep your stomach from doing somersaults.'

I finished speaking to find Shay staring at me. 'Did you ever wonder if you're dead wrong?'

'About what?'

'All of it. What Jesus said. What Jesus meant. I mean, he didn't even write the Bible, did he? In fact, the people who *did* write the Bible weren't even alive when Jesus was.' I must have looked absolutely stricken, because Shay hurried to continue. 'Not that Jesus wasn't a really cool guy – great teacher, excellent speaker, yadda yadda yadda. But . . . Son of God? Where's the proof?'

'That's what faith is,' I said. 'Believing without seeing.'

'Okay,' Shay argued. 'But what about the folks who think Allah's the one to put your money on? Or that the right path is the eight-fold one? I mean, how can a guy who walked on water even get *baptized*?'

'We know Jesus was baptized because—'

'Because it's in the Bible?' Shay laughed. 'Someone wrote the Bible, and it wasn't God. Just like someone wrote the Quran, and the Talmud. And he must have made decisions about what went in and what didn't. It's like when you write a letter, and you put in all the stuff you did during vacation but you leave out the part where your wallet got stolen and you got food poisoning.'

'Do you really need to know if Jesus got food poisoning?' I asked.

'You're missing the point. You can't take Matthew 26:39 or Luke 500:43 or whatever and read it as fact.'

'See, Shay, that's where you're wrong. I *can* take Matthew 26:39 and know it's the word of God. Or Luke 500:43, if it went up that high.'

By now, other inmates on the pod were eavesdropping. Some of them – like Joey Kunz, who was Greek Orthodox, and Pogie, who was Southern Baptist – liked to listen when I visited Shay and read scripture; a few of them had even asked if I'd stop by and pray with them when I came in to see Shay. 'Shut your piehole, Bourne,' Pogie yelled out. 'You're going to hell as soon as they push that needle in your arm.'

'I'm not saying I'm right,' Shay said, his voice escalating. 'I'm just saying that if *you're* right, it still doesn't mean *I'm* wrong.'

'Shay,' I said, 'you have to stop shouting, or they're going to ask me to leave.'

He walked toward me, flattening his hands on the other side of the steel mesh door. 'What if it didn't matter if you were a

Christian or a Jew or a Buddhist or a Wiccan or a . . . a transcen-
dentalist? What if all those roads led to the same place?'

'Religion brings people together,' I said.

'Yeah, right. You can track every polarizing issue in this country
to religion. Stem cell research, the war in Iraq, the right to die,
gay marriage, abortion, evolution, even the death penalty – what's
the fault line? That Bible of yours.' Shay shrugged. 'You really
think Jesus would be happy with the way the world's turned out?'

I thought of suicide bombers, of the radicals who stormed into
Planned Parenthood clinics. I thought of the news footage of the
Middle East. 'I think God would be horrified by some of the things
that are done in His name,' I admitted. 'I think there are places
His message has been distorted. Which is why I think it's even
more important to spread the one He meant to give.'

Shay pushed away from the cell door. 'You look at a guy like
Calloway—'

'Fuck you, Bourne,' Reece called out. 'I don't want to be part
of your speech. I don't even want your filthy-ass mouth speaking
my name—'

'— an AB guy, who burned down a temple—'

'You're dead, Bourne,' Reece said. 'D-E-A-D.'

'— or the CO who walks you to the shower and knows he can't
look you in the eye, because if his life had gone just a little different,
he might be the one wearing the cuffs. Or the politicians who
think that they can take someone they don't really want in society
anymore and lock him away—'

At this, the other inmates began to cheer. Texas and Pogie picked
up their dinner trays and began to bang them against the steel
doors of their cells. On the intercom, an officer's voice rang through.
'What's going on in there?'

Shay was standing at the front of his house now, preaching to
his congregation, disconnected from linear thought and everything
but his moment of grandstanding. 'And the ones who are really
monsters, the ones they don't ever want walking around near their
wives and children again – the ones like *me* – well, those they get

to dispose of. Because it's easier than admitting there isn't much difference between them and me.'

There were catcalls; there were cheers. Shay backed up as if he were on a stage, bent at the waist, bowed. Then he came back for his encore.

'The joke's on them. One little hypodermic won't be enough. Split a piece of wood, and they'll find me. Lift up a stone, and they'll find me. Look in the mirror, and they'll find me.' Shay gazed squarely at me. 'If you really want to know what makes someone a killer,' he said, 'ask yourself what would make *you* do it.'

My hands tightened on the Bible I always brought when I came to visit Shay. As it turned out, Shay wasn't railing about nothing. He wasn't disconnected from reality.

That would have been me.

Because, as Shay was suggesting, we weren't as different as I would have liked to think. We were both murderers.

The only distinction was that the death I'd caused had yet to happen.

Maggie

That week, when I showed up at the ChutZpah for lunch with my mother, she was too busy to see me. 'Maggie,' she said when I was standing at the threshold of her office door. 'What are you doing here?'

It was the same day, the same time, we met for our habitual lunch – the same lunch I never wanted to go to. But today, I was actually looking forward to zoning out while my cuticles were being cut and shaped. Ever since Father Michael had barreled into my office talking about a meeting between Shay and June Nealon, I'd been doubting myself and my intentions. By trying to make it possible for Shay to donate his heart, was I carrying out what was in his best interests, or my own? Sure, it would be a media boon for the anti–death penalty movement if Shay's last act on earth was as selfless as organ donation . . . but wasn't it morally wrong to try to legally hasten a man's execution, even if it was what he'd asked for? After three sleepless nights, all I wanted was to close my eyes, soak my hands in warm water, and think of anything *but* Shay Bourne.

My mother was wearing a cream-colored skirt so tiny it might as well have come from the American Girl doll store, and her hair was twisted up in a chignon. 'I have an investor coming in,' she said. 'Remember?'

What I remembered was her vague mention of adding another wing to the ChutZpah. And that there was some very rich lady from Woodbury, New York, who wanted to talk about financing it.

'You never told me it was going to be today,' I said, and I sank down in one of the chairs opposite her desk.

'You're crushing the pillows,' my mother said. 'And I *did* tell you. I called you at work, and you were typing, like you always do when I call even though you think I can't hear it in the background. And I told you I had to postpone lunch till Thursday, and you yessed me and said you were really busy, and did I have to call you at work?'

My face flushed. 'I don't type while I'm on the phone with you.'

Okay, I do. But it's my mother. And she calls for the most ridiculous reasons: Is it okay if she makes Chanukah dinner on Saturday, December 16, never mind that it's currently March? Do I remember the name of the librarian in my elementary school, because she thinks she ran into her at the grocery store? In other words, my mother phones for reasons that are completely trivial compared to writing up a brief to save the life of a man who's going to be executed.

'You know, Maggie, I realize that nothing I do here could possibly be as important as what *you* do, but it does hurt me to know that you don't even listen when I talk to you.' Her eyes were tearing up. 'I can't believe you came here to upset me before I have to sit down with Alicia Goldman-Hirsch.'

'I didn't come here to upset you! I came here because I always come here the second Tuesday of every month! You can't blame me because of a stupid phone conversation we probably had six months ago!'

'A stupid phone conversation,' my mother said quietly. 'Well, it's good to know what you really think of our relationship, Maggie.'

I held up my hands. 'I can't win here,' I said. 'I hope your meeting goes well.' Then I stormed out of her office, past the white secretary's desk with the white computer and the nearly albino receptionist, all the way to my car in the parking lot, where I tried to tell myself that the reason I was crying had nothing to do with the fact that even when I wasn't trying, all I did was let people down.

*   *   *

I found my father in his office – a rental space in a strip mall, since he was a rabbi without a temple – writing his sermon for Shabbat. As soon as I walked in, he smiled, then lifted a finger to beg a moment's time to finish whatever brilliant thought he was scribbling down. I wandered around, trailing my fingers over the spines of books written in Hebrew and Greek, Old Testaments and New Testaments, books on theurgy and theology and philosophy. I palmed an old paperweight I'd made him in nursery school – a rock painted to look like a crab, although now it seemed to more closely resemble an amoeba – and then took down one of my baby photos, tucked in an acrylic frame.

I had fat cheeks, even then.

My father closed his laptop. 'To what do I owe this surprise?'

I set the photo back on the mahogany shelf. 'Did you ever wonder if the person in the picture is the same one you see when you look in the mirror?'

He laughed. 'That's the eternal question, isn't it? Are we born who we are, or do we make ourselves that way?' He stood up and came around his desk, kissed my cheek. 'Did you come here to argue philosophy with your old man?'

'No, I came here because . . . I don't know why I came here.' That was the truth; my car had sort of pointed itself in the direction of his office, and even when I realized where it was headed I didn't correct my course. Everyone else came to my father when they were troubled or wanted counseling, why shouldn't I? I sank down onto the old leather couch that he'd had for as long as I could remember. 'Do you think God forgives murderers?'

My father sat down next to me. 'Isn't your client Catholic?'

'I was talking about me.'

'Well, gosh, Mags. I hope you got rid of the weapon.'

I sighed. 'Daddy, I don't know what to do. Shay Bourne doesn't want to become the poster child against capital punishment, he *wants* to die. And yeah, I can tell myself a dozen times that we can both have our cake and eat it, too – Shay gets to die on his own terms; I get the death penalty put under a microscope and maybe even repealed by the Supreme Court – but it doesn't cancel out the fact that at the end of the day, Shay will be dead, and I'll be just as responsible as the state that signed the warrant in the first place. Maybe I should be trying to convince Shay to get his conviction overturned, to fight for his life, instead of his death.'

'I don't think he'd want that,' my father said. 'You're not murdering him, Maggie. You're fulfilling his last wishes – to help him make amends for what he's done wrong.'

'Repentance through organ donation?'

'More like *teshuvah*.'

I stared at him.

'Oh, right,' he smirked. 'I forgot about the post-Hebrew School amnesia. For Jews, repentance is about conduct – you realize you've done something wrong, you resolve to change it in the future. But *teshuvah* means *return*. Inside each of us is some spark of God – the real us. It's there whether you're the most pious Jew or the most marginal. Sin, evil, murder – all those things have the ability to cover up our true selves.

Teshuvah means turning back to the part of God that's gotten concealed. When you repent, usually, you feel sad – because of the regret that led you there. But when you talk about *teshuvah,* about making that connection with God again – well, it makes you happy,' my father said. 'Happier even than you were before, because your sins separated you from God . . . and distance always makes the heart grow fonder, right?'

He walked toward the baby picture I'd put back on the shelf. 'I know Shay's not Jewish, but maybe that's what's at the root of this desire to die, and to give up his heart. *Teshuvah* is all about reaching for something divine – something beyond the limitations of a body.' He glanced at me. 'That's the answer to your question about the photo, by the way. You're a different person on the outside than you were when this picture was snapped, but not on the inside. Not at the *core*. And not only is that part of you the same as it was when you were six months old . . . it's also the same as me and your mother and Shay Bourne and everyone else in this world. It's the part of us that's connected to God, and at that level, we're all identical.'

I shook my head. 'Thanks, but that didn't really make me feel any better. I want to save him, Daddy, and he – he doesn't want that at all.'

'Restitution is one of the steps a person has to take for *teshuvah*,' my father said. 'Shay has apparently taken a very literal interpretation of this – he took a child's life; therefore he owes that mother the life of a child.'

'It's not a perfect equation,' I said. 'He'd have to bring Elizabeth Nealon back for that.'

My father nodded. 'That's something rabbis have talked about for years since the Holocaust – if the victim is dead, does the family really have the power to forgive the killer? The victims are the ones with whom he has to make amends. And those victims – they're ashes.'

I sat up, rubbing my temples. 'It's really complicated.'

'Then ask yourself what's the right thing to do.'

'I can't even answer that much.'

'Well,' my father said, 'then maybe you should ask Shay.'

I blinked up at him. It was that simple. I hadn't seen my client since that first meeting in the prison; the work I'd been doing to set up a restorative justice meeting had been on the phone. Maybe what I really needed was to find out why Shay Bourne was so sure he'd come to the right decision, so that I could start explaining it to myself.

I leaned over and gave him a hug. 'Thanks, Daddy.'

'I didn't do anything.'

'Still, you're a better conversationalist than Oliver.'

'Don't tell the rabbit that,' he said. 'He'd scratch me twice as hard as he already does.'

I stood up, heading for the door. 'I'll call you later. Oh, and by the way,' I said, 'Mom's mad at me again.'

*   *   *

I was sitting under the harsh fluorescent lights of the attorney-client conference room when Shay Bourne was brought in to meet with me. He backed up to the trap so that his handcuffs could be removed, and he sat down across the table. His hands were small, I realized, maybe even smaller than mine.

'How's it going?' he asked.

'Fine. How's it going with you?'

'No, I meant my lawsuit. My heart.'

'Well, we're waiting until after you speak to June Nealon tomorrow.' I hesitated. 'Shay, I need to ask you a question, as your lawyer.' I waited until he looked me in the eye. 'Do you really believe that the only way to atone for what you've done is to die?'

'I just want to give her my heart—'

'I get that. But in order to do that, you've basically agreed to your own execution.'

He smiled faintly. 'And here I thought my vote didn't count.'

'I think you know what I mean,' I said. 'Your case is going to shine a beacon on the issue of capital punishment, Shay – but you'll be the sacrificial lamb.'

His head snapped up. 'Who do you think I am?'

I hesitated, not quite sure what he was asking.

'Do you believe what they all believe?' he asked. 'Or what Lucius believes? Do you think I can make miracles happen?'

'I don't believe anything I haven't seen,' I said firmly.

'Most people just want to believe what someone else tells them,' Shay said.

He was right. It was why, in my father's office, I'd had a break-down: because even as a confirmed atheist, I sometimes found it just too frightening to think that there might not be a God who was watching out for our greater good. It was why a country as enlightened as the United States could still have a death penalty statute in place: it was just too frightening to think about what justice – or lack of it – would prevail if we didn't. There was comfort in facts, so much so that we stopped questioning where those facts had come from.

Was I trying to figure out who Shay Bourne was for myself? Probably. I didn't buy the fact that he was the Son of God, but if it was getting him media attention, then I thought he was brilliant for encouraging that line of thought. 'If you can get June to forgive you at this meeting, Shay, maybe you don't have to give up your heart. Maybe you'll feel good about connecting with her again, and then we can get her to talk to the governor on your behalf to commute your sentence to life in prison—'

'If you do that,' Shay interrupted, 'I will kill myself.'

My jaw dropped. 'Why?'

'Because,' he said, 'I have to get out of here.'

At first I thought that he was talking about the prison, but then I saw he was clutching his own arms, as if the penitentiary he was referring to was his own body. And that, of course, made me think of my father and *teshuvah*. Could I truly be helping him by letting him die on his own terms?

'Let's take it one step at a time,' I conceded. 'If you can get June Nealon to understand why you want to do this, then I'll work on making a court understand it, too.'

But Shay was suddenly lost in his thoughts, wherever they happened to be taking him. 'I'll see you tomorrow, Shay,' I said, and I went to touch his shoulder to let him know I was leaving. As soon as I stretched out my arm, though, I found myself flat on the floor. Shay stood over me, just as shocked by the blow he'd dealt me as I was.

An officer bolted into the room, driving Shay down to the floor with a knee in the small of his back so that he could be handcuffed. 'You all right?' he called out to me.

'I'm fine . . . I just slipped,' I lied. I could feel a welt rising on my left cheekbone, one that I was sure the officer would see as well. I swallowed the knot of fear in my throat. 'Could you just give us a couple more minutes?'

I did not tell the officer to remove Shay's handcuffs; I wasn't quite that brave. But I struggled to my feet and waited until we were alone in the room again. 'I'm sorry,' Shay blurted out. 'I'm sorry, I didn't mean it, I sometimes, when you . . .'

'Shay,' I ordered. 'Sit down.'

'I didn't mean to do it. I didn't see you coming. I thought you were – would—' He broke off, choking on the words. 'I'm sorry.'

I was the one who'd made the mistake. A man who had been locked up alone for a decade, whose only human contact was having his handcuffs chained and removed, would be completely unprepared for a small act of kindness. He would have instinctively seen it as a threat to his personal space, which was how I'd wound up sprawled on the floor.

'It won't happen again,' I said.

He shook his head fiercely. 'No.'

'See you tomorrow, Shay.'

'Are you mad at me?'

'No.'

'You are. I can tell.'

'I'm not,' I said.

'Then will you do something for me?'

I had been warned about this by other attorneys who worked with inmates: they will bleed you dry. Beg you for stamps, for money, for food. For phone calls, made by you to their family, on their behalf. They are the ultimate con artists; no matter how much sympathy you feel for them, you have to remind yourself that they will take whatever they can get, because they have nothing.

'Next time, will you tell me what it feels like to walk barefoot on grass?' he asked. 'I used to know, but I can't remember anymore.' He shook his head. 'I just want to . . . I want to know what that's like again.'

I folded my notebook beneath my arm. 'I'll see you tomorrow, Shay,' I repeated, and I motioned to the officer who would set me free.

Michael

Shay Bourne was pacing in his cell. Every fifth turn, he pivoted and started circling the other way. 'Shay,' I said, to calm myself down as much as him, 'it's going to be all right.'

We were awaiting his transportation down to the room where our restorative justice meeting with June Nealon would take place, and we were both nervous.

'Talk to me,' Shay said.

'All right,' I said. 'What do you want to talk about?'

'What I'm going to say. What *she's* going to say . . . the words won't come out right, I just know it.' He looked up at me. 'I'm going to fuck this up.'

'Just say what you need to, Shay. Words are hard for everyone.'

'Well, it's worse when you know the person you're talking to thinks you're full of shit.'

'Jesus managed to do it,' I pointed out, 'and it wasn't like He was attending the Tuesday Toastmasters meeting in Nineveh.' I opened my Bible to the book of Isaiah. 'The Spirit of the Lord is on me, because he has anointed me to preach good news . . .'

'Could we just this once *not* have a Bible study moment?' Shay groaned.

'It's an example,' I said. 'Jesus said that when He came back to the synagogue where He'd grown up. Let me tell you, that congregation had a lot of questions – after all, they'd grown up with Him, and knew Him before He started the miracle train – so before they could doubt Him, what did He do? He gave them the words they'd been waiting to hear. He gave them hope.' I looked at Shay. 'That's what you need to do, with June.'

The door to I-tier opened, and six officers in flak jackets and full face shields entered. 'Don't talk until the mediator asks you to. And make sure you tell her why this is so important to you,' I urged, last-minute quarterbacking.

Just then the first officer reached the cell door. 'Father,' he said, 'we're going to have to ask you to meet us down there.'

I watched them move Shay down the tier. *Speak from your heart*, I thought, watching him go. *So that she knows it's worth taking.*

I had already been told what they would do with him. He'd be handcuffed and cuffed at the ankles. Both of these would be linked to a belly chain, so that he'd shuffle along inside the human box of officers. He would be taken to the cafeteria, which was now set up for offender counseling. Basically, the warden had explained, when they needed to have group sessions with violent offenders, they bolted several individual metal boxes to the floor – and prisoners were put into these miniature cells along with a counselor, who would sit on a chair in the cafeteria with them. 'It's group therapy,' Warden Coyne had proudly explained, 'but they're still incarcerated.'

Maggie had lobbied for a face-to-face visit. Failing that, she wanted to know if we could meet on opposite sides of a glass visiting booth. But there were too many of us, when you added in the moderator and June, or so the administration said (never mind I'd seen families of ten cram into one of those little noncontact booths for a visit with an inmate). Although I – like Maggie – thought that we were starting at a grave disadvantage if one of the participants was restrained and bolted to the floor like Hannibal Lecter, this was the best we were going to get.

The mediator was a woman named Abigail Herrick, who'd come from the attorney general's victim's assistance office and had been trained to do this kind of thing. She and June were talking quietly on one side of the anteroom. I walked up to June as soon as I entered. 'Thank you. This means a lot to Shay.'

'Which is the last reason I'd ever do it,' June said, and she turned back to Abigail.

I slunk across the room to the seat beside Maggie. She was painting a run in her stocking with pink nail polish. 'We are in serious trouble,' I said.

'Yeah? How's he doing?'

'He's panicked.' I squinted in the dim light as she lifted her head. 'How'd you get that shiner?'

'In my spare time I'm the welterweight champion of New Hampshire.'

There was a buzzing, and Warden Coyne walked in. 'Everything's set.'

He led us into the cafeteria by way of the metal detector. Maggie and I had already emptied our pockets and taken off our jackets before June and Abigail even realized what was going on; this is the difference between someone who has intimate experience with a detention facility and those who lead normal lives. An officer, still dressed in full riot gear, opened a door for June, who continued to stare at him in horror as she walked inside.

Shay was sitting in what looked like a telephone booth permanently sealed shut with nuts and bolts and metal. Bars vivisected his face; his eyes searched for mine as soon as I walked into the room. When he saw us, he stood up.

At that moment, June froze.

Abigail took her arm and led her to one of the four chairs that were arranged in a semicircle in front of the booth. Maggie and I filled in the remaining seats. Two officers stood behind us; in the distance I could hear the sizzle of something cooking on a grill.

'Well. Let's get started,' Abigail said, and she introduced herself. 'Shay, I'm Abigail Herrick. I'm going to be the mediator today. Do you understand what that means?'

He hesitated. He looked like he was going to faint.

'Victim-offender mediation is a process that gives a victim the chance to meet her offender in a safe and structured setting,' Abigail explained. 'The victim will he able to tell the offender about the crime's physical, emotional, and financial impact. The victim also has the chance to receive answers to any lingering questions about the crime, and to be directly involved in trying to develop a plan for the offender to pay back a debt if possible – emotional or monetary. In return, the offender gets the opportunity to take responsibility for his behavior and actions. Everyone with me so far?'

I started to wonder why this wasn't used for every crime committed. Granted, it was labor-intensive for both the AG's office and the prison, but wasn't it better to come face-to-face with the opposing party, instead of having the legal system be the intermediary?

'Now, the process is strictly voluntary. That means if June wants to leave at any time, she should feel free to do so. But,' Abigail added, 'I also want to point out that this meeting was initiated by Shay, which is a very good first step.'

She glanced at me, at Maggie, and then at June, and finally Shay. 'Right now, Shay,' Abigail said, 'you need to listen to June.'

June

They say you get over your grief, but you don't really, not ever. It's been eleven years, and it hurts just as much as it did that first day.

Seeing his face – sliced into segments by those metal bars, like he was some kind of Picasso portrait that couldn't be put together again – brought it all back. That face, his *fucking* face, was the last one Kurt and Elizabeth saw.

When it first happened, I used to make bargains with myself. I'd say that I could handle their deaths, as long as – and here I'd fill in the blank. As long as they had been quick and painless. As long as Elizabeth had died in Kurt's arms. I'd be driving, and I'd tell myself that if the light turned green before I reached the intersection, surely these details were true. I did not admit that sometimes I slowed down to stack the odds.

The only reason I was able to drag myself out of bed at all those first few months was because there was someone more needy than I was. As a newborn, Claire didn't have a choice. She had to be fed and diapered and held. She kept me so grounded in the present that I had to let go of my hold on the past. I credit her with saving my life. Maybe that's why I am so determined to reciprocate.

But even having Claire to care for was not foolproof. The smallest things would send me into a downward spiral: while pressing seven birthday candles into her cake, I'd think of Elizabeth, who would have been fourteen. I'd open a box in the garage and breathe in the scent of the miniature cigars Kurt liked to smoke every now and then. I'd open up a pot of Vaseline and see Elizabeth's tiny fingerprint, preserved on the surface. I would pull a book off a shelf and a shopping list would flutter out of it, in Kurt's handwriting: *thumbtacks, milk, rock salt.*

What I would like to tell Shay Bourne about the impact this crime had on my family is that it erased my family, period. What I would like to do is bring him back to the moment Claire, four, perched on the stairs to stare at a picture of Elizabeth and asked where the girl who looked like her lived. I would like him to know what it feels like to have to run your hand up the terrain of your own body, and underneath your nightshirt, only to realize that you cannot surprise yourself with your own touch.

I would like to show him the spot in the room he built, Claire's old nursery, where there is a bloodstain on the floorboards that I cannot scrub clean. I'd like to tell him that even though I carpeted the room years ago and turned it into a guest bedroom, I still do not walk across it, but instead tiptoe around the perimeter when I have to go inside.

I would like to show him the bills that came from the hospital every time Claire was sent there, which quickly consumed the money we received from the insurance company after Kurt died. I'd like him to come with me to the bank, the day I broke down in front of the teller and told her that I wanted to liquidate the college fund of Elizabeth Nealon.

I would like to feel that moment when Elizabeth was sitting in my lap and I was reading to her, and she went boneless and soft, asleep in my arms. I would like to hear Kurt call me Red again, for my hair, and tangle his fingers in it as we watch television in the bedroom at night. I would like to pick up the dirty socks that Elizabeth strewed about the house, a tiny tornado, the same reason I once yelled at her. I would love to fight with Kurt over the size of the MasterCard bill.

If they had to die, I would have loved to have known in advance, so that I could take each second spent with them and know to hold on to it, instead of assuming there would be a million more.

If they had to die, I would have loved to have been there, to be the last face they saw, instead of his.

I would like to tell Shay Bourne to go to hell, because wherever he winds up after he dies, it had better not be anywhere close to my daughter and my husband.

Michael

'Why?' June Nealon asked. Her voice was striped with rust and sorrow, and in her lap, her hands twisted. 'Why did you do it?' She lifted her gaze, staring at Shay. 'I let you into my home. I gave you a job. I *trusted* you. And you, you took everything I had.'

Shay's mouth was working silently. He moved from side to side in his little booth, hitting his forehead sometimes. His eyes fluttered, as if he was trying hard to organize what he had to say. 'I can fix it,' he said finally.

'You can't fix anything,' she said tightly.

'Your other little girl—'

June stiffened. 'Don't you talk about her. Don't you even breathe her name. Just tell me. I've waited eleven years to hear it. Tell me why you did this.'

He squeezed his eyes shut; sweat had broken out on his brow. He was whispering, a litany meant to convince himself, or maybe June. I leaned forward, but the noise from the kitchen obliterated his words. And then whatever had been sizzling was taken off the grill, and we all heard Shay, loud and clear: 'She was better off dead.'

June shot to her feet. Her face was so pale that I feared she would fall over, and I rose just in case. Then blood rushed, hot, into her cheeks. 'You bastard,' she said, and she ran outside.

Maggie tugged on my jacket. 'Go,' she mouthed.

I followed June past the two officers and through the anteroom. She burst through the double doors and into the parking lot without even bothering to pick up her driver's license at the control booth, trading back her visitor's pass. I was certain she would rather go to the DMV and pay for a replacement than set foot in this prison again.

'June,' I yelled. 'Please. Wait.'

I finally cornered her at her car, an old Ford Taurus with duct tape around the rear bumper. She was sobbing so hard that she couldn't get the key into the lock.

'Let me.' I opened the door and held it for her so that she could sit down, but she didn't. 'June, I'm sorry—'

'How could he say that? She was a little girl. A beautiful, smart, perfect little girl.'

I gathered her into my arms and let her cry on my shoulder. Later, she would regret doing this; later, she would feel that I had manipulated the situation. But for right now, I held her until she could catch her breath.

Redemption had very little to do with the big picture, and far more to do with the particulars. Jesus might forgive Shay, but what good was that if Shay didn't forgive himself? It was that impetus that drove him to give up his heart, just as I was driven to help him do it because it would cancel out my vote to execute him in the first place. We couldn't erase our mistakes, so we did the next best thing and tried to do something that distracted attention from them.

'I wish I could have met your daughter,' I said softly.

June pulled away from me. 'I wish you could have, too.'

'I didn't ask you here to hurt you all over again. Shay truly does want to make amends. He knows the one good thing to come out of his life might be his death.' I looked at the Constantine wire running along the top of the prison fence: a crown of thorns for a man who wanted to be a savior. 'He's taken away the rest of your family,' I said. 'If nothing else, let him help you keep Claire.'

June ducked into her car. She was crying again as she lurched out of the parking spot. I watched her pause at the exit of the prison, her blinker marking time.

Then, suddenly, her brake lights came on. She sped backward, stopping beside me with only inches to spare. She unrolled the window on the driver's side. 'I'll take his heart,' June said, her voice thick. 'I'll take it, and I'll watch that son of a bitch die, and we *still* won't be even.'

Too stunned to find any words, I nodded. I watched June drive off, her taillights winking as red as the eyes of any devil.

Maggie

'Well,' I said when I saw Father Michael walking back into the prison, dazed, 'that sucked.'

At the sound of my voice, he looked up. 'She's taking the heart.'

My mouth dropped open. 'You're kidding.'

'No. She's taking it for all the wrong reasons . . . but she's taking it.'

I could not believe it. Following the debacle in the restorative justice meeting, I would have more easily accepted that she'd gone out to buy an Uzi to exact her own justice against Shay Bourne. My mind began to kick into high gear: if June Nealon wanted Shay's heart – for whatever reason – then there was a great deal I had to do.

'I'll need you to write an affidavit, saying that you're Shay's spiritual advisor and that his religious beliefs include donating his heart.'

He drew in his breath. 'Maggie, I can't put my name on a court document about Shay—'

'Sure you can. Just lie,' I said, 'and go to confession afterward. You're not doing this for you; you're doing it for Shay. And we'll need a cardiologist to examine Shay, to see if his heart's even a match for Claire.'

The priest closed his eyes and nodded. 'Should I go in and tell him?'

'No,' I said, smiling. 'Let me.'

After a slight detour, I walked through the metal detectors again and was taken to the attorney-client room outside I-tier. A few minutes later, a grumbling officer showed up with Shay. 'He keeps getting moved around like this, the state's going to have to hire him a chauffeur.'

I rubbed my thumb and forefinger together, the world's smallest violin.

Shay ran his hands through his hair, making it stand on end; the shirt of his prison scrubs was untucked. 'I'm sorry,' he said immediately.

'I'm not the one who could have used the apology,' I replied.

'I know.' He squinched his eyes shut, shook his head. 'There were eleven years of words in my head, and I couldn't get them out the way I wanted.'

'Amazingly, June Nealon is willing to accept your heart for Claire.'

A few times in my career, I'd been the messenger of information that would change a client's life: the victim of a hate crime whose store was destroyed, receiving reparation and damages that would allow him to build a bigger, better venue; the gay couple who were given the legal stamp of approval to be listed as parents in the elementary school directory. A smile blossomed across Shay's face, and I remembered, at that moment, that *gospel* is another word for good news.

'It's not a done deal yet,' I said. 'We don't know, medically, if this is viable. And there are a whole bunch of legal hoops to jump through . . . which is what I need to talk to you about, Shay.'

I waited until he sat down across from me at the table, and was calm enough to stop grinning and look me in the eye. I had gotten to this point with clients before: you drew them a map and explained where the exit hatch was, and then you waited to see if they understood you needed them to crawl there on their own. That was legitimate, in law; you were not telling them to alter their truth, just explaining the way the courts worked, and hoping they would choose to massage it themselves. 'Listen carefully,' I said. 'There's a law in this country that says the state has to let you practice your own religion, as long as it doesn't interfere with safety in the prison. There's also a law in New Hampshire that says even though the court has sentenced you to die by lethal injection, which wouldn't allow you to donate your heart . . . in certain circumstances, death row inmates can be hanged instead. And if you're hanged, you'd be able to donate your organs.'

It was a lot for him to take in, and I could see him ingesting the words as if they were being fed on a conveyor.

'I might be able to convince the state to hang you,' I said, 'if I can prove to a judge in federal court that donating your organs is part of your religion. Do you understand what I'm saying?'

He winced. 'I didn't like being Catholic.'

'You don't have to say you're Catholic.'

'Tell that to Father Michael.'

'Gladly.' I laughed.

'Then what *do* I have to say?'

'There are a lot of people outside this prison, Shay, who have no trouble believing that what you're doing in here has some sort of religious basis. But I need you to believe it, too. If this is going to work, *you* have to tell me donating your organs is the only way to salvation.'

He stood up and started to pace. 'My way of saving myself may not be someone else's way.'

'That's okay,' I said. 'The court doesn't care about anyone else. They just want to know if *you* think that giving your heart to Claire Nealon is going to redeem you in God's eyes.'

When he stopped in front of me and caught my eye, I saw something that surprised me. Because I had been so busy crafting an escape hatch for Shay Bourne, I had forgotten that sometimes the outrageous is actually the truth. 'I don't think it,' he said. 'I *know* it.'

'Then we're in business.' I slipped my hands into my suit pockets and suddenly remembered what else I had to tell Shay. 'It's prickly,' I said. 'Like walking on a board full of needles. But somehow it doesn't hurt. It smells like Sunday morning, like a mower outside your window when you're trying to pretend the sun's not up yet.'

As I spoke, Shay closed his eyes. 'I think I remember.'

'Well,' I said. 'Just in case you don't.' I withdrew the handfuls of grass I'd torn from outside the prison grounds and sprinkled the tufts onto the floor.

A smile broke over Shay's face. He kicked off his prison-issued tennis shoes and began to move back and forth, barefoot, over the grass. Then he bent down to gather the cuttings and funneled them into the breast pocket of his scrubs, against a heart that was still beating strong. 'I'm going to save them,' he said.

'I know God will not give me anything I can't handle.
I just wish He didn't trust me so much.'

— *MOTHER TERESA*

June

Everything comes with a price.

You can have the man of your dreams, but only for a few years.

You can have the perfect family, but it turns out to be an illusion.

You can keep your daughter alive, but only if she hosts the heart of the person you hate most in this world.

I could not go straight home from the prison. I was shaking so hard that at first, I couldn't even drive; and even afterward, I missed the exit off the highway twice. I had gone to that meeting to tell Shay Bourne we didn't want his heart. So why had I changed my mind? Maybe because I was angry. Maybe because I was so shocked by what Shay Bourne had said. Maybe because if we waited for UNOS to find Claire a heart, it could be too late.

Besides, I told myself, this was all likely a moot point. The chance of Bourne even being a good physical match for Claire was negligible; his heart was probably far too large for a child's body; there could be all sorts of compromising diseases or long-term drug use that would prohibit him from being a donor.

And yet, there was another part of me that kept thinking: *But what if?*

Could I let myself hope? And could I stand it if, once again, that hope was shattered by Shay Bourne?

By the time I felt calm enough to drive home and face Claire, it was late at night. I had arranged for a neighbor to check on her hourly throughout the afternoon and evening, but Claire flatly refused a formal babysitter. She was fast asleep on the couch, the dog curled over her feet. Dudley lifted his head when I walked in, a worthy sentry. *Where were you when Elizabeth was taken?* I thought, not for the first time, rubbing Dudley between the ears. For days after the murders, I had held the puppy, staring into his eyes and pretending he could give me the answers I so desperately needed.

I turned off the television that was chattering to nobody and sat down beside Claire. If she received Shay Bourne's heart, would I look at my daughter but see him staring back at me?

Could I survive that?

And if I couldn't . . . would Claire survive at all?

I fitted myself around Claire's body, stretching beside her on the couch. In her sleep, she curled against me, a puzzle piece fitting back where it belonged. I kissed my daughter's forehead, unconsciously reading it for fever. This was my life now, and Claire's: a waiting game. Like Shay Bourne sitting in his cell, waiting for his turn to die, we sat imprisoned by the limitations of Claire's body, waiting for her turn to live.

So don't judge me, unless you've fallen asleep on a couch with your ill child, thinking this night might be her last.

Ask instead: would you do it?

Would you give up your vengeance against someone you hate if it meant saving someone you love?

Would you want your dreams to come true if it meant granting your enemy's dying wish?

Maggie

In school, I was the kind of kid who crossed her *t*'s and dotted her *i*'s. I made sure to right-justify my papers, so that the type didn't look ragged. I'd craft elaborate covers – a tiny, two-dimensional working guillotine for my essay on *A Tale of Two Cities*; a science lab on prisms with the header rainbowed in multiple colors; a scarlet letter for . . . well, you get the picture.

To that end, putting together a letter to the commissioner of corrections reminded me a little of my days as a student. There were multiple parts involved: the transcript of Shay Bourne attesting that he wanted to donate his heart to the sister of his victim; an affidavit from Claire Nealon's cardiac surgeon, stating that she did indeed need a heart to survive. I had made a call to facilitate a medical visit for Shay, to see if he was a match for Claire; and I had spent an hour on the phone with a UNOS coordinator, to confirm that if Shay gave up his heart, he could pick the recipient. I fastened all these letters together with a shiny silver butterfly clip and then turned back to the computer to finish my note to Commissioner Lynch.

As evidenced by the letter from the defendant's spiritual advisor, Father Michael Wright, execution by lethal injection will not only prevent the defendant from his intention of donating his heart to Claire Nealon – it also interferes with his practice of religion – a blatant violation of his First Amendment rights. Therefore, under the New Hampshire criminal code 630:5, subsection XIV, it would be impractical for the commissioner of corrections to carry out the

punishment of death by lethal injection. A sentence of death carried
out by hanging, however, would not only be allowed by the criminal
code, but also would allow the defendant to practice his religion up to
the moment of his execution.

I could imagine, at this moment, the commissioner's jaw drop-
ping as he realized that I had managed to piece together two
disparate laws in a way that would make the next few weeks a
living hell.

Furthermore, this office would be pleased to work in conjunction with
the commissioner of corrections to facilitate what needs to be done, as
there are tissue matches and medical testing to be completed prior to
the donation, and because time is of the essence during the organ
harvest.

Not to mention – I don't trust you.

It is imperative to settle this matter swiftly, for obvious reasons.

We don't have a lot of time to work this out. Because neither Shay
Bourne nor Claire Nealon have a lot of time left, period.

> *Sincerely,*
> *Maggie Bloom, Attorney*

I printed out the letter and slipped it into a manila envelope I'd
already addressed. As I licked the envelope, I thought: *Please make*
this work.
    Who was I talking to?
    I didn't believe in God. Not anymore.
    I was an atheist.
    Or so I told myself, even if there was a secret part of me that
hoped I'd be proven wrong.

Lucius

People always think they know what they'd miss the most if they had to trade places with me in this cell. Food, fresh air, your favorite pair of jeans, sex – believe me, I've heard them all, and they're all wrong. What you miss the most in prison is choice. You have no free will: your hair is cut in one style, like everyone else's. You eat what's being served when it is given to you. You are told when you can shower, shit, shave. Even our conversations are prescribed: If someone bumps into you in the real world, he says 'Excuse me.' If someone bumps into you in here, you say 'What the fuck, motherfucker' before he can even speak. If you *don't* do this, you become a mark.

The reason we have no choice now is because we made a bad one in the past – which is why we were all energized by Shay's attempt to die on his own terms. It was still an execution, but even that tiny sliver of preference was more than we had on a daily basis. I could only imagine how my world would change if we were given an option to choose between orange scrubs and yellow ones; if we were asked whether we'd like a spoon or a fork with our meal trays, instead of the universal plastic 'spork.' But the more animated we got at the possibility of, well, possibility . . . the more depressed Shay grew.

'Maybe,' he said to me one afternoon when the air-conditioning had broken and we were all wilting in our cells, 'I should just let them do what they want.'

The officers, in an act of mercy, had opened the door that led to the exercise cell. It was supposed to afford us a breeze, but that hadn't happened. 'Why would you say that?'

'Because it feels like I've started a war,' Shay said.

'Well, imagine that,' Crash laughed. 'Since I'm over here practicing my shooting.'

This afternoon Crash had been injecting Benadryl. Many of the inmates here had made their own points – homemade hypodermics that could be sharpened every few uses by scraping them against a matchbook. Benadryl was given out by the prison nurse; you could accumulate a stash and open up a capsule, then cook down the tiny beads of medicine in a spoon over a soda-can stove. It was a speed high, but the buffers used in the medicine would also make you crazy.

'Whaddya say, Mistah Messiah . . . you want a hit?'

'He most certainly does not,' I answered.

'I don't think he was talking to *you*,' Shay said. And then, to Crash: 'Give it to me.'

Crash laughed. 'Guess you don't know him as well as you think you do, Liberace. Ain't that right, Death Row?'

Crash had no moral compass. He aligned himself with the Aryan Brotherhood when it suited his needs. He talked of terrorist attacks; he'd cheered when we were watching the news footage of the World Trade Center collapsing. He had a list of victims, should he ever get out. He wanted his kids to grow up to be addicts or dealers or whores, and said he would be disappointed if they turned out to be anything else. Once, I heard him describing a visit with his three-year-old daughter: he told her to punch another kid at school to make him proud, and not to come back till she did. Now I watched him fish Shay the hype kit, hidden neatly inside a dismantled battery, ready for a hit with the liquefied Benadryl inside it. Shay put the needle to the crook of his elbow, set his thumb on the plunger.

And squirted the precious drug onto the floor of the catwalk.

'What the fuck!' Crash exploded. 'Gimme that back.'

'Haven't you heard? I'm Jesus. I'm *supposed* to save you,' Shay said.

'I don't want to be saved,' Crash yelled. 'I want my kit back!'

'Come and get it,' Shay said, and he pushed the kit under his door, so that it landed square on the catwalk. 'Hey, CO,' he yelled. 'Come see what Crash made.'

As the COs entered to confiscate the hype kit – and write him a ticket that would include a stay in solitary – Crash slammed his hand against the metal door. 'I swear, Bourne, when you least expect it . . .'

He was interrupted by the sound of Warden Coyne's voice out in the courtyard. 'I just bought a goddamn death gurney,' the warden cried, conversing with someone we could not see. 'What am I supposed to do with *that*?' And then, when he stopped speaking, we all noticed something – or the lack of something. The incessant hammering and sawing that had been going on outside for months, as the prison built a death chamber to accommodate Shay's sentence, had fallen silent. All we heard was a simple, blissful quiet.

'. . . you're gonna wind up dead,' Crash finished, but now we were starting to wonder if that would still be true.

Michael

The Reverend Arbogath Justus preached at the Drive-In Church of Christ in God in Heldratch, Michigan. His congregation arrived in their cars on Sunday mornings and received a blue flyer with the day's scripture, and a note to tune in to AM 1620 in order to hear the good reverend when he took the pulpit – formerly the snack bar, when it was a movie theater. I would have ridiculed this, but his flock was six hundred strong, which led me to believe that there were enough people in this world who wanted to tuck their prayer requests beneath windshield wipers to be collected, and to receive Communion from altar girls on roller skates.

I suppose it wasn't a big stretch to go from the movie screen to the small one, which is why Reverend Justus ran a television ministry site, too, on a cable station called SOS (Save Our Souls). I'd caught it a few times, while I was flipping through channels. It was fascinating to me, in the same way Shark Week was fascinating on the Discovery Channel – I was curious to learn more, but from a nice, secure distance. Justus wore eyeliner on television, and suits in a range of lollipop colors. His wife played the accordion when it came time to sing hymns. It all seemed like a parody of what faith was supposed to be – quiet and heart-settling, not grandiose and dramatic – which is why I always eventually changed the channel.

One day, when I went to visit Shay, my car was stopped in traffic leading to the prison. Shiny, scrubbed Midwestern faces worked their way from car to car. They were wearing green T-shirts with the name of Justus's church on the back, scrawled above a rudimentary drawing of a '57 Chevy convertible. When one girl approached, I unrolled the window. 'God bless you!' she said, and offered me a slip of yellow paper.

There was a picture of Jesus, arms outstretched and palms raised, floating in the oval of a sideview car mirror. The caption read: OBJECTS IN MIRROR ARE CLOSER THAN THEY APPEAR.

And then below it: *Shay Bourne: A Wolf in Sheep's Clothing? Don't Let a False Prophet Lead You Astray!*

The line of cars chugged forward, finally, and I turned into the parking lot. I had to pull my car onto the grass; it was that crowded. The throngs of people waiting for Shay, and the media covering his story, had not dissipated.

However, by the time I came close to the prison, I realized that the attention of most of these people was not held by Shay at that moment, but by a man in a three-piece lime-green suit, wearing a clerical collar. I got close enough to see the pancake makeup and the eyeliner, and realized that Reverend Arbogath Justus had now moved into the realm of satellite ministries . . . and had chosen the prison as his first stop. 'Miracles mean nothing,' Justus announced. 'The world is full of false prophets. In Revelations, we're told of a beast that uses miracles to fool men into worshipping it. Do you know what happens to that beast on Judgment Day? He and the people who were fooled are all thrown into a lake of fire. Is that what you want?'

A woman fell forward from the cliff-edge of the crowd. 'No,' she sobbed. 'I want to go with God.'

'Jesus can hear you, sister,' Reverend Justus said. 'Because He's here, with us. Not inside that prison, like the false prophet Shay Bourne!'

There was a roar from his converts. But just as quickly, it was matched by those who hadn't given up on Shay. 'How do we know *you're* not the false prophet?' one young man called out.

Beside me, a mother tucked her sick child into her arms more tightly. She looked at my collar and frowned. 'Are you with him?'

'No,' I said. 'Definitely not.'

She nodded. 'Well, I'm not taking advice from a man whose church has a concession stand.'

I started to agree, but was distracted by a burly man who grabbed the reverend from his makeshift pulpit and yanked him into the crowd.

The cameras, of course, were all rolling.

Without thinking twice about what I was doing, or that I was doing it on film, I pushed forward and rescued Reverend Arbogath Justus from the clutches of the mob. He wrapped his arms around me, gasping, as I pulled us both up onto a granite ledge that ran along the edge of the parking lot.

In retrospect, I didn't know why I had chosen to play the hero. And I *really* didn't know why I said what I did next. Philosophically, Reverend Justus and I were on the same team – even if we pitched religion with very different styles. But I also knew that Shay was – maybe for the first time in his life – attempting to do something honorable. He didn't deserve to be slandered for that.

I might not believe *in* Shay – but I believed him.

I felt the wide, white eye of a television camera swing toward me, and a herd of others followed. 'Reverend Justus came here, I'm sure, because he thinks he's telling you the truth. Well, so does Shay Bourne. He wants to do one thing in this world before he leaves it: save the life of a child. The Jesus *I* know would endorse that, I think. And,' I said, turning to the reverend, 'the Jesus *I* know wouldn't send people to some fiery hell if they were trying to atone for their sins. The Jesus *I* know believed in second chances.'

As Reverend Justus realized that I might have saved him from the mob to sacrifice him all over again, his face reddened. 'There's one true word of God,' he proclaimed in his camera-ready voice, 'and Shay Bourne isn't speaking it.'

Well, I couldn't argue with that. In all the time I'd been with Shay, he had never quoted the New Testament. He was far more likely to swear or go off on a tangent about Hanta virus and government conspiracy. 'You're absolutely right,' I said. 'He's trying to do something that's never been done before. He's asking questions of the status quo. He's trying to suggest another way – a better way. And he's willing to die for it to happen.' I raised a brow. 'Come to think of it, I bet Jesus might find a lot in common with a guy like Shay Bourne.'

I nodded, stepped down from the granite ledge, and shoved my way through the crowd to the security partition, where a correctional officer let me through. 'Father,' he said, shaking his head, 'you got no idea how big a pile of you-know-what you just stepped into.' And as if I needed proof, my cell phone rang: Father Walter's angry summons back to St Catherine's, immediately.

I sat in the front pew of the church as Father Walter paced in front of me. 'What if I blamed it all on being moved by the Holy Spirit?' I offered, and received a withering glare.

'I don't understand,' Father Walter said. 'Why would you say something like that . . . on live television, for the love of God—'

'I didn't mean to—'

'— when you had to know that it was going to bring the heat down on St Catherine's?' He sank down beside me and tipped his head back, as if he were praying to the carved statue of Jesus on the Cross that rose above us. 'Michael, seriously, what were you thinking?' he said softly. 'You're a young, handsome, smart, straight guy. You could write your ticket in the Church – get your own parish, wind up in Rome . . . be whatever you want. And instead, I get a copy of an affidavit from the attorney general's office, saying that as Shay Bourne's spiritual advisor you believe in salvation through organ donation? And then I turn on the midday news and see you on a soapbox, sounding like some kind of . . . some kind of . . .'

'What?'

He shook his head, but stopped short of calling me a heretic. 'You've read Tertullian,' he said.

We all had, in seminary. He was a famous orthodox Christian historian whose text *The Prescription Against Heretics* was a forerunner of the Nicene Creed. Tertullian had coined the idea of a deposit of faith – that we take what Christ taught and believe it as is, without adding to or taking away from it.

'You want to know why Catholicism's been around for two thousand years?' Father Walter said. '*Because* of people like Tertullian, who understood that you can't mess around with truth. People were upset with the changes of Vatican II. The Pope's even reinstated the Latin Mass.'

I took a deep breath. 'I thought being a spiritual advisor meant doing what Shay Bourne needs to face his death with peace – not what *we* need him to do, as a good Catholic.'

'Good Lord,' Father Walter said. 'He's conned you.'

I frowned. 'He hasn't conned me.'

'He's got you eating out of the palm of his hand! Look at you – you practically acted like his press secretary today on the news –'

'Do you think Jesus died for a reason?' I interrupted.

'Of course.'

'Then why shouldn't Shay Bourne be allowed to do the same?'

'Because,' Father Walter said, 'Shay Bourne is not dying for anyone's sins, except his own.'

I flinched. Well, didn't I know that better than anyone else?

Father Walter sighed. 'I don't agree with the death penalty, but I understand this sentence. He murdered two people. A police officer, and a little girl.' He shook his head. 'Save his soul, Michael. Don't try to save his life.'

I glanced up. 'What do you think would have happened if just one of the apostles had stayed awake in the garden with Jesus? If they'd kept Him from being arrested? If they'd tried to save *His* life?'

Father Walter's mouth dropped open. 'You don't *really* think Shay Bourne is Jesus, do you?'

I didn't.

Did I?

Father Walter sank down onto the pew and took off his glasses.

He rubbed his eyes. 'Mikey,' he said, 'take a couple weeks off. Go somewhere and pray. Think about what you're doing – what you're *saying*.' He looked up at me. 'And in the meantime, I don't want you going to the prison on behalf of St Catherine's.'

I looked around this church, which I had grown to love – with its polished pews and the spatter of light from the stained glass, the whispering silk of the chalice veil, the dancing flames on the candles lit in offering. *Where your treasure is, there your heart will be.*

'I won't go to the prison on behalf of St Catherine's,' I said, 'but I will go on behalf of Shay.'

I walked down the aisle, past the holy water, past the bulletin board with the information about the young boy from Zimbabwe the congregation supported with their donations. When I stepped outside the double doors of the church, the world was so bright that for a moment, I couldn't see where I was headed.

Maggie

There were four ways to hang someone. The short drop involved a prisoner falling just a few inches; their body weight and physical struggling tightened the noose and caused death by strangulation. Suspension hanging required the prisoner to be raised upward and strangled. Standard drop hanging – popular in America in the late nineteenth and twentieth centuries – meant the prisoner fell four to six feet, which might or might not break his neck. Long drop hanging was a more personal execution: the distance the prisoner fell was determined by weight and body type. The body was still accelerating due to gravity at the end of the drop, but the head was restricted by the noose – which broke the neck and ruptured the spinal cord, rendering instant unconsciousness, and a quick death.

I'd learned that next to shooting, hanging was the world's most popular form of execution. It was introduced in Persia twenty-five hundred years ago for male criminals (females were strangled at the stake, because it was less indecent) – a nice alternative to the blood and guts of a typical beheading, with all the same punch as any public spectacle.

It was not, however, foolproof. In 1885, a British murderer named Robert Goodale was hanged, but the force of the drop decapitated him. Most recently, Saddam Hussein's half brother had suffered the same grisly fate in Iraq. This was a legal conundrum: if the sentence of death was to be carried out by hanging, then the prisoner could not be decapitated, or the sentence wasn't fulfilled.

I had to do my homework – which explained why I was reading the Official Table of Drops and estimating Shay Bourne's weight when Father Michael came into my office. 'Oh, good,' I said, motioning to the seat across from my desk. 'If the noose is positioned right – there's something about a brass eyelet – the fall causes an instant fracture of the C2 vertebra. It says here brain death occurs in six minutes, and whole-body death within ten to fifteen minutes. That means we've got a four-minute window to get him back on a respirator before the heart stops beating and oh, I almost forgot – I heard back from the AG's office. They denied our request to have Shay hanged instead of executed with lethal injection. They even included the original sentence, as if I haven't read it a bazillion times, and told me if I wanted to challenge it, I had to file the appropriate motions. Which,' I said, 'I did five hours ago.'

Father Michael didn't even seem to hear me. 'Listen,' I said gently, 'it's easier if you think about this hanging business as science . . . and stop connecting it personally to Shay.'

'I'm sorry,' the priest said, shaking his head. 'It's just – it's been a pretty bad day.'

'You mean the showdown you had with the televangelist?'

'You saw that?'

'You're the talk of the town, Father.'

He closed his eyes. 'Great.'

'I'm sure Shay saw it, too, if that's any consolation.'

Father Michael looked up at me. 'Thanks to Shay, my supervising priest thinks I'm a heretic.'

I thought about what my father would say if a member of his congregation came to him to ease his soul. 'Do *you* think you're a heretic?'

'Does *any* heretic?' he said. 'Honestly, I'm the last person who ought to be helping you win Shay's case, Maggie.'

'Hey,' I said, trying to boost his spirits. 'I was just about to go to my parents' house for dinner. It's a standing engagement on Friday nights. Why don't you come with me?'

'I couldn't impose—'

'Believe me, there's always enough food to feed a third world country.'

'Well, then,' the priest said, 'that would be great.'

I switched off my desk lamp. 'We can take my car,' I said.

'Can I leave my motorcycle parked in the lot here?'

'You're allowed to ride a motorcycle, but you can't eat meat on Friday?'

He still looked as if the world had been pulled out from beneath him. 'I guess the Church forefathers found it easier to abstain from beef than Harleys.'

I led him through the maze of file cabinets in the ACLU office and headed outside. 'Guess what I found out today,' I said. 'The trapdoor from the old gallows at the state prison is in the chaplain's office.'

When I glanced at Father Michael, I was pretty sure I saw the ghost of a smile.

June

One of the things I liked about Dr Wu's office was the wall of pictures. An enormous corkboard held photographs of patients who had beaten the odds after having Dr Wu operate on their failing hearts. There were babies propped up on pillows, Christmas card portraits, and boys wielding Little League bats. It was a mural of success.

When I'd first come to tell Dr Wu about Shay Bourne's offer, he listened carefully and then said that in his twenty-three years of practice, he had yet to see a grown man's heart that would be a good match for a child. Hearts grew to fit the needs of their host body – which was why every other potential organ that had been offered to Claire for transplant had come from another child. 'I'll examine him,' Dr Wu promised, 'but I don't want you to get your hopes up.'

Now I watched Dr Wu take a seat and flatten his palms on the desk. I always marveled at the fact that he walked around shaking hands and waving as if the appendages were totally normal, instead of miraculous. Those ridiculous celebrities who insured their breasts and their legs had nothing on Dr Wu and his hands. 'June . . .'

'Just say it quickly,' I said, full of false cheer.

Dr Wu met my gaze. 'He's a perfect match for Claire.'

I had already gathered the strap of my purse in my fist, planning to thank him hastily and beat a retreat out of the office before I started crying again over yet another lost heart; but these words rooted me to my seat. 'I . . . I'm sorry?'

'They have the same blood type – B positive. The tissue cross-match we did of their blood was nonreactive. But – here's the remarkable part – his heart is just the right size.'

I knew they looked for a donor who was within 20 percent of the patient's weight – which for Claire meant anyone between sixty and a hundred pounds. Shay Bourne was a small man, but he was still an adult. He had to weigh 120 or 130 pounds.

'Medically, it doesn't make sense. Theoretically, his heart is too tiny to be doing the job his own body needs . . . and yet he seems to be healthy as a horse.' Dr Wu smiled. 'It looks like Claire's got herself a donor.'

I stilled. This was supposed to be wonderful news – but I could barely breathe. How would Claire react if she knew the circumstances behind the donation? 'You can't tell her,' I said.

'That she's going to have a transplant?'

I shook my head. 'Where it came from.'

Dr Wu frowned. 'Don't you think she'll find out? This is all over the news.'

'Organ donations are always done anonymously. Plus, she doesn't want a boy's heart. She always says that.'

'That's not really the issue here, is it?' The cardiologist stared at me. 'It's a muscle, June. Nothing more, and nothing less. What makes a heart worthy for transplant has nothing to do with the donor's personality.'

I looked up at him. 'What would you do, if she was your daughter?'

'If she was my daughter,' Dr Wu replied, 'I would already have scheduled the surgery.'

Lucius

I tried to tell Shay that he was the topic on *Larry King Live* that night, but either he was asleep or he just didn't feel like answering me. Instead, I took out my stinger from where it was hidden behind a cement block in the wall and heated up some water for tea. The guests that night were the nutcase reverend that Father Michael had sparred with outside the prison, and some stuffed-shirt academic named Ian Fletcher. It was hard to tell who had the more intriguing backstory – Reverend Justus with his drive-in church, or Fletcher – who'd been a television atheist until he'd run across a little girl who could apparently perform miracles and raise the dead. He wound up marrying the girl's single mother, which in my opinion, greatly diluted the credibility of his commentary.

Still, he was a better speaker than Reverend Justus, who kept rising out of his seat as if he were filled with helium. 'There's an old proverb, Larry,' the reverend said. 'You can't keep trouble from coming, but you don't have to make out a place card.'

Larry King tapped his pen on the desk twice. 'And by that you mean . . . ?'

'Miracles don't make a man into God. Dr Fletcher ought to know that better than anyone.'

Unrattled, Ian Fletcher smiled. 'The more you think you're right, the likelier you are to be wrong. That's a proverb Reverend Justus probably hasn't encountered yet.'

'Tell us about being a television atheist,' Larry said.

'Well, I used to do what Jerry Falwell did, except instead of saying there's a God, I said there wasn't one. I went around debunking claims of miracles all over the country. Eventually, when I found one that I couldn't discredit, I started wondering if it was really God I objected to . . . or just the sense of entitlement that seems to be part of affiliating with a religious group. Like the way you'll hear that a person is a good Christian – well, who says Christians corner the market on virtue? Or when the president ends a speech with 'God bless the United States of America' . . . why just us?'

'Are you still an atheist?' King asked.

'Technically, I suppose you'd call me an agnostic.'

Justus scoffed. 'Splitting hairs.'

'Not true; an atheist's got more in common with a Christian, since he believes you can know whether or not God exists – but where a Christian says absolutely, the atheist says absolutely not. For me, and any other agnostic – the jury's still out. Religion is intriguing, but in a historical sense. A man should live his life a certain way not because of some divine authority, but because of a personal moral obligation to himself and others.'

Larry King turned to Reverend Justus. 'And you, sir, your congregation meets in a former drive-in movie theater? Don't you think that takes some of the pomp and circumstance out of religion?'

'What we've found, Larry, is that for some people the obligation of getting up and going to church is too overwhelming. They don't like having to see or be seen by others; they don't enjoy being indoors on a beautiful Sunday; they prefer to worship in private. Coming to the Drive-In Church allows a person to do whatever it is he needs to do while communing with God – whether that's wearing pajamas, or eating an Egg McMuffin, or dozing off during my sermon.'

'Now, Shay Bourne isn't the first person to come along and stir the pot,' King said. 'Few years back, a Florida State football quarterback was found lying in the street, claiming to be God. And a fellow in Virginia wanted his driver's license changed to reflect that he was a resident of the Kingdom of Heaven. What do you think it is about Shay Bourne that makes people believe he might be the real deal?'

'As far as I understand,' Fletcher said, 'Bourne's not claiming to be the Messiah or Mary Poppins or Captain America – it's the people supporting him who have christened him, no pun intended. Ironically, that's very similar to what we see in the Bible – Jesus doesn't go around claiming to be God.'

'"*I am the way, the truth, and the life; no man cometh unto the Father, but by me*,"' Justus quoted. 'John, 14:6.'

'There's also evidence in the gospels that Jesus appeared in different forms to different people,' Fletcher said. 'The apostle James talks about seeing Jesus standing on the shore in the form of a child. He points it out to John, who thinks he's nuts, because the person on the shore isn't a child but a handsome young man. They go to investigate, and although one sees an old, bald man, the other sees a young guy with a beard.'

Reverend Justus frowned. 'I can quote the Gospel of John forward and backward,' he said, 'and that's *not* in there.'

Fletcher smiled. 'I never said it was from the Gospel of John. I said it was from *a* gospel. A Gnostic one, called the *Acts of John*.'

'There's no Acts of John in the Bible,' Justus huffed. 'He's making this up.'

'The reverend's right – it's not in the Bible. And there are dozens of others like it. Through a series of editorial decisions, they were excluded – and considered heresy by the early Christian church.'

'That's because the Bible is the Word of God, period,' Justus said.

'Actually, Matthew, Mark, Luke, and John weren't even written by the apostles Matthew, Mark, Luke, and John. They were written in Greek, by authors who had a modicum of education – unlike Jesus's fishermen disciples, who were illiterate, like ninety percent of the population. Mark is based on the apostle Peter's preaching. Matthew's author was probably a Jewish Christian from Antioch, Syria. The Gospel of Luke was allegedly written by a doctor. And the author of the Gospel of John never mentions his own name . . . but it was the latest of the four synoptic gospels to be written, roughly around A.D. 100. If the apostle John *was* the author, he would have been extremely old.'

'Smoke and mirrors,' Reverend Justus said. 'He's using rhetoric to distract us from the basic truth here.'

'Which is?' King asked.

'Do you truly believe that if the Lord chose to grace us with his earthly presence again – and that is a big *if*, in my humble opinion – he would willingly choose to inhabit a convicted murderer, two times over?'

My hot water started to boil, and I disconnected the stinger. Then I turned off the television without hearing Fletcher's answer. Why would God choose to inhabit *any* of us?

What if it was the other way around . . . if we were the ones who inhabited God?

Michael

During the drive to Maggie's parents' home, I wallowed in various degrees of guilt. I had let down Father Walter and St Catherine's. I'd made a fool of myself on TV. And although I'd started to tell Maggie that Shay and I had some history between us that he didn't know about — I had chickened out. Again.

'So here's the thing,' Maggie said, distracting me from my thoughts as we pulled into the driveway. 'My parents are going to be a little excited when they see you in my car.'

I glanced around at the quiet, wooded retreat. 'Don't get much company here?'

'Don't get many *dates* is more like it.'

'I don't want to burst your bubble, but I'm not exactly boyfriend material.'

Maggie laughed. 'Yeah, thanks, but I'd like to think even *I'm* not that desperate. It's just that my mother's got radar or something — she can sniff out a Y chromosome from miles away.'

As if Maggie had conjured her, a woman stepped out of the house. She was petite and blond, with her hair cut into a neat bob and pearls at her neck. Either she'd just come home from work, or she was headed out — my mother, on a Friday night, would have been wearing one of my dad's flannel shirts with the sleeves rolled up, and what she called her Weekend Fat Jeans. She squinted, glimpsing me through the windshield. 'Maggie!' she cried. 'You didn't tell us you were bringing a *friend* for dinner.'

Just the way she said the word *friend* made me feel a rush of sympathy for Maggie.

'Joel!' she called into the house behind her. 'Maggie's brought a guest!'

I stepped out of the car and adjusted my collar. 'Hello,' I said. 'I'm Father Michael.'

Maggie's mother's hand went to her throat. 'Oh, God.'

'Close,' I replied, 'but no cigar.'

At that moment, Maggie's father came hurrying out the front door, tucking in his dress shirt. 'Mags,' he said, folding her into a bear hug, which was when I noticed his yarmulke. Then he turned to me and held out a hand. 'I'm Rabbi Bloom.'

'You could have *told* me your father was a rabbi,' I whispered to Maggie.

'You didn't *ask*.' She looped her arm through her father's. 'Daddy, this is Father Michael. He's a heretic.'

'Please tell me you're not dating him,' Mrs Bloom murmured.

'Ma, he's a priest. Of course I'm not.' Maggie laughed as they headed toward the house. 'But I bet that street performer who asked me out is starting to look a lot more palatable to you . . .'

That left two of us, men of God, standing awkwardly on the driveway. Rabbi Bloom led the way into the house, toward his study. 'So,' he said. 'Where's your congregation?'

'Concord,' I said. 'St Catherine's.'

'And you met my daughter how?'

'I'm Shay Bourne's spiritual advisor.'

He glanced up. 'That must be unnerving.'

'It is,' I said. 'On many levels.'

'So is he or isn't he?'

'Donating his heart? That's going to be up to your daughter, I think.'

The rabbi shook his head. 'No, no. Maggie, she could move a mountain if she wanted to, one molecule at a time. I meant is he or isn't he Jesus?'

I blinked. 'I never figured I'd hear that question from a rabbi.'

'Jesus *was* a Jewish man, after all. Just look at the evidence: he lived at home, went into his dad's business, thought his mother was a virgin, and his mother thought he was God.' Rabbi Bloom grinned, and I started to smile.

'Well, Shay's not preaching what Jesus did.'

The rabbi laughed. 'And you were around the first time to know this for sure?'

'I know what it says in scripture.'

'I never understood people – Jewish *or* Christian – who read the Bible as if it were hard evidence. Gospel means good *news*. It's a way to update the story, to fit the audience you're telling it to.'

'I don't know if I'd say that Shay Bourne's here to update the story of Christ for the modern generation,' I replied.

'It makes you wonder, then, why so many people have jumped on his bandwagon. It's almost like who he is matters less than what all of them need him to be.' Rabbi Bloom began to scour his bookshelves, finally lighting on one dusty tome, which he skimmed through until he found a certain page. *'Jesus said to his disciples, "Compare me to someone and tell me whom I am like." Simon Peter said to him, "You are like a righteous angel." Matthew said to him, "You are like a wise philosopher." Thomas said to him, "Master, my mouth is wholly incapable of saying whom you are like." Jesus said, "I am not your master. Because you have drunk, you have become intoxicated from the bubbling spring which I have measured out."'*

He snapped the book shut again as I tried to place the scripture. 'History's always written by the winners,' Rabbi Bloom said. 'This was one of the losers.' He handed me the book just as Maggie poked her head into the room.

'Dad, you're not trying to pawn off another copy of *The Best Jewish Knock-Knock Jokes*, are you?'

'Unbelievably, Father Michael already has a signed copy. Is dinner ready?'

'Yes.'

'Thank goodness. I was beginning to think your mother had cremated the tilapia.' As Maggie ducked back into the kitchen,

Rabbi Bloom turned to me. 'Well, in spite of how Maggie introduced you, you don't seem like a heretic to me.'

'It's a long story.'

'I'm sure you already know that *heresy* comes from the Greek
word for *choice*.' He shrugged. 'Makes you wonder. What if the
ideas that have always been considered sacrilegious aren't sacrilegious at all – just ideas we haven't come across before? Or ideas
we haven't been *allowed* to come across?'

In my hands, the book the rabbi had given me felt as if it were
burning. 'You hungry?' Bloom asked.

'Starving,' I admitted, and I let him lead the way.

June

When I was pregnant with Claire, I was told that I had gestational diabetes. I still don't think that was true, frankly – an hour before I had the test, I'd taken Elizabeth to McDonald's and finished her orange Hi-C drink, which is enough to put anyone into a sugar coma. However, when the obstetrician told me the results, I did what I had to do: stuck to a strict diet that left me hungry all the time, got blood drawn twice a week, held my breath at every visit while my doctor checked the baby's growth.

The silver lining? I was treated to numerous ultrasounds. Long after most moms-to-be had gotten their twenty-week preview of the baby inside them, I continued to get updated portraits. It got to be so commonplace for Kurt and I to see our baby that he stopped coming to the weekly OB visits. He'd watch Elizabeth while I drove to the hospital, lifted up my shirt, and let the wand roll over my belly, illuminating on a monitor a foot, an elbow, the slope of this new child's nose. By then, in my eighth month, the picture wasn't the stick-figure skeleton you see at twenty weeks – you could see her hair, the ridges on her thumb, the curve of her cheek. She looked so real on the ultrasound screen that sometimes I'd forget she was still inside me.

'Not much longer,' the technician had said to me that last day as she wiped the gel off my belly with a warm washcloth.

'Easy for you to say,' I told her. 'You're not the one chasing around a seven-year-old in your eighth month.'

'Been there done that,' she said, and she reached beneath the screen to hand me that day's printout of the baby's face.

When I saw it, I drew in my breath: that's how much this new baby looked like Kurt – completely unlike me, unlike Elizabeth. This new baby had his wide-set eyes, his dimples, the point of his chin. I folded the picture into my purse so that I could show it to him, and then I drove home.

There were cars backed up on the street leading to mine. I assumed it was construction; they'd been repaving the roads around here. We sat in a line, idling, listening to the radio. After five minutes, I started to worry – Kurt was on duty today, and had taken his lunch break early so that I could go to the ultrasound without dragging Elizabeth along. If I didn't get home soon, he'd be late for work.

'Thank God,' I said when the traffic slowly began to move. But as I drew closer, I saw the detour signs set up at the end of my block, the police car sprawled sideways across the street. I felt that small tumble in my heart, the way you do when you see a fire engine racing toward the general vicinity of your home.

Roger, an officer I knew only marginally, was diverting traffic. I unrolled my window. 'I live here,' I said. 'I'm married to Kurt Nea—'

Before I could finish, his face froze, and that was how I knew something had happened. I'd seen Kurt's face do the same thing when he'd told me that my first husband had been killed in the car wreck.

I snapped off my seat belt and pushed my way out of the car, ungainly and awkward in my pregnancy. 'Where is she?' I cried, the car still running. 'Where's Elizabeth?'

'June,' Roger said as he wrapped an arm around me firmly. 'Why don't you just come with me?'

He walked me down the road where I lived, until I could see what I hadn't been able to from the crossroads: the glare of police cruiser lights, blinking like a holiday. The yawning mouths of the ambulances. The door to my house wide open. One officer held the dog in his arms; when Dudley saw me, he began to bark like mad.

'Elizabeth!' I yelled, and I shoved away from Roger, running as fast as I could given my shape and size. 'Elizabeth!!'

I was intercepted by someone who knocked the breath from me – the chief of police. 'June,' he said softly. 'Come with me.'

I struggled against Irv – scratching, kicking, pleading. I thought maybe if I put up a fight, it would keep me from hearing what he was about to say. 'Elizabeth?' I whispered.

'She's been shot, June.'

I waited for him to say *But she'll be just fine*, except he didn't. He shook his head. Later, I would remember that he had been crying.

'I want to see her,' I sobbed.

'There's something else,' Irv said, and as I watched, a brace of paramedics wheeled Kurt out on a stretcher. His face was white, leached of blood – all of which seemed to be soaking the makeshift bandage around his midsection.

I reached for Kurt's hand, and he turned toward me, his eyes glassy. 'I'm sorry,' he choked out. 'I'm so sorry.'

'What happened?' I shrieked, frantic. 'Sorry for what? What happened to her!'

'Ma'am,' a paramedic said, 'we've got to get him to a hospital.'

Another paramedic pulled me back. I watched them take Kurt away from me.

As Irv led me to the steps of another ambulance, he spoke, words that at the time felt as solid and square as bricks, layered sentence upon sentence to build a wall between life as I'd known it and the one I would now be forced to lead. *Kurt gave us a statement . . . found the carpenter sexually abusing Elizabeth . . . standoff . . . shots were fired . . . Elizabeth got in the way.*

Elizabeth, I used to say, when she was following me around the tiny kitchen as I cooked dinner, *I'm tripping over you.*

Elizabeth, your father and I are trying to have a conversation.

Elizabeth, not now.

Never.

My legs were numb as Irv led me into a second ambulance.

'She's the mother,' he said as one of the paramedics came forward. A small form lay on a stretcher in the central cavity of the ambulance, covered with a thick gray blanket. I reached out, shaking, and pulled the cloth down. As soon as I saw Elizabeth, my knees gave out; if not for Irv, I would have fallen.

She looked like she was sleeping. Her hands were tucked on either side of her body; her cheeks were flushed.

They'd made a mistake, that was all.

I leaned over the stretcher, touching her face. Her skin was still warm. 'Elizabeth,' I whispered, the way I did on school days to wake her. 'Elizabeth, time to get up.'

But she didn't stir; she didn't hear me. I broke down over her body, pulling her against me. The blood on her chest was garish. I tried to draw her closer, but I couldn't – this baby inside me was in the way. 'Don't go,' I whispered. 'Please don't go.'

'June,' Irv said, touching my shoulder. 'You can ride with them if you want, but you'll have to put her down.'

I did not understand the great hurry to take her to a hospital; later, I would learn that only a doctor could pronounce Elizabeth dead, no matter how obvious it was.

The paramedics gently strapped Elizabeth to the gurney and offered me a seat beside it. 'Wait,' I said, and I unclasped a barrette from my hair. 'She doesn't like her bangs in her eyes,' I murmured, and I clipped them back. I left my hand on her forehead for a moment, a benediction.

On the interminable ride to the hospital, I looked down at my shirt. It was stained with blood, a Rorschach of loss. But I was not the only one who had been marked, permanently changed. It was no surprise when a month later I gave birth to Claire – an infant who looked nothing like her father, as she had that day at the ultrasound, but who instead was the spitting image of the sister she would never meet.

Maggie

Oliver and I were enjoying a glass of Yellow Tail and a TiVo'd *Grey's Anatomy* when there was a knock on the door. Now, this was alarming on several counts:

1. It was Friday night, and no one ever stopped by on Friday night.
2. People who ring the doorbell at ten p.m. are either
   a. stranded with a dead battery in their car
   b. serial killers
   c. all of the above
3. I was in my pajamas.
4. The ones with a hole on the butt, so that my underwear showed.

I looked at the rabbit. 'Let's not get it,' I said, but Oliver hopped off my lap and began to sniff around the bottom of the door.

'Maggie?' I heard. 'I know you're in there.'

'Daddy?' I got off the couch and unlocked the door to let him in. 'Shouldn't you be at services?'

He took off his coat and hung it on an antique rack that my mother had given me for my birthday one year, and that I really hated, but that she looked for every time she came to my house (*Oh, Maggie, I'm so glad you've still got this!*). 'I stayed for the important parts. Your mother's kibitzing with Carol; I'll probably make it home before she will.'

Carol was the cantor – a woman with a voice that made me

think of falling asleep in the summertime sun: strong, steady, utterly relaxing. When she wasn't singing, she collected thimbles. She went to conventions as far away as Seattle to trade them, and had one entire forty-foot wall of her house divvied up by a contractor into minuscule display shelves. Mom said that Carol had more than five thousand thimbles. I didn't think I had five thousand of anything, except maybe daily calories.

He walked into the living room and glanced at the television. 'I wish that skinny girl would just ditch McDreamy.'

'You watch *Grey's Anatomy*?'

'Your mother watches. I absorb by osmosis.' He sat down on the couch, while I mulled over the fact that I actually did have something in common with my mother.

'I liked your friend the priest,' my father said.

'He's not my friend. We work together.'

'I can still like him, can't I?'

I shrugged. 'Something tells me you didn't come all the way here to tell me how fabulous Father Michael is.'

'Well, in part. How come you brought him over tonight?'

'Why?' I bristled. 'Did Mom complain?'

'Will you just stop with the Mom thing?' My father sighed. 'I'm asking you a question.'

'He had a hard day. Being on Shay's side isn't easy for him.'

My father looked at me carefully. 'How about for you?'

'You told me to ask Shay what he wanted,' I said. 'He doesn't want his life saved. He wants his death to mean something.'

My father nodded. 'A lot of Jews think you can't donate organs, because it violates Jewish law – you're not supposed to mutilate the body after death; you're supposed to bury it as soon as possible. But *pikkuah nefesh* takes precedence over that. It says that the duty to save life trumps everything. Or in other words – a Jew is *required* to break the law, if it means saving a life.'

'So it's okay to commit murder in order to save someone else?' I asked.

'Well, God's not stupid; He sets parameters. But if there's any karmic *pikkuah nefesh* in the world—'

'To mix metaphors, no less religions . . .'

'—then the fact that you can't stop an execution is at least balanced by the fact that you'll be saving a life.'

'At what cost, Daddy? Is it okay to kill someone who's a criminal, someone society really doesn't want around anymore, so that a little girl can live? What if it wasn't a little girl who needed that heart? What if it was some other criminal? Or what if it wasn't Shay who had to die in order to donate his organs? What if it was *me*?'

'God forbid,' my father said.

'It's semantics.'

'It's morality. You're doing good.'

'By doing bad.'

My father shook his head. 'There's something else about *pikkuah nefesh* . . . it clears the slate of guilt. You can't feel remorse about breaking the law, because ethically, you're obligated to do it.'

'See, that's where you're wrong. I *can* feel remorse. Because we're not talking about not fasting on Yom Kippur since you happen to be sick . . . we're talking about a man dying.'

'And saving your life.'

I looked up at him. '*Claire's* life.'

'Two birds with one stone,' my father said. 'Maybe it's not literal in your case, Maggie. But this lawsuit – it's fired you up. It's given you something to look forward to.' He looked around my home – the place setting for one, the bowl of popcorn on the table, the rabbit cage.

I suppose there was a point in my life when I wanted the package deal – the chuppah, the husband, the kids, the carpools – but somewhere along the line, I'd just stopped hoping. I had gotten used to living alone, to saving the other half of the can of soup for the next night's dinner, to only changing the pillowcases on my side of the bed. I had become overly comfortable with myself, so much so that anyone else would have felt like an intrusion.

Pretending, it turned out, took much less effort than hoping.

One of the reasons I loved my parents – and hated them – is that they still thought I had a chance at all that. They only wanted me to be happy; they didn't see how on earth I could be happy by myself. Which, if you read between the lines, meant they found me just as lacking as I did.

I could feel my eyes filling with tears. 'I'm tired,' I said. 'You should go now.'

'Maggie—'

When he reached for me, I ducked away. 'Good night.'

I punched buttons on the remote control until the television went black. Oliver crept out from behind my desk to investigate, and I scooped him up. Maybe this was why I chose to spend my free time with a rabbit: he didn't offer unwanted advice. 'You forgot one little detail,' I said. '*Pikkuah nefesh* doesn't apply to an atheist.'

My father paused in the act of taking his coat from the world's ugliest coat rack. He slipped it over his arm and walked toward me. 'I know it sounds strange for a rabbi,' he said, 'but it's never mattered to me what you believe in, Mags, as long as you believe in yourself as much as I do.' He settled his hand on top of Oliver's back. Our fingers brushed, but I didn't look up at him. 'And that's not semantics.'

'Daddy—'

He held up a hand to shush me and opened the door. 'I'll tell your mother to get you new pajamas for your birthday,' he said, pausing at the threshold. 'Those have a hole in the butt.'

Michael

In 1945, two brothers were digging beneath cliffs in Nag Hammadi, Egypt, trying to find fertilizer. One – Mohammed Ali – struck something hard as he dug. He unearthed a large earthenware jug, covered with a red dish. Afraid that a jinn would be inside it, Mohammed Ali didn't want to open the jar. Finally, the curiosity of finding gold instead led him to break it open – only to find thirteen papyrus books inside, bound in gazelle leather.

Some of the books were burned for firewood. The others made their way to religious scholars, who dated them to have been written around A.D. 140, about thirty years after the New Testament – and deciphered them to find the names of gospels not found in the Bible, full of sayings that were in the New Testament . . . and many that weren't. In some, Jesus spoke in riddles; in others, the Virgin birth and bodily resurrection were dismissed. They came to be known as the Gnostic gospels, and even today, they are given short shrift by the Church.

In seminary, we learned about the Gnostic gospels. Namely, we learned that they were heresy. And let me tell you, when a priest hands you a text and tells you this is what *not* to believe, it colors the way you read it. Maybe I skimmed the text, saving the careful close analysis for the Bible. Maybe I whiffed completely and told the priest who was teaching that course that I'd done my homework when in fact I didn't. Whatever the excuse, that night when I cracked open Joel Bloom's book, it was as if I'd never seen the words before, and although I planned to only read the foreword by the scholar who'd compiled the texts – a man named Ian Fletcher – I found myself devouring the pages as if it were the latest Stephen King novel and not a collection of ancient gospels.

The book had been earmarked to the Gospel of Thomas. Any mentions of Thomas I knew from the Bible certainly weren't flattering: He doesn't believe Lazarus will rise from the dead. When Jesus tells His disciples to follow Him, Thomas points out that they don't know where to go. And when Jesus rises after the crucifixion, Thomas isn't even *there* – and won't believe it until he can touch the wounds with his own hands. He's the very definition of faithless – and the origin of the term *doubting Thomas*.

Yet in Rabbi Bloom's book, this page began:

These are the secret words which the living Jesus spoke, and the twin, Didymos Judas Thomas, wrote them down.

Twin? Since when did Jesus have a twin?

The rest of the 'gospel' was not a narrative of Jesus's life, like Matthew, Mark, Luke, and John, but a collection of quotes by Jesus, all beginning with the words *Jesus said*. Some were lines similar to those in the Bible. Others were completely unfamiliar and sounded more like logic puzzles than any scripture:

If you bring forth what is within you, what is within you will save you. If you don't bring forth what is within you, what is within you will destroy you.

I read the line over twice and rubbed my eyes. There was something about it that made me feel as if I'd heard it before.

Then I realized where.

Shay had said it to me the first time I'd met with him, when he'd explained why he wanted to donate his heart to Claire Nealon.

I kept reading intently, hearing Shay's voice over and over again:

The dead aren't alive, and the living won't die.

We come from the light.

Split a piece of wood; I am there. Lift up the stone; you will find me there.

The first time I had gone on a roller coaster, I felt like this – like the ground had been pulled out from beneath my feet, like I was going to be sick, like I needed something to grab hold of.

If you asked a dozen people on the street if they'd ever heard of the Gnostic gospels, eleven would look at you as if you were crazy. In fact most people today couldn't even recite the Ten Commandments. Shay Bourne's religious training had been minimal and fragmented; the only thing I'd ever seen him 'read' was the *Sports Illustrated* Swimsuit Issue. He couldn't write; he could barely follow a thought through to the end of one sentence. His formal schooling ended at a GED he'd gotten while at the juvenile detention facility.

How, then, could Shay Bourne have memorized the Gospel of Thomas? Where would he even have stumbled across it in his lifetime?

The only answer I could come up with was that he hadn't.

It could have been coincidence.

I could have been remembering the conversations incorrectly.

Or – maybe – I could have been wrong about him.

The past three weeks, I had pushed past the throngs of people camped out in front of the prison. I had turned off the television when yet another pundit suggested that Shay might be the Messiah. After all, I knew better. I was a priest; I had taken vows; I understood that there was one God. His message had been recorded in the Bible, and above all else, when Shay spoke, he did *not* sound like Jesus in any of the four gospels.

But here was a fifth. A gospel that hadn't made it into the Bible but was equally as ancient. A gospel that espoused the beliefs of at least *some* people during the birth of Christianity. A gospel that Shay Bourne had quoted to me.

What if the Church forefathers had gotten it wrong?

What if the gospels that had been dismissed and debunked were the real ones, and the ones that had been picked for the New Testament were the embellished versions? What if Jesus had actually said the quotations listed in the Gospel of Thomas?

It would mean that the allegations being made about Shay Bourne might not be that far off the mark.

And it would explain why a Messiah might return in the guise of a convicted murderer – to see if this time, we might get it right.

I got out of my chair, folding the book by my side, and started to pray.

Heavenly Father, I said silently, *help me understand.*

The telephone rang, making me jump. I glanced at the clock – who would call after three in the morning?

'Father Michael? This is CO Smythe, from the prison. Sorry to disturb you at this hour, but Shay Bourne had another seizure. We thought you'd want to know.'

'Is he all right?'

'He's in the infirmary,' Smythe said. 'He asked for you.'

At this hour, the vigilant masses outside the prison were tucked into their sleeping bags and tents, underneath the artificial day created by the enormous spotlights that flooded the front of the building. I had to be buzzed in; when I entered the receiving area, CO Smythe was waiting for me. 'What happened?'

'No one knows,' the officer said. 'It was Inmate DuFresne who alerted us again. We couldn't see what happened on the security cameras.'

We entered the infirmary. In a distant, dark corner of the room, Shay was propped up in a bed, a nurse beside him. He held a cup of juice that he sipped through a straw; his other hand was cuffed to the bed's railing. There were wires coming out from beneath his medical johnny. 'How is he?' I asked.

'He'll live,' the nurse said, and then, realizing her mistake, blushed fiercely. 'We hooked him up to monitor his heart. So far, so good.'

I sat down on a chair beside Shay and looked up at Smythe and the nurse. 'Can we have a minute?'

'That's about all you've got,' the nurse said. 'We just gave him something to knock him out.'

They moved to the far side of the room, and I leaned closer to Shay. 'Are you okay?'

'You wouldn't believe it if I told you.'

'Oh, try me,' I said.

He glanced over to make sure no one else was listening. 'I was just watching TV, you know? This documentary on how they make movie theater candy, like Dots and Milk Duds. And I started to get tired, so I went to turn it off. But before I could push the button, all the light in the television, it shot into me like electricity. I mean, I could feel those things inside my blood moving around, what are they called again, corporals?'

'Corpuscles.'

'Yeah, right, those. I hate that word. Did you ever see that *Star Trek* where those aliens are sucking the salt out of everything? I always thought they should be called corpuscles. You say the word, and it sounds like you're eating a lemon . . .'

'Shay. You were talking about the light.'

'Oh, right, yeah. Well, it was like I started boiling inside, and my eyes, they were going to jelly, and I tried to call out but my teeth were wired shut and then I woke up in here, feeling like I'd been sucked dry.' He looked up at me. 'By a *corpuscle*.'

'The nurse said it was a seizure. Do you remember anything else?'

'I remember what I was thinking,' Shay said. 'This was what it would feel like.'

'What?'

'Dying.'

I took a deep breath. 'Remember when you were little, a kid – and you'd fall asleep in the car? And someone would carry you out and put you into bed, so that when you woke up in the morning, you knew automatically you were home again? That's what I think it's like to die.'

'That would be good,' Shay said, his voice deeper, groggy. 'It'll be nice to know what home looks like.'

A phrase I'd read just an hour ago slipped into my mind like a splinter: *The Father's kingdom is spread out upon the earth, and people don't see it.*

Although I knew it wasn't the right time, although I knew I was supposed to be here for Shay, instead of the other way around, I leaned closer, until my words could fall into the shell of his ear. 'Where did you find the Gospel of Thomas?' I whispered.

Shay stared at me blankly. 'Thomas who?' he said, and then his eyes drifted shut.

As I drove away from the prison, I heard Father Walter's voice: *He's conned you.* But when I'd mentioned the Gospel of Thomas, I hadn't seen even the slightest flicker of recognition in Shay's eyes, and he'd been drugged – it would have been awfully hard to keep dissembling.

Was this what it had felt like for the Jews who met Jesus and recognized him as more than just a gifted rabbi? I had no point of comparison. I'd grown up Catholic; I'd become a priest. I could not remember a time that I hadn't believed Jesus was the Messiah.

I knew someone, though, who could.

Rabbi Bloom didn't have a temple, because it had burned down, but he did rent office space close to the school where services were held. I was waiting in front of the locked door when he arrived just before eight a.m.

'Wow,' he said, taking in the vision in front of him – a red-eyed, rumpled priest clutching a motorcycle helmet and the Nag Hammadi texts. 'I would have let you borrow it longer than one night.'

'Why don't Jews believe Jesus was the Messiah?'

He unlocked the door to the office. 'That's going to take at least a cup and a half of coffee,' Bloom said. 'Come on in.'

He started brewing a pot and offered me a seat. His office looked a lot like Father Walter's at St Catherine's – inviting, comfortable. A place you'd want to sit and talk. Unlike Father Walter's, though, Rabbi Bloom's plants were the real thing. Father Walter's were

plastic, bought by the Ladies' Aid, when he kept killing everything from a ficus to an African violet.

'It's a wandering Jew,' the rabbi said when he saw me checking
out the flowerpot. 'Maggie's little idea of a joke.'

'I just got back from the prison. Shay Bourne had another
seizure.'

'Did you tell Maggie?'

'Not yet.' I looked at him. 'You didn't answer my question.'

'I haven't had my coffee.' He got up and poured us each a cup,
putting milk and sugar in mine without asking first. 'Jews don't
think Jesus was the Messiah because he didn't fulfill the criteria
for a Jewish messiah. It's really pretty simple, and it's all laid out
by Maimonides. A Jewish *moshiach* will bring the Jews back to
Israel and set up a government in Jerusalem that's the center of
political power for the world, for both Jews and Gentiles. He'll
rebuild the Temple and reestablish Jewish law as the governing
law of the land. He'll raise the dead – all of the dead – and usher
in a great age of peace, when everyone believes in God. He'll be
a descendant of David, a king and a warrior, a judge, and a great
leader . . . but he'll also be firmly, unequivocally *human*.' Bloom
set the cup down in front of me. 'We believe that in every generation, a person's born with the potential to become the *moshiach*.
But if the messianic age doesn't come and that person dies, then
that person isn't him.'

'Like Jesus.'

'Personally, I've always seen Jesus as a great Jewish patriot. He
was a good Jew, who probably wore a yarmulke and obeyed the
Torah, and never planned to start a new religion. He hated the
Romans and wanted to get them out of Jerusalem. He got charged
with political rebellion, sentenced to execution. Yes, a Jewish
high priest carried it out – Caiaphas – but most Jews back then
hated Caiaphas anyway because he was the henchman for the
Romans.' He looked up at me over the edge of his coffee mug.
'Was Jesus a good guy? Yeah. Great teacher? Sure. Messiah?
Dunno.'

'A lot of the Bible's predictions for the messianic era *were* fulfilled by Jesus—'

'But were they the crucial ones?' Rabbi Bloom asked. 'Let's say you didn't know who I was and I asked you to meet me. I told you I'd be standing outside the Steeplegate Mall at ten o'clock wearing a Hawaiian shirt and that I'd have curly red hair and be listening to Outkast on my iPod. And at ten o'clock, you saw someone standing outside the Steeplegate Mall who had curly red hair and was wearing a Hawaiian shirt and listening to Outkast on an iPod . . . but it was a woman. Would you still think it was me?'

He stood up to refill his coffee. 'Do you know what I heard on NPR on the way over here today? Another bus blew up in Israel. Three more kids from New Hampshire died in Iraq. And the cops just arrested some guy in Manchester who shot his ex-wife in front of their two kids. If Jesus ushered in the messianic era, and the world I hear about on the news is one of peace and redemption . . . well, I'd rather wait for a different *moshiach*.' He glanced back at me. 'Now, if you don't mind me asking *you* a question . . . what's a priest doing at a rabbi's office at eight in the morning asking questions about the Jewish Messiah?'

I got up and began to walk around the little room. 'The book you loaned me – it got me thinking.'

'And that's a bad thing?'

'Shay Bourne has said things, verbatim, that I read last night in the Gospel of Thomas.'

'Bourne? He's read Thomas? I thought Maggie said he—'

'— has no religious training to speak of, and a minimal education.'

'It's not like the Gideons leave the Gospel of Thomas in hotel rooms,' Rabbi Bloom said. 'Where would he have—'

'Exactly.'

He steepled his fingers. 'Huh.'

I placed the book he'd loaned me on his desk. 'What would you do if you began to second-guess everything you believed?'

Rabbi Bloom leaned forward and riffled through his Rolodex. 'I would ask more questions,' he said. He scribbled down something on a Post-it and handed it to me.

Ian Fletcher, I read. *603-555-1367.*

Lucius

The night Shay had his second seizure, I was awake, gathering ink that I planned to use to give myself another tattoo. If I do say so myself, I'm rather proud of my homemade tattoos. I had five – my rationale being that my body, up until three weeks ago, wasn't worth much more than being a canvas for my art; plus the threat of getting AIDS from a dirty needle was obviously a moot point. On my left ankle was a clock, with the hands marking the moment of Adam's death. On my left shoulder was an angel, and below it an African tribal design. On my right leg was a bull, because I was a Taurus; and swimming beside it was a fish, for Adam, who was a Pisces. I had grand plans for this sixth one, which I planned to put right on my chest: the word BELIEVE, in Gothic letters. I'd practiced the art in reverse multiple times in pencil and pen, until I felt sure that I could replicate it with my tattoo gun as I worked in the mirror.

My first gun had been confiscated by the COs, like Crash's hype kit. It had taken me six months to amass the parts for the new one. Making ink was hard to do, and harder to get away with – which was why I had chosen to work on this during the deadest hours of the night. I had lit a plastic spoon on fire, keeping the flame small so I could catch the smoke in a plastic bag. It stank horribly, and just as I was getting certain the COs would literally get wind of it and shut down my operation, Shay Bourne collapsed next door.

This time, his seizure had been different. He'd screamed – so loud that he woke up the whole pod, so loud that the finest dust of plaster drifted down from the ceilings of our cells. To be honest, Shay was such a mess when he was wheeled off I-tier that none of us were sure whether or not he'd be returning – which is why I was stunned to see him being led back to his cell the very next day.

'Po-lice,' Joey Kunz yelled, just in time for me to hide the pieces of my tattoo gun underneath the mattress. The officers locked Shay into his cell, and as soon as the door to I-tier shut behind them, I asked Shay how he was feeling.

'My head hurts,' he said. 'I have to go to sleep.'

With Crash still off the tier after the hype kit transgression, things were quieter. Calloway slept most days and stayed up nights with his bird; Texas and Pogie played virtual poker; Joey was listening to his soaps. I waited an extra few minutes to make sure the officers were otherwise occupied out in the control booth and then I reached underneath my mattress again.

I had unraveled a guitar string to its central core, a makeshift needle. This was inserted into a pen whose ink cartridge had been removed – and a small piece of its tip sawed off and attached to the other end of the needle, which was attached to the motor shaft of a cassette player. The pen was taped to a toothbrush bent into an L shape, which let you hold the contraption more easily. You could adjust the needle length by sliding the pen casing back and forth; all that was left was plugging in the AC adapter of the cassette player, and I had a functional tattoo gun again.

The soot I'd captured the previous night had been mixed with a few drops of shampoo to liquefy it. I stood in front of the stainless steel panel that served as a mirror, and scrutinized my chest. Then, gritting my teeth against the pain, I turned on the gun. The needle moved back and forth in an elliptical orbit, piercing me hundreds of times per minute.

There it was, the letter B.

'Lucius?' Shay's voice drifted into my house.

'I'm sort of busy, Shay.'

'What's that noise?'

'None of your business.' I lifted it to my skin again, felt the needle working against me, a thousand arrows striking.

'Lucius? I can still hear that noise.'

I sighed. 'It's a tattoo gun, Shay, all right? I'm giving myself a tattoo.'

There was a hesitation. 'Will you give me one?'

I had done this for multiple inmates when I was housed on different tiers – ones that had a bit more freedom than I-tier, which offered twenty-three rollicking hours of lockdown. 'I can't. I can't reach you.'

'That's okay,' Shay said. 'I can reach *you*.'

'Yeah, whatever,' I said. I squinted back into the mirror and set the tattoo gun against my skin. Holding my breath, I carefully formed the curves and flourishes around the letters *E* and *L*.

I thought I heard Shay whimpering when I started on the letter *I*, and surely he cried out when I tattooed the *V*. My gun must not have been helping his headache any. Shrugging off his moans, I stepped closer to the mirror and surveyed my handi-work.

God, it was gorgeous. The letters moved with every breath I took; even the angry red swelling of my skin couldn't take away from the clean lines of the letters.

'B-believe,' Shay stammered.

I turned around, as if I could see him through the wall between our cells. 'What did you say?'

'It's what *you* said,' Shay corrected. 'I read it right, didn't I?'

I had not told anyone of my plans for my sixth tattoo. I hadn't shared the prototype artwork. I knew for a fact that Shay, from where he stood, could not have seen into my cell as I worked.

Fumbling behind the brick that served as my safe, I took out the shank that I used as a portable mirror. I stepped up to the front of my cell and angled it so that I could see Shay's beaming face in the reflection. 'How did you know what I was writing?'

Shay smiled wider, and then raised his fist. He unfolded his fingers, one at a time.

His palm was red and inflamed, and printed across it, in Gothic script, was the same exact tattoo I'd just given myself.

Michael

Shay paced his cell in figure eights. 'Did you see him?' he asked, wild-eyed.

I sank down on the stool I'd dragged in from the control booth. I was sluggish today – not only was my head buzzing with questions about what I'd read, but I was also – for the first time in a year – not officiating at this evening's midnight Mass. 'See who?' I replied, distracted.

'Sully. The new guy. Next door.'

I glanced into the other cell. Lucius DuFresne was still on Shay's left; on his right, the formerly empty cell now had someone occupying it. Sully, however, wasn't there. He was in the rec yard, repeatedly running full tilt across the little square yard and leaping up against the far wall, hands splayed, as if hitting it hard enough meant he'd go right through the metal.

'They're going to kill me,' Shay said.

'Maggie's working on writing a motion at this very—'

'Not the state,' Shay said. 'One of *them*.'

I did not know anything about prison politics, but there was a fine line between Shay's paranoia and what might pass for the truth. Shay was receiving more attention than any other inmate at the prison, as a result of his lawsuit and the media frenzy. There was every chance he might be targeted by the general prison population.

Behind me, CO Smythe passed in his flak jacket, carrying a broom and some cleaning supplies. Once a week, the inmates were required to clean their own cells. It was one-at-a-time,

supervised cleaning: after an inmate came in from rec, the supplies
would be waiting for him in his cell, and a CO would stand
guard at the doorway until the work was finished – close by,
because even Windex could become a weapon in here. I watched
the empty cell door open, so that Smythe could leave the spray
bottles and the toweling and the broom; then he walked to the
far end of the tier to get the new inmate from the rec yard. 'I'll
talk to the warden. I'll make sure you're protected,' I told Shay,
which seemed to mollify him. 'So,' I said, changing the subject,
'what do you like to read?'

'What, you're Oprah now? We're having a book club?'

'No.'

'Good, because I'm not reading the Bible.'

'I know that,' I said, seizing this inroad. 'Why not?'

'It's lies.' Shay waved a hand, a dismissal.

'What do you read that *isn't* a lie?'

'I don't,' he replied. 'The words get all knotted up. I have to
stare at a page for a year before I can make sense of it.'

'"*There's light inside a person of light,*'" I quoted, "'*and it shines on
the whole world.*'"

Shay hesitated. 'Can you see it, too?' He held his hands up in
front of his face, scrutinizing his fingertips. 'The light from the television – the stuff that went into me – it's still there. It glows, at night.'

I sighed. 'It's from the Gospel of Thomas.'

'No, I'm pretty sure it came from the television . . .'

'The *words*, Shay. The ones I just said. They came from a gospel
I was reading last night. And so does a lot of stuff you've been
saying to me.'

His eyes met mine. 'What do you know,' he said softly, and I
couldn't tell if it was a statement or a question.

'I *don't* know,' I admitted. 'That's why I'm here.'

'That's why we're *all* here,' Shay said.

*If you bring forth what is within you, what is within you will save
you.* It was one of Jesus's sayings in the Gospel of Thomas; it was
one of the first things Shay Bourne had ever told me, when he

was explaining why he needed to donate his heart. Could it really be this simple? Could salvation be not a passive acceptance, like I'd been led to believe, but an active pursuit?

Maybe it was saying the rosary, for me, and receiving Holy Communion, and serving God. Maybe for Maggie's father, it was meeting with a bunch of die-hard congregants who wouldn't let the lack of a physical temple dissuade them from prayer. Maybe for Maggie, it was mending whatever kept her focused on her faults instead of her strengths.

Maybe for Shay, maybe it was offering his heart – literally and figuratively – to the mother who'd lost hers years ago because of him.

Then again, Shay Bourne was a killer; his sentences curled like a puppy chasing its tail; he thought he had something phosphorescent coursing through his veins because a television had zapped him in the middle of the night. He did not sound messianic – just delusional.

Shay looked at me. 'You should go,' he said, but then his attention was distracted by the sound of the rec yard door being opened. Officer Smythe led the new inmate back onto I-tier.

He was an enormous tower of muscle with a swastika tattooed on his scalp. His hair, sprouting out from a buzz cut, grew over it like moss.

The inmate's cell door was closed, and his handcuffs removed. 'You know the drill, Sully,' the officer said. He stood in the doorway as Sully slowly picked up the spray bottle and washed down his sink. I heard the squeak of paper toweling on metal.

'Hey, Father – you watch the game last night?' CO Smythe said, and then he rolled his eyes. 'Sully, what are you doing? You don't need to sweep the—'

Suddenly the broom in Sully's hands was no longer a broom but a broken spear that he jutted into the officer's throat. Smythe grabbed his neck, gurgling. His eyes rolled back in his head; he stumbled toward Shay's cell. As he fell beside me, I clasped my hands over the wound and screamed for help.

The tier came to life. The inmates were all clamoring to see what had happened; CO Whitaker was suddenly there and hauling me to my feet, taking my place as another officer started CPR. Four more officers ran past me with pepper spray and shot it into Sully's face. He was dragged out of the tier shrieking as the closest physician arrived – a psychiatrist I'd seen around the prison. But by now, Smythe had stopped moving.

No one seemed to notice that I was there; there was far too much happening, too much at stake. The psychiatrist tried to find a pulse in Smythe's neck, but his hand came away slick with blood. He lifted the CO's wrist and, after a moment, shook his head. 'He's gone.'

The tier had gone absolutely silent; the inmates were all staring in shock at the body in front of them. Blood had stopped flowing from Smythe's neck; he was perfectly still. To my right, I could see an argument going on in the control booth – the EMTs who'd arrived too late and were trying to gain admission to the tier. They were buzzed in, still shrugging into their flak jackets, and knelt beside Smythe's body, repeating the same ineffective tests that the psychiatrist had.

Behind me, I heard weeping.

I turned around to find Shay crouched on the floor of his cell. His face was streaked with tears and blood; his hand slipped beneath his cell door so that his fingers brushed Smythe's.

'You here for last rites?' one of the medics asked, and for the first time, everyone seemed to realize I was still present.

'I, uh—'

'What's he doing here?' CO Whitaker barked.

'Who the hell is he?' another officer said. 'I don't even work this tier.'

'I can go,' I said. 'I'll . . . just go.' I glanced once more at Shay, who was curled into a ball, whispering. If I hadn't known better, I would have thought he was praying.

As the two EMTs got ready to move the body onto a stretcher, I prayed over Smythe. 'In the Name of God the Father Almighty who created you . . . in the Name of Jesus Christ who redeemed you; in the Name of the Holy Spirit who sanctifies you. May your rest be this day in peace, and your dwelling place in the Paradise of God. Amen.'

I made the sign of the cross and started to get to my feet.

'On three,' the first EMT said.

The second one nodded, his hands on the slain officer's ankles. 'One, two . . . holy *shit*,' he cried as the dead man began to struggle against him.

'One of the proofs of the immortality
of the soul is that myriads have believed it.
They also believed the world was flat.'

— *MARK TWAIN, NOTEBOOK*

June

Claire would be cut in half, her sternum buzzed open with a saw and held open with a metal spreader so that she could be made, literally, heartless – and this was not what terrified me the most.

No, what scared me to death was the idea of cellular memory.

Dr Wu had said that there was no scientific evidence that the personality traits of heart donors transferred to their recipients. But science could only go so far, I figured. I'd read the books and done the research, and I didn't see why it was such a stretch to think that living tissue might have the ability to remember. After all, how many of us had tried to forget something traumatic . . . only to find it printed on the back of our eyelids, tattooed on our tongues?

There were dozens of cases. The baby with a clubfoot who drowned and gave his heart to another infant, who began to drag her left leg. The rapper who started playing classical music, and then learned his donor had died clutching a violin case. The cattle rancher who received the heart of a sixteen-year-old vegetarian, and could not eat meat again without getting violently ill.

Then there was the twenty-year-old organ donor who wrote music in his spare time. A year after he died, his parents found a CD of a love song he'd recorded, about losing his heart to a girl named Andi. His recipient, a twenty-year-old girl, was named Andrea. When the boy's parents played the song for her, she could complete the chorus, without ever having heard it.

Most of these stories were benign – a strange coincidence, an intriguing twist. Except for one: a little boy received the heart of another boy who'd been murdered. He began to have nightmares about the man who killed his donor – with details about the clothing the man wore, how he'd abducted the boy, where the murder weapon had been stashed. Using this evidence, the police caught the killer.

If Claire received Shay Bourne's heart, it would be bad enough if she were to harbor thoughts of murder. But what would absolutely wreck me was if, with that heart in her, she had to *feel* her own father and sister being killed.

In that case, better to have no heart at all.

Maggie

Today, I decided, I was going to do everything right. It was Sunday, and I didn't have to go to work. Instead, I got up and unearthed my *One Minute Workout* video (which was not nearly as slacker as it sounds – you could add minutes to your own liking, and no one was here to notice if I chose the four-minute option over the more grueling eight-minute one). I picked Focus on Abs, instead of the easier Upper Arm. I sorted my recyclables and flossed and shaved my legs in the shower. Downstairs, I cleaned Oliver's cage and let him have the run of the living room while I made myself scrambled egg whites for breakfast.

With *wheat germ*.

Well. I lasted forty-seven minutes, anyway, before I had to break out the Oreos that I hid in the box with my skinny jeans, a last-ditch attempt at utter guilt before I ripped open the package and indulged.

I gave Oliver an Oreo, too, and was starting my third cookie when the doorbell rang.

As soon as I saw the bright pink T-shirt of the man standing on the porch, with the words JOYOUS FOR JESUS printed boldly across it, I knew this was my punishment for falling off the wagon into the snack foods.

'If you're not gone in the next ten seconds, I'm calling 911,' I said.

He grinned at me, a big platinum orthodontically enhanced grin. 'I'm not a stranger,' he said. 'I'm a friend you haven't met yet.'

I rolled my eyes. 'Why don't we just cut to the chase – you give me the pamphlets, I politely refuse to talk to you, and then I close the door and throw them in the trash.'

He held out his hand. 'I'm Tom.'

'You're *leaving*,' I corrected.

'I used to be bitter, too. I'd go to work in the mornings and come home to an empty house and eat half a can of soup and wonder why I had even been put on this earth. I thought I had no one, but myself—'

'And then you offered Jesus the rest of your soup,' I finished. 'Look, I'm an atheist.'

'It's not too late to find your faith.'

'What you really mean is that it's not too late for me to find *your* faith,' I answered, scooping up Oliver as he made a mad dash for the open door. 'You know what I believe? That religion served its historical purpose – it was a set of laws to live by, before we had a justice system. But even when it starts out with the best of intentions, things get screwed up, don't they? A group bands together because they believe the same things, and then somehow that gets perverted so that anyone who doesn't believe those things is wrong. Honestly, even if there was a religion founded on the principle of doing good for other people, or helping them with their personal rights, like I do every day, I wouldn't join . . . because it would still be a *religion*.'

I had rendered Tom speechless. This was probably the most heated debate he'd had in months; mostly, he'd have doors closed in his face. Inside my house, the phone began to ring.

Tom pushed a pamphlet into my hand and beat a hasty retreat off my porch. As I closed the door behind him I glanced down at the cover.

GOD + YOU = ∞

'If there's any math to religion,' I muttered, 'it's division.' I slipped the pamphlet onto the liner of newspaper beneath Oliver's cage as I hurried to the phone, which was on the verge of rolling over to the answering machine. 'Hello?'

The voice was unfamiliar, halting. 'Is Maggie Bloom there?'

'Speaking.' I geared up for a zinger to put a telemarketer in her place for disturbing me on a Sunday morning.

As it turned out, she wasn't a telemarketer. She was a nurse at Concord Hospital, and she was calling because I had been listed as Shay Bourne's emergency contact, and an emergency had occurred.

Lucius

You would not have believed it possible, but when CO Smythe came back to life, things actually got worse.

The remaining officers had to give statements to the warden about the stabbing. We were kept in lockdown, and the next day a team of officers who did not normally work on I-tier were brought in on duty. They started our one-hour rotations on the exercise yard and the shower, and Pogie was the first to go.

I hadn't showered since the stabbing, although the COs had given both Shay and me a fresh set of scrubs. We had gotten Smythe's blood on us, and a quick wash in our cell basins didn't go very far to making me feel clean. While we were waiting for our turns in the shower, Alma showed up to give us both blood tests. They tested anyone who came in contact with an inmate's blood, and since that included CO Smythe, *his* blood apparently was only one step removed from questionable. Shay was moved in handcuffs, ankle cuffs, and a belly chain to a holding room outside the tier, where Alma was waiting.

In the middle of all this, Pogie slipped in the shower. He lay there, moaning about his back. Two more COs dragged in the backboard and handcuffed Pogie to it, then carried him to a gurney so he could be transported all the way to Medical. But because they were not used to I-tier, and because COs are supposed to follow us, not lead, they did not realize that Shay was already being brought back to the tier at the same time Pogie was going out.

Tragedies happen in a split second in prison; that's all it took for Pogie to use the handcuff key he'd hidden to free himself, jump off the backboard, grab it, and slam it into Shay's skull, so that he flew face-first into the brick wall.

'*Weiss macht!*' Pogie yelled – *White pride!* – which was how I realized Crash – from where he was still being kept in solitary – had used his connections to order a hit on Shay in retaliation for ratting him out and giving his hype kit to the COs. Sully's attack on CO Smythe had just been collateral damage, meant to shake up the staffing on our tier so that part two of the plan could be carried out. And Pogie – a probate – had jumped at the chance to earn his bones by carrying out a murder sanctioned by the Aryan Brotherhood.

Six hours after this fiasco, Alma returned to finish drawing my blood. I was taken to the holding cell and found her still shaken by what had happened, although she would not tell me anything – except that Shay had been taken to the hospital.

When I saw something silver winking at me, I waited until Alma drew the needle from my arm. Then I put my head down between my knees.

'You all right, sugar?' Alma asked.

'Just feeling a little dizzy.' I let my fingers trail along the floor.

If magicians are the best at sleight of hand, then inmates have to be a close second. As soon as I was back in my cell, I pulled my booty out of the seam in my scrubs where I'd hidden it. Pogie's handcuff key was tiny, shiny, formed from the fastener of a manila envelope.

I crawled beneath my bunk and wriggled the loose brick that concealed my prized possessions. In a small cardboard box were my bottles of paint and my Q-tip brushes. There were packets of candy, too, that I planned to extract pigment from in the future – a half-empty pack of M&M's, a roll of LifeSavers, a few loose Starbursts. I unwrapped one of the Starbursts, the orange one that tasted like St Joseph children's aspirin, and kneaded the square with my thumbs until the taffy became pliable. I pressed the hand-cuff key into the center, then reshaped a careful square and folded it into its original wrapping.

I did not like the thought of profiting in some way from an incident that had hurt Shay so badly, but I was also a realist. When Shay ran out of his nine lives and I was left alone, I would need all the help I could get.

Maggie

Even if I hadn't been listed as Shay Bourne's emergency contact, I would have found him quickly enough at the hospital: he was the only patient with armed guards standing outside his door. I glanced at the officers, then turned my attention to the nurse at the desk. 'Is he all right? What happened?'

Father Michael had called me after the attack on CO Smythe and told me Shay hadn't been hurt. Somewhere between now and then, however, something must have gone drastically wrong. I had tried calling the priest now, but he wasn't answering his cell – I assumed he was on his way, that he'd been called, too.

If Shay hadn't been treated at the prison hospital, whatever had happened must've been pretty awful. Inmates weren't moved off-site unless absolutely necessary, because of cost and security. With the hoopla Shay had generated outside the prison walls, it must have been a matter of life or death.

Then again, maybe *everything* was when it came to Shay. Here I was literally shaking over the news that he'd been seriously injured, when I had spent yesterday filing motions that would streamline his execution.

The nurse looked up at me. 'He's just come back from surgery.'

'*Surgery?*'

'Yes,' said a clipped British voice behind me. 'And no, it wasn't an appendectomy.'

When I turned around, Dr Gallagher was standing there.

'Are you the *only* doctor who works here?'

'It certainly feels that way sometimes. I'm happy to answer your questions. Mr Bourne is my patient.'

'He's my client.'

Dr Gallagher glanced at the nurse and at the armed officers. 'Why don't we go somewhere to talk?'

I followed him down the hall to a small family waiting lounge that was empty. When the doctor gestured for me to take a seat, my heart sank. Doctors only made you sit down when they delivered bad news.

'Mr Bourne is going to be fine,' Dr Gallagher said. 'At least in terms of this injury.'

'*What* injury?'

'I'm sorry, I thought you knew – apparently, it was an inmate fight. Mr Bourne sustained a severe blow to the maxillary sinus.'

I waited for him to translate.

'His maxilla's broken,' Dr Gallagher said, and he leaned forward, touching my face. His fingers brushed over the bone below my eye socket, tracing toward my mouth. 'Here,' he said, and I absolutely, positively stopped breathing. 'There was a bit of a trauma during the operation. As soon as we saw the injuries we knew that the anesthesia would be intravenous, instead of inhalational. Needless to say, when Mr Bourne heard the anesthesiologist say that she'd begun Sodium Pentothal drip, he grew quite agitated.' The doctor looked up at me. 'He asked if this was a dry run for the real thing.'

I tried to imagine how it would feel to be Shay – hurt, aching, and confused – whisked away to an unfamiliar place for what seemed to be a prelude to his own execution. 'I want to see him.'

'If you can tell him, Ms Bloom, that if I'd realized who he was – what his circumstances are, I mean – well, I would never have allowed the anesthesiologist to use that drug, much less an IV tube. I'm deeply sorry for putting him through that.'

I nodded and stood up.

'One more thing,' Dr Gallagher said. 'I really admire you. For doing this sort of thing.'

I was halfway to Shay's room when I realized that Dr Gallagher had remembered my name.

It took several cell phone calls to the prison before I was allowed in to see Shay, and even then, the warden insisted that the officer inside the room would have to stay. I walked inside, acknowledged the CO, and sat down on the edge of Shay's bed. His eyes were blackened, his face bandaged. He was asleep, and it made him look younger.

Part of what I did for a living meant championing the causes of my clients. I was the strong arm, fighting on their behalf, the bullhorn broadcasting their voices. I could feel the angry discomfort of the Abenaki boy whose school team was called the Redskins; I could identify with the passion of the teacher who'd been fired for being Wiccan. Shay, though, had sent me reeling. Although this was arguably the most important case I would ever bring to court, and although – as my father pointed out – I hadn't been this motivated in my career in ages, there was an inherent paradox. The more I got to know him, the better chance I had of winning his organ donation case. But the more I got to know him, the harder it would be for me to see him executed.

I dragged my cell phone out of my purse. The officer's eyes flicked toward me. 'You're not supposed to use that in here—'

'Oh, piss off,' I snapped, and for the hundredth time I dialed Father Michael, and reached his voice mail. 'I don't know where you are,' I said, 'but call me back *immediately*.'

I had left the emotional component of Shay Bourne's welfare to Father Michael, figuring (a) my talents were better put to use in a courtroom, and (b) my interpersonal relationship skills had grown so rusty I needed WD-40 before employing them. But now, Father Michael was MIA, Shay was hospitalized, and I was here, for better or for worse.

I stared at Shay's hands. They were cuffed at the wrist to the metal bars of the hospital gurney. The nails were clean and clipped, the tendons ropy. It was hard to imagine the fingers curled around a pistol, pulling a trigger twice. And yet, twelve jurors had been able to picture it.

Very slowly, I reached across the knobby cotton blanket. I threaded my fingers with Shay's, surprised at how warm his skin was. But when I was about to pull away, his grip tightened. His eyes slitted open, another shade of blue amid the bruising. 'Gracie,' he said, in a voice that sounded like cotton caught on thorns. 'You came.'

I did not know who he thought I was. 'Of *course* I came,' I said, squeezing his hand. I smiled at Shay Bourne and pretended that I was the person he needed me to be.

Michael

Dr Vijay Choudhary's office was filled with statues of Ganesha, the Hindu deity with a potbellied human body and an elephant's head. I had to move one in order to sit down, in fact. 'Mr Smythe was extremely lucky,' the doctor said. 'A quarter inch to the left, and he wouldn't have survived.'

'About that . . .' I took a deep breath. 'A doctor at the prison pronounced him dead.'

'Between you and me, Father, I wouldn't trust a psychiatrist to find his own car in a parking lot, much less a hypotensive victim's pulse. Reports of Mr Smythe's death were, as they say, greatly exaggerated.'

'There was a lot of blood—'

'Many structures in the neck can bleed a great deal. To a layman, a pool of blood may look like a huge quantity, even when it's not.' He shrugged. 'What I imagine happened was a vasovagal reaction. Mr Smythe saw blood and passed out. The body compensates for shock due to blood loss. Blood pressure lowers, and vasoconstriction occurs, and both tend to stop the bleeding. They also lead to a loss of palpable pulses in the extremities – which is why the psychiatrist couldn't find one in his wrist.'

'So,' I said, pinkening. 'You don't think it's possible that Mr Smythe was . . . well . . . resurrected?'

'No,' he chuckled. 'Now, in medical school, I saw patients who'd frozen to death, in the vernacular, come back to life when they were warmed up. I saw a heart stop beating, and then start up by itself again. But in neither of those cases – or in Mr Smythe's

– did I consider the patient clinically dead before his or her recovery.'

My phone began to vibrate, as it had every ten minutes for the past two hours. I'd turned the ringer off when I came into the hospital, as per their policy. 'Nothing miraculous, then,' I said.

'Perhaps not by your standards . . . but I think that Mr Smythe's family might disagree.'

I thanked him, set the statue of Ganesha back on my chair, and left Dr Choudhary's office. As soon as I exited the hospital building, I turned on my cell phone to see fifty-two messages.

Call me right back, Maggie said on her message. *Something's happened to Shay*. Beep.

Where are you?? Beep.

Okay, I know you probably don't have your phone on but you have to call me back immediately. Beep.

Where the fuck are you? Beep.

I hung up and dialed her cell phone. 'Maggie Bloom,' she whispered, answering.

'What happened to Shay?'

'He's in the hospital.'

'What?! *Which* hospital?'

'Concord. Where are you?'

'Standing outside the ER.'

'Then for God's sake, get up here. He's in room 514.'

I ran up the stairs, pushing past doctors and nurses and lab technicians and secretaries, as if my speed now could make up for the fact that I had not been available for Shay when he needed me. The armed officers at the door took one look at my collar – a free pass, especially on a Sunday afternoon – and let me inside. Maggie was curled up on the bed, her shoes off, her feet tucked underneath her. She was holding Shay's hand, although I would have been hard-pressed to recognize the patient as the man I'd talked to just yesterday. His skin was the color of fine ash; his hair had been shaved in one patch to accommodate stitches to close a gash. His nose – broken, from the looks of it – was covered with gauze, and the nostrils were plugged with cotton.

'Dear God,' I breathed.

'From what I can understand, he came out on the short end of a prison hit,' Maggie said.

'That's not possible. I was *there* during the prison hit—'

'Apparently, you left before Act Two.'

I glanced at the officer who stood like a sentry in the corner of the hospital room. The man looked at me and nodded in confirmation.

'I already called Warden Coyne at home to give him hell,' Maggie said. 'He's meeting me at the prison in a half hour to talk about additional security measures that can be put in place to protect Shay until his execution – when what he really means is "What can I do to keep you from suing?" She turned to me. 'Can you sit here with Shay?'

It was a Sunday, and I was utterly, absolutely lost. I was on an unofficial leave of absence from St Catherine's, and although I had always known I'd feel adrift without God, I had underestimated how aimless I would feel without my church. Usually at this time, I would be hanging my robes after celebrating Mass. I would go with Father Walter to have lunch with a parishioner. Then we'd head back to his place and watch the preseason Sox game on TV, have a couple of beers. What religion did for me went beyond belief – it made me part of a community.

'I can stay,' I answered.

'Then I'm out of here,' Maggie said. 'He hasn't woken up, not really, anyway. And the nurse said he'll probably have to pee when he does, and that we should use this torture device.' She pointed at a plastic jug with a long neck. 'I don't know about you, but I'm not getting paid enough for that.' She paused in the doorway. 'I'll call you later. Turn on your damn phone.'

When she left, I pulled a chair closer to Shay's bed. I read the plastic placard about how to raise and lower the mattress, and the list of which television channels were available. I said an entire rosary, and still Shay didn't stir.

At the edge of the bed, Shay's medical chart hung on a metal clip. I skimmed through the language that I didn't understand – the injury, the medications, his vital statistics. Then I glanced at the patient name at the top of the page:

I. M. Bourne

Isaiah Matthew Bourne. We had been told this at his trial, but I had forgotten that Shay was not his Christian name. 'I. M. Bourne,' I said aloud. 'Sounds like a guy Trump would hire.'

I am born.

Was this a hint, another puzzle piece of evidence?

There were two ways of looking at any situation. What one person sees as a prisoner's babble, another might recognize as words from a long-lost gospel. What one person sees as a medically viable stroke of luck, another might see as a resurrection. I thought of Lucius being healed, of the water into wine, of the followers who had so easily believed in Shay. I thought of a thirty-three-year-old man, a carpenter, facing execution. I thought of Rabbi Bloom's idea – that every generation had a person in it capable of being the Messiah.

There is a point when you stand at the edge of the cliff of hard evidence, look across to what lies on the other side, and step forward. Otherwise, you wind up going nowhere. I stared at Shay, and maybe for the first time, I didn't see who he was. I saw who he might be.

As if he could feel my gaze, he began to toss and turn. Only one of his eyes could slit open; the other was swollen shut. 'Father,' he rasped in a voice still cushioned with medication. 'Where am I?'

'You were hurt. You're going to be all right, Shay.'

In the corner of the room, the officer was staring at us. 'Do you think we could have a minute alone? I'd like to pray in private with him.'

The officer hesitated – as well he should have: what clergyman isn't accustomed to praying in front of others? Then he shrugged. 'Guess a priest wouldn't do anything funny,' he said. 'Your boss is tougher than mine.'

People anthropomorphized God all the time – as a boss, as a lifesaver, as a justice, as a father. No one ever pictured him as a convicted murderer. But if you put aside the physical trappings of the body – something that all the apostles had had to do after Jesus was resurrected – then maybe anything was possible.

As the officer backed out of the room, Shay winced. 'My face . . .' He tried to lift up his hand to touch the bandages, but found that he was handcuffed to the bed. Struggling, he began to pull harder.

'Shay,' I said firmly, 'don't.'

'It hurts. I want drugs . . .'

'You're already on drugs,' I told him. 'We only have a few minutes till the officer comes back in, so we have to talk while we can.'

'I don't want to talk.'

Ignoring him, I leaned closer. 'Tell me,' I whispered. 'Tell me who you are.'

A wary hope lit Shay's eyes; he'd probably never expected to be recognized as the Lord. He went very still, never taking his eyes off mine. 'Tell me who you are.'

In the Catholic Church, there were lies of commission and lies of omission. The first referred to telling an outright falsehood, the second to withholding the truth. Both were sins.

I had lied to Shay since before the moment we met. He'd counted on me to help him donate his heart, but he'd never realized how black mine was. How could I expect Him to reveal Himself when I hadn't done the same?

'You're right,' I said quietly. 'There's something I haven't told you . . . about who I used to be, before I was a priest.'

'Let me guess . . . an altar boy.'

'I was a college student, majoring in math. I didn't even go to church until after I served on the jury.'

'What jury?'

I hesitated. 'The one that sentenced you to death, Shay.'

He stared at me for a long minute, and then he turned away. 'Get out.'

'Shay—'

'Get the fuck away from me!' He flailed against his handcuffs, yanking at the bonds so that his skin rubbed raw. The sound he made was wordless, primordial, the noise that had surely filled the world before there was order and light.

A nurse came running in, along with the two officers who were standing outside. 'What happened?' the nurse cried, as Shay continued to thrash, his head whipping from side to side on the pillow. The gauze in his nose bloomed with fresh blood.

The nurse pushed a call button on the panel behind Shay's head, and suddenly the room was filled with people. A doctor yelled at the officers to unlock his damn hands, but as soon as they did, Shay began swatting at everything he could reach. An aide plunged a hypodermic into his arm. 'Get him out of here,' someone said, and an orderly pulled me out of the room; the last thing I saw was Shay going boneless, sliding away from the people who were desperately trying to save him.

June

Claire was standing in front of a full-length mirror, naked. Her chest was crisscrossed with black ribbon, like the lacing on a football. As I watched, she untied the bow, unraveled the ribbons, and peeled back both halves of her chest. She unhooked a tiny brass hinge on her rib cage and it sprang open.

Inside, the heart was beating sure and strong, a clear sign that it wasn't hers. Claire lifted a serving spoon and began to carve at the organ, trying to sever it from the veins and arteries. Her cheeks went pale; her eyes were the color of agony – but she managed to pull it free: a bloody, misshapen mass that she placed in my outstretched hand. 'Take it back,' she said.

I woke up from the nightmare, sweat-soaked, pulse racing. After speaking with Dr Wu about organ compatibility, I'd realized he was right – what was at issue here was not where this heart came from, but whether it came at all.

But I still hadn't told Claire a donor heart had become available. We had yet to go through the legal proceedings, anyway – and although I told myself I didn't want to get her hopes up until the judge ruled, another part of me realized that I just didn't want to have to tell her the truth.

After all, it was *her* chest that would be hosting this man's heart.

Even a long shower couldn't get the nightmare of Claire out of my mind, and I realized that we had to have the conversation I had been so studiously avoiding. I dressed and hurried downstairs to find her eating a bowl of cereal on the couch and watching television. 'The dog needs to go out,' she said absently.

'Claire,' I said, 'I have to talk to you.'

'Let me just see the end of this show.'

I glanced at the screen – it was *Full House*, and Claire had watched this episode so often that even *I* could have told you Jesse came home from Japan realizing being a rock star was not what it was cracked up to be.

'You've seen it before,' I said, turning off the television.

Her eyes flashed, and she used the remote to turn the show back on.

Maybe it was a lack of sleep; maybe it was just the weight of the imminent future on my shoulders – for whatever reason, I snapped. I whirled around and yanked the cable feed out of the wall.

'What is *wrong* with you?' Claire cried. 'Why are you being such a bitch!'

Both of us fell silent, stunned by Claire's language. She'd never called me that before; she'd never really even argued with me: *Take it back*, I thought, and I remembered that image of Claire, holding out her heart.

'Claire,' I said, backpedaling. 'I'm sorry. I didn't mean to—'

I broke off as Claire's eyes rolled back in her head.

I'd seen this before – too often. The AICD in her chest was firing: when Claire's heart skipped a beat, or several, it automatically defibrillated her. I caught her as she collapsed, settling her on the couch, waiting for her heart to restart, for Claire to come to.

Except this time, she didn't.

On the ambulance ride to the hospital, I counted all the reasons I hated myself: For picking a fight with Claire. For accepting Shay Bourne's offer to donate his heart, without asking her first. For turning off *Full House* before the happy ending.

Just stay with me, I begged silently, *and you can watch TV twenty-four hours a day. I will watch it with you. Don't give up, we've come so close.*

Although the EMTs had gotten Claire's heart beating again by the time we reached the hospital, Dr Wu had admitted her, with the unspoken agreement that this was her new home until a new heart arrived – or hers gave out. I watched him check Claire, who was fast asleep in the oceanic blue light of the darkened room. 'June,' he said, 'let's talk outside.'

He closed the door behind us. 'There's no good news here.'

I nodded, biting my lip.

'Obviously, the AICD isn't functioning correctly. But in addition, the tests we've done show her urine output decreasing and her creatinine levels rising. We're talking about renal failure, June. It's not just her heart that's giving out – her whole body is shutting down.'

I looked away, but I couldn't stop a tear from rolling down my cheek.

'I don't know how long it's going to take to get a court to agree to that heart donation,' the doctor said, 'but Claire can't wait around for the docket to clear.'

'I'll call the lawyer,' I said softly. 'Is there anything else I can do?'

Dr Wu touched my arm. 'You should think about saying goodbye.'

I held myself together long enough for Dr Wu to disappear into an elevator. Then, I rushed down the hallway and blindly plunged into a doorway that stood ajar. I fell to my knees and let the grief bleed out of me – one great, low keening note.

Suddenly I felt a hand on my shoulder. I blinked through my tears to find the priest who was Shay Bourne's ally staring at me. 'June? Is everything all right?'

'No,' I said. 'No, everything is most definitely *not* all right.'

I could see then what I hadn't noticed when I first came into the room – the gold cross on the long dais in the front of the room, one flag with the star of David, another with a Muslim crescent moon: this was the hospital chapel, a place to ask for what you wanted the most.

Was it wrong to wish for someone's death so that Claire could have his heart sooner?

'Is it your daughter?' the priest asked.

I nodded, but I couldn't look him in the eye.

'Would it be all right – I mean, would you mind if I prayed for her?'

Although I did not want his assistance – had not *asked* for his assistance – this one time, I was willing to put aside how I felt about God, because Claire could use all the help she could get. Almost imperceptibly, I nodded.

Beside me, Father Michael's voice began to move over the hills and valleys of the simplest of prayers: '*Our Father, who art in heaven, hallowed be thy name. Thy kingdom come, thy will be done, on earth as it is in heaven.*'

Before I realized what I was doing, my own mouth had started to form the words, a muscle memory. And to my surprise, instead of it feeling false or forced, it made me relieved, as if I had just passed the baton to someone else.

'*Give us this day our daily bread and lead us not into temptation. Forgive us our trespasses, as we forgive others who trespass against us; and lead us not into temptation, but deliver us from evil.*'

It felt like putting on flannel pajamas on a snowy night; like turning on your blinker for the exit that you know will take you home.

I looked at Father Michael, and together we said 'Amen.'

Michael

Ian Fletcher, former tele-atheist and current academic, lived in New Canaan, New Hampshire, in a farmhouse on a dirt road where the mailboxes were not numbered. I drove up and down the street four times before turning down one driveway and knocking on the door. When I did, no one answered, although I could hear strains of Mozart through the open windows.

I had left June in the hospital, still shaken by my encounter with Shay. Talk about irony: just when I allowed myself to think that I *might* be in God's company, after all – He flatly rejected me. The whole world felt off-kilter; it is an odd thing to start questioning the framework that's ordered your life, your career, your expectations – and so I had placed a phone call to someone who'd been through it before.

I knocked again, and this time the door swung open beneath my fist. 'Hello? Anyone home?'

'In here,' a woman called out.

I stepped into the foyer, taking note of the colonial furniture, the photo on the wall that showed a young girl shaking hands with Bill Clinton and another of the girl smiling beside the Dalai Lama. I followed the music to a room off the kitchen, where the most intricate dollhouse I'd ever seen was sitting on a table, surrounded by bits of wood and chisels and glue gun sticks. The house was made of bricks no bigger than my thumbnail, the windows had miniature shutters that could be louvered to let in light; there was a porch with Corinthian columns. 'Amazing,' I murmured, and a woman stood up from behind the dollhouse, where she'd been hidden.

'Oh,' she said. 'Thanks.' Seeing me, she did a double take, and I realized her eyes were focused on my clerical collar.

'Bad parochial school flashback?'

'No . . . it's just been a while since I've had a priest in here.' She stood up, wiping her hands on a white butcher's apron. 'I'm Mariah Fletcher,' she said.

'Michael Wright.'

'*Father* Michael Wright.'

I grinned. 'Busted.' Then I gestured to her handiwork. 'Did you make this?'

'Well. Yeah.'

'I've never seen anything like it.'

'Good,' Mariah said. 'That's what the client's counting on.'

I bent down, scrutinizing a tiny door knocker with the head of a lion. 'You're quite an artist.'

'Not really. I'm just better at detail than I am at the big picture.' She turned off the CD player that was trilling *The Magic Flute*. 'Ian said I was supposed to keep an eye out for you. And – Oh, shoot.' Her eyes flew to the corner of the room, where a stack of blocks had been abandoned. 'You didn't come across two hellions on your way in?'

'No . . .'

'That's not a good sign.' Pushing past me, she ran into the kitchen and threw open a pantry door. Twins – I figured them to be about four years old – were smearing the white linoleum with peanut butter and jelly.

'Oh, God,' Mariah sighed as their faces turned up to hers like sunflowers.

'You told us we could finger-paint,' one of the boys said.

'Not on the floor; and not with food!' She glanced at me. 'I'd escort you, but—'

'You have to take care of a sticky situation?'

She smiled. 'Ian's in the barn; you can just head down there.'

She lifted each boy and pointed him toward the sink. 'And you two,' she said, 'are going to clean up, and then go torture Daddy.'

I left her washing the twins' hands and walked down the path toward the barn. Having children was not in the cards for me – I knew that. A priest's love for God was so all-encompassing that it should erase the human craving for a family – my parents, brothers, sisters, and children were *all* Jesus. If the Gospel of Thomas was right, however, and we were more *like* God than *unlike* Him, then having children should have been mandatory for everyone. After all, God had a son and had given Him up. Any parent whose child had gone to college or gotten married or moved away would understand this part of God more than me.

As I approached the barn, I heard the most unholy sounds – like cats being dismembered, calves being slaughtered. Panicked – was Fletcher hurt? – I threw open the door to find him watching a teenage girl play the violin.

Really badly.

She took the violin from her chin and settled it into the slight curve of her hip. 'I don't understand why I have to practice in the barn.'

Fletcher removed a pair of foam earplugs. 'What was that?'

She rolled her eyes. 'Did you even hear my piece at *all*?'

Fletcher paused. 'You know I love you, right?' The girl nodded. 'Well, let's just say if God was hanging around here today, that last bit probably sent Her running for the hills.'

'Tryouts for band are tomorrow,' she said. 'What am I going to *do*?'

'Switch to the flute?' Fletcher suggested, but he put his arm around the girl and hugged her as he spoke. As he turned, he noticed me. 'Ah. You must be Michael Wright.' He shook my hand and introduced the girl. 'This is my daughter, Faith.'

Faith shook my hand, too. 'Did *you* hear me play? Am I as bad as he says I am?'

I hesitated, and Fletcher came to my rescue. 'Honey, don't put the priest in a position where he's going to have to lie – he'll waste his whole afternoon at confession.' He grinned at Faith. 'I think it's your turn to watch the demon twins from hell.'

'No, I remember very clearly that it's *your* turn. I was doing it all morning while Mom worked.'

'Ten bucks,' Ian said.

'Twenty,' Faith countered.

'Done.' She put her violin back in its case. 'Nice to meet you,' she said to me, and she slipped out of the barn, heading toward the house.

'You have a beautiful family,' I said to Fletcher.

He laughed. 'Appearances can be deceiving. Spending an afternoon with Cain and Abel is a whole new form of birth control.'

'Their names are—'

'Not really,' Fletcher said, smiling. 'But that's what I call them when Mariah's not listening. Come on back to my office.'

He walked me past a generator and a snowblower, two abandoned horse stalls, and through a pine door. Inside, to my surprise, was a finished room with paneled walls and two stories of bookshelves. 'I have to admit,' Fletcher said, 'I don't get very many calls from the Catholic clergy. They aren't quite the prevalent audience for my book.'

I sat down on a leather wing chair. 'I can imagine.'

'So what's a nice priest like you doing in the office of a rabble-rouser like me? Can I expect a blistering commentary in the *Catholic Advocate* with your byline on it?'

'No . . . this is more of a fact-finding mission.' I thought about how much I should admit to Ian Fletcher. The confidentiality relationship between a parishioner and a priest was as inviolable as the one between a patient and his doctor, but was telling Fletcher what Shay had said breaking a trust if the same words were already in a gospel that had been written two thousand years ago? 'You used to be an atheist,' I said, changing the subject.

'Yeah.' Fletcher smiled. 'I was pretty gifted at it, too, if I do say so myself.'

'What happened?'

'I met someone who made me question everything I was so sure I knew about God.'

'That,' I said, 'is why I'm in the office of a rabble-rouser like you.'

'And what better place to learn more about the Gnostic gospels,' Fletcher said.

'Exactly.'

'Well, then, the first thing is that you shouldn't call them that. It would be like calling someone a spic or a Hebe – the label Gnostic was made up by the same people who rejected them. In my circles, we call them noncanonical gospels. *Gnostic* literally means *one who knows* – but the people who coined the term considered its followers *know-it-alls*.'

'That's what we pretty much learn in seminary.'

Fletcher looked at me. 'Let me ask you a question, Father – in your opinion, what's the purpose of religion?'

I laughed. 'Wow, thank goodness you picked an easy one.'

'I'm serious . . .'

I considered this. 'I think religion brings people together over a common set of beliefs . . . and makes them understand why they matter.'

Fletcher nodded, as if this was the answer he'd been expecting. 'I think it's there to answer the really hard questions that arise when the world doesn't work the way it's supposed to – like when your child dies of leukemia, or you're fired after twenty years of hard work. When bad things happen to good people, and good things happen to bad people. The really interesting thing, to me, is that somehow religion stopped being about trying to find honest solutions . . . and started being about ritual. Instead of everyone searching for understanding on their own, orthodox religion came along and said, "Do x, y, and z – and the world will be a better place."'

'Well, Catholicism's been around for thousands of years,' I replied, 'so it must be doing something right.'

'You have to admit, it's done a lot *wrong*, too,' Fletcher said.

Anyone who'd had limited religious instruction or a thorough college education knew about the Catholic Church and its role in politics and history – not to mention the heresies that had been squelched over the centuries. Even sixth graders studied the Inquisition. 'It's a corporation,' I said. 'And sure, there have been times when it's been staffed badly, with people who think ambition trumps faith. But that doesn't mean you throw the baby out with the bathwater. No matter how screwed up God's servants are in the Church, His message has managed to get through.'

Fletcher tilted his head. 'What do you know about the birth of Christianity?'

'Did you want me to start with the Holy Ghost visiting Mary, or skip ahead to the star in the East . . .'

'That's the birth of *Jesus*,' Fletcher said. 'Two very different things. Historically, after Jesus's death, his followers weren't exactly welcomed with open arms. By the second century A.D., they were literally dying for their beliefs. But even though they belonged to groups that called themselves Christians, the groups weren't unified, because they were all very different from one another. One of these groups was the so-called Gnostics. To them, being Christian was a good first step, but to truly reach enlightenment, you had to receive secret knowledge, or *gnosis*. You *started* with faith, but you *developed* insight – and for these people, Gnostics offered a second baptism. Ptolemy called it *apolutrosis* – the same word used when slaves were legally freed.'

'So how did people get this secret knowledge?'

'There's the rub,' Fletcher said. 'Unlike the church, you couldn't be taught it. It had nothing to do with being told what to believe, and everything to do with figuring it out on your own. You had to reach inside yourself, understand human nature and its destiny, and at that moment you'd know the secret – that there's divinity in you, if you're willing to look for it. And the path would be different for everyone.'

'That sounds more Buddhist than Christian.'

'*They* called themselves Christians,' Fletcher corrected. 'But

Irenaeus, who was the bishop of Lyons at the time, disagreed. He saw three huge differences between Orthodox Christianity and Gnosticism. In Gnostic texts, the focus wasn't on sin and repentance, but instead on illusion and enlightenment. Unlike in the Orthodox Church, you couldn't be a member simply by joining – you had to show evidence of spiritual maturity to be accepted. And – this was probably the biggest stumbling block for the bishop – Gnostics didn't think Jesus's resurrection was literal. To them, Jesus was never really human – he just appeared in human form. But that was just a technicality to the Gnostics, because unlike Orthodox Christians, they didn't see a gap between the human and the divine. To them, Jesus wasn't a one-of-a-kind savior – he was a guide, helping you find your individual spiritual potential. And when you reached it, you weren't redeemed by Christ – you *became* a Christ. Or in other words: you were *equal* to Jesus. Equal to God.'

It was easy to see why, in seminary, this had been taught as heresy: the basis of Christianity was that there was only one God, and He was so different from man that the only way to reach Him was through Jesus. 'The biggest heresies are the ones that scare the Church to death.'

'Especially when the Church is going through its own identity crisis,' Fletcher said. 'I'm sure you remember how Irenaeus decided to unify the Orthodox Christian Church – by figuring out who was a true believer, and who was faking. Who was speaking the word of God, and who was speaking . . . well . . . just words?'

On a pad in front of him, Fletcher wrote GOD = WORD = JESUS, then spun it around so I could see. 'Irenaeus came up with this little gem. He said that we can't be divine, because Jesus's life and death were so different from that of any man – which became the very beginning of Orthodox Christianity. What didn't fit this equation became heretical – if you weren't worshipping the right way, you were out. It was sort of the first reality show, if you want to think of it that way: who had the purest form of Christianity? He condemned the folks who got creative with faith, like Marcus and his followers, who spoke in prophecies and had visions of a feminine divinity clothed in the letters of the Greek alphabet. He condemned the groups that swore by only one gospel – like the Ebionites, who were attached to Matthew; or the Marcionites, who studied only Luke. Just as bad were the groups like the Gnostics, who had too *many* texts. Instead, Irenaeus decided that Matthew, Mark, Luke, and John should be the four cornerstone gospels of what to believe—'

'— because they all had a narrative of Christ's Passion in them . . . which the Church needed, in order for the Eucharist to mean something.'

'Exactly,' Fletcher said. 'Then Irenaeus appealed to all those people who were trying to decide which Christian group was right for them. Basically, he said: 'We know how hard it is to figure out what's true, and what's not. So we're going to make it easy for you, and tell you what to believe.' People who did that were true Christians. People who didn't were not. And the things Irenaeus told people to believe became the foundation for the Nicene Creed, years later.'

Every priest knew that what we were taught in seminary had a Catholic spin put on it – yet there was an incontrovertible truth behind it. I had always believed that the Catholic Church was evidence of religious survival of the fittest: the truest, most powerful ideas were the ones that had prevailed over time. But Fletcher was saying that the most powerful ideas had been *subjugated* . . . because they jeopardized the existence of the Orthodox Church. That the reason they'd had to be crushed was because – at one point – they'd been as or more popular than Orthodox Christianity.

Or in other words, the reason the Church had survived and flourished was not because its ideas were the most valid, but because it had been the world's first bully.

'Then the books of the New Testament were just an editorial decision someone once had to make,' I said.

Fletcher nodded. 'But what were those decisions based on? The gospels aren't the word of God. They're not even the apostles' firsthand accounts of the word of God. They're simply the stories that best supported the creed that the Orthodox Church wanted people to follow.'

'But if Irenaeus hadn't done that,' I argued, 'chances are there would be no Christianity. Irenaeus united a whole mass of fragmented followers and their beliefs. When you're in Rome in A.D. 150 and you're being arrested because you confess Christ as your savior, you want to make sure that the people beside you aren't going to turn around at the last minute and say they believe something different. In fact, it's *still* important today to figure out who's a believer and who's just a nutcase – read any paper and you'll see how anger, prejudice, or ego are all routinely passed off as the Word of God, usually with a bomb strapped to it.'

'Orthodoxy takes the risk away,' Fletcher agreed. 'We tell you what's real and what's not, so you don't have to worry about getting it wrong. The problem is that the minute you do it, you start separating people into groups. Some get favored, some don't. Some gospels get picked, others get hidden away underground for thousands of years.' He looked at me. 'Somewhere along the line, organized religion stopped being about faith, and started being about who had the power to *keep* that faith.' Fletcher ripped off the sheet of paper with Irenaeus's equation, leaving a clear, blank slate beneath. He crumpled the paper, tossed it into his trash can. 'You said that the purpose of religion was to bring people together. But does it, really? Or does it – knowingly, purposefully, and intentionally – break them apart?'

I took a deep breath. And then I told him everything I knew about Shay Bourne.

Lucius

None of us were getting any sleep, but it wasn't for lack of trying.

Crowds have their own pH, and the remarkable thing is that they can change in an instant. The people who had been camping out outside the prison – who were featured in a countdown every night on the local news (MR MESSIAH: DAY 23) – had somehow gotten word that Shay had been hospitalized for an injury. But now, in addition to the camp that was holding a prayer vigil for Shay, there was a very vocal group of people who felt that this was a sign, that the reason Shay had been hurt so badly was because God decided he had it coming to him.

They got louder, for some reason, after dark. Insults were hurled, fights were picked, punches were thrown. Someone sent the National Guard down to patrol the perimeter of the prison and keep the peace, but no one could shut them up. Shay's supporters would sing gospel to drown out the chants of the disbelievers ('Jesus lives! Bourne dies!'). Even with headphones on, I could still hear them, a headache that wouldn't go away.

Watching the eleven o'clock news that night was surreal. To see the prison and hear the resonant shouts of the mob outside echoing the broadcast on my television – well, it was like déjà vu, except it was happening now.

There's only one God, people shouted.

They carried signs: JESUS IS MY HOMEBOY – NOT SATAN.

LET HIM DIE FOR *HIS* SINS.

NO CROWN OF THORNS FOR SHAY BOURNE.

They were separated from the Shay loyalists by armed guards toting guns, who walked the fault line of public opinion between them.

'As you can see,' the reporter said, 'sentiment in support of Shay Bourne and his unprecedented case to donate his heart is waning in the wake of his hospitalization. A recent poll done by WNRK news shows only thirty-four percent of New Hampshire residents still convinced that the courts should allow Bourne to be an organ donor; and even less than that – sixteen percent – agree that his miracles are divinely inspired. Which means that an overwhelming eighty-four percent of the state agrees with Reverend Arbogath Justus, who's joining us again this evening. Reverend, you and the members of your church have been here for nearly a week now and have been instrumental in turning the tide of public opinion. What's your take on the Bourne hospitalization?'

The Reverend Justus was still wearing that green suit. 'Ninety-nine percent of the state thinks you should burn that outfit,' I said out loud.

'Janice,' the reverend replied, 'we at the Drive-In Church of Christ in God have of course been praying for Shay Bourne's speedy and full recovery in the wake of the prison attack. However, when we pray, we pray to the one and only Lord: Jesus Christ.'

'Is there any message you have for those who still don't agree with you?'

'Why, yes.' He leaned closer to the camera. 'I *told* you so.'

The reporter took back the microphone. 'We've been told that Bourne will be released from the hospital in the next few hours, but doctors haven't commented on his condition . . .' Suddenly, a roar went up from both sides of the crowd, and the reporter covered her earpiece with one hand. 'This is unconfirmed,' she said over the din, 'but apparently an ambulance has just driven into the rear entrance of the prison . . .'

On the screen, the camera swung past her to catch a man decking a woman in a purple caftan. The armed guards stepped in, but by then other fights had broken out between the camps.

The line separating the two bled, until the guards had to call in reinforcements. The cameras captured a teenager being trampled, a man being smacked in the head by the butt of a guard's rifle and collapsing.

'Lights-out,' a CO said over the loudspeaker. Lights-out never really meant lights-out – there was always some residual bulb shining somewhere in the prison. But I pulled off my headphones, lay down on my bunk – and listened to the riot going on outside the brick walls of the prison.

This is what it always comes down to, I realized. There are the ones who believe, and the ones who don't, and caught in the space between them are guns.

Apparently, I wasn't the only one being disturbed. Batman the Robin began to squawk, in spite of Calloway's efforts to hush him.

'Shut that freaking bird up already!' Texas yelled.

'*You* shut up,' Calloway said. 'Fucking Bourne. Wish he'd never come onto this fucking tier.'

As if he'd been summoned, the door to I-tier opened, and in the half-light, Shay moved toward his cell, escorted by a flock of six officers. He had a bandage on his face, and two black eyes. Part of his scalp had been shaved. He did not look at any of us as he passed. 'Hey,' I murmured as he walked by my cell, but Shay didn't respond. He moved like a zombie, like someone in a sci-fi film whose frontal lobe has been removed by the mad scientist.

Five of the officers left. The sixth stood outside Shay's cell door, his own personal security guard. The presence of the CO prevented me from talking to Shay. In fact, the presence of the CO prevented any of us from talking, period.

I guess we were all so focused on his return that it took us several moments to realize that the quiet wasn't just a lack of conversation. Batman the Robin had fallen asleep in Calloway's breast pocket. And outside, that din – that god-awful din – had gone spectacularly, blissfully silent.

Maggie

America was founded on religious freedom, on the separation of church and state, and yet I will be the first to tell you that we're not much better off than those Puritans were in the 1770s over in England. Religion and politics get into bed with each other all the time: the first thing we do in a courtroom is swear on a Bible; public school classes begin with the Pledge of Allegiance, which declares us one nation under God; even our currency is stamped with the words *In God We Trust*. You'd think that of all people, a lawyer like me from the ACLU would be violently opposed to this on principle, but no. I had spent thirty minutes in the shower and another twenty driving downtown to the federal courthouse trying to figure out the best way to drag religion smack into the middle of a courtroom.

I was just determined to do it without offending the personal beliefs of the judge.

In the parking lot, I called the ChutZpah and reached my mother on the first try.

'What kind of name is Haig?'

'You mean like the general?'

'Yeah.'

'Sounds German, maybe,' she mused. 'I don't know. Why?'

'I was talking religious affiliation.'

'Is that what you think I do?' my mother said. 'Judge people on their last names?'

'Does *everything* have to be an accusation? I just need to know before I go into chambers, so that I can tailor what I say to the justice sitting on the case.'

'I thought the whole point of being a judge was being impartial.'

'Right. Just like the whole point of being crowned Miss America is to promote world peace.'

'I can't remember if Alexander Haig is Jewish. I know your father liked him because he supported Israel . . .'

'Well, even if he is, that doesn't mean that my judge is. Haig isn't quite as easy to figure out as someone named O'Malley or Hershkowitz.'

'Your father once dated a Jewish girl named Barbara O'Malley, for your information,' my mother said.

'Hopefully before he married you . . .'

'Very funny. I'm just saying that your theory isn't airtight.'

'Well, you don't meet many Jewish O'Malleys.'

My mother hesitated. 'I think her grandparents had their surname legally changed from Meyer.'

I rolled my eyes. 'I've got to go. No matter what his religion is, no judge likes a lawyer who's late.'

I had received a call from my secretary when I was meeting with Warden Coyne about Shay's protection in the prison – Judge Haig wanted to see counsel in federal court the very next morning, a mere four days after I'd filed my complaint there. I should have realized things were going to move blisteringly fast. Shay already had an execution date scheduled, so the court had put us on an expedited trial calendar.

As I turned the corner, I saw the AAG from the appellate division, Gordon Greenleaf, already waiting. I nodded at him, and then felt my cell phone vibrating in my purse with a text message.

GOOGLED HAIG-ROM CATH. XO MOM

I snapped the phone shut as the clerk arrived to lead us into Judge Haig's chambers.

The judge had thinning gray hair and a distance-runner's body. I peered at the collar of his shirt, but he was wearing a tie: for all I knew, he might be wearing a crucifix, a star of David, or even a rope of garlic to ward off vampires. 'All right, boys and girls,' he said, 'who can tell us why we're here today?'

'Your Honor,' I answered, 'I'm suing the commissioner of corrections of the State of New Hampshire on behalf of my client, Shay Bourne.'

'Yes, thank you, Ms Bloom, I already breathlessly read your complaint from cover to cover. What I meant was that Mr Bourne's impending execution is already a zoo. Why is the ACLU turning it into a bigger one?'

Gordon Greenleaf cleared his throat. He had always reminded me of Bozo the Clown, with his tufted red hair and allergies that left his nose red more often than not. 'He's a death row inmate trying to delay the inevitable, Your Honor.'

'He's not trying to delay anything,' I argued. 'He's just trying to make amends for his sins, and he believes this is the way he needs to die in order to reach salvation. He'd be the first to tell you you can execute him tomorrow, as long as it's by hanging.'

'This is 2008, Ms Bloom. We execute people by lethal injection. We're not going back to a more archaic form of execution,' Judge Haig said.

I nodded. 'But, Judge, with all due respect, if the Department of Corrections finds lethal injection impractical, the sentence may be carried out by hanging.'

'The Department of Corrections doesn't have a problem with lethal injection!' Greenleaf said.

'It does when Mr Bourne's First Amendment rights are being violated. He has the right to practice his religious beliefs, even in a prison setting – up to and including during the moment of his execution.'

'What are you talking about?' Greenleaf exploded. '*No* religion insists on organ donation. Just because one individual gets some crazy set of rules into his head to live – or die – by, that doesn't qualify it as a religious belief.'

'Gee, Gordon,' I said. 'Who died and left *you* God?'

'Counselors, back to your corners,' Judge Haig said. He pursed his lips, deep in thought. 'There are some factual issues here that need to be fleshed out,' he began, 'but the first of these is, Mr Greenleaf, whether the state will agree to hang Mr Bourne in lieu of giving him a lethal injection.'

'Absolutely not, Judge. Preparations are already in place for the method of execution that was specified at his sentencing.'

Judge Haig nodded. 'Then we'll set this down for trial. Given the very real deadline we're working under, it will be an expedited hearing. We're going to pretend that there's no such thing as federal discovery; we're going to pretend that there's no such thing as summary judgment motions – we don't have time for them. Instead, I want witness lists on my desk in a week, and I want you prepared to go straight to trial in two weeks.'

Gordon and I gathered our belongings and stepped outside chambers. 'Do you have any idea how much money the taxpayers of New Hampshire have spent on that death chamber?'

'Take it up with the governor, Gordon,' I said. 'If the rich towns in New Hampshire have to pay for public education, maybe the poor towns can cough up the funds for future death row inmates.'

He folded his arms. 'What's the ACLU's game here, Maggie? You can't get the death penalty declared unconstitutional, so you use religion as a fallback position?'

I smiled at him. 'You do if it *helps* you get the death penalty declared unconstitutional. See you in two weeks, Gordon,' I said, and I walked off, leaving him staring after me.

Three times, I picked up the phone and dialed. Three times, I hung up just as the line connected.

I couldn't do this.

But I had to. I had two weeks to get the facts; and if I was going to fight on Shay's behalf to donate his heart, I needed to understand exactly how this was going to work – and be able to explain that in court.

When the hospital switchboard connected, I asked to speak to Dr Gallagher's office. I left my name and number with a secretary, fully anticipating the fact that it would take some time before he returned my call, during which I might actually develop the courage to speak to him. So when the phone rang almost as soon as I put down the receiver, I was shocked to hear his voice. 'Ms Bloom,' he said. 'What can I do for you?'

'You weren't supposed to call back this fast,' I blurted out.

'Ah, I'm sorry. I really should be less punctual with my patients.'

'I'm not your patient.'

'Right. You were only masquerading as one.' He was silent, and then said, 'I believe you called me?'

'Yes. Yes, I did. I was wondering if you might be willing to meet with me – professionally, of course—'

'Of course.'

'— to talk about hanging and organ donation.'

'If only I had a dime for every time I've been asked to do that,' Dr Gallagher said. 'I'd be delighted to meet with you. Professionally, of course.'

'Of course,' I said, deflated. 'The catch is, I have to meet you fairly soon. My client's trial starts in two weeks.'

'Well, then, Ms Bloom, I'll pick you up at seven.'

'Oh – you don't have to do that. I can meet you at the hospital.'

'Yes, but I really prefer to not eat the cafeteria Jell-O on my days off.'

'It's your day off?' *He called me back on his day off?* 'Well, we can do it some other time . . .'

'Didn't you just tell me this was something that needed to be done quickly?'

'Well,' I said. 'Yeah.'

'Then seven o'clock it is.'

'Excellent,' I said in my finest courtroom voice. 'I look forward to it.'

'Ms Bloom.'

'Yes?'

I held my breath, waiting for him to lay down the parameters of this meeting. Do not expect this to be any more than it is on the surface: two professionals doing business. Do not forget that you could have asked any number of doctors, even ones who don't have eyes the color of a moonless night and an accent that tugs like a fishing hook. Do not delude yourself into pretending this is a real date.

'I don't know where you live.'

Whoever said that black makes you look thinner obviously did not have the same clothes that were hanging in *my* closet. First I tried on my favorite black pants, which were no longer my favorite because they only buttoned if I stopped breathing and didn't intend to sit at all during the meal. The black turtleneck that still had tags on it made me look like I had a double chin, and the black crochet shrug that had looked so cute in the catalog showed every inch of bra roll. *Red*, I thought. *I'll be bold and make a statement.* I tried on a crimson silk camisole, but the only statement I seemed to be sending was Frederick's of Hollywood. I sifted through wraps and cardigans and shells and blazers, A-line skirts and pleated ones and cocktail dresses, tossing them off one by one onto the floor as Oliver hopped away in vain, trying not to get trapped underneath. I tried on every single pair of trousers in my possession and decided that my ass was well on its way to being declared one of Saturn's moons. Then I marched myself to the bathroom mirror. 'Here's the thing,' I said to myself. 'You don't have to look like Jennifer Aniston to discuss the best way to execute someone.'

Although, I imagined, it probably helped.

Finally I decided on my favorite pair of jeans, and a flowing pale green tunic that I'd found for five dollars at an Asian boutique, so I always felt good about wearing it, even when I didn't look perfect. I twisted my hair up and stabbed it with a hair stick, hoping it looked artful and Grecian instead of just messy and out of time.

At exactly seven, the doorbell rang. I took one last look at myself in the mirror – the outfit clearly said casual, together, not trying too hard – and opened the door to find Dr Gallagher wearing a coat and tie.

'I can change,' I said quickly. 'I didn't know we were going somewhere nice. Not that I wouldn't expect you to take me somewhere nice. Or that you're *taking* me. I mean, I'm taking myself. And you're taking you. We're just going in the same car.'

'You look lovely,' he said. 'This is how I dress all the time.'

'On your day off?'

'Well, I *am* British,' he replied, an explanation; but he hooked his finger in his collar and slipped the tie from his shirt. He draped it over the inside knob of the front door.

'When I was in college and someone did that it meant—' I broke off, remembering what it did mean: don't enter, because your roommate is getting lucky. 'It meant that, um, you were busy studying for a test.'

'Really?' Dr Gallagher said. 'How strange. At Oxford it meant your roommate was inside having sex.'

'Maybe we should go,' I said quickly, hoping he didn't notice that I was blushing fiercely, or that I lived alone with a rabbit, or that my hips were so big that they probably wouldn't fit into the seat of the little sports car he'd parked in my driveway.

He opened the car door for me and didn't turn the ignition until my seat belt was fastened. As he sped off, he cleared his throat. 'There's something I'd like to get out of the way before we go any further,' he said. 'I'm Christian.'

I stared at him. Was he some kind of fundamentalist who limited his extracurricular conversations to people of the same faith? Did he think that I harbored some secret desire to elope, and was he giving me the lay of the land? (All right. So maybe that last one wasn't far off the mark.)

Well, whatever. I'd been eating, sleeping, breathing religion with Shay's case; I was even more sensitive now about religious tolerance than I'd been before I took up this mantle. And if religion was so vitally important to Gallagher that he had to bring it up as the first point of conversation, I could give as good as I got. 'I'm an atheist,' I said, 'but you might as well know right now that my father's a rabbi, and if you have a problem with that I'm sure I can find another physician to talk to me, and I'd really appreciate it if you didn't make a joke right now about Jewish doctors.'

I exhaled.

'Well,' he said, and glanced at me. 'Perhaps you'd rather call me Chris?'

I was pretty sure Emily Post wouldn't have covered this topic, but it seemed more discreet to wait until after we were served our main course to start talking about how to kill a man.

The restaurant was inside an old colonial home in Orford, with floorboards that rolled like the seas beneath my feet and a bustling kitchen off to one side. The hostess had a husky, mellifluous voice and greeted the doctor by name.

Christian.

The room we were sitting in had only six tables, covered with mismatched linen and dishes and glasses; candles burned in recycled wine bottles. On the wall were mirrors in every shape and size – my own personal version of the ninth circle of hell – but I hardly even noticed them. Instead, I drank water and wine and pretended that I did not want to spoil my appetite by eating the freshly baked bread they'd served us along with dipping oil – or by talking about Shay's execution.

Christian smiled at me. 'I've always imagined one day I'd be forced to consider how one went about losing one's heart, but I must admit, I didn't think it would be quite so literal.'

The waiter arrived with our plates. The menu had been full of the most delectable cuisine: Vietnamese bouillabaisse, escargot tortellini, chorizo dumplings. Even the descriptions of the entrées made me salivate: *Handmade to order, fresh Italian parsley pasta filled with fresh artichoke hearts, roasted eggplant, a medley of cheeses, and sweet roasted red and yellow pepper, tossed with a sun-dried tomato cream sauce. Slices of boneless chicken lined with thin slices of prosciutto filled with fresh spinach, Asiago cheese, and sweet onion rolled and served with fresh fettuccine and a tomato marsala wine reduction. Boneless breast of duck roasted, thinly sliced, served with a sun-dried cherry sauce and a wild rice pancake.*

In the wild hope that I might fool Christian into thinking my waist size was not what it seemed to be, I'd swallowed hard and ordered an appetizer. I'd fervently wished that Christian would order the braised leg of lamb or the steak frites so that I could beg a taste, but when I explained I wasn't all that hungry (a colossal lie), he said an appetizer was all he really wanted, too.

'From what I imagine,' Christian said, 'the inmate would be hanged in such a way that the spine would be fractured at C2/C3, which would arrest all spontaneous respiration.'

I was trying very hard to follow along. 'You mean he'd break his neck and stop breathing?'

'Right.'

'So then he's brain-dead?'

A couple at the next table glanced at me, and I realized I'd been talking too loudly. That some people didn't like to mix death with dinner.

'Well, not quite. It takes some time for anoxic changes to the brain to result in a loss of reflexes . . . which is how you test for brain-stem function. The problem is that you can't leave your man hanging for a great period of time, or his heart will stop, and that disqualifies him as a donor.'

'So what has to happen?'

'The state needs to agree that the fact that respiration's ceased is enough to justify taking the body down from the noose on likely suspicion of death, then intubate him so that the heart is protected, and *then* test for brain death.'

'Intubating him isn't the same as resuscitating him, then?'

'No. It's the equivalent of someone brain-dead being on a venti-
lator. It preserves the organs, but there won't be any brain function once that spinal cord is severed and hypoxia sets in, no matter
how much oxygen you pump into his system.'

I nodded. 'So how do you determine brain death?'

'There are multiple ways. You can do a physical exam first –
check to make sure there are no corneal reflexes, no spontaneous
respirations, no gag reflex – and then repeat it twelve hours later.
But since time is of the essence, I'd recommend a transcranial
Doppler test, which uses ultrasound to measure blood flow through
the carotid arteries at the base of the brain. If there's no blood
flow for ten minutes, you can legally declare brain death.'

I imagined Shay Bourne – who could barely string together a
coherent sentence, who bit his fingernails to the quick – being
led to a gallows. I pictured the noose being drawn tight around
his neck and felt the hair stand up on the back of my own.

'It's brutal,' I said softly, and put down my fork.

Christian was quiet for a moment. 'I was a resident in
Philadelphia the first time I had to tell a mother her child had
died. He was the victim of a gang shooting – eight years old. He'd
gone to the corner store to get a quart of milk, and was in the
wrong place at the wrong time. I will never forget the look in her
eyes when I told her we weren't able to save her son. When a
child is killed, two people die, I think. The only difference is that
his mother still had to suffer a heartbeat.' He looked up at me. 'It
will be brutal for Mr Bourne. But it was brutal for June Nealon
first.'

I sat back in my chair. This, then, was the catch. You meet a
well-educated, intensely gorgeous, charming Oxford-educated
man, and he turns out to be so right-wing he's nearly pointed
backward. 'Then you're in favor of capital punishment?' I asked,
trying to keep my voice level.

'I think it's easy to take the moral high road when it's all theory,'
Christian said. 'As a physician, do I think it's right to kill someone?
No. But then again, I don't have children yet. And I'd be lying

if I said that when I do, this issue will still seem crystal clear to me.'

I didn't have children yet, either; at the rate I was going, I might never have them. And the only time I'd seen June Nealon, face-to-face, we'd been at the restorative justice meeting and she had been so filled with righteous anger that I found it hard to look at her. I didn't know what it felt like to carry a child underneath my heart for nine months, to feel my body give way to make room for hers. I didn't know what it felt like to hold an infant and rock her to sleep, to find a lullaby in her breathing. But I knew what it was like to be the daughter.

My mother and I hadn't always argued. I could still remember wishing that I was as glamorous as she was – trying on her high-heeled shoes, pulling her sheer satin slips up to my armpits as if they were strapless dresses, diving into the wondrous mystery of her makeup bag. She had, at one point, been the person I wanted to grow up to be.

It was so damn hard to find love in this world, to locate someone who could make you feel that there was a reason you'd been put on this earth. A child, I imagined, was the purest form of that. A child was the love you didn't have to look for, didn't have to prove anything to, didn't have to worry about losing.

Which is why, when it happened, it hurt so badly.

Suddenly, I wanted to call my mother. I wanted to call June Nealon. I was on my first date since the dinosaurs had roamed the planet, a date that was really just a business dinner, and I felt like bursting into tears.

'Maggie?' Christian leaned forward. 'Are you all right?' And then he put his hand on top of mine.

Arrest all spontaneous respiration, he had said.

The waiter appeared at the side of the table. 'I hope you've left room for dessert.'

I had nothing *but* room; my appetizer had been a crab cake the size of my thumbnail. But I could feel the warmth of Christian's skin on mine, and it was like heat at the tip of a candle – only a matter of time before the rest of me melted, too. 'Oh, I couldn't,' I said. 'I'm stuffed.'

'Right,' Christian said, and he slipped his hand away from mine. 'I guess just the bill, then.'

Something had changed in his features – and there was a chill to his voice that hadn't been there a moment before. 'What's the matter?' I asked. He shook his head, dismissive, but I knew what it was: the death penalty. 'You think I'm on the wrong side.'

'I don't think there are sides,' Christian said, 'but that's not it.'

'Then what did I do wrong?'

The waiter sidled over with the bill, tucked into a leather folder. Christian reached for it. 'My last steady girlfriend was a principal dancer for the Boston Ballet.'

'Oh,' I said feebly. 'She must have been . . .' Beautiful. Graceful. Skinny.

Everything I wasn't.

'Every time we went out for a meal I felt like some sort of . . . *glutton* . . . because I had an appetite, and she never ate a damn thing. I suppose I thought – well, *hoped* – that you'd be different.'

'But I *love* chocolate,' I blurted out. 'And apple fritters and pumpkin pie and mousse and tiramisu and I probably would have eaten everything on this menu if I didn't think it would make me look like a pig. I was trying to be . . .' My voice trailed off.

'. . . what you thought I was looking for?'

I focused my attention on the napkin on my lap. Leave it to me to ruin a date that wasn't even really one.

'What if all I was looking for,' Christian asked, 'was you?'

I lifted my head slowly as Christian summoned back our waiter. 'Tell us about dessert,' he said.

'We have a crème brûlée, a fresh blueberry tart, warm peach puff pastries with homemade ice cream and caramel sauce, and my personal favorite,' the waiter said. 'Chocolate French toast with

a thin pecan crust, served with mint ice cream, and our own rasp-
berry sauce.'

'What shall we try?' Christian asked.

I turned to the waiter. 'Maybe we could skip back to the main
course first,' I said, and smiled.

'This is my simple religion.
There is no need for temples;
no need for complicated philosophy.
Our own brain, our own heart is our temple;
the philosophy is kindness.'

– HIS HOLINESS THE 14TH DALAI LAMA

June

As it turned out, in spite of the deathbed promises, I didn't tell Claire about her potential new heart when she first awakened after the episode that had brought us back to this hospital. Instead, I made a hundred excuses: When she wasn't running a temperature. When she had a little more energy. When we knew for sure that a judge was going to allow the donation to happen. The longer I put off the conversation, the more I was able to convince myself that Claire would have another hour, day, week with me in which to have it.

And in the meantime, Claire was failing. Not just her body, but her spirit. Dr Wu told me every day that she was stable, but I saw changes. She didn't want me to read from *Teen People*. She didn't want to watch television. She lay on her side, staring at a blank wall.

'Claire,' I said one afternoon, 'want to play cards?'

'No.'

'How about Scrabble.'

'No thanks.' She turned away. 'I'm tired.'

I smoothed her hair back from her face. 'I know, baby.'

'No,' she said. 'I mean I'm *tired*, Mom. I don't want to do this anymore.'

'Well, we can take a walk – I mean, *I* can take a walk and push you in a wheelchair. You don't have to stay in bed—'

'I'm going to die in here. You and I both know it. Why can't I just go home and do it there, instead of hooked up to all of this stuff?'

I stared at her. Where was the child in that sentence, the one who had believed in fairies and ghosts and all sorts of impossible things? *But we're so close to fixing that*, I started to say, and then I realized that if I did, I would have to tell her about the heart that might or might not be coming.

And whose it was.

'I want to sleep in my own bed,' Claire said, 'instead of one with stupid plastic sheets and a pillow that crackles every time I move my head. I want to eat meat loaf, instead of chicken soup in a blue plastic cup and Jell-O—'

'You hate when I serve meat loaf.'

'I know, and I want to get mad at you for cooking it again.' She flopped onto her back and looked at me. 'I want to drink from the orange juice container. I want to throw a tennis ball for my dog.'

I hesitated. 'Maybe I can talk to Dr Wu,' I said. 'We can get your own sheets and pillow, I bet . . .'

Something in Claire's eyes dimmed. 'Just forget it,' she said, and that was how I realized she'd already begun to die, before I had a chance to save her.

As soon as Claire fell asleep that afternoon, I left her in the capable hands of the nursing staff and exited the hospital for the first time in a week. I was stunned to see how much the world had changed. There was a nip in the air that whispered of winter; the trees had begun to turn color, sugar maples first, their bright heads like torches that would light the rest of the woods on fire. My car felt unfamiliar, as if I were driving a rental. And most shocking – the road that led past the state prison had been rerouted with policemen on traffic detail. I inched through the cones, gaping at the crowds that had been cordoned off by police tape: SHAY BOURNE WILL BURN IN HELL, read one sign. Another banner said SATAN IS ALIVE AND KICKING ON I-TIER.

Once, when Claire was tiny, she'd raised the blackout shade in her bedroom window when she woke up. At the sight of the sunrise, with its outstretched crimson fingers, she'd gasped. *Did I do that?*

Now, looking at the signs, I had to wonder: Could you believe something so fiercely that it actually happened? Could your thoughts change the minds of others?

Keeping my eyes on the road, I passed the prison gates and continued toward my house. But my car had other intentions – it turned right, and then left, and into the cemetery where Elizabeth and Kurt were buried.

I parked and started walking to their shared grave. It was underneath an ash tree; in the light wind, the leaves shimmered like golden coins. I knelt on the grass and traced my finger over the lettering on the headstone:

BELOVED DAUGHTER.

TREASURED HUSBAND.

Kurt had bought his plot after we'd been married for a year. *That's macabre*, I had said, and he had just shrugged it off; he saw the business of death and dying every day. *Here's the thing, though*, he had said. *There's room for you, if you want.*

He had not wanted to impose, because he didn't know if I'd want to be buried near my first husband. Even that tiny bit of consideration – the fact that he wanted me to choose, instead of making an assumption – had made me realize why I loved him. *I want to be with you*, I had told him. I wanted to be where my heart was.

After the murders, I would sleepwalk. I'd find myself the next morning in the gardening shed, holding a spade. In the garage, with my face pressed against the metal cheek of a shovel. In my subconscious, I was making plans to join them; it was only when I was awake and alert and felt Claire kicking me from within that I realized I had to stay.

Would she be the next one I'd bury here? And once I did, what would keep me from carrying things through to their natural conclusion, from putting my family back together in one place?

I lay down for a minute, prone on the grass. I pressed my face into the stubbled moss at the edge of the headstone and pretended I was cheek-to-cheek with my husband; I felt the dandelions twine through my fingers and pretended I was holding my daughter's hand.

In the elevator of the hospital, the duffel bag started to move itself across the floor. I crouched down, unzipped the top of it. 'Good boy,' I said, and patted the top of Dudley's head. I'd retrieved him from my neighbor, who had been kind enough to play foster parent while Claire was sick. Dudley had fallen asleep in the car, but now he was alert and wondering why I had zipped him into a piece of luggage. The doors opened and I hoisted him up, approaching the nurse's desk near Claire's room. I tried to smile normally. 'Everything all right?'

'She's been sleeping like a baby.'

Just then, Dudley barked.

The nurse's eyes flew up to mine, and I pretended to sneeze. 'Wow,' I said, shaking my head. 'Is that pollen count something or *what*?'

Before she could respond, I hurried into Claire's room and closed the door behind me. Then I unzipped the bag and Dudley shot out like a rocket. He ran a lap around the room, nearly knocking over Claire's IV pole.

There was a reason dogs weren't allowed in hospitals, but if Claire wanted *normal*, then she was going to get it. I wrapped my arms around Dudley and hoisted him onto Claire's bed, where he sniffed the cotton blanket and began to lick her hand.

Her eyes fluttered open, and when she saw the dog, a smile split her face. 'He's not allowed in here,' she whispered, burying her hands in the fur at his neck.

'Are you going to tell on me?'

Claire pushed herself to a sitting position and let the dog crawl into her lap. She scratched behind his ears while he tried to chew on the wire that ran from beneath Claire's hospital gown to the heart monitor.

'We won't have a lot of time,' I said quickly. 'Someone's going to—'

Just then, a nurse walked in holding a digital thermometer. 'Rise and shine, missy,' she began, and then she saw the dog on the bed. '*What* is that doing in here?'

I looked at Claire, and then back at the nurse. 'Visiting?' I suggested.

'Mrs Nealon, not even service dogs are allowed onto this ward without a letter from the vet stating that the vaccinations are up to date and the stool's tested negative for parasites —'

'I was just trying to make Claire feel better. He won't leave this room, I swear.'

'I'll give you five minutes,' the nurse said. 'But you have to promise you won't bring him in again before the transplant.'

Claire, who had a death grip on the dog, glanced up. 'Transplant?' she repeated. '*What* transplant?'

'She was being theoretical,' I said quickly.

'Dr Wu doesn't schedule theoretical transplants,' the nurse said.

Claire blinked at me. 'Mom?' There was a thread in her voice that had started to unravel.

The nurse turned on her heel. 'I'm counting,' she said, and left the room.

'Is it true?' Claire asked. 'There's a heart for me?'

'We're not sure. There's a catch . . .'

'There's *always* a catch,' Claire said. 'I mean, how many hearts have turned out to not be as great as Dr Wu expected?'

'Well, this one . . . it's not ready for transplant yet. It's sort of still being used.'

Claire laughed a little. 'What are you planning to do? *Kill* someone?'

I didn't answer.

'Is the donor really sick, or old? How could she even *be* a donor if she's sick or old?' Claire asked.

'Honey,' I said. 'We have to wait for the donor to be executed.'

Claire was not stupid. I watched her put together this new information with what she'd heard on television. Her hands tightened on Dudley. 'No *way*,' she said quietly. 'I am not taking a heart from the guy who killed my father and my sister.'

'He wants to *give* it to you. He offered.'

'This is sick,' Claire said. 'You're sick.' She struggled to get up, but she was tethered to the bed with tubes and wires.

'Even Dr Wu said that it's an amazing match for you and your body. I couldn't just say no.'

'What about me? Don't *I* get to say no?'

'Claire, baby, you know donors don't come along every day. I *had* to do it.'

'Then *undo* it,' she demanded. 'Tell them I don't want his stupid heart.'

I sank down on the edge of the hospital bed. 'It's just a muscle. It doesn't mean you'll be like him.' I paused. 'And besides, he *owes* this to us.'

'He doesn't owe us anything! Why don't you get that?' Her eyes filled with tears. 'You can't tie the score, Mom. You just have to start over.'

Her monitors began to sound an alert; her pulse was rising, her heart pumping too hard. Dudley began to bark. 'Claire, you have to calm down . . .'

'This isn't about him,' Claire said. 'This isn't even about me. It's about *you*. *You* need to get payment for what happened to Elizabeth. *You* need to make him pay for what he did. Where do *I* fit into that?'

The nurse flew into the room like a great white heron, fussing over Claire. 'What's going on in here?' she said, checking the connections and tubes and drips.

'Nothing,' we both said simultaneously.

The nurse gave me a measured glance. 'I highly recommend you take that dog away and let Claire get some rest.'

I reached for Dudley and wrestled him back into the duffel bag. 'Just think about it,' I pleaded.

Ignoring me, Claire reached into the bag and patted the dog. 'Good-bye,' she whispered.

Michael

I had gone back to St Catherine's. I told Father Walter that I had not been seeing clearly, and that God had opened my eyes to the truth.

I just neglected to mention that God happened to be sitting on I-tier about three miles away from our church, awaiting an expedited trial that began this week.

Each night, I said three consecutive rosaries – penance for lying to Father Walter – but I *had* to be there. I had to do something constructive with my time, now that I wasn't spending it with Shay. Since I'd confessed to him at the hospital that I'd served on the jury that had convicted him, he'd refused to see me.

There was a part of me that understood his reaction – imagine how it would feel to know your confidant had betrayed you – but there was another part of me that spent hours trying to figure out why divine forgiveness hadn't kicked in yet. Then again, if the Gospel of Thomas was to be believed, no matter how much time and space Shay put between us, we were never really separate: mankind and divinity were flip sides of the same coin.

And so, every day at noon, I told Father Walter I was meeting a fictional couple at their house to try to guide them away from the path of divorce. But instead, I rode my Trophy to the prison, burrowed through the crowds, and went inside to try to see Shay.

CO Whitaker was called to escort me to I-tier after I'd passed through the metal detectors at the visitor's booth. 'Hi, Father. You here to sell Girl Scout cookies?'

'You know it,' I replied. 'Anything exciting happen today?'

'Let's see. Joey Kunz got a medical visit for diarrhea.'

'Wow,' I said. 'Sorry I missed that.'

As I suited up in my flak jacket, Whitaker went into I-tier to tell Shay I'd come. Again. But no more than five seconds had passed before he returned, a sheepish look on his face. 'Not today, Father,' he said. 'Sorry.'

'I'll try again,' I replied, but we both knew that wasn't possible. We had run out of time: Shay's trial began tomorrow.

I left the prison and walked back to my motorcycle. All modesty aside, I was the closest thing Shay had to a disciple; and if that was true, it meant learning from the mistakes of history. At Jesus's crucifixion, His followers had scattered – except for Mary Magdalene, and his mother. So even if Shay didn't acknowledge me in court, I would still be there. I would bear witness for him.

For a long time, I sat on my bike in the parking lot, going nowhere.

In fairness, it wasn't like I wanted to spring this all on Maggie a few days before the trial. The truth of the matter was that if Shay didn't want me as his spiritual advisor anymore, I had no excuse for not telling Maggie that I'd been on the jury that convicted him. I'd tried to contact her several times over the past week, but she was either out of her office, not at home, or not answering her cell. And then, out of the blue, she called me. 'Get your ass down here,' she said. 'You have some explaining to do.'

In twenty minutes, I was sitting in her ACLU office. 'I had a meeting with Shay today,' Maggie said. 'He said you'd lied to him.'

I nodded. 'Did he go into detail?'

'No. He said I deserved to hear it firsthand.' She crossed her arms. 'He also said he didn't want you testifying on his behalf.'

'Right,' I mumbled. 'I don't blame him.'

'Are you really a priest?'

I blinked at her. 'Of course I am—'

'Then I don't care what you're lying about,' Maggie said. 'You can unburden your soul *after* we win Shay's case.'

'It's not that simple . . .'

'Yes it is, Father. You are the only character witness we've got for Shay; you're credible because you're wearing that collar. I don't care if you and Shay had a fight; I don't care if you moonlight as a drag queen; I don't care if you have enough secrets to last a lifetime. It's don't ask, don't tell until the trial starts, okay? All I care about is that you wear that collar, get on the stand, and make Shay sound like a saint. If you walk, the whole case goes down the toilet. Is that simple enough for you?'

If Maggie was right — if my testimony was the only thing that would help Shay — then how could I tell her something now that would ruin the case? A sin of omission could be understandable if you were helping someone by holding back. I could not give Shay his life back, but I could make sure his death was what he wanted.

Maybe it would be enough for him to forgive me.

'It's normal to be a little freaked out about going to court,' Maggie said, misreading my silence.

During my testimony, I was supposed to explain in layman's terms how donating a heart to Claire Nealon was one of Shay's spiritual beliefs. Having a *priest* say this was a stroke of genius on Maggie's part — who wouldn't believe a member of the clergy when it came to religion?

'You don't have to be worried about the cross-exam,' Maggie continued. 'You tell the judge that while a Catholic would believe that salvation comes solely through Jesus Christ, Shay believes organ donation's necessary for redemption. That's perfectly true, and I can promise you that lightning isn't going to crash through the ceiling when you say it.'

My head snapped up. 'I can't tell the court that Shay will find Jesus,' I said. 'I think he might *be* Jesus.'

She blinked. 'You think *what*?'

The words began to spill out of me, the way I always imagined it felt to be speaking in tongues: truths that tumbled before you even realized they'd left your mouth. 'It makes perfect sense. The age, the profession. The fact that he's on death row. The miracles. And the heart donation – he's literally giving himself away for our sins, again. He's giving the part that matters the least – the body – in order to become whole in spirit.'

'This is *way* worse than having cold feet,' Maggie murmured. 'You're crazy.'

'Maggie, he's been quoting a gospel that was written two hundred years after Christ's death – a gospel that most people don't even know exists. Word for word.'

'I've listened to his words, and frankly, they're unintelligible. Do you know what he was doing yesterday when I briefed him on his testimony? Playing tic-tac-toe. With himself.'

'You have to read between the lines.'

'Yeah, right. And I bet when you listen to Britney Spears records backward, you hear 'Sleep with me, I'm not too young.' For God's sake – no pun intended – you're a Catholic *priest*. Whatever happened to the Father, Son, and Holy Ghost? I don't remember Shay being part of the Trinity.'

'What about everyone camped outside the prison? Are they all crazy, too?'

'They want Shay to cure their kid's autism or reverse their husband's Alzheimer's. They're in it for *themselves*,' Maggie said. 'The only people who think Shay Bourne is the Messiah are so desperate that they'd be able to find salvation beneath the lid of a two-liter bottle of Pepsi.'

'Or through a heart transplant?' I countered. 'You've worked up a whole legal theory based on individual religious beliefs. So how can you tell me, categorically, that I'm wrong?'

'Because it's not a matter of right or wrong. It's life or death – namely, Shay's. I'd say whatever I had to to win this case for him; it's my job. And it was supposed to be *yours*, too. This isn't about some revelation; it's not about who Shay might have been or might be in the future. It's about who he is right now: a convicted murderer who's going to be executed unless I can do something about it. It doesn't matter to me if he's a vagrant or Queen Elizabeth or Jesus Christ – it just matters that we win this case for him, so that he can die on his own terms. That means that you will get on that damn stand and swear on that Bible – which, for all I know, might not even be relevant to you now that you've found Jesus on I-tier. And if you screw this up for Shay by sounding like a nut job when I question you, I will make your life miserable.' By the time Maggie finished, she was red in the face and breathless. 'This old gospel,' she said. 'Word for word?'

I nodded.

'How did you find out about it?'

'From your father,' I said.

Maggie's brows rose. 'I'm not putting a priest *and* a rabbi on the stand. The judge will be waiting for a punch line.'

I looked up at her. 'I have an idea.'

Maggie

In the client-attorney conference room outside I-tier, Shay climbed on the chair and started talking to flies. 'Go left,' he urged as he craned his neck toward the air vent. 'Come on. You can do it.'

I looked up from my notes for a moment. 'Are they pets?'

'No,' Shay said, stepping down from the chair. His hair was matted, but only on the left side, which made him look absent-minded at best and mentally ill at worst. I wondered what I could say to convince him to let me brush it before we went out in front of the judge tomorrow.

The flies were circling. 'I have a pet rabbit,' I said.

'Last week, before I was moved to I-tier, I had pets,' Shay said, then shook his head. 'It wasn't last week. It was yesterday. I can't remember.'

'It doesn't matter—'

'What's its name?'

'Sorry?'

'The rabbit.'

'Oliver,' I said, and took out of my pocket what I'd been holding for Shay. 'I brought you a gift.'

He smiled at me, his eyes piercing and suddenly focused. 'I hope it's a key.'

'Not quite.' I passed him a Snack Pack butterscotch pudding. 'I figured you don't get the good stuff in prison.'

He opened the foil top, licked it, and then carefully folded it into his breast pocket. 'Is there butter in it?'

'I don't know.'

'What about Scotch?'

I smiled. 'I truly doubt it.'

'Too bad.'

I watched him take the first bite. 'Tomorrow's going to be a big day,' I said.

In the wake of Michael's crisis of faith, I had contacted the witness he recommended – an academic named Ian Fletcher whom I vaguely remembered from a television show he used to host, where he'd go around debunking the claims of people who saw the Virgin Mary in their toast burn pattern and things like that. At first, putting him on the stand seemed to be a sure way to lose a case – but the guy had a PhD from the Princeton Theological Seminary, and there had to be some merit in putting a former atheist on the stand. If Fletcher could be convinced there was a God – be it Jesus, Allah, Yahweh, Shay, or none of the above – then surely *any* of us could.

Shay finished his pudding and handed the empty cup back to me. 'I need the foil, too,' I said. The last thing I wanted was to find out a few days from now that Shay had fashioned a shank out of the aluminum and hurt himself or someone else. He took it out of his pocket meekly and handed it back to me. 'You *do* know what's happening tomorrow, right?'

'Don't *you?*'

'Well. About the trial,' I began, 'all you have to do is sit patiently and listen. A lot of what you'll hear probably won't make sense to you.'

He looked up. 'Are you nervous?'

I was nervous, all right – and not just because this was a high-profile death penalty case that might or might not have found a constitutional loophole. I lived in a country where 85 percent of the residents called themselves Christians and about half went regularly to some form of church – religion was not about the individual to the average American; it was about the community of believers, and my whole case was about to turn that on its ear. 'Shay,' I said. 'You understand that we might lose.'

Shay nodded, dismissive. 'Where is she?'

'Who?'

'The girl. The one who needs the heart.'

'She's in the hospital.'

'Then we have to hurry,' he said.

I exhaled slowly. 'Right. I'd better go get my game face on.'

I stood up, summoning the CO to let me out of the conference room, but Shay's voice called me back. 'Don't forget to say you're sorry,' he said.

'To whom?'

By then, though, Shay was standing on the chair again, his attention focused on something else. And as I watched, seven flies landed in quick succession on the palm of his outstretched hand.

When I was five, all I wanted was a Christmas tree. My friends had them, and the menorah we lit at night paled in comparison. My father pointed out that we got eight presents, but my friends got even more than that, if you added up what was sitting underneath their tree. One cold December afternoon, my mother told my father we were heading to the movies, and instead, she drove me to the mall. We waited in line with little girls who had ribbons in their hair and fancy lace dresses, so that I could sit on Santa's lap and tell him I wanted My Pretty Pony. Then, with a candy cane fisted in my hand, we walked to the decoration display where there were fifteen Christmas trees set up – white ones with glass balls, fake balsam ones strung with red beads and bows, one that had Tinker Bell at the top and all the Disney characters dotted as ornaments. 'Like this,' my mother said, and right in the middle of the department store we lay down at a crossroads of the trees and gazed up at the blinking light displays. I thought it was the most beautiful thing I'd ever seen. 'I won't tell Daddy,' I promised, but she said that didn't matter. This wasn't about another religion, my mother explained. These were just the trappings. You could admire the wrapping, without ever taking out what was inside the box.

After I left Shay, I sat in my car and called my mother at the ChutZpah. 'Hi,' I said when she answered. 'What are you doing?'

There was a beat of silence. 'Maggie? What's wrong?'

'Nothing. I felt like calling you.'

'Did something happen? Did you get hurt?'

'Can't I call my mother just because I feel like it?'

'You *can*,' she said, 'but you *don't*.'

Well. There was just no arguing with the truth. I took a deep breath and forged ahead. 'Do you remember the time you took me to see Santa?'

'Please don't tell me you're converting. It'll kill your father.'

'I'm not converting,' I said, and my mother sighed with relief. 'I just was remembering it, that's all.'

'So you called to tell me?'

'No,' I said. 'I called to say I'm sorry.'

'For what?' My mother laughed. 'You haven't done anything.'

In that moment, I remembered us lying on the floor of the department store, gazing at the lit trees, as a security guard loomed over us. *Just give her another few minutes,* my mother had begged. June Nealon's face flashed before me. Maybe this was the job of a mother: to buy time for her child, no matter what. Even if it meant doing something she'd rather not; even if it left her flat on her back.

'Yes,' I answered. 'I know.'

'Desiring religious freedom is nothing new,' I said, standing up in front of Judge Haig at the opening of Shay Bourne's trial. 'One of the most famous cases happened more than two hundred years ago, and it didn't take place in our country – namely, because there *was* no country. A group of people who dared to hold religious beliefs different from the status quo found themselves being forced to adopt the policies of the Church of England – and instead, they chose to strike off to an unknown place across the ocean. But the Puritans liked religious freedom so much they kept it all to themselves – often persecuting people who didn't believe what they did. This is precisely why the founders of the new nation of the United States decided to put an end to religious intolerance by making religious freedom a cornerstone of this country.'

This was a nonjury trial, which meant that the only person I had to preach to was the judge; but the courtroom was still filled. There were reporters there from four networks the judge had preapproved, there were victim's rights advocates, there were death penalty supporters and death penalty opponents. The only party present in support of Shay – and my first witness – was Father Michael, seated just behind the plaintiff's table.

Beside me, Shay sat in handcuffs and ankle cuffs, linked to a belly chain. 'Thanks to the forefathers who crafted the Constitution, everyone in this country has the freedom to practice his own religion – even a prisoner on death row in New Hampshire. In fact, Congress went so far as to pass a law about it. The Religious Land Use and Institutionalized Persons Act guarantees an inmate the opportunity to worship whatever he likes as long as it doesn't impede the safety of others in the prison or affect the running of the prison. Yet Shay Bourne's constitutional right to practice his religion has been denied by the State of New Hampshire.'

I looked up at the judge. 'Shay Bourne is not a Muslim, or a Wiccan; he's not a secular humanist or a member of the Baha'i faith. In fact, his system of beliefs may not be familiar to any common world religion you can name off the top of your head. But they *are* a system of beliefs, and they include the fact that – to Shay – salvation depends on being able to donate his heart after his execution to the sister of his victim . . . an outcome that's not possible if the state uses lethal injection as a method of execution.'

I walked forward. 'Shay Bourne has been convicted of possibly the most heinous crime in the history of this state. He has appealed that conviction, and those appeals have been denied – yet he is not contesting that decision. He knows he is going to die, Your Honor. All he asks is that, again, the laws of this country be upheld – in particular, the laws that say anyone has the right to practice their religion, wherever, whenever, however. If the state agrees to his execution by hanging, and provides for the subsequent donation of his organs, the safety of other inmates isn't impeded; the running of the prison isn't affected – but it would offer a very significant personal outcome for Shay Bourne: to save a little girl's life, and in the process, to save his own soul.'

I sat back down and glanced at Shay. He had a legal pad in front of him. On it, he'd doodled a picture of a pirate with a parrot on his shoulder.

At the defense table, Gordon Greenleaf was seated beside the New Hampshire commissioner of corrections, a man with both hair and complexion the color of a potato. Greenleaf tapped his pencil twice on the desk. 'Ms Bloom brought up the founding fathers of this country. Thomas Jefferson, in fact, coined a phrase in a letter in 1789 – 'a wall of separation between church and state.' He was explaining the First Amendment – in particular the clauses about religion. And his words have been used by the Supreme Court many times – in fact, the Lemon test, which the high court has used since 1971, says that for a law to be constitutional, it must have a secular purpose, must neither advance nor inhibit religion, and must not result in excessive government entanglement with religion. That last part's an interesting bit – since Ms Bloom is both crediting the forefathers of this nation with the noble division of church and state . . . and yet simultaneously asking Your Honor to join them together.'

He stood up, walking forward. 'If you were to take her claim seriously,' Greenleaf said, 'you'd see that what she's really asking for is a legally binding sentence to be massaged, because of a loophole called religion. What's next? A convicted drug dealer asking that his sentence be overturned because heroin helps him reach nirvana? A murderer insisting that his cell door face Mecca?' Greenleaf shook his head. 'The truth is, Judge, this petition has been filed by the ACLU not because it's a valid and troublesome concern – but because it will purposefully create a three-ring circus during the state's first execution in sixty-nine years.' He waved his arm around the crowded gallery. 'And all of you are proof that it's already working.'

Greenleaf glanced at Shay. 'Nobody takes the death penalty lightly, least of all the commissioner of corrections in the State of New Hampshire. The sentence in Shay Bourne's case was death by lethal injection. That's exactly what the state has prepared and intends to carry out – with dignity and respect for all parties involved.

'Let's look at the facts here. No matter what Ms Bloom says, there is no organized religion that mandates organ donation after death as a means of reaching the afterlife. According to his records, Shay Bourne was raised in foster homes, so he can't claim that he was reared in one religious tradition that fostered organ donation. If he's converted to some religion that is now claiming that organ donation is part of its tenets, we submit to this court that it's pure bunk.' Greenleaf spread his hands. 'We know you'll listen carefully to the testimony, Your Honor, but the reality is that the Department of Corrections is not required to submit to the whim of every misguided prisoner that comes through its doors – especially one who has committed the monstrous torture and murders of two New Hampshire citizens, a child and a police officer. Don't let Ms Bloom and the ACLU take a grave matter and turn it into a spectacle. Allow the state to impose the penalty that was set forth by the court, in as civilized and professional a manner as possible.'

I glanced at Shay. On his legal pad, he'd added his initials, and the logo for the band AC/DC.

The judge pushed his glasses up his nose and looked at me. 'Ms Bloom,' he said, 'you may call your first witness.'

Michael

As soon as I was asked to approach the witness stand, I locked my gaze on Shay's. He stared back at me, silent, blank. The clerk approached, holding a Bible. 'Do you swear to tell the truth, the whole truth, and nothing but the truth, so help you God?'

The leather cover of the book was finely grained and black, worn smooth by the palms of thousands who'd recited a vow just like this one. I thought of all the times I'd held a Bible for comfort, a religious man's security blanket. I used to think it contained all the answers; now I wondered whether the right questions had even been asked. *So help me God,* I thought.

Maggie's hands were clasped lightly in front of her. 'Can you state your name and address for the record?'

'Michael Wright,' I said, clearing my throat. 'Thirty-four twenty-two High Street, in Concord.'

'How are you employed?'

'I'm a priest at St Catherine's.'

'How does one become a priest?' Maggie asked.

'You go to seminary for a certain number of years, and then you become a member of the transitional deaconate . . . learning the ropes under the guidance of a more experienced parish priest. Finally, you get ordained.'

'How long ago did you take your vows, Father?'

'It's been two years,' I said.

I could still remember the ordainment ceremony, my parents watching from the pews, their faces lit as if they had stars caught in their throats. I had been so certain, then, of my calling – of serving Jesus Christ, of who Jesus Christ was. Had I been wrong then? Or was it simply that there was more than one kind of *right*?

'As part of your duties at St Catherine's, Father, have you been a spiritual advisor for an inmate named Shay Bourne?'

'Yes.'

'And is Shay here in the courtroom today?'

'He is.'

'In fact,' Maggie said, 'he's the plaintiff in this case who was sitting beside me at that table, isn't that correct?'

'Yes.' I smiled at Shay, who looked down at the table.

'During the course of your training to become a priest, did you speak with parishioners about their religious beliefs?'

'Of course.'

'Is it part of your duty as a priest to help others become familiar with God?'

'Yes.'

'How about deepening their faith in God?'

'Absolutely.'

She turned to the judge. 'I'm going to offer up Father Michael as an expert on spiritual advice and religious beliefs, Your Honor.'

The other attorney shot up. 'Objection,' he said. 'With all due respect, is Father Michael an expert on Jewish beliefs? Methodist beliefs? Muslim ones?'

'Sustained,' the judge said. 'Father Michael may not testify as an expert on religious beliefs outside of the Catholic faith, except in his role as a spiritual advisor.'

I had no idea what that meant, and from the looks on their faces, neither did either attorney. 'What's the role of a spiritual advisor in the prison?' Maggie asked.

'You meet with inmates who would like a friend to talk to, or a voice to pray with,' I explained. 'You offer them counseling, direction, devotional materials. Basically, you're a priest making a house call.'

'How was it that you were chosen to become a spiritual advisor?'

'St Catherine's – my parish – received a request from the state prison.'

'Is Shay Catholic, Father?'

'One of his foster mothers had him baptized Catholic, so in the eyes of the Church, yes, he is. However, he does not consider himself a practicing Catholic.'

'How does that work, then? If you're a priest and he's not Catholic, how are you able to be his spiritual advisor?'

'Because my job isn't to preach to him, but to listen.'

'When was the first time you met with Shay?' Maggie asked.

'March eighth of this year,' I said. 'I've seen him once or twice a week since then.'

'At some point, did Shay discuss his desire to donate his heart to Claire Nealon, the sister of one of his victims?'

'It was the very first conversation we had,' I replied.

'How many times since have you discussed with Shay his feelings about this transplant?'

'Maybe twenty-five, thirty.'

Maggie nodded. 'There are people here today who think that Shay's desire to become an organ donor has everything to do with buying himself time, and nothing to do with religion. Do you agree with that?'

'Objection,' the other attorney said. 'Speculation.'

The judge shook his head. 'I'll allow it.'

'He'd die today, if you let him donate his heart. It's not time he wants; it's the chance to be executed in a way that would allow for a transplant.'

'Let me play devil's advocate,' Maggie said. 'We all know donating organs is selfless . . . but where's the link between donation and salvation? Was there something that convinced you this wasn't just altruism on Shay's part . . . but part of his faith?'

'Yes,' I said. 'When Shay told me what he wanted to do, he said it in a very striking way. It almost sounded like a weird riddle: "If I bring forth what's inside me, what's inside me will save me. If I don't bring forth what's inside me, what's inside me will destroy me." I found out later that Shay's statement wasn't original. He was quoting someone pretty important.'

'Who, Father?'

I looked at the judge. 'Jesus Christ.'

'Nothing further,' Maggie said, and she sat back down beside Shay.

Gordon Greenleaf frowned at me. 'Forgive my ignorance, Father. Is that from the Old Testament or the New Testament?'

'Neither,' I replied. 'It's from the Gospel of Thomas.'

This stopped the attorney in his tracks. 'Aren't all gospels *somewhere* in the Bible?'

'Objection,' Maggie called out. 'Father Michael can't respond, because he's not a religious expert.'

'*You* offered him up as one,' Greenleaf said.

Maggie shrugged. 'Then you shouldn't have objected to it.'

'I'll rephrase,' Greenleaf said. 'So, Mr Bourne quoted something that is not actually in the Bible, but you're claiming it's proof that he's motivated by religion?'

'Yes,' I said. 'Exactly.'

'Well, then, what religion does Shay practice?' Greenleaf asked.

'He doesn't label it.'

'You said he's not a practicing Catholic. Is he a practicing Jew, then?'

'No.'

'A Muslim?'

'No.'

'A Buddhist?'

'No,' I said.

'Is Mr Bourne practicing any type of organized religion that the court might be familiar with, Father?'

I hesitated. 'He's practicing a religion, but it isn't formally organized.'

'Like what? Bourneism?'

'Objection,' Maggie interrupted. 'If Shay can't name it, why do we have to?'

'Sustained,' Judge Haig said.

'Let me clarify,' Greenleaf said. 'Shay Bourne is practicing a religion you can't name, and quoting from a gospel that's not in the Bible . . . and yet somehow his desire to be an organ donor is grounded in the concept of religious salvation? Does that not strike you, Father, as the slightest bit *convenient* on Mr Bourne's part?'

He turned, as if he hadn't really expected me to give an answer, but I wasn't going to let him off that easy. 'Mr Greenleaf,' I said, 'there are all sorts of experiences that we can't really put a name to.'

'I beg your pardon?'

'The birth of a child, for one. Or the death of a parent. Falling in love. Words are like nets – we hope they'll cover what we mean, but we know they can't possibly hold that much joy, or grief, or wonder. Finding God is like that, too. If it's happened to you, you know what it feels like. But try to describe it to someone else – and language only takes you so far,' I said. 'Yes, it sounds convenient. And yes, he's the only member of his religion. And no, it doesn't have a name. But . . . I believe him.' I looked at Shay until he met my gaze. 'I believe.'

June

When Claire was awake, which was less and less often, we did not talk about the heart that might be coming for her or whether or not she'd take it. She didn't want to; I was afraid to. Instead, we talked about things that didn't matter: who'd been voted off her favorite reality TV show; how the Internet actually worked; if I'd reminded Mrs Walloughby to feed Dudley twice a day instead of three times, because he was on a diet. When Claire was asleep, I held her hand and told her about the future I dreamed of. I told her that we'd travel to Bali and live for a month in a hut perched over the ocean. I told her that I would learn to water-ski barefoot while she drove the boat, and then we'd swap places. How we would climb Mt. Katahdin, get our ears double pierced, learn how to make chocolate from scratch. I imagined her swimming up from the sandy bottom of unconsciousness, bursting through the surface, wading to where I was waiting onshore.

It was during one of Claire's afternoon drug-induced marathon naps that I began to learn about elephants. That morning, when I had gone down to the hospital cafeteria for a cup of coffee, I passed the same three retail establishments I'd passed every day for the past two weeks – a bank, a bookstore, a travel agency. Today, though, for the first time, I was magnetically drawn to a poster in the window. EXPERIENCE AFRICA, it said.

The bored college girl staffing the office was talking to her boyfriend on the phone when I walked inside, and was more than happy to send me on my way with a brochure, in lieu of actually telling me about the destination herself. 'Where were we?' I heard her say as she picked up the phone again when I left the office, and then she giggled. 'With your *teeth*?'

Upstairs in Claire's room, I pored over pictures of rooms with beds as wide as the sea, covered with crisp white linens and draped with a net of gauze. Of outside showers, exposed to the bush, so that you were as naked as the animals. Of Land Rovers and African rangers with phosphorescent smiles.

And oh, the animals – sleek leopards, with their Rorschach spots; a lioness with eyes like amber; the massive monolith of an elephant yanking a tree out of the ground.

Did you know, the brochure read, *that elephants live in a society much like ours?*

That they travel in matriarchal packs, and gestate for 22 months?

That they can communicate over a distance of 50 km?

Come track the amazing elephant in its natural habitat, the Tuli Block . . .

'What are you reading?' Claire squinted at the brochure, her voice groggy.

'Something on safaris,' I said. 'I thought maybe you and I might go on one.'

'I'm not taking that stupid heart,' Claire said, and she rolled on her side, closing her eyes again.

I would tell Claire about the elephants when she woke up, I decided. About a country where mothers and daughters walked side by side for years with their aunts and sisters. About how elephants were either right-handed or left-handed. How they could find their way home years after they'd left.

Here is what I wouldn't tell Claire, ever: That elephants know when they're close to dying, and they make their way to a riverbed for nature to take its course. That elephants bury their dead, and grieve. That naturalists have seen a mother elephant carry a dead calf for miles, cradled in her trunk, unwilling and unable to let it go.

Maggie

Nobody wanted Ian Fletcher to testify, including me.

When I'd called an emergency meeting with the judge days earlier, asking to add Fletcher to my witness list as an expert on the history of religion, I thought Gordon Greenleaf would burst a blood vessel in chambers. 'Hello?' he said. 'Rule 26(c)?'

He was talking about the Federal Rules of Civil Procedure, which said that witnesses had to be disclosed thirty days before a trial, unless otherwise directed by the court. I was banking on that last clause. 'Judge,' I said, 'we've only had two weeks to prepare for this trial – neither of us disclosed *any* of our witnesses within thirty days.'

'You don't get to sneak in an expert just because you happened to stumble over one,' Greenleaf said.

Federal court judges were notorious for trying to keep their cases on the straight and narrow. If Judge Haig allowed Fletcher to testify, it opened up a whole can of worms – Greenleaf would need to prepare his cross, and would most likely want to hire a counterexpert, which would delay the trial . . . and we all knew that couldn't happen, since we had a deadline in the strictest sense of the word. But – here was the crazy thing – Father Michael had been right. Ian Fletcher's book dovetailed so neatly with the hook I was using to drag Shay's case to a victory that it would have been a shame not to try. And even better – it provided the one element I'd been lacking in this case: a historical precedent.

I had fully convinced myself that Judge Haig would laugh in my face anyway when I tried to include a new witness at the last minute, but instead, he looked down at the name. 'Fletcher,' he said, testing the word in his mouth as if it were made of sharp stones. '*Ian* Fletcher?'

'Yes, Your Honor.'

'Is he the one who used to have a television show?'

I sucked in my breath. 'I believe so.'

'I'll be damned,' the judge said. He said this in a voice that wasn't wish-I-had-his-autograph, but more he-was-like-a-train-wreck-I-couldn't-turn-away-from.

The good news was, I was allowed to bring in my expert witness. The bad news was that Judge Haig didn't like him very much – and had in the forefront of his mind my witness's former incarnation as an atheist showboat, when I really wanted him to be seen as a grave and credible historian. Greenleaf was furious that he'd only had days to figure out what tune Fletcher was singing these days; the judge regarded him as a curiosity, and me – well, I was just praying that my whole case didn't self-destruct in the next ten minutes.

'Before we begin, Ms Bloom,' the judge said, 'I have a few questions for Dr Fletcher.'

He nodded. 'Shoot, Judge.'

'How does a man who was an atheist a decade ago convince a court that he's an expert on religion now?'

'Your Honor,' I interjected. 'I'm planning on going through Dr Fletcher's credentials . . .'

'I didn't ask *you*, Ms Bloom,' he said.

But Ian Fletcher wasn't rattled. 'You know what they say, Your Honor. Sinners make the best reformed saints.' He grinned, a slow and lazy smile that reminded me of a cat in the sunlight. 'I guess finding God is like seeing a ghost – you can be a skeptic until you come face-to-face with what you said doesn't exist.'

'So you're a religious man now?' the judge asked.

'I'm a *spiritual* man,' Fletcher corrected. 'And I do think there's a difference. But being spiritual doesn't pay the rent, which is why I have degrees from Princeton and Harvard, three *New York Times* bestselling nonfiction books, forty-two published articles on the origins of world religions, and positions on six interfaith councils, including one that advises the current administration.'

The judge nodded, making notes; and Greenleaf stipulated to the list of Fletcher's credentials. 'I might as well start with where Judge Haig left off,' I said, beginning the direct examination. 'It's pretty rare for an atheist to get interested in religion. Did you just sort of wake up one day and find Jesus?'

'It's not like you're vacuuming under the sofa cushions and bingo, there he is. My interest grew more from a historical standpoint, because these days, people act like faith grows in a vacuum. When you break down religions and look politically and economically and socially at what was going on during their births, it changes the way you think.'

'Dr Fletcher, do you have to be part of a group to be part of a religion?'

'Not only *can* religion be individualized – it *has* been, in the past. In 1945, a discovery was made in Egypt: fifty-two texts that were labeled gospels – and that weren't part of the Bible. Some of them were full of sayings that would be familiar to anyone who's gone to Sunday school . . . and some of them, to be honest, were really bizarre. They were scientifically dated from the second century, roughly thirty to eighty years younger than the gospels in the New Testament. And they belonged to a group called Gnostic Christians – a splinter group from Orthodox Christianity, who believed that true religious enlightenment meant undertaking a very personal, individual quest to know yourself, not by your socioeconomic status or profession, but at a deeper core.'

'Hang on,' I said. 'After Jesus's death, there was more than one kind of Christian?'

'Oh, there were dozens.'

'And they had their own Bibles?'

'They had their own *gospels*,' Fletcher corrected. 'The New Testament – in particular, Matthew, Mark, Luke, and John – were the ones that the orthodoxy chose to uphold. The Gnostic

Christians preferred texts like the Gospel of Thomas, and the
Gospel of Truth, and the Gospel of Mary Magdalene.'

'Did those gospels talk about Jesus, too?'

'Yes, except the Jesus they describe isn't the one you'd recognize from the Bible. *That* Jesus is very different from the humans
he's come here to save. But the Gospel of Thomas – my personal
favorite from Nag Hammadi – says Jesus is a guide to help you
figure out all you have in *common* with God. So if you were a
Gnostic Christian, you would have *expected* the road to salvation
to be different for everyone.'

'Like donating your heart to someone who needs it . . . ?'

'Exactly,' Fletcher said.

'Wow,' I said, playing dumb. 'How come this stuff isn't taught
in Sunday school?'

'Because the Orthodox Christian Church felt threatened by the
Gnostics. They called their gospels heresy, and the Nag Hammadi
texts were hidden for two thousand years.'

'Father Wright said that Shay Bourne quoted from the Gospel
of Thomas. Do you have any idea where he would have stumbled
over that text?'

'Maybe he read my book,' Fletcher said, smiling widely, and the
people in the gallery laughed.

'In your opinion, Doctor, could a religion that only one person
believes and follows still be valid?'

'An individual can have a religion,' he said. 'He can't have a
religious *institution*. But it seems to me that Shay Bourne is standing
in a tradition similar to the ones the Gnostic Christians did nearly
two thousand years ago. He's not the first to say that he can't name
his faith. He's not the first to find a path to salvation that is different
from others you've heard about. And he's certainly not the first to
mistrust the body – to literally want to give it away, as a means
to finding divinity inside oneself. But just because he doesn't have
a church with a white steeple over his head, or a temple with a
six-pointed star surrounding him, doesn't mean that his beliefs
are any less worthy.'

I beamed at him. Fletcher was easy to listen to, interesting, and he didn't sound like a left-wing nutcase. Or so I thought, until I heard Judge Haig exhale heavily and say court was recessed until the next day.

Lucius

I was painting when Shay returned from his first day of trial, huddled and withdrawn, as going to court made most of us. I'd been working on the portrait all day, and I was quite pleased with the way it was turning out. I glanced up when Shay was escorted past my cell, but didn't speak to him. Better to let him come back to us on his own time.

Not twenty minutes afterward, a long, low keen filled the tier. At first I thought Shay was crying, letting the stress of the day bleed from him, but then I realized that the sound was coming from Calloway Reece's cell. 'Come on,' he moaned. He started smacking his fists against the door of his cell. 'Bourne,' he called out. 'Bourne, I need your help.'

'Leave me alone,' Shay said.

'It's the bird, man. I can't get him to wake up.'

The fact that Batman the Robin had survived inside I-tier for several weeks on crusts of toast and bits of oatmeal was a wonder in its own right, not to mention the fact that he'd cheated death once before.

'Give him CPR,' Joey Kunz suggested.

'You can't do fucking CPR on a bird,' Calloway snapped. 'They got *beaks.*'

I put down the makeshift brush I was using to paint – a rolled wad of toilet paper – and angled my mirror-shank out my door so that I could see. In his enormous palm, Calloway cradled the bird, which lay on its side, unmoving.

'Shay,' he begged, *'please.'*

There was no response from Shay's cell. 'Fish him to me,' I said, and crouched down with my line. I was worried that the bird had grown too big to make it through the little slit at the bottom, but Calloway wrapped him in a handkerchief, roped the top, and sent the slight weight in a wide arc across the floor of the catwalk. I knotted my string with Calloway's and gently drew the bird toward me.

I couldn't resist unwrapping the kerchief to peek. Batman's eyelid was purple and creased, his tail feathers spread like a fan. The tiny hooks on the ends of his claws were as sharp as pins. When I touched them, the bird did not even twitch. I placed my forefinger beneath the wing – did birds have hearts where we did? – and felt nothing.

'Shay,' I said quietly. 'I know you're tired. And I know you've got your own stuff going on. But please. Just take a look.'

Five whole minutes passed, long enough for me to give up. I wrapped the bird in the cloth again and tied him to the end of my fishing line, cast him onto the catwalk for Calloway to retrieve. But before his line could tangle with mine, another whizzed out, and Shay intercepted the bird.

In my mirror, I watched Shay take Batman from the kerchief, hold him in his hand. He stroked the head with his finger; he gingerly covered the body with his other hand, as if he had caught a star between his palms. I held my breath, watching for that flutter or feather or the faintest cheep, but after a few moments Shay just wrapped the bird up again.

'Hey!' Calloway had been watching, too. 'You didn't *do* anything!'

'Leave me alone,' Shay repeated. The air had gone bitter as almonds; I could barely stand to breathe it. I watched him fish back that dead bird, and all of our hopes along with it.

Maggie

When Gordon Greenleaf stood up, his knees creaked. 'You've studied comparative world religions in the course of your research?' he asked Fletcher.

'Yes.'

'Do different religions take a stand on organ donation?'

'Yes,' Fletcher said. 'Catholics believe only in transplants done after death – you can't risk killing the donor, for example, during the donation. They fully support organ donation, as do Jews and Muslims. Buddhists and Hindus believe organ donation is a matter of individual conscience, and they put high value on acts of compassion.'

'Do any of those religions *require* you to donate organs as a means to salvation?'

'No,' Fletcher said.

'Are there Gnostic Christians practicing today?'

'No,' Fletcher said. 'The religion died out.'

'How come?'

'When you have a belief system that says you shouldn't listen to the clergy, and that you should continually ask questions, instead of accepting doctrine, it's hard to form a community. On the other hand, the Orthodox Christians were delineating the steps to being card-carrying members of the group – confess the creed, accept baptism, worship, obey the priests. Plus, *their* Jesus was someone the average Joe could relate to – someone who'd been born, had an overprotective mom, suffered, and died. That was a much easier sell than the Gnostic Jesus – who was never even human. The rest of the Gnostics' decline,' Fletcher said, 'was political. In A.D. 312, Constantine, the Roman emperor, saw a crucifix in the sky and converted to Christianity. The Catholic Church became part of the Holy Roman Empire . . . and having Gnostic texts and beliefs were punishable by death.'

'So, it's fair to say no one's practiced Gnostic Christianity for fifteen hundred years?' Greenleaf said.

'Not formally. But there are elements of Gnostic belief in other religions that have survived. For example, Gnostics recognized the difference between the reality of God, which was impossible to describe with language, and the image of God as we knew it. This sounds a lot like Jewish mysticism, where you find God being described as streams of energy, male and female, which pool together into a divine source; or God as the source of all sounds at once. And Buddhist enlightenment is very much like the Gnostic idea that we live in a land of oblivion, but can waken spiritually right here while we're still part of this world.'

'But Shay Bourne can't be a follower of a religion that no longer exists, isn't that true?'

He hesitated. 'From what I understand, donating his heart is Shay Bourne's attempt to learn who he is, who he wants to be, how he is connected to others. And in that very basic sense, the Gnostics would agree that he's found the part of him that comes closest to being divine.' Fletcher looked up. 'A Gnostic Christian would tell you that a man on death row is more like us than unlike us. And that – as Mr Bourne seems to be trying to suggest – he still has something to offer the world.'

'Yeah. Whatever.' Greenleaf raised a brow. 'Have you ever even met Shay Bourne?'

'Actually,' Fletcher said, 'no.'

'So for all you know, he doesn't have any religious beliefs at all. This could all be some grand plan to delay his execution, couldn't it?'

'I've spoken with his spiritual advisor.'

The lawyer scoffed. 'You've got a guy practicing a religion by

himself that seems to hearken back to a religious sect that died
out thousands of years ago. Isn't it possible that this is a bit too
. . . easy? That Shay Bourne could just be making it all up as he
goes along?'

Fletcher smiled. 'A lot of people thought that about Jesus.'

'Dr Fletcher,' Greenleaf said, 'are you telling this court that Shay
Bourne is a messiah?'

Fletcher shook his head. 'Your words, not mine.'

'Then how about your stepdaughter's words?' Greenleaf asked.
'Or is this some kind of family trait you all have, running into
God in state prisons and elementary schools and Laundromats?'

'Objection,' I said. 'My witness isn't on trial here.'

Greenleaf shrugged. 'His ability to discuss the history of
Christianity is—'

'Overruled,' Judge Haig said.

Fletcher narrowed his eyes. 'What my daughter did or didn't
see has no bearing on Shay Bourne's request to donate his heart.'

'Did you believe she was a fake when you first met her?'

'The more I spoke with her, the more I—'

'When you *first* met her,' Greenleaf interrupted, 'did you believe
she was a fake?'

'Yes,' Fletcher admitted.

'And yet, with no personal contact, you were willing to testify
in a court of law that Mr Bourne's request to donate his organs
could be massaged to fit your loose definition of a religion.'
Greenleaf glanced at him. 'I guess, in your case, old habits die
fairly easy.'

'Objection!'

'Withdrawn.' Greenleaf started back to his seat, but then turned.
'Just one more question, Dr Fletcher – this daughter of yours. She
was seven years old when she found herself at the center of a religious media circus not unlike this one, correct?'

'Yes.'

'Are you aware that's the same age of the little girl Shay Bourne
murdered?'

A muscle in Fletcher's jaw twitched. 'No. I wasn't.'

'How do you think you'd feel about God if your stepdaughter was the one who'd been killed?'

I shot to my feet. *'Objection!'*

'I'll allow it,' the judge answered.

Fletcher paused. 'I think that kind of tragedy would test anyone's faith.'

Gordon Greenleaf folded his arms. 'Then it's not faith,' he said. 'It's being a chameleon.'

Michael

During the lunch recess, I went to see Shay in his holding cell. He was sitting on the floor, near the bars, while a U.S. marshal sat outside on a stool. Shay held a pencil and scrap of paper, as if he were conducting an interview.

'H,' the marshal said, and Shay shook his head. 'M?'

Shay scribbled something on the paper. 'I'm down to your last toe, dude.'

The marshal sucked in his breath. 'K.'

Shay grinned. 'I win.' He scrawled something else on the page and passed it through the bars – only then did I notice that it had been a game of hangman, and that this time around, Shay was the executioner.

Scowling, the marshal stared down at the paper. '*Szygszyg* isn't a real word.'

'You didn't say that it had to be *real* when we started playing,' Shay replied, and then he noticed me standing at the threshold of the door.

'I'm Shay's spiritual advisor,' I told the marshal. 'Can we have a minute?'

'No problem. I have to take a whiz.' He stood up, offering me the stool he was vacating, and headed out of the room.

'How are you doing?' I said quietly.

Shay walked to the back of the cell, where he lay down on the metal bunk and faced the wall.

'I want to talk to you, Shay.'

'Just because you want to talk doesn't mean I want to listen.'

I sank down on the stool. 'I was the last one on your jury to vote for the death penalty,' I said. 'I was the reason we deliberated so long. And even after I'd been convinced by the rest of the jury that this was the best sentence, I didn't feel good about it. I kept having panic attacks. One day, during one, I stumbled into a cathedral and started to pray. The more I did it, the fewer panic attacks I had.' I clasped my hands between my knees. 'I thought that was a sign from God.'

Still with his back to me, Shay snorted.

'I still think it's a sign from God, because it's brought me back into your life.'

Shay rolled onto his back and flung one arm over his eyes. 'Don't kid yourself,' he said. 'It's brought you back into my death.'

Ian Fletcher was already standing at a urinal when I ran into the men's room. I had been hoping it would be empty. Shay's comment – the bald truth – had made me so sick to my stomach that I'd rushed out of the holding cell without explanation. I pushed into a stall, fell to my knees, and got violently ill.

No matter how much I wanted to fool myself – no matter what I said about atoning for my past sins – the bottom line was that for the second time in my life, my actions were going to result in the death of Shay Bourne.

Fletcher pushed the door of the stall open and put his hand on my shoulder. 'Father? You all right?'

I wiped my mouth, slowly got to my feet. 'I'm fine,' I said, then shook my head. 'No, actually, I'm awful.'

I walked to the sink, turned on the faucet, and splashed water on my face as Fletcher watched. 'Do you need to sit down or something?'

I dried my face with a paper towel he passed me. And suddenly, I wanted someone else to bear this burden. Ian Fletcher was a man who'd unraveled secrets from two thousand years ago; surely he could keep one of mine. 'I was on his jury,' I murmured into the recycled brown paper.

'I'm sorry?'

No, I am, I thought. I met Fletcher's gaze. 'I was on the jury that sentenced Shay Bourne to death. Before I joined the priesthood.'

Fletcher let out a long, low whistle. 'Does he know?'

'I told him a few days ago.'

'And his lawyer?'

I shook my head. 'I keep thinking that this must be how Judas felt after turning Jesus in.'

Fletcher's mouth turned up at the corners. 'Actually, there's a recently discovered Gnostic gospel – the Gospel of Judas – and there's very little in there about betrayal. In fact, this gospel paints Judas as Jesus's confidant – the only one he trusted to make what needed to happen, happen.'

'Even if it was an assisted suicide,' I said, 'I'm sure Judas felt like crap about it afterward. I mean, he *killed* himself.'

'Well,' Fletcher said, 'there was *that*.'

'What would you do if you were me?' I asked. 'Would you carry through with this? Help Shay donate his heart?'

'I guess that depends on why you're helping him,' Fletcher said slowly. 'Is it to save him, like you said on the stand? Or are you really just trying to save yourself?' He shook his head. 'If man had the answers for questions like those, there wouldn't be a need for religion. Good luck, Father.'

I went back into the stall and closed the lid of the toilet, sat down. I slipped my rosary out of my pocket and whispered the familiar words of the prayers, sweet in my mouth like sucking candies. Finding God's grace wasn't like locating missing keys or the forgotten name of a 1940s pinup girl – it was more of a feeling: the sun breaking through an overcast morning, the softest bed sinking under your weight. And, of course, you couldn't find God's grace unless you admitted you were lost.

A bathroom stall at the federal courthouse might not be the most likely spot to find God's grace, but that didn't mean it couldn't be done.

Find God's grace.

Find Grace.

If Shay was willing to give up his heart, then the least I could do was make sure he'd be remembered in someone else's. Someone who – unlike me – had never condemned him.

That was when I decided to find Shay's sister.

June

It is not an easy thing to pick the clothes in which your child will be buried. I had been told by the funeral director, after the murders, to think about it. He suggested something that represented her, a beautiful girl – such as a nice little dress, one that opened up the back, preferably. He asked me to bring in a picture of her so that he could use makeup to match the blush of her cheek, the natural color of her skin, her hairstyle.

What I had wanted to say to him was: Elizabeth hated dresses. She would have worn pants without buttons, because they were frustrating, or possibly last year's Halloween costume, or the tiny set of doctors' scrubs she got for Christmas – I had, just days before, found her 'operating' on an overgrown zucchini that was the size of a newborn. I would have told him that Elizabeth did not have a hairstyle, because you could not ground her long enough to brush it, much less braid or curl. And that I did not want him putting makeup on her face, not when I would never have that bonding moment between a mother and daughter in a bathroom before an elegant night on the town, when I could let her try the eye shadow, a smudge of mascara, pink lipstick.

The funeral director told me that it might be nice to have a table of mementos that meant something to Elizabeth – stuffed animals or family vacation photos, chocolate chip cookies. To play her favorite music. To let her school friends write messages to her, which could be buried in a silk satchel inside the coffin.

What I wanted to say to him was: Don't you realize that by telling me the same things you tell everyone else about how to make a meaningful funeral, you are making it meaningless? That Elizabeth deserved fireworks, an angel choir, the world turning backward on its axis.

In the end, I had dressed Elizabeth in a ballerina's tutu, one she somehow always wanted to wear when we went grocery shopping, and that I always made her take off before we left. I let the funeral director put makeup on her face for the first time. I gave her a stuffed dog, her stepfather, and most of my heart to take with her.

It was not an open-casket funeral; but before we left for the graveside service, the funeral director lifted the cover to make final adjustments. At that moment, I pushed him out of the way. *Let me*, I had said.

Kurt was wearing his uniform, as befitted a police officer killed in the line of duty. He looked exactly like he did every day, except for the fine white line around his finger where his wedding ring had been. That, I now wore on a chain around my neck.

Elizabeth looked delicate, angelic. Her hair was tied up in matching ribbons. Her arm was around her stepfather's waist.

I reached into the coffin, and the moment my hand brushed my daughter's cheek I shivered, because somehow I had still expected it to be warm – not this fake-flesh, this cool-to-the-touch skin. I tugged the ribbons out of her hair, gently lifted her head, fanned her hair on both sides of her face. I tugged the left leotard sleeve down a quarter inch, to match the one on the right.

I hope you're pleased, the funeral director had said.

It didn't look like Elizabeth, not one bit, because she was too perfect. My daughter would have been rumpled and untucked, her hands dirty from chasing frogs, her socks mismatched, her wrists ringed with bracelets she'd beaded herself.

But in a world where things happen that shouldn't, you find yourself saying and doing things that are the complete opposite of what you mean. So I had nodded, and watched him seal away the two people I loved most in this world.

Now I found myself in the same position I'd been in eleven

years ago, standing in the middle of my daughter's bedroom and sifting through her clothes. I sorted through shirts and skirts and tights, jeans as soft as flannel and a sweatshirt that still smelled like the apple orchard where she last wore it. I chose a pair of flared black leggings and a long-sleeved tee that had Tinker Bell printed on it – clothes that I had seen Claire wear on the laziest of Sundays, when it was snowing and there was nothing to be done but read the Sunday paper and doze with your cheek pressed against the wall of heat thrown by the fireplace. I picked out a pair of underwear – SATURDAY, it read across the front, but I couldn't find any other days of the week scattered in the drawer. It was when I was looking that I found, wrapped in a red bandanna, the photograph. In a tiny silver oval frame, I thought at first it was one of Claire's baby pictures – and then I realized it was Elizabeth.

The frame used to sit on top of the piano that nobody played anymore, gathering dust. The fact that I never even noticed it was missing was a testament to the fact that I must have learned how to live again.

Which is why I collected the clothes and put them into a shopping bag to take to the hospital: an outfit in which I sincerely hoped I would not bury my daughter, but instead, bring her back home.

Lucius

These nights, I slept well. There were no more sweats, no diarrhea, no fevers to keep me thrashing in my bunk. Crash Vitale was still in solitary, so his rants didn't wake me. From time to time, the extra officer who'd been assigned to Shay for protection would prowl through the tier, his boots a soft-soled shuffle on the catwalk.

I had been sleeping so well, in fact, that I was surprised I woke up to the quiet conversation going on in the cell next door to mine. 'Will you just let me explain?' Shay asked. 'What if there's another way?'

I waited to hear whom he was talking to, but there was no answer.

'Shay?' I said. 'Are you okay?'

'I tried to give away my heart,' I heard him say. 'And look at what it turned into.' Shay kicked at the wall; something heavy in his cell tumbled to the floor. 'I know what you want. But do you know what *I* want?'

'Shay?'

His voice was just a braid of breath. '*Abba?*'

'It's me. Lucius.'

There was a beat of silence. 'You were listening to my conversation.'

Was it a conversation if you were having a monologue in your own cell? 'I didn't mean to . . . you woke me up.'

'Why were you asleep?' Shay asked.

'Because it's three in the morning?' I replied. 'Because that's what you're supposed to be doing?'

'What I'm supposed to be doing,' Shay repeated. 'Right.'

There was a thud, and I realized Shay had fallen. The last time that had happened, he'd been having a seizure. I scrabbled underneath the bunk and pulled out the mirror-shank. 'Shay,' I called out. 'Shay?'

In the reflection, I could see him. He was on his knees in the front of the cell, with his hands spread wide. His head was bowed, and he was bathed in sweat, which – from the dim crimson light on the catwalk – looked like beads of blood.

'Go away,' he said, and I withdrew the mirror from the slats of my own door, giving him privacy.

As I hid away my makeshift mirror, I caught a glimpse of my own reflection. Like Shay's, my skin looked scarlet. And yet even that didn't stop me from noticing the familiar ruby sore that had opened up once again across my forehead – a scar, a stain, a planet's moving storm.

Michael

Shay's last foster mother, Renata Ledoux, was a Catholic who lived in Bethlehem, New Hampshire, and as I'd traveled up to meet with her, the irony of the name of the town where Shay had spent his teenage years did not escape me. I was wearing my collar and had on my gravest priest demeanor, because I was pulling out all the stops. I was going to say whatever was necessary to find out what had happened to Grace.

As it turned out, though, it hardly took any work at all. Renata invited me in for tea, and when I told her I had a message for Grace from a person in my congregation, she simply wrote out an address and handed it to me. 'We're still in touch,' she said simply. 'Gracie was a good girl.'

I couldn't help but wonder what she thought of Shay. 'Didn't she have a brother?'

'That boy,' Renata had said, 'deserves to burn in hell.'

It was ludicrous to believe that Renata had not heard about Shay's death sentence – the news would have reached up here, even in rural Bethlehem. I had thought, maybe, as his foster mother, she'd at least harbor some soft spot for him. But then again, the boy she'd raised had left her home to go to juvenile prison, and had grown up to become a convicted murderer. 'Yes,' I'd said. 'Well.'

Now, twenty minutes later, I was approaching Grace's house, and hoping for a better reception. It was the pink one with gray shutters and the number 131 on a carved stone at the end of the drive – but the shades were drawn, the garage door was closed. There were no plants hanging on the porch, no doors open for a breeze, no outgoing mail in the box – nothing to indicate that the inhabitant was home.

I got out of my car and rang the doorbell. Twice.

Well, I could leave a note and ask her to call me. It would take more time – time Shay did not really have – but if it was the best I could do, then so be it.

Just then the door opened just a crack. 'Yes?' a voice inside murmured.

I tried to see into the foyer, but it was pitch-dark. 'Does Grace Bourne live here?'

A hesitation. 'That's me.'

'I'm Father Michael Wright. I have a message for you, from one of the parishioners in my congregation.'

A slender hand slipped out. 'You can give it to me,' Grace said.

'Actually, could I just come in for a bit – use your restroom? It's been a long drive from Concord . . .'

She hesitated – I suppose I would, too, if a strange man showed up at my door and I was a woman living alone, even if he was wearing a collar. But the door opened wide and Grace stepped back to let me in. Her head was ducked to the side; a long curtain of black hair hung over her face. I caught a glimpse of long dark lashes and a ruby of a mouth; you could tell, even at first glance, how pretty she must be. I wondered if she was agoraphobic, painfully shy. I wondered who had hurt her so much that she was afraid of the rest of the world.

I wondered if it was Shay.

'Grace,' I said, reaching for her hand. 'It's nice to meet you.'

She lifted her chin then, and the screen of hair fell back. The entire left side of Grace Bourne's face was ravaged and pitted, a lava flow of skin that had been stretched and sewed to cover an extensive burn.

'Boo,' she said.

'I . . . I'm sorry. I didn't mean . . .'

'Everyone stares,' Grace said quietly. 'Even the ones who try not to.'

There was a fire, Shay had said. *I don't want to talk about it.*

'I'm sorry.'

'Yeah, you said that already. The bathroom's down the hall.'

I put a hand on her arm. There were patches of skin there, too, that were scarred. 'Grace. That message – it's from your brother.'

She took a step away from me, stunned. 'You know Shay?'

'He needs to see you, Grace. He's going to die soon.'

'What did he say about me?'

'Not a lot,' I admitted. 'But you're the only family he has.'

'Do you know about the fire?' Grace asked.

'Yes. It was why he went to juvenile prison.'

'Did he tell you that our foster father died in it?'

This time, it was my turn to be surprised. A juvenile record would be sealed, which is why I hadn't known during the capital murder trial what Shay had been convicted of. I'd assumed, when fire had been mentioned, that it was arson. I hadn't realized that the charges might have included negligent homicide, or even manslaughter. And I understood exactly why, now, Renata Ledoux might viscerally hate Shay.

Grace was staring at me intently. 'Did he ask to see me?'

'He doesn't actually know I'm here.'

She turned away, but not before I saw that she had started to cry. 'He didn't want me at his trial.'

'He probably didn't want you to have to witness that.'

'You don't know anything.' She buried her face in her hands.

'Grace,' I said, 'come back with me. Come see him.'

'I can't,' she sobbed. 'I can't. You don't understand.'

But I was beginning to: Shay had set the fire that had disfigured her. 'That's all the more reason to meet with him. Forgive him, before it's too late.'

'Forgive him? Forgive *him?*' Grace parroted. 'No matter what I say, it won't change what happened. You don't get to do your life over.' She glanced away. 'I think . . . I just . . . you should go.'

It was my dismissal. I nodded, accepting.

'The bathroom's the second door on the right.'

Right – my ruse to get inside. I walked down the hall to a restroom that was floral, overpowering in a scent of air freshener and
rose potpourri. There were little crocheted toilet paper holders, a
crocheted bra for the toilet tank, and a crocheted cover for the
Kleenex box. There were roses on the shower curtain, and art on
the walls – framed prints of flowers, except for one of a child's
drawing – a dragon, or maybe a lizard. The room felt like the
kind of abode for an elderly lady who'd lost count of her cats. It
was stifling; slowly, Grace Bourne was suffocating herself to death.

If Shay knew that his sister forgave him for the fire, then maybe
– even if he wasn't allowed to donate his heart – it would be
enough to let him die in peace. Grace was in no condition to be
convinced right now, but I could work on her. I'd get her phone
number and call her, until I'd worn down her resistance.

I opened the sliding mirrored medicine cabinet, looking for a
prescription with Grace's phone number so that I could copy it
down. There were lotions and creams and exfoliants, toothpaste
and floss and deodorant. There was also a medicine bottle of
Ambien, with Grace's phone number across the top of the label.
I wrote it on the inside of my palm with a pen and set the pills
back on the shelf, beside a small pewter frame. Two tiny children
sat at a table: Grace in a high chair with a glass of milk in front
of her, and Shay hunched over a picture he was drawing. A dragon,
or maybe a lizard.

He was smiling, so wide it looked like it might hurt.

Every inmate is someone's child. And so is every victim.

I walked out of the bathroom. Handing Grace a card with my
name and number on it, I thanked her. 'Just in case you change
your mind.'

'Mine was never the one that needed changing,' Grace said, and
closed the door behind me. Immediately I heard the bolt slide
shut, the curtain in the front window rustle. I kept envisioning
the dragon picture, which was carefully matted and framed in the
bathroom. TO GRACIE, it had said in the upper left-hand corner.

I was all the way to Crawford Notch before I realized what had been niggling in my mind about that photo of Shay as a child. In it, he'd been holding a pen in his right hand. But in prison – when he ate, when he wrote – he was a lefty.

Could someone change so radically over a lifetime? Or could all of these changes in Shay – from his dominant hand to his miracles to his ability to quote the Gospel of Thomas – have come from some . . . possession? It sounded like some bad science fiction movie, but that wasn't to say it couldn't happen. If prophets could be overtaken by the Holy Spirit, why not a murderer?

Or, maybe it was simpler than that. Maybe who we were in the past informed who we chose to be in the future. Maybe Shay had intentionally shifted his writing hand. Maybe he cultivated miracles, to make up for a sin as horrible as setting a fire that took the lives of two people – one literal, one metaphorical. It struck me that even in the Bible, there was no record of Jesus's life between the ages of eight and thirty-three. What if he'd done something awful; what if his later years were a response to that?

You could do a horrible thing, and then spend your whole natural life trying to atone.

I knew that better than anyone.

Maggie

The last conversation I had with Shay Bourne, before putting him on the stand as a witness, had not gone well. In the holding cell, I'd reminded him what was going to happen in court. Shay didn't deal well with curves being thrown at him; he could just as likely become belligerent as curl up in a ball beneath the wooden stand. Either way, the judge would think he was crazy – and that couldn't happen.

'So after the marshal helps you into the seat,' I had explained, 'they're going to bring you a Bible.'

'I don't need one.'

'Right. But they need you to swear on it.'

'I want to swear on a comic book,' Shay had replied. 'Or a *Playboy* magazine.'

'You have to swear on a Bible,' I'd said, 'because we have to play by their rules before we're allowed to change the game.'

Just then, a U.S. marshal had come to tell me that court was about to convene. 'Remember,' I had said to Shay, 'focus only on me. Nothing else in that courtroom's important. It's just us, having a chat.'

He had nodded, but I could see that he was jittery. And now, as I watched him being brought into the courtroom, everyone else could see it, too. He was bound at the ankles and the wrists, with a belly chain to link the others; the links rattled as he shuddered into his seat beside me. His head was ducked, and he was murmuring words no one but I could hear. He was actually cursing out one of the U.S. marshals who'd led him into the courtroom, but with any luck, people who watched his mouth moving silently would think he was praying.

As soon as I put him on the witness stand, a quiet pall fell over the people in the gallery. *You are not like us,* their silence seemed to say. *You never will be.* And there, without me asking a single question, was my answer: no amount of piousness could erase the stain on the hands of a murderer.

I walked in front of Shay and waited until he caught my eye. *Focus,* I mouthed, and he nodded. He gripped the front of the witness box railing, and his chains clinked.

Dammit. I'd forgotten to tell him to keep his hands in his lap. It would be less of a reminder to the judge and the gallery that he was a convicted felon.

'Shay,' I asked, 'why do you want to donate your heart?'

He stared right at me. Good boy. 'I have to save her.'

'Who?'

'Claire Nealon.'

'Well,' I said, 'you're not the only person in the world who can save Claire. There are other suitable heart donors.'

'I'm the one who took the most away from her,' Shay said, just like we had practiced. 'I have the most to give back to her.'

'Is this about clearing your conscience?' I asked.

Shay shook his head. 'It's about clearing the slate.'

So far, I thought, *so good.* He sounded rational, and clear, and calm.

'Maggie?' Shay said just then. 'Can I stop now?'

I smiled tightly. 'Not quite yet, Shay. We've got a few more questions.'

'The questions are bullshit.'

There was a gasp in the rear of the gallery – probably one of the blue-haired ladies I'd seen filing in with their Bibles wrapped in protective quilted cozies, who hadn't stumbled across a cuss word since before menopause. 'Shay,' I said, 'we don't use that language in court. Remember?'

'Why is it called court?' he asked. 'It's not like a tennis court or a basketball court, where you're playing a game. Or maybe you are, and that's why there's a winner and a loser, except it has nothing to do with how well you make a three-point shot or how fast your serve is.' He looked at Judge Haig. 'I bet you play golf.'

'Ms Bloom,' the judge said. 'Control your witness.'

If Shay didn't shut up, I was going to personally cover his mouth with my hand. 'Shay, tell me about your religious upbringing as a child,' I said firmly.

'Religion's a cult. You don't get to choose your own religion. You're what your parents tell you you are; it's not upbringing at all, just a brainwashing. When a baby's getting water poured over his head at a christening he can't say, "Hey, man, I'd rather be a Hindu," can he?'

'Shay, I know this is hard for you, and I know that being here is very distracting,' I said. 'But I need you to listen to the question I'm asking, and answer it. Did you go to church when you were a kid?'

'Part of the time. And part of the time I didn't go anywhere at all, except hide in the closet so I wouldn't get beat up by another kid or the foster dad, who'd try to keep everyone in line with a metal hairbrush. It kept us in line, all right, all the way down our backs. The whole foster care system in this country is a joke; it ought to be called foster *don't* care, don't give a shit except for the stipend you're getting from the—'

'Shay!' I warned him with a flash of my eyes. 'Do you believe in God?'

This question, somehow, seemed to calm him down. 'I *know* God,' Shay said.

'Tell me how.'

'Everyone's got a little God in them . . . and a little murder in them, too. It's how your life turns out that makes you lean to one side or the other.'

'What's God like?'

'Math,' Shay said. 'An equation. Except when you take everything away, you get infinity, instead of zero.'

'And where does God live, Shay?'

He leaned forward, lifted his chained hands so that the metal chinked. He pointed to his heart. 'Here.'

'You said you used to go to church when you were a kid. Is the God you believe in today the same God you were taught about at church?'

Shay shrugged. 'Whatever road you take, the view is going to be the same.'

I was nearly a hundred percent certain I'd heard that phrase before, at the one and only Bikram yoga class I'd attended, before I decided that my body wasn't meant to bend in certain ways. I couldn't believe Greenleaf wasn't objecting, on the grounds that channeling the Dalai Lama wasn't the same as answering a question. Then again, I *could* believe Greenleaf wasn't objecting. The more Shay said, the crazier he appeared. It was hard to take someone's claims about religion seriously when he sounded delusional; Shay was digging a grave big enough for both of us.

'If the judge orders you to die by lethal injection, Shay, and you can't donate your heart — will that upset God?' I asked.

'It'll upset me. So yeah, it'll upset God.'

'Well, then,' I said, 'what is it about giving your heart to Claire Nealon that will *please* God?'

He smiled at me then — the sort of smile you see on the faces of saints in frescoes, and that makes you wish you knew their secret. 'My end,' Shay said, 'is her beginning.'

I had a few more questions, but to be honest, I was terrified of what Shay might say. He already was talking in riddles. 'Thank you,' I replied, and sat down.

'I have a question, Mr Bourne,' Judge Haig said. 'There's a lot of talk about odd things that have occurred at the prison. Do you believe you can perform miracles?'

Shay looked at him. 'Do *you*?'

'I'm sorry, but that's not how a courtroom works. I'm not allowed to answer your question, but you still need to answer mine. So,' the judge said, 'do you believe you can perform miracles?'

'I just did what I was supposed to. You can call that whatever
you want.'

The judge shook his head. 'Mr Greenleaf, your witness.'

Suddenly, a man in the gallery stood up. He unzipped his jacket,
revealing a T-shirt that had been emblazoned with the numbers
3:16. He started yelling, his voice hoarse. 'For God so loved the
world that he gave his only son—' By then, two U.S. marshals
had descended, hauling him out of his seat and dragging him up
the alley, as the news cameras swiveled to follow the action. 'His
only son!' the man yelled. '*Only!* You are going to hell once they
pump your veins full of—' The doors of the courtroom banged
shut behind him, and then it was utterly silent.

It was impressive that this man had gotten into the court in the
first place – there were checkpoints with metal detectors and
marshals in place before you entered. But his weapon had been
the fundamental fury of his righteousness, and at that moment, I
would have been hard-pressed to decide whether he or Shay had
come off looking worse.

'Yes,' Gordon Greenleaf said, getting to his feet. 'Well.' He walked
toward Shay, who rested his chained hands on the witness stand
rail again. 'You're the only person who subscribes to your religion?'

'No.'

'No?'

'I don't belong to a religion. Religion's the reason the world's
falling apart – did you see that guy get carted out of here? *That's*
what religion does. It points a finger. It causes wars. It breaks
apart countries. It's a petri dish for stereotypes to grow in. Religion's
not about being holy,' Shay said. 'Just holier-than-thou.'

At the plaintiff's table, I closed my eyes – at the very least, Shay
had surely just lost the case for himself; at the most, I was going
to wind up with a cross being burned on my lawn. 'Objection,' I
said feebly. 'It's not responsive.'

'Overruled,' the judge replied. 'He's not your witness now, Ms
Bloom.'

Shay continued muttering, more quietly now. 'You know what religion does? It draws a big fat line in the sand. It says, "If you don't do it my way, you're out."'

He wasn't yelling, he wasn't out of control. But he wasn't *in* control, either. He brought his hands up to his neck, started scratching at it as the chains jangled down his chest. 'These words,' he said, 'they're cutting my throat.'

'Judge,' I said immediately, alert to a rapidly approaching meltdown. 'Can we take a recess?'

Shay started rocking back and forth.

'Fifteen minutes,' Judge Haig said, and the U.S. marshals approached to remand Shay into custody. Panicking, Shay cowered and raised his arms in defense. And we all watched as the chains he was wearing – the ones that had secured him at the wrists and the ankles and the waist, the ones that had jangled throughout his testimony – fell to the floor with a clatter, as if they'd been no more substantial than smoke.

'Religion often gets in the way of God.'

— *BONO, AT THE NATIONAL PRAYER
BREAKFAST, FEBRUARY 2, 2006*

Maggie

Shay stood, his arms akimbo, looking just as surprised to be unshackled as we were to see him that way. There was a collective moment of disbelief, and then chaos exploded in the courtroom. Screams rang out from the gallery. One marshal dragged the judge off the bench and into his chambers while the other drew his weapon, yelling for Shay to put his hands up. Shay froze, only to have the marshal tackle and handcuff him. 'Stop!' Father Michael cried behind me. 'He doesn't know what's happening!' As the marshal pushed Shay's head against the wooden floor, he looked up at us, terrified.

I whipped around to face the priest. 'What the hell's going on? He's gone from being Jesus to being Houdini?'

'This is the kind of thing he does,' Father Michael said. Was it me, or did I hear a note of satisfaction in his voice? 'I tried to tell you.'

'Let me tell *you*,' I shot back. 'Our friend Shay just earned himself a one-way ticket to the lethal injection gurney, unless one of us can convince him to say something to Judge Haig to explain what just happened.'

'You're his lawyer,' Michael said.

'*You're* his advisor.'

'Remember how I told you Shay won't talk to me?'

I rolled my eyes. 'Could we just pretend we're not in seventh grade anymore, and do our jobs?'

He let his gaze slide away, and immediately I knew that whatever else this conversation had to hold, it wasn't going to be pleasant.

By now, the courtroom had emptied. I had to get to Shay and put a solitary, cohesive thought in his head, one that I hoped he could retain long enough to take to the witness stand. I didn't have time for Father Michael's confessions right now.

'I was on the jury that convicted Shay,' the priest said.

My mother had a trick she'd employed since I was a teenager – if I said something that made her want to (a) scream, (b) whack me, or (c) both, she would count to ten, her lips moving silently, before she responded. I could feel my mouth rounding out the syllables of the numbers, and with some dismay I realized that finally, I *had* become my mother. 'Is that all?' I asked.

'Isn't that *enough*?'

'Just making sure.' My mind raced. I could get into a lot of trouble for not telling Greenleaf that fact in advance. Then again, I hadn't *known* in advance. 'Is there a reason you waited so long to mention this?'

'Don't ask, don't tell,' he said, parroting my own words. 'At first I thought I'd just help Shay understand redemption, and then I'd tell you the truth. But Shay wound up teaching *me* about redemption, and you said my testimony was critical, and I thought maybe it was better you didn't know. I thought it wouldn't screw up the trial quite as much . . .'

I held up my hand, stopping him. 'Do you support it?' I asked. 'The death penalty?'

The priest hesitated before he spoke. 'I *used* to.'

I would have to tell Greenleaf. Even if Father Michael's testimony was stricken from the record, though, you couldn't make the judge forget hearing it; the damage had been done. Right now, however, I had more important things to do. 'I have to go.'

In the holding cell, I found Shay still distraught, his eyes squinched shut. 'Shay?' I said. 'It's Maggie. Look at me.'

'I can't,' he cried. 'Turn the volume down.'

The room was quiet; there was no radio playing, no sound at all. I glanced at the marshal, who shrugged. 'Shay,' I commanded, coming up to the bars of the cell. 'Open your goddamn eyes.'

One eye squinted open a crack, then the other.

'Tell me how you did it.'

'Did what?'

'Your little magic act in there.'

He shook his head. 'I didn't do anything.'

'You managed to get out of handcuffs,' I said. 'What did you do, make a key and hide it in a seam?'

'I don't have a key. I didn't unlock them.'

Well, technically, this was true. What I'd seen were the still-fastened cuffs, clattering to the floor, while Shay's hands were somehow free of them. He certainly could have unfastened the locks and snapped them shut again – but it would have been noisy, something we all would have heard.

And we hadn't.

'I didn't do anything,' Shay repeated.

I'd read somewhere of magicians who learned to dislocate their shoulders to get out of straitjackets; maybe this had been Shay's secret. Maybe he could double-joint his thumbs or resettle the bones of his fingers and slide out of the metal fittings without anyone being the wiser. 'Okay. Whatever.' I exhaled heavily. 'Here's the thing, Shay. I don't know if you're a magician, or a messiah. I don't know very much about salvation, or miracles, or any of those things that Father Michael and Ian Fletcher talked about. I don't even know if I believe in God. But what I do know is the law. And right now, everyone in that courtroom thinks you're a raving lunatic. You have to pull it together.' I glanced at Shay and saw him looking at me with utter focus, his eyes clear and shrewd. 'You have one chance,' I said slowly. 'One chance to speak to the man who will decide how you die, and whether Claire Nealon gets to live. So what are you going to tell him?'

Once, when I was in sixth grade, I let the most popular girl in the school cheat off my paper during a math test. 'You know what,' she said afterward, 'you're not totally uncool.' She let me sit with her at the lunch table and for one glorious Saturday, I was invited to the mall with her Gordian knot of friends, who spritzed perfume onto their wrists at department stores and tried on expensive skinny jeans that didn't even come in my size. (I told them I had my period, and I didn't ever shop for jeans when I was bloated – a total lie, and yet one of the girls offered to show me how to make myself throw up in the bathroom to take off that extra five.) It was when I was getting a makeover at the Clinique counter, with no intent of buying any of the makeup, that I looked in a mirror and realized I did not like the girl staring back. To be the person they wanted me to be, I'd lost myself.

Watching Shay take the witness stand again, I thought about that sixth-grade thrill I'd gotten when, for a moment, I'd been part of the in-crowd; I'd been popular. The gallery, hushed, waited for another outburst – but Shay was mild-mannered and calm, quiet to a fault. He was triple-chained, and had to hobble to the stand, where he didn't look at anyone and simply waited for me to address him with the question we had practiced. I wondered whether remaking him in the image of a viable plaintiff said more about who *he* was willing to be, or whom *I* had become.

'Shay,' I said. 'What do you want to tell this court?'

He looked up at the ceiling, as if he were waiting for the words to drift down like snow. 'The Spirit of the Lord is on me, because he has anointed me to preach good news,' he murmured.

'Amen,' said a woman in the gallery.

I'll be honest, this was not quite what I had had in mind when I had told Shay he could make one final attempt to sway this court. To me, religious scripture sounded just as wacky and zealous as the diatribe Shay had given on the nature of organized religion. But maybe Shay was smarter than I was, because his quote made the judge purse his lips. 'Is that from the Bible, Mr Bourne?'

'I don't know,' Shay replied. 'I don't remember where it comes from.'

A tiny paper airplane torpedoed over my shoulder to land in my lap. I opened it up, read Father Michael's hastily scrawled note. 'Yes, Judge,' I said quickly. 'It is.'

'Marshal,' Judge Haig said, 'bring me the Bible.' He began to thumb through the onionskin pages. 'Do you happen to know where, Ms Bloom?'

I didn't know when or if Shay Bourne had been reading scripture. This quote could have come from the priest; it could have come from God; it could have been the only line he knew in the whole Old Testament. But somehow, he'd piqued the interest of Judge Haig, who was no longer dismissing my client outright, but instead tracing the pages of the Bible as if it were written in Braille.

I stood, armed with Father Michael's citation. 'It's in Isaiah, Your Honor,' I said.

During the lunch recess, I drove to my office. Not because I had such an inviolable work ethic (although technically I had sixteen other cases going at the same time as Shay's, my boss had given me his blessing to put them on the back burner of the largest metaphorical stove *ever*), but because I just needed to get away from the trial completely. The secretary at the ACLU office blinked when I walked through the door. 'Aren't you supposed to be—'

'Yes,' I snapped, and I walked through the maze of filing cabinets to my desk.

I didn't know how Shay's outburst would affect the judge. I didn't know if I'd already lost this case, before the defense had even presented its witnesses. I did know that I hadn't slept well in three weeks and was flat out of rabbit food for Oliver, and I was having a really bad hair day. I rubbed my hands down my face, and then realized I'd probably smeared my mascara.

With a sigh, I glanced at the mountain of paperwork on my desk that had been steadily growing without me there to act as clearinghouse. There was an appeal that had been filed in the Supreme Court by the attorneys of a skinhead who'd written the word *towelhead* in white paint on the driveway of his employer, a Pakistani convenience store owner who'd fired him for being drunk on the job; some research about why the words *under God* had been added to the Pledge of Allegiance in 1954 during the

McCarthy era; and a stack of mail equally balanced between desperate souls who wanted me to fight on their behalf and right-wing conservatives who berated the ACLU for making it criminal to be a white churchgoing Christian.

One letter sifted through my hands and dropped onto my lap – a plain envelope printed with the address of the New Hampshire State Prison, the Office of the Warden. I opened it and found inside a pressed white sheet of paper, still bearing its watermark.

It was an invitation to attend the execution of Isaiah Bourne. The guest list included the attorney general, the governor, the lawyer who originally prosecuted Shay's case, me, Father Michael, and several other names I didn't recognize. By law, there had to be a certain number of people present for an execution from both the inmate's and the victim's sides. In this, it was a bit like organizing a wedding. And just like a wedding, there was a number to call to RSVP.

It was fifteen days before Shay was scheduled to die.

Clearly, I was the only one who found it remotely hilarious that the first and only witness the defense called – the commissioner of corrections – was a man named Joe Lynch. He was a tall, thin man whose sense of humor had apparently dissipated along with the hair on his scalp. I was quite sure that when he took the job, he'd never dreamed that he would be faced with New Hampshire's first execution in more than half a century.

'Commissioner Lynch,' the assistant attorney general said, 'what preparations have been made for the execution of Shay Bourne?'

'As you're aware,' Lynch said, 'the State of New Hampshire was not equipped to deal with the death sentence handed down to Inmate Bourne. We'd hoped that the job could be done at Terre Haute, but found out that wasn't going to happen. To that end, we've had to construct a lethal injection chamber – which now occupies a good corner of what used to be our exercise yard at the state penitentiary.'

'Can you give us a breakdown of the costs involved?'

The commissioner began to read from a ledger. 'The architectural and construction fees for the project were $39,100. A lethal injection gurney cost $830. The equipment associated with lethal injection cost $684. In addition, the human cost included meeting with staff, training the staff, and attending hearings – totaling $48,846. Initial supplies were $1,361, and the chemicals cost $426. In addition to this, several physical improvements were made to the space where the execution would occur: vertical blinds in the witness area, a dimmer switch in the chamber, a tinted one-way mirror, air-conditioning and an emergency generator, a wireless microphone and amplifier into the viewing area, a mono plug phone jack. These ran up to $14,669.'

'You've done the math, Commissioner. By your calculation, what do you estimate you've spent on Shay Bourne's execution so far?'

'$105,916.'

'Commissioner,' Greenleaf asked, 'does the State of New Hampshire have a gallows that could be used if the court ordered Mr Bourne to be hanged?'

'Not anymore,' Lynch replied.

'Would it be correct to assume, then, that there would be an additional outlay for the taxpayers of New Hampshire if a new gallows had to be constructed?'

'That's correct.'

'What specifications are needed to build a gallows?'

The commissioner nodded. 'A floor height of at least nine feet, a crossbeam of nine feet, with a clearance of three feet above the inmate being executed. The opening in the trapdoor would have to be at least three feet to ensure proper clearance. There would have to be a means of releasing the trapdoor and stopping it from swinging after it has been opened, and a fastening mechanism for the rope with the noose.'

In a few short sentences, Gordon Greenleaf had recentered this trial from the woo-woo touchy-feely freedom-of-religion aspect, to the inevitability of Shay's imminent death. I glanced at Shay.

He had gone white as the blank sheet of paper framed between his chained hands.

'You're looking at no less than seventy-five hundred for construction and materials,' the commissioner said. 'In addition, there would be the investment of a body restraint.'

'What's that, exactly?' Greenleaf asked.

'A waist strap with two wrist restraints, made of three-thousand-pound test nylon, and another leg restraint made from the same materials. We'd need a frame – basically, a human dolly that enables the officers to transport the inmate to the gallows in the event of a physical collapse – and a hood, and a mechanical hangman's knot.'

'You can't just use rope?'

'Not if you're talking about a humane execution,' the commissioner said. 'This knot is made from a Delran cylinder and has two longitudinal holes and a steel U-clamp to fasten the rope, as well as a noose sleeve, a rope in thirty-foot lengths, knot lubricant . . .'

Even I was impressed at how much time and thought had gone into the death of Shay Bourne. 'You've done a great deal of research,' Greenleaf said.

Lynch shrugged. 'Nobody wants to execute a man. It's my job to do it with as much dignity as possible.'

'What would be the cost of constructing and purchasing all this equipment, Commissioner Lynch?'

'A bit less than ten thousand.'

'And you said the State of New Hampshire has already invested over a hundred thousand on the execution of Shay Bourne?'

'That's correct.'

'Would it be a burden on the penitentiary system if you were required to construct a gallows at this time, in order to accommodate Mr Bourne's so-called religious preferences?'

The commissioner puffed out a long breath. 'It would be more than a burden. It would be damn near impossible, given the date of the execution.'

'Why?'

'The law said we were to execute Mr Bourne by lethal injection, and we are ready and able to do it, after much preparation. I wouldn't feel personally and professionally comfortable cutting corners to create a last-minute gallows.'

'Maggie,' Shay whispered, 'I think I'm going to throw up.'

I shook my head. 'Swallow it.'

He lay his head down on the table. With any luck a few sympathetic people would assume that he was crying.

'If you were ordered by the court to construct a gallows,' Greenleaf asked, 'how long would it delay Mr Bourne's execution?'

'I'd say six months to a year,' the commissioner said.

'A whole year that Inmate Bourne would live past his execution warrant date?'

'Yes.'

'Why so long?'

'You're talking about construction going on inside a working penitentiary system, Mr Greenleaf. Background checks have to be done before a crew can come to work inside our gates – they're bringing in tools from the outside, which can be security threats; we have to have officers standing guard to watch them to make sure they don't wander into insecure areas; we have to make sure they're not trying to pass contraband to the inmates. It would be a substantial burden on the correctional institution if we had to, well, start from scratch.'

'Thank you, Commissioner,' Greenleaf said. 'Nothing further.'

I rose from my seat and approached the commissioner. 'Your estimate for constructing the gallows is about ten thousand dollars?'

'Yes.'

'So in fact, the cost to hang Shay Bourne would be one-tenth the cost of executing him by lethal injection.'

'Actually,' the commissioner said, 'it would be a hundred and ten percent. You can't get a lethal injection chamber at Nordstrom with a satisfaction guarantee, Ms Bloom. I can't return what we've already built.'

'Well, you needed to construct that chamber anyway, didn't you?'

'Not if Inmate Bourne isn't going to be executed that way.'

'The Department of Corrections didn't have the lethal injection chamber available for any other death row prisoners, however.'

'Ms Bloom,' the commissioner said, 'New Hampshire doesn't *have* any other death row prisoners.'

I couldn't very well suggest that in the future we might – no one wanted to entertain that option. 'Would executing Shay Bourne by hanging affect the safety of the other inmates in the prison?'

'No. Not during the actual process.'

'Would it impinge on the safety of the officers there?'

'No.'

'And in terms of the personnel – there would be, in fact, less manpower needed for an execution by hanging than an execution by lethal injection, correct?'

'Yes,' the commissioner said.

'So there's no safety issue involved in changing Shay's method of execution. Not for staff, and not for inmates. The only thing you can point to as a burden on the Department of Corrections, really, is a cost of just under ten thousand dollars to construct a gallows. Ten thousand lousy bucks. Is that right, Commissioner?'

The judge caught the commissioner's eye. 'Do you have that in the budget?'

'I don't know,' Lynch said. 'Budgets are always tight.'

'Your Honor, I have here a copy of the budget of the Department of Corrections, to be entered into evidence.' I handed it to Greenleaf, to Judge Haig, and finally, to Commissioner Lynch. 'Commissioner, does this look familiar?'

'Yes.'

'Can you read me the line that's highlighted?'

Lynch settled his spectacles on his nose. 'Supplies for capital punishment,' he said. 'Nine thousand eight hundred and eighty dollars.'

'By supplies, what did you mean?'

'Chemicals,' the commissioner said. 'And whatever else came along.'

What he meant, I was sure, was a fudge line in the budget. 'By your own testimony, chemicals would only cost four hundred and twenty-six dollars.'

'We didn't know what else might be involved,' Lynch said. 'Police blocks, traffic direction, medical supplies, extra manpower on staff . . . this is our first execution in nearly seventy years. We budgeted conservatively, so that we wouldn't find ourselves short when it actually came to pass.'

'If that money was going to be spent on Shay Bourne's execution no matter what, does it really matter whether it's used to purchase Sodium Pentothal . . . or to construct a gallows?'

'Uh,' Lynch stammered. 'It's still not ten thousand dollars.'

'No,' I admitted. 'You're a hundred and twenty dollars short. Tell me . . . is that worth the price of a man's soul?'

June

Someone once told me that when you give birth to a daughter, you've just met the person whose hand you'll be holding the day you die. In the days after Elizabeth was born, I would watch those minuscule fingers, the nail beds like tiny shells, the surprisingly firm grip she had on my index finger – and wonder if, years from now, I'd be the one holding on so tight.

It is unnatural to survive your child. It is like seeing an albino butterfly, or a bloodred lake; a skyscraper tumbling down. I had already been through it once; now I was desperate to keep from experiencing that again.

Claire and I were playing Hearts, and don't think I didn't appreciate the irony. The deck of cards showcased Peanuts characters; my game strategy had nothing to do with the suit, and everything to do with collecting as many Charlie Browns as I could. 'Mom,' Claire said, 'play like you mean it.'

I looked up at her. 'What are you talking about?'

'You're *cheating*. But you're doing it so you'll lose.' She shuffled the remaining deck and turned over the top card. 'Why do you think they're called clubs?'

'I don't know.'

'Do you think it's the kind you want to join? Or the kind that you use to beat someone up?'

Behind her, on the cardiac monitor, Claire's failing heart chugged a steady rhythm. At moments like these, it was hard to believe that she was as sick as she was. But then, all I had to do was witness her trying to swing her legs over the bed to go to the bathroom, see how winded she became, to know that looks could be deceiving.

'Do you remember when you made up that secret society?' I asked. 'The one that met behind the hedge?'

Claire shook her head. 'I never did that.'

'Of course you did,' I said. 'You were little, that's why you've forgotten. But you were absolutely insistent about who could and couldn't be a member of the club. You had a stamp that said CANCELED and an ink pad – you put it on the back of my hand, and if I even wanted to tell you dinner was ready I had to give a password first.'

Across the room, my cell phone began to ring in my purse. I made a beeline for it – mobile phones were strictly verboten in the hospital, and if a nurse caught you with one, you would be given the look of death. 'Hello?'

'June. This is Maggie Bloom.'

I stopped breathing. Last year, Claire had learned in school that there were whole segments of the brain devoted to involuntary acts like digesting and oxygen intake, which was so evolutionarily clever; and yet, these systems could be felled by the simplest of things: love at first sight; acts of violence; words you did not want to hear.

'I don't have any formal news yet,' Maggie said, 'but I thought you'd want to know: closing arguments start tomorrow morning. And then, depending on how long the judge deliberates, we'll know if and when Claire will have the heart.' There was a crackle of silence. 'Either way, the execution will take place in fifteen days.'

'Thank you,' I said, and closed the clamshell of the phone. In twenty-four hours, I might know if Claire would live or die.

'Who called?' Claire asked.

I slipped the phone into the pocket of my jacket. 'The dry cleaner,' I said. 'Our winter coats are ready to be picked up.'

Claire just stared at me; she knew I was lying. She gathered up the cards, although we were not finished with our game. 'I don't want to play anymore,' she said.

'Oh. Okay.'

She rolled onto her side, turning her face away from me. 'I never had stamps and an ink pad,' Claire murmured. 'I never had a secret club. You're thinking of Elizabeth.'

'I'm not thinking of—' I said automatically, but then I broke off. I could clearly picture Kurt and I standing at the bathroom sink, grinning as we scrubbed off the temporary tattoos we'd been given, wondering if our daughter would speak to us at breakfast without that mark of faith. Claire could not have initiated her father into her secret world; she had never even met him.

'I told you so,' Claire said.

Lucius

Shay was not on I-tier often, but when he was, he was transported to conference rooms and the infirmary. He'd tell me,
when he came back, about the psych tests they ran on him; about
the way they tapped at the crooks of his elbows, checking his
veins. I supposed it was important for them to dot their i's and
cross their t's before the Big Event, so that they didn't look stupid
when the rest of the world was watching.

The real reason they kept shuttling Shay around for medical
tests, though, was to get him out of the pod so that they could
have their practice runs. They'd done a couple of these in August.
I'd been in the exercise cage when the warden led a small group
of COs to the lethal injection chamber that was being built. I
watched them in their hard hats. 'What we need to figure out,
people,' Warden Coyne had said, 'is how long it'll take the victim's
witnesses to get from my office to the chamber. We can't have
them crossing paths with the inmate's witnesses.'

Now that the chamber was finished, they had even more to
check and double-check: if the phone lines to the governor's
office worked; if the straps on the gurney were secure. Twice
now, while Shay was at Medical, a group of officers – the special
ops team, who had volunteered to be part of the execution –
arrived on I-tier. I'd never seen any of them before. I suppose
that there is humanity in not having the man who kills you
be the same guy who has brought you your breakfast for the
past eleven years. And likewise: it must be easier to push the
plunger on that syringe if you haven't had a conversation with

the inmate about whether the Patriots would win another Super Bowl.

This time, Shay had not wanted to go to Medical. He put up a fight, saying that he was tired, that he didn't have any blood left for them to draw. Not that he had a choice, of course – the officers would have dragged him there kicking and screaming. Eventually, Shay agreed to be chained so that he could make the trip off I-tier, and fifteen minutes after he was gone, the special ops team showed up. They put an officer pretending to be Shay into his cell, and then one of the other COs started a stopwatch. 'We're rolling,' he said.

I don't know how the mistake happened, to be honest. I mean, I suppose that was the whole point of a practice run – you were leaving room for human error. But somehow, just as the special ops team was escorting Fake-Shay off the pod as part of their training, the real Shay was entering I-tier again. For a moment, they hesitated at the door, gazing at one another.

Shay stared at his faux counterpart, until Officer Whitaker had to drag him through the door of I-tier, and even then, he craned his neck, trying to see where his future was heading.

In the middle of the night, the officers came for Shay. He was banging his head against the walls of his cell, speaking in a river of gibberish. Usually, I would have heard all of this – I was often the first to know that Shay was upset – but I had slept through it. I woke up when the officers arrived in their goggles and shields, swarming over him like a clot of black cockroaches.

'Where are you taking him?' I yelled, but the words sliced my throat to ribbons. I thought of the run-through and wondered if it was time for the real thing.

One of the officers turned to me – a nice one, but in that instant I could not grasp his name, although I had seen him every week for the past six years. 'It's okay, Lucius,' he said. 'We're just taking him to an observation cell, so he doesn't hurt himself.'

When they left, I lay down on my bunk and pressed my palm

against my forehead. Fever: it was a school of fish swimming through my veins.

Once before, Adam had cheated on me. I found a note in his pocket when I went to take his shirts to the dry cleaner. *Gary*, and a phone number. When I asked him about it, he said it had only been one night, after a show at the gallery where he worked. Gary was one of the artists, a man who created miniature cities out of plaster of Paris. New York was currently on display. He told me about the art-deco detail on the top of the Chrysler Building; the individual leaves that were hand-fastened to the trees on Park Avenue. I imagined Adam standing with Gary, their feet planted in Central Park, their arms around each other, monstrous as Godzilla.

It was a mistake, Adam had said. *It was just so exciting, for a minute, to know someone else was interested.*

I could not imagine how people would not be interested in Adam, with his pale green eyes, his mocha skin. I saw heads turn all the time, gay and straight, when we walked down the street.

It felt all wrong, he said, *because it wasn't you.*

I had been naive enough to believe then that you could take something toxic and poisonous, and contain it so that you'd never be burned by it again. You'd think, after all that happened later with Adam, I had learned my lesson. But things like jealousy, rage, and infidelity – they don't disappear. They lie in wait, like a cobra, to strike you again when you least expect it.

I looked down at my hands, at the dark blotches of Kaposi's sarcoma that had already begun to blend into one another, turning my skin as dark as Adam's, as if my punishment were to reinvent myself in his image.

'Please don't do this,' I whispered. But I was begging to stop something that had already started. I was praying, although I couldn't remember to whom.

Maggie

After court had adjourned for the weekend, I took a trip to the ladies' room. I was sitting in a stall when suddenly a microphone snaked underneath the metal wall from the cubicle beside mine. 'I'm Ella Wyndhammer from FOX News,' a woman said. 'I wonder if you have a comment about the fact that the White House has given a formal statement about the Bourne trial and the separation of church and state?'

I hadn't been aware that the White House had given a formal statement; there was a part of me that shivered with a thrill to know that we'd attracted that much attention. Then I considered what the statement most likely had been, and how it probably wouldn't help my case at all. And *then* I remembered that I was in the bathroom.

'Yeah, I've got a comment,' I said, and flushed.

Because I didn't want to be ambushed by Ella Wyndhammer or any of the other hundred reporters crawling over the steps of the courthouse like lichen, I retreated into a foxhole – okay, an attorney-client conference room – and locked the door. I took out a legal pad and began to write my closing for Monday, hoping that by the time I finished, the reporters would have moved onto a fresher kill.

It was dark when I slipped on my heels again and packed away my notes. The lights had been turned off in the courthouse; distantly, I could hear a custodian buffing the floors. I walked through the lobby, past the dormant metal detectors, took a deep breath, and opened the door.

The majority of the media had packed up for the night. In the distance, though, I could see one tenacious reporter holding his microphone. He called out my name.

I forged past him. 'No comment,' I muttered, and then I realized he wasn't a reporter, and he wasn't holding a microphone.

'It's about time,' Christian said, and he handed me the rose.

Michael

'You're his spiritual advisor,' Warden Coyne said when he phoned me at three in the morning. 'Go give him some advice.'

I had tried to explain to the warden that Shay and I weren't quite on speaking terms, but he hung up before I got the chance. Instead, with a sigh, I dragged myself out of bed and rode to the prison. Instead of taking me to I-tier, however, the CO led me elsewhere. 'He's been moved,' the officer explained.

'Why? Did someone hurt him again?'

'Nah, he was doing a good job of that on his own,' he said, and as we stopped in front of Shay's cell, I understood.

Bruises mottled most of his face. His knuckles were scraped raw. A trickle of blood ran down his left temple. He was chained at the wrists and ankles and belly, even though he was inside the cell. 'Why haven't you called a doctor?' I demanded.

'He's been here three times,' the CO said. 'Our boy, here, keeps ripping off the bandages. That's why we had to cuff him.'

'If I promise you that he'll stop doing whatever he's doing—'

'Slamming his head into the wall?'

'Right. If I give you my word, will you take off the handcuffs?' I turned to Shay, who was studiously avoiding me. 'Shay?' I said. 'How does that sound?'

He didn't react one way or another, and I had no idea how I was going to convince Shay to stop harming himself, but the CO motioned him toward the cell door and removed the cuffs from his wrists and ankles. The belly chain, however, stayed on. 'Just in case,' he said, and left.

'Shay,' I said. 'Why are you doing this?'

'Get the fuck away from me.'

'I know you're scared. And I know you're angry,' I said. 'I don't blame you.'

'Then I guess something's changed. Because you sure *did*, once. You, and eleven other people.' Shay took a step forward. 'What was it like, in that room? Did you sit around talking about what kind of monster would do those horrible things? Did you ever think that you hadn't gotten the whole story?'

'Then why didn't you tell it?' I burst out. 'You gave us *nothing*, Shay. We had the prosecution's explanation of what had happened; we heard from June. But you didn't even stand up and ask us for a lenient sentence.'

'Who would believe what I had to say, over the word of a dead cop?' he said. 'My own lawyer didn't. He kept talking about how we ought to use my troubled childhood to get me off – not my story of what happened. He said I didn't look like someone the jury would trust. He didn't care about me; he just wanted to get his five seconds on the news at night. He had a *strategy*. Well, you know what his strategy was? First he told the jury I didn't do it. Then it comes time for sentencing and he says: "Okay, he did it, but here's why you shouldn't kill him for it." You might as well admit that pleading not guilty in the first place was a lie.'

I stared at him; stunned. It had never occurred to me during the capital murder trial that all this might be whirling around in Shay's head; that the reason he did not get up and beg for clemency during sentencing was because in order to do that, it felt like he'd also be admitting to the crime. Now that I looked back on it, it *had* felt like the defense had changed their tune between the penalty phase and the sentencing phase of the trial. It *had* made it harder to believe anything they said.

And Shay? Well, he'd been sitting right *there*, with his unwashed hair and his vacant eyes. His silence – which I'd read as pride, or shame – might only have been the understanding that for people like him, the world did not work the way it should. And I, like the other eleven jurors, had judged him before any verdict was given. After all, what kind of man gets put on trial for a double murder? What prosecutor seeks the death penalty without good reason?

Since I'd become his spiritual advisor, he'd told me that what had happened in the past didn't matter now, and I'd taken that to mean that he wouldn't accept responsibility for what he'd done. But it could also have meant that in spite of his innocence, he knew he was still going to die.

I'd been present at that trial; I'd heard all the testimony. To think Shay might not have deserved a death sentence seemed ridiculous, impossible.

Then again, so were miracles.

'But Shay,' I said quietly, 'I heard that evidence. I saw what you did.'

'I didn't *do* anything.' He ducked his head. 'It was because of the tools. I left them at the house. No one came when I knocked on the door so I just went inside to get them . . . and then I saw her.'

I felt my stomach turn over. 'Elizabeth.'

'She used to play with me. A staring game. Whoever smiled first, that was the loser. I used to get her every time, and then one day while we were staring she lifted up my screwdriver – I didn't even know she'd taken it – and waved it around like a maniac with a knife. I burst out laughing. *I got you*, she said. *I got you*. And she did – she had me, one hundred percent.' His face twisted. 'I never would have hurt her. When I came in that day, she was with *him*. He had his pants down. And she was – she was crying . . . he was supposed to be her *father*.' He flung an arm up over his face, as if he could stop himself from seeing the memory. 'She looked up at me, like it was a staring contest, but then she smiled. Except this time, it wasn't because she lost. It was because she knew she was going to win. Because I was there. Because I could rescue her. My whole life, people looked at me like I was a fuckup, like I couldn't do anything right – but she, it was like she believed in me,' Shay said. 'And I wanted – God, I wanted to believe her.'

He took a deep breath. 'I grabbed her and ran upstairs, to the room I was finishing. I locked the door. I told her we would be safe there. But then there was a shot, and the whole door was gone, and he came in and pointed his gun at me.'

I tried to imagine what it would be like to be Shay – easily confused and unable to communicate well – and to suddenly have a pistol thrust in my face.

I would have panicked, too.

'There were sirens,' Shay said. 'He'd called them in. He said they were coming for me and that no cop would believe any story from a freak like me. She was screaming, "Don't shoot, don't shoot." He said, "Get over here, Elizabeth," and I grabbed the gun so he couldn't hurt her and we were fighting and both our hands were on it and it went off and went off again.' He swallowed. 'I caught her. The blood, it was everywhere; it was on me, it was on her. He kept calling her name but she wouldn't look at him. She stared at me, like we were playing our game; she stared at me, except it wasn't a game . . . and then even though her eyes were open, she stopped staring. And it was over even though I didn't smile.' He choked on a sob, pressed his hand against his mouth. 'I didn't smile.'

'Shay,' I said softly.

He glanced up at me. 'She was better off dead.'

My mouth went dry. I remembered Shay saying that same sentence to June Nealon at the restorative justice meeting, her storming out of the room in tears. But what if we'd taken Shay's words out of context? What if he truly believed Elizabeth's death was a blessing, after what she'd suffered at the hands of her step-father?

Something snagged in the back of my mind, a splinter of memory. 'Her underpants,' I said. 'You had them in your pocket.'

Shay stared at me as if I were an idiot. 'Well, that's because she didn't have a chance to put them back *on* yet, before everything else happened.'

The Shay I had grown to know was a man who could close an open wound with a brush of his hand, yet who also might have a breakdown if the mashed potatoes in his meal platter were more yellow than the day before. That Shay would not see anything suspicious about the police finding a little girl's underwear in his possession; it would make perfect sense to him to grab them when he grabbed Elizabeth, for the sake of her modesty.

'Are you telling me the shootings were accidental?'

'I never said I was guilty,' he answered.

The pundits who downplayed Shay's miracles were always quick to point out that if God were to return to earth, He wouldn't choose to be a murderer. But what if He hadn't? What if the whole situation had been misunderstood; what if Shay had not willfully, intentionally killed Elizabeth Nealon and her stepfather – but in fact had been trying to save her from him?

It would mean that Shay was about to die for someone else's sins.

Again.

'*Not* a good time,' Maggie said when she came to the door.

'It's an emergency.'

'Then call the cops. Or pick up your red phone and dial God directly. I'll give you a call tomorrow morning.' She started to close the door, but I stuck my foot inside.

'Is everything all right?' A man with a British accent was suddenly standing beside Maggie, who had turned beet red.

'Father Michael,' she said. 'This is Christian Gallagher.'

He held out his hand to me. 'Father. I've heard all about you.'

I hoped not. I mean, if Maggie was having a date, clearly there were better topics of conversation.

'So,' Christian asked amiably. 'Where's the fire?'

I felt heat rising to the back of my neck. In the background, I could hear soft music playing; there was half a glass of red wine in the man's hand. There was no fire; it was already burning, and I had just thrown a bucket of sand on it. 'I'm sorry. I didn't mean—' I stepped backward. 'Have a nice night.'

I heard the door close behind me, but instead of walking to my bike, I sat down on the front stoop. The first time I'd met Shay, I'd told him that you can't be lonely if God is with you all the time, but that wasn't entirely true. *He's lousy at checkers*, Shay had said. Well, you couldn't take God out to a movie on a Friday night, either. I knew that I could fill the space a companion normally would with God; and it was more than enough. But that wasn't to say I didn't feel that phantom limb sometimes.

The door opened, and into the slice of light stepped Maggie. She was barefoot, and she had her power-suit coat draped over her shoulders. 'I'm sorry,' I said. 'I didn't mean to ruin your night.'

'That's okay. I should have known better than to assume all the planets had aligned for me.' She sank down beside me. 'What's up?'

In the dark, with her face lit in profile by the moon, she was as beautiful as any Renaissance Madonna. It struck me that God had chosen someone just like Maggie when He picked Mary to bear His Son: someone willing to take the weight of the world on her shoulders, even when it wasn't her own burden. 'It's Shay,' I said. 'I think he's innocent.'

Maggie

I was not particularly surprised to hear what Shay Bourne had told the priest.

No, what surprised me was how fervently he'd fallen for it – hook, line, and sinker.

'It's not about protecting Shay's rights anymore,' Michael said. 'Or letting him die on his own terms. We're talking about an innocent man being killed.'

We had moved into the living room, and Christian – well, he was sitting on the other end of the couch pretending to do a Sudoku puzzle in the newspaper, but actually listening to every word we said. He'd been the one to come outside and invite me back into my own home. I fully intended to pop Father Michael's bubble of incensed righteousness and get back to the spot I'd been in before he arrived.

Which was flat on my back, with Christian's hand moving over my side, showing me where you made the incision to remove a gallbladder – something that, in person, was far more exciting than it sounds.

'He's a convicted murderer,' I said. 'They learn how to lie before they learn how to walk.'

'Maybe he never should have been convicted,' Michael said.

'*You* were on the jury that found him guilty!'

Christian's head snapped up. 'You *were*?'

'Welcome to my life,' I sighed. 'Father, you sat through days of testimony. You saw the evidence firsthand.'

'I know. But that was before he told me that he walked in on

Kurt Nealon molesting his own stepdaughter; and that the gun went off repeatedly while he was struggling to get it out of Kurt's hand.'

At that, Christian leaned forward. 'Well. That makes him a bit of a hero, doesn't it?'

'Not when he still kills the girl he's trying to rescue,' I said. 'And why, pray tell, did he not gift his defense attorney with this information?'

'He said he tried, but the lawyer didn't think it would fly.'

'Well, gee,' I said. 'Doesn't *that* speak volumes?'

'Maggie, you know Shay. He doesn't look like a clean-cut American boy, and he didn't back then, either. Plus, he'd been found with a smoking gun, and a dead cop and girl in front of him. Even if he told the truth, who would have listened? Who's more likely to be cast as a pedophile – the heroic cop and consummate family man . . . or the sketchy vagrant who was doing work in the house? Shay was doomed before he ever walked into a courtroom.'

'Why would he take the blame for someone else's crime?' I argued. 'Why not tell someone – anyone – in eleven years?'

He shook his head. 'I don't know the answer to that. But I'd like to keep him alive long enough to find out.' Father Michael glanced at me. '*You're the* one who says the legal system doesn't always work for everyone. It was an *accident*. Manslaughter, not murder.'

'Correct me if I'm wrong,' Christian interrupted. 'But you can't be sentenced to death for manslaughter, can you?'

I sighed. 'Do we have any new evidence?'

Father Michael thought for a minute. 'He told me so.'

'Do we have any *evidence*,' I repeated.

His face lit up. 'We have the security camera outside the observation cell,' Michael said. 'That's got to be recorded somewhere, right?'

'It's still just a tape of him telling you a story,' I explained. 'It's different if you tell me, oh, that there's semen we can link to Kurt Nealon . . .'

'You're an ACLU lawyer. You must be able to do *something* . . .'

'Legally, there's nothing we *can* do. We can't reopen his case unless there's some fantastic forensic proof.'

'What about calling the governor?' Christian suggested.

Our heads both swiveled toward him.

'Well, isn't that what always happens on TV? And in John Grisham novels?'

'*Why* do you know so much about the American legal system?' I asked.

He shrugged. 'I used to have a torrid crush on the Partridge girl from *L.A. Law.*'

I sighed and walked to the dining room table. My purse was slogged across it like an amoeba. I dug inside for my cell phone, punched a number. 'This better be good,' my boss growled on the other end of the line.

'Sorry, Rufus. I know it's late—'

'Cut to the chase.'

'I need to call Flynn, on behalf of Shay Bourne,' I said.

'Flynn? As in Mark Flynn the governor? Why would you want to waste your last appeal before you even get a verdict back from Haig?'

'Shay Bourne's spiritual advisor is under the impression that he was falsely convicted.' I looked up to find Christian and Michael both watching me intently.

'Do we have any new evidence?'

I closed my eyes. 'Well. No. But this is really important, Rufus.'

A moment later, I hung up the phone and pressed the number I'd scrawled on a paper napkin into Michael's hand. 'It's the governor's cell number. Go call him.'

'Why me?'

'Because,' I said. 'He's Catholic.'

'I have to leave,' I had told Christian. 'The governor wants us to come to his office right now.'

'If I had a quid for every time a girl's used that one on me,' he said. And then, just as if it were the most normal thing in the world, he kissed me.

Okay, it had been a quick kiss. And one that could have ended a G-rated movie. And it had been performed in front of a priest. But still, it looked completely natural, as if Christian and I had been kissing at the ends of sentences for ages, while the rest of the world was still hung up on punctuation.

Here's where it all went wrong. 'So,' I had said. 'Maybe we could get together tomorrow?'

'I'm on call for the next forty-eight hours,' he'd said. 'Monday?'

But Monday I was in court again.

'Well,' Christian said. 'I'll call.'

I was meeting Father Michael at the statehouse, because I wanted him to go home and get clothing that was as priestly as possible – the jeans and button-down shirt in which he'd come to my door weren't going to win us any favors. Now, as I waited for him in the parking lot, I replayed every last syllable of my conversation with Christian . . . and began to panic. Everyone knew that when a guy said he'd call, it really meant that he wouldn't – he just wanted a swift escape. Maybe it had been the kiss, which was the precursor to that whole line of conversation. Maybe I had garlic breath. Maybe he'd just spent enough time in my company to know I wasn't what he wanted.

By the time Father Michael rode into the parking lot, I'd decided that if Shay Bourne had cost me my first shot at a relationship since the Jews went to wander the desert, I would execute him *myself*.

I was surprised that Rufus had wanted me to go to meet Governor Flynn alone; I was even more surprised that he thought Father Michael should be the one to finesse the interview in the first place. But Flynn wasn't a born New Englander; he was a transplanted southern boy, and he apparently preferred infor-mality to pomp and circumstance. *He'll be expecting you to come to him for a stay of execution after the trial,* Rufus had mused. *So maybe catching him off guard is the smartest thing you can do.* He

suggested that instead of a lawyer putting through the call, maybe
a man of the cloth should do it instead. And, within two minutes
of conversation, Father Michael had discovered that Governor
Flynn had heard him preach at last year's Christmas Mass at St
Catherine's.

We were let into the statehouse by a security guard, who put
us through the metal detectors and then escorted us to the
governor's office. It was an odd, eerie place after hours; our footsteps rang like gunshots as we hustled up the steps. At the top
of the landing, I turned to Michael. 'Do *not* do anything inflam-
matory,' I whispered. 'We get one shot at this.'

The governor was sitting at his desk. 'Come in,' he said, getting
to his feet. 'Pleasure to see you again, Father Michael.'

'Thanks,' the priest said. 'I'm flattered you remembered me.'

'Hey, you gave a sermon that didn't put me to sleep – that puts
you into a *very* small category of clergymen. You run the youth
group at St Catherine's, too, right? My college roommate's kid was
getting into some trouble a year ago, and then he started working
with you. Joe Cacciatone?'

'Joey,' Father Michael said. 'He's a good kid.'

The governor turned to me. 'And you must be . . . ?'

'Maggie Bloom,' I said, holding out my hand. 'Shay Bourne's
attorney.' I had never been this close to the governor before. I
thought, irrationally, that he looked taller on television.

'Ah, yes,' the governor said. 'The infamous Shay Bourne.'

'If you're a practicing Catholic,' Michael said to the governor,
'how can you condone an execution?'

I blinked at the priest. Hadn't I just told him *not* to say anything
provocative?

'I'm doing my job,' Flynn said. 'There's a great deal that I don't
agree with, personally, that I have to carry out professionally.'

'Even if the man who's about to be killed is innocent?'

Flynn's gaze sharpened. 'That's not what a court decided,
Father.'

'Come talk to him,' Michael said. 'The penitentiary – it's a five-minute drive. Come listen to him, and then tell me if he deserves to die.'

'Governor Flynn,' I interrupted, finally finding my voice. 'During a . . . confession, Shay Bourne made some revelations that indicate there are details of his case that weren't revealed at the time – that the deaths occurred accidentally while Mr Bourne was in fact trying to protect Elizabeth Nealon from her father's sexual abuse. We feel that with a stay of execution, we'll have time to gather evidence of Bourne's innocence.'

The governor's face paled. 'I thought priests couldn't reveal confessions.'

'We're obligated to, if there's a law about to be broken, or if a life is in danger. This qualifies on both counts.'

The governor folded his hands, suddenly distant. 'I appreciate your concerns – both religious and political. I'll take your request under advisement.'

I knew a dismissal when I heard one; I nodded and stood. Father Michael looked up at me, then scrambled to his feet, too. We shook the governor's hand again and groveled our way out of the office. We didn't speak until we were outside, beneath a sky spread with stars. 'So,' Father Michael said. 'I guess that means no.'

'It means we have to wait and see. Which probably means no.' I dug my hands into the pockets of my suit jacket. 'Well. Seeing as my entire evening has been shot to hell, I'm just going to call it a night—'

'You don't believe he's innocent, do you?' Michael said.

I sighed. 'Not really.'

'Then why are you willing to fight so hard for him?'

'On December twenty-fifth, when I was a kid, I'd wake up and it would be just another day. On Easter Sunday, my family was the only one in the movie theater. The reason I fight so hard for Shay,' I finished, 'is because I know what it's like when the things you believe make you feel like you're on the outside looking in.'

'I . . . I didn't realize . . .'

'How could you?' I said, smiling faintly. 'The guys at the top of the totem pole never see what's carved at the bottom. See you Monday, Father.'

I could feel his gaze on me as I walked to my car. It felt like a cape made of light, like the wings of the angels I'd never believed in.

My client looked like he'd been run over by a truck. Somehow, in the middle of trying to get me to save his life, Father Michael had neglected to mention that Shay had begun a course of self-mutilation. His face was scabbed and bloomed with bruises; his hands – cuffed tightly to his waist after last week's fiasco – were scratched. 'You look like crap,' I murmured to Shay.

'I'm going to look worse after they hang me,' he whispered back.

'We have to talk. About what you said to Father Michael—' But before I could go any further, the judge called on Gordon Greenleaf to offer his closing argument.

Gordon stood up heavily. 'Your Honor, this case has been a substantial waste of the court's time and the state's money. Shay Bourne is a convicted double murderer. He committed the most heinous crime in the history of the state of New Hampshire.'

I glanced at Shay beneath my lashes. If what he'd said was true – if he'd seen Elizabeth being abused – then the two murders became manslaughter and self-defense. DNA testing had not been in vogue when he was convicted – was it possible that there was some shred of carpet or couch fabric left that could corroborate Shay's account?

'He's exhausted all legal remedies at every level,' Gordon continued. 'State, first circuit, Supreme Court – and now he's desperately trying to extend his life by filing a bogus lawsuit that claims he believes in some bogus religion. He wants the State of New Hampshire and its taxpayers to build him his own special gallows so that he can donate his heart to the victims' family – a group that he suddenly has feelings for. He certainly didn't have feelings for them the day he murdered Kurt and Elizabeth Nealon.'

It was, of course, highly unlikely that there would still be evidence. By now, even the underwear that had been found in his pocket had been destroyed or given back to June Nealon – this was a case that had closed eleven years ago, in the minds of the investigators. And all the eyewitnesses had died at the scene – except for Shay.

'Yes, there is a law that protects the religious freedom of inmates,' Greenleaf said. 'It exists so that Jewish inmates can wear yarmulkes in prison, and Muslims can fast during Ramadan. The commissioner of corrections always makes allowances for religious activity in compliance with federal law. But to say that this man – who's had outbursts in the courtroom, who can't control his emotions, who can't even tell you what the name of his religion is – deserves to be executed in some special way to comply with federal law is completely inappropriate, and is not what our system of justice intended.'

Just as Greenleaf sat down, a bailiff slipped a note to me. I glanced at it and took a deep breath.

'Ms Bloom?' the judge prompted.

'One hundred and twenty dollars,' I said. 'You know what you can do with one hundred and twenty dollars? You can get a great pair of Stuart Weitzman shoes on sale. You can buy two tickets to a Bruins game. You can feed a starving family in Africa. You can purchase a cell phone contract. Or, you can help a man reach salvation – and rescue a dying child.'

I stood up. 'Shay Bourne is not asking for freedom. He's not asking for his sentence to be overturned. He's simply asking to die in accordance with his religious beliefs. And if America stands for nothing else, it stands for the right to practice your own religion, even if you die in the custody of the state.'

I began to walk toward the gallery. 'People still flock to this country because of its religious freedom. They know that in America, you won't be told what God should look like or sound like. You won't be told there is one right belief, and yours isn't it. They want to speak freely about religion, and to ask questions. Those rights were the foundation of America four hundred years ago, and they're still the foundation today. It's why, in this country, Madonna can perform on a crucifix, and *The Da Vinci Code* was a bestseller. It's why, even after 9/11, religious freedom flourishes in America.'

Facing the judge again, I pulled out all the stops. 'Your Honor, we're not asking you to remove the wall between church and state by ruling in favor of Shay Bourne. We just want the law upheld – the one that promises Shay Bourne the right to practice his religion even in the state penitentiary, unless there's a compelling governmental interest to keep him from doing so. The only governmental interest that the state can point to here is one hundred and twenty dollars – and a matter of a few months.' I walked back to my seat, slipped into it. 'How do you weigh lives and souls against two months, and a hundred and twenty bucks?'

Once the judge returned to chambers to reach his verdict, two marshals came to retrieve Shay. 'Maggie?' he said, getting to his feet. 'Thanks.'

'Guys,' I said to the marshals, 'can you give me a minute with him in the holding cell?'

'Make it quick,' one of them said, and I nodded.

'What do you think?' Father Michael said, still seated in the gallery behind me. 'Does he have a chance?'

I reached into my pocket, retrieved the note the bailiff had passed me just before I began my closing, and handed it to Michael. 'You better hope so,' I said. 'The governor denied his stay of execution.'

He was lying on the metal bunk, his arm thrown over his eyes, by the time I reached the holding cell. 'Shay,' I said, standing in front of the bars. 'Father Michael came to talk to me. About what happened the night of the murders.'

'It doesn't matter.'

'It does matter,' I said urgently. 'The governor denied your stay of execution, which means we're up against a brick wall. DNA evidence is used routinely now to overturn capital punishment verdicts. There was some talk about sexual assault during the trial, wasn't there, before that charge was dropped? If that semen sample still exists, we can have it tested and matched to Kurt . . . I just need you to give me the details about what happened, Shay, so that I can get the ball rolling.'

Shay stood up and walked toward me, resting his hands on the bars between us. 'I can't.'

'Why not?' I challenged. 'Were you lying when you told Father Michael you were innocent?'

He glanced up at me, his eyes hot. 'No.'

I cannot tell you why I believed him. Maybe I was naive, because I hadn't been a criminal defense attorney; maybe I just felt that a dying man had very little left to lose. But when Shay met my gaze, I knew that he was telling me the truth – and that executing an innocent man was even more devastating, if possible, than executing a guilty one. 'Well, then,' I said, my head already swimming with possibilities. 'You told Father Michael your first lawyer wouldn't listen to you – but I'm listening to you now. Talk to me, Shay. Tell me something I can use to convince a judge you were wrongly convicted. Then I'll write up the request for DNA testing, you just have to sign—'

'No.'

'I can't do this alone,' I exploded. 'Shay, we're talking about overturning your conviction, do you understand that? About you walking out of here, free.'

'I know, Maggie.'

'So instead of trying, you're just going to die for a crime you didn't commit? You're okay with that?'

He stared at me and slowly nodded. 'I told you that the first day I met you. I didn't want you to save me. I wanted you to save my heart.'

I was stunned. 'Why?'

He struggled to get the words out. 'It was still my fault. I tried to rescue her, and I couldn't. I wasn't there in time. I never liked Kurt Nealon – I used to try to not be in the same room as him when I was working, so I wouldn't feel him looking at me. But June, she was so nice. She smelled like apples and she'd make me tuna fish for lunch and let me sit at the kitchen table like I belonged there with her and the girl. After Elizabeth . . . afterward . . . it was bad enough that June wouldn't have them anymore. I didn't want her to lose the past, too. Family's not a thing, it's a place,' Shay said softly. 'It's where all the memories get kept.'

So he took the blame for Kurt Nealon's crimes, in order to allow the grieving widow to remember him with pride, instead of hate. How much worse would it have been for June if DNA testing had existed back then – if the alleged rape of Elizabeth had proved Kurt as the perpetrator?

'You go looking for evidence now, Maggie, and you'll rip her wide open again. This way – well, this is the end, and then it's over.'

I could feel my throat closing, a fist of tears. 'And what if one day June finds out the truth? And realizes that you were executed, even though you were innocent?'

'Then,' Shay said, a smile breaking over him like daylight, 'she'll remember me.'

I had gone into this case knowing that Shay and I wanted different outcomes; I had expected to be able to convince him that an overturned conviction was a cause for celebration, even if living meant organ donation would have to be put on hold for a while. But Shay was ready to die; Shay *wanted* to die. He wasn't just giving Claire Nealon a future; he was giving one to her mother, too. He wasn't trying to save the world, like me. Just one life at a time – which is why he had a fighting chance of succeeding.

He touched my hand, where it rested on the bars. 'It's okay, Maggie. I've never done anything important. I didn't cure cancer or stop global warming or win a Nobel Prize. I didn't do anything with my life, except hurt people I loved. But dying – dying will be different.'

'How?'

'They'll see their lives are worth living.'

I knew that I would be haunted by Shay Bourne for a very long time, whether or not his sentence was carried out. 'Someone who thinks like that,' I said, 'does not deserve to be executed. Please, Shay. Help me help you. You don't have to play the hero.'

'Maggie,' he said. 'Neither do you.'

June

*C*ode blue, the nurse had said.

A stream of doctors and nurses flooded Claire's room. One began chest compressions.

I don't feel a pulse.

We need an airway.

Start chest compressions.

Can we get an IV access . . .

What rhythm is she in?

We need to shock her . . . put on the patches . . .

Charge to two hundred joules.

All clear . . . fire!

Hold compressions . . .

No pulse.

Give epi. Lidocaine. Bicarb.

Check for a pulse . . .

Dr Wu flew through the door. 'Get the mother out of here,' he said, and a nurse grasped my shoulders.

'You need to come with me,' she said, and I nodded, but my feet would not move. Someone held the defibrillator to Claire's chest again. Her body jackknifed off the bed just as I was dragged through the doorway.

I had been the one present when Claire flatlined; I was the one who'd run to the nurse's desk. And I was the one sitting with her now that she'd been stabilized, now that her heart, battered and ragged, was beating again. She was in a monitored bed, and I stared at the screens, at the mountainous terrain of her cardiac rhythm, sure that if I didn't blink we'd be safe.

Claire whimpered, tossing her head from side to side. The monitors cast her skin an alien green.

'Baby,' I said, moving beside her. 'Don't try to talk. You've still got a tube in.'

Her eyes slitted open; she pleaded to me with her eyes and mimed holding a pen.

I gave her the white board Dr Wu had given me; until Claire was extubated tomorrow morning she would have to use this to communicate. Her writing was shaky and spiked. WHAT HAPPENED?

'Your heart,' I said, blinking back tears. 'It wasn't doing so well.'
MOMMY, DO SOMETHING.

'Anything, honey.'
LET GO OF ME.

I glanced down; I was not touching her.

Claire circled the words again; and this time, I understood.

Suddenly I remembered something Kurt had told me once: you could only save someone who wanted to be saved; otherwise, you'd be dragged down for the count, too. I looked at Claire, but she was asleep again, the marker still curled in her hand.

Tears slipped down my cheeks, onto the hospital blanket. 'Oh, Claire . . . I'm so sorry,' I whispered, and I was.

For what I had done.

For what I knew I had to do.

Lucius

When I coughed it turned me inside out. I could feel the tendons tangle on the outside of my skin and the fever in my head steaming against the pillow. You put ice chips on my tongue and they vanished before I swallowed isn't it funny how now things come back that I was so sure I'd forgotten like this moment of high school chemistry. Sublimation that's the word the act of turning into something you never expected to become.

The room it was so white that it hurt the backs of my eyeballs. Your hands were like hummingbirds or butterflies *Stay with us Lucius* you said but it was harder and harder to hear you and I could only feel you instead your hummingfly hands your butter-bird fingers.

They talk about white lights and tunnels and there was a part of me expecting to see oh I'll just say it outright Shay but none of that was true. Instead it was Him and He was holding out His hand and reaching for me. He was just like I remembered coffee skin ebony eyes five o'clock shadow that dimple too deep for tears and I saw how foolish I had been. How could I not have known it would be Him how could I not have known that you see God every time you look at the face of the person you love.

There were so many things I expected Him to say to me now when it counted the most. *I love you. I missed you.* But instead He smiled at me with those white teeth those white wolf's teeth and He said *I forgive you Lucius I forgive you.*

Your hands pounded and pumped at me your electricity shot through my body but you could not reclaim my heart it already belonged to someone else. He spread the fingers of His hand a star a beacon and I went to him. *I am coming I am coming.*

Wait for me.

Maggie

'I wouldn't have called you in here on a Sunday, normally,' Warden Coyne said to me, 'but I thought you'd want to know . . .' He closed the door to his office for privacy. 'Lucius DuFresne died last night.'

I sank down into one of the chairs across from the warden's desk. 'How?'

'AIDS-related pneumonia.'

'Does Shay know?'

The warden shook his head. 'We thought that might not be the best course of action at this moment.'

What he meant, of course, was that Shay was already in an observation cell for slamming his own head into a wall – they didn't need to give him even more reason to be upset. 'He could hear about it from someone else.'

'That's true,' Coyne said. 'I can't stop rumors.'

I remembered the reporters glorifying Lucius's initial cure – how would this turn the tide of public opinion against Shay even more? If he wasn't a messiah, then – by default – he was only a murderer. I glanced up at the warden. 'So you asked *me* here so I could break the bad news to him.'

'That's your call, Ms Bloom. I asked you here to give you this.' He reached into his desk and removed an envelope. 'It was with Lucius's personal effects.'

The manila envelope was addressed to Father Michael and me in shaky, spiderweb handwriting. 'What is it?'

'I didn't open it,' the warden said.

I unhinged the clasp of the envelope and reached inside. At first I thought I was looking at a magazine advertisement of a painting – the detail was that precise. But a closer look showed that this was a piece of card stock; that the pigment wasn't oil, but what seemed to be watercolor and pen.

It was a copy of Raphael's *Transfiguration*, something I only knew because of an art history course I'd taken when I fancied myself in love with the TA who ran the class sessions – a tall, anemic guy with ski-slope cheekbones who wore black, smoked clove cigarettes, and wrote Nietzsche quotes on the back of his hand. Although I didn't really care about sixteenth-century art, I'd gotten an A, trying to impress him – only to discover he had a live-in lover named Henry.

The *Transfiguration* was thought to be Raphael's last painting. It was left unfinished and was completed by one of his students. The upper part of the painting shows Jesus floating above Mt Tabor with Moses and Elijah. The bottom part of the painting shows the miracle of the possessed boy, waiting for Jesus to cure him, along with the Apostles and the other disciples.

Lucius's version looked exactly like the painting I'd seen slides of in a darkened amphitheater – until you looked closely. Then you noticed that my face was superimposed where Moses's should have been. Father Michael was standing in for Elijah. The possessed boy – there, Lucius had drawn his self-portrait. And Shay rose in white robes above Mt Tabor, his face turned upward.

I slipped the painting back into the envelope carefully and looked at the warden. 'I'd like to see my client,' I said.

Shay stepped into the conference room. 'Did you get the verdict?'

'Not yet. It's still the weekend.' I took a deep breath. 'Shay, I have some bad news for you. Lucius died last night.'

The light faded from his face. 'Lucius?'

'I'm sorry.'

'He was . . . getting better.'

'I guess he wasn't, really. It only looked that way,' I said. 'I know you thought you helped him. I know you *wanted* to help him. But Shay, you couldn't have. He was dying from the moment you met him.'

'Like me,' Shay said.

He bent over, as if the hand of grief were pushing hard on him, and started to cry – and that, I realized, was going to be my undoing. Because when you got right down to it, what was different between Shay and everyone else in this world was not nearly as profound as what we had in common. Maybe my hair was brushed, and I could string words together to make a sentence. Maybe I hadn't been convicted of murder. But if someone told me that the only friend I really had in this world had left it, I'd sink to my knees, sobbing, too.

'Shay,' I said, at a loss, approaching him. How come there were no words for this kind of comfort?

'Don't touch me,' Shay growled, his eyes feral. I ducked at the last moment as he swung at me, and his fist punched through the double pane of glass that separated us from the officer standing watch. 'He wasn't supposed to die,' Shay cried, as his hand bled down the front of his prison scrubs like a trail of regret. A small army of officers rushed in to save me and secure him, and then haul him off to the infirmary for stitches, proof – as if either of us needed it – that Shay was not invincible.

One year in junior high, during a sex-ed unit, our teacher discussed the painfully obvious fact that some of us would not mature as quickly as our classmates. This was not a lesson you had to teach someone like me, whose waistline was larger than her bra size; or Cheryl Otenski, who had gotten her period in full view of every other sixth grader during an assembly where she happened to be wearing white pants. 'Late bloomers,' the teacher called it – that was close enough to my last name for me to be the butt of every joke for the remaining week.

I had told my mother I had the bubonic plague and refused to get out of bed for three days, spending most of it under the covers and wishing I could just miraculously skip ahead ten or fifteen years to when my life surely would be more pleasant.

After seeing Shay, I was sorely tempted to pull the same act. If I stayed in bed when the verdict was read, did that mean the plaintiff lost by default?

Instead of driving to my house, however, I found myself pointing in the opposite direction and turned into the emergency entrance of the hospital. I felt as if I'd been poleaxed, which surely qualified me for medical attention – but I didn't think that even the most gifted physician could cure a skeptic who'd come to see the light: I could not remain as emotionally unattached from my client as I'd believed. This wasn't, as I'd told myself, about the death penalty in America. It wasn't about my career as a litigator. It was about a man I'd been sitting next to – a man whose scent I could recognize (Head & Shoulders shampoo and pungent industrial soap); whose voice was familiar (rough as sandpaper, with words dropped like stepping-stones) – who would, very shortly, be dead. I did not know Shay Bourne well, but that didn't mean he would not leave a hole in my life when he exited his own.

'I need to see Dr Gallagher,' I announced to the triage nurse. 'I'm a personal . . .'

What?

Friend?

*Girl*friend?

Stalker?

Before the nurse could rebuff me, however, I saw Christian coming down the hall with another doctor. He noticed me and – before I could even make a decision to go to him – he came to me. 'What's wrong, sweetheart?'

No one except my father had ever called me that. For this reason, and a dozen others, I burst into tears.

Christian folded me into his arms. 'Follow me,' he said, and led me by the hand into an empty family waiting room.

'The governor denied Shay's stay of execution,' I said. 'And Shay's best friend died, and I was the one who had to tell him.

And *he's* going to die, Christian, because he won't let me try to find new evidence to exonerate him.' I drew away from him, wiping my eyes on my sleeve. 'How do you do it? How do you let go?'

'The first patient who died on my table,' Christian said, 'was a seventy-six-year-old woman who came in complaining of abdominal pain after a meal at a posh London restaurant. A half hour into the surgery, she coded, and we couldn't bring her back.' He looked up at me. 'When I went into the family waiting area to speak with her husband, the man just kept staring at me. Finally, I asked him if he had any questions, and he said he'd taken his wife to dinner to celebrate their fiftieth wedding anniversary.' Christian shook his head. 'That night, I sat with her body in the morgue. Silly, I know, but I thought that on one's fiftieth anniversary, one didn't deserve to spend the night alone.'

If I hadn't been swayed before by Christian's charm, good looks, or the way he called the trunk of his car a boot and the hood a bonnet, I was now completely smitten.

'Here's the thing,' Christian added. 'It doesn't get any easier, no matter how many times you go through it. And if it does – well, I suspect that means you've lost some part of yourself that's critically important.' He reached for my hand. 'Let me be the attending physician at the execution.'

'You can't,' I said automatically. Killing a man was a violation of the Hippocratic oath; doctors were contacted privately by the Department of Corrections, and the whole event was kept secret. In fact, in the other executions I'd studied before Shay's trial, the doctor's name was never mentioned – not even on the death certificate.

'Let me worry about that,' Christian said.

I felt a fresh wave of tears rising. 'You would do that for Shay?'

He leaned forward and kissed me lightly. 'I would do that for you,' he said.

*   *   *

If this had been a trial, here were the facts I'd present to the jury:

1. Christian had suggested that he swing by my house after his shift, just to make sure I wasn't falling apart at the seams.
2. He was the one who brought the bottle of Penfolds.
3. It would have been downright rude to refuse to have a glass. Or three.
4. I truly could not establish the causal line between how we went from kissing on the couch to lying on the carpet with his hands underneath my shirt, and me worrying about whether or not I was wearing underwear that was a step above granny panties.
5. Other women – those who have sex with men more often than once during a senatorial term, for example – probably have a whole set of underwear just for moments like these, like my mother has a set of Sabbath china.
6. I was truly hammered if I had just thought of *sex* and *my mother* in the same sentence.

Maybe the details here weren't nearly as important as the outcome – I had a man in my bed, right now, waiting for me. He was even more beautiful without clothes on than he was in them. And where was I?

Locked in the bathroom, so paralyzed by the thought of my disgusting, white, fish-bellied body being seen by him that I couldn't open the door.

I had been discreet about it – lowering my lashes and murmuring something about changing. I'm sure Christian assumed I meant slipping into lingerie. Me, I was thinking more along the lines of morphing into Heidi Klum.

Bravely, I unbuttoned my blouse and stepped out of my jeans. There I was in the mirror, in my bra and panties, just like a bikini – except I wouldn't be caught dead in a bikini. *Christian sees a hundred bodies a day,* I told myself. *Yours can't be any worse than those.*

But. Here was the ripple of cottage cheese cellulite that I usually avoided by dressing in the dark. Here was the inch (or two) that I could pinch with my fingers, which vanished beneath a waistband. Here was my butt, large enough to colonize, which could so craftily be camouflaged by black trousers. Christian would take one look at the acoustic version of me and run screaming for the hills.

His voice came, muffled, through the bathroom door. 'Maggie?' Christian said. 'Are you all right in there?'

'I'm fine!' *I'm fat.*

'Are you coming out?'

I didn't answer that. I was looking inside the waistband of my pants. They were a twelve, but that didn't count, because this label had resized downward so that fourteens like me could feel better about themselves for being able to squeeze into the brand at all. But hadn't Marilyn Monroe been a size fourteen? Or was that back when a size fourteen was really an eight – which meant that comparatively, I was a behemoth compared to your average 1940s starlet?

Well, hell. I was a behemoth compared to your average 2008 starlet, too.

Suddenly I heard scratching outside the door. It couldn't have been Oliver – I'd put him in his cage when he kept sniffing around our heads as we'd rolled across the living room carpet having our *From Here to Eternity* moment. To my horror, the locked doorknob popped open and began to twist.

I grabbed my ratty red bathrobe from the back of the door and wrapped it around myself just in time to see the door swing open. Christian stood there, holding a wire hanger with its neck straightened.

'You can pick locks, too?' I said.

Christian grinned. 'I do laparoscopic surgery through belly buttons,' he explained. 'This isn't dramatically different.'

He folded his arms around me and met my gaze in the mirror. 'I can't say come back to bed, because you haven't been in it yet.'

His chin notched over my shoulder. 'Maggie,' he murmured, and at that moment he realized that I was wearing a robe.

Christian's eyes lit up and his hands slipped down to the belt. Immediately, I started to tug him away. 'Please. Don't.'

His hands fell to his sides, and he took a step back. The room must have cooled twenty degrees. 'I'm sorry,' Christian said, all business. 'I must have misread—'

'No!' I cried, facing him. 'You didn't misread anything. I want this. I want *you*. I'm just afraid that . . . that . . . you won't want *me*.'

'Are you *joking*? I've wanted you since the moment I didn't get to examine you for appendicitis.'

'Why?'

'Because you're smart. And fierce. And funny. And so beautiful.'

I smiled wryly. 'I almost believed you, until that last part.'

Christian's eyes flashed. 'You truly think you're not?' In one smooth motion, before I could stop him, he yanked the wide shawl collar of the robe down to my elbows, and my blouse along with it. My arms were trapped; I stood before him in my underwear. 'Look at you, Maggie,' he said with quiet awe. 'My God.'

I could not look at myself in the mirror, so instead, I looked at Christian. He wasn't scrutinizing breasts that sagged or a waist that was too thick or thighs that rubbed together when the temperature climbed above eighty degrees. He was just staring at me, and as he did, his hands began to shake where they touched me.

'Let me show you what I see when I look at you,' Christian said quietly. His fingers were warm as they played over me, as they coaxed me into the bedroom and under the covers, as they traced the curves of my body like a roller coaster, a thrill ride, a wonder. And somewhere in the middle of it all, I stopped worrying about sucking in my stomach, or if he could see me in the half-light of the moon, and instead noticed how seamlessly we fit together; how when I let go of me, there was only room for us.

*   *   *

Wow.

I woke up with the sun slicing the bed like a scalpel, and every muscle in my body feeling like I'd started training for a triathlon. Last night could effectively be classified as a workout, and to be honest, it was the first exercise routine I could see myself really looking forward to on a daily basis.

I smoothed my hand over the side of the bed where Christian had slept. In the bathroom, I heard the shower being turned off. The door opened, and Christian's head popped out. He was wearing a towel. 'Hi,' he said. 'I hope I didn't knock you up.'

'Well. I, uh, hope so, too . . .' Christian frowned, confused, and I realized that we were not speaking the same language. 'Let me guess,' I said. 'Where you come from, that doesn't mean getting a girl pregnant?'

'Good God, no! It's, you know, rousing someone from their sleep.'

I rolled onto my back and started laughing, and he sank down beside me, the towel slipping dangerously low. 'But since I've knocked you up,' he said, leaning down to kiss me, 'maybe I could try my hand at knocking you up . . .'

I had morning breath and hair that felt like a rat had taken nest in it, not to mention a courtroom verdict to attend, but I wrapped my arms around Christian's neck and kissed him back. Which was about the same moment that a phone began to ring.

'Bloody hell,' Christian muttered, and he swung over the far side of the bed to where he'd folded his clothes in a neat pile, his cell phone and pager resting on top. 'It's not mine,' he said, but by then I'd wrapped his discarded towel around me and hiked to my purse in the living room to dig out my own.

'Ms Bloom?' a woman's voice said. 'This is June Nealon.'

'June,' I said, immediately sobering. 'Is everything all right?'

'Yes,' she said, and then, 'No. Oh, God. I can't answer that question.' There was a beat of silence. 'I can't take it,' June whispered.

'I can't imagine how difficult all this waiting has been for you,'

I said, and I meant it. 'But we should know definitively what's going to happen by lunchtime.'

'I can't take it,' June repeated. 'Give it to someone else.'

And she hung up the phone, leaving me with Shay's heart.

Michael

There were only seven people attending Monday morning Mass, and I was one of them. I wasn't officiating – it was my day off, so Father Walter was presiding, along with a deacon named Paul O'Hurley. I participated in the Lord's Prayer and the sign of peace, and I realized these were the moments Shay had missed: when people came *together* to celebrate God. You might be able to find Him on your own spiritual journey, but it was a lonelier trip. Coming to church felt like validation, like a family where everyone knew your flaws, and in spite of that was still willing to invite you back.

Long after Father Walter finished Mass and said his good-byes to the congregants, I was still sitting in a pew. I wandered toward the votive candles, watching the tongues of their flames wag like gossips. 'I didn't think we'd see you today, with the verdict and all,' Father Walter said, walking up to me.

'Yeah,' I said. 'Maybe that's why I needed to come.'

Father Walter hesitated. 'You know, Mikey, you haven't been fooling anyone.'

I felt the hair stand up on the back of my neck. 'No?'

'You don't have to be embarrassed about having a crisis of faith,' Father Walter said. 'That's what makes us human.'

I nodded, not trusting myself to respond. I wasn't having a crisis of faith; I just didn't particularly think Father Walter was any more right in his faith than Shay was.

Father Walter reached down and lit one of the candles, murmuring a prayer. 'You know how I see it? There's always going to be bad stuff out there. But here's the amazing thing – light trumps darkness, every time. You stick a candle into the dark, but you can't stick the dark into the light.' We both watched the flame reach higher, gasping for oxygen, before settling comfortably. 'I guess from my point of view, we can choose to be in the dark, or we can light a candle. And for me, Christ is that candle.'

I faced him. 'But it's not just candles, is it? There are flashlights and fluorescent bulbs and bonfires . . .'

'Christ says that there are others doing miracles in His name,' Father Walter agreed. 'I never said there might not be a million points of light out there – I just think Jesus is the one who strikes the match.' He smiled. 'I couldn't quite understand why you were so surprised when you thought God had showed up, Mikey. I mean, when *hasn't* He been here?'

Father Walter started to walk back down the church aisle, and I fell into step beside him. 'You got time for lunch in the next few weeks?' he asked.

'Can't,' I said, grinning. 'I'll be doing a funeral.' It was a joke between priests – you couldn't schedule anything when your plans were likely to be changed by the lives and deaths of your parishioners.

Except this time, as I said it, I realized it wasn't a joke. In days, I'd be presiding over Shay's funeral.

Father Walter met my gaze. 'Good luck today, Mike. I'll be praying.'

Out of the blue I remembered the Latin words that had been combined to create *religion*: *re + ligere*. I had always assumed they translated to *reconnect*. It was only when I was at seminary that I learned the correct translation was to *bind*.

Back then, I hadn't seen a difference.

When I first arrived at St Catherine's, I was given the task of hosting a heart: St Jean Marie Baptiste Vianney's, to be precise – a French priest who'd died in 1859, at the age of seventy-three. Forty-five years later, when his body was exhumed, the priest's heart had not decayed. Our parish had been chosen as the U.S. location for the heart's veneration; thousands of Catholics from the Northeast were expected to view the organ.

I remembered being very stressed out, and wondering why I had to battle police lines and roadblocks when I had turned to the priesthood to get *closer* to God. I watched Catholics file into our little church and disrupt our Mass schedule and our confession schedule. But after the doors were locked and the onlookers gone, I'd stare down at the glass case with the organ sealed inside. The real wonder, to me, was the course of events that had brought this ancient relic all the way across an ocean to be venerated. Timing was everything. After all, if they hadn't dug up the saint's body, they never would have known about his heart, or told others. A miracle was only a miracle if someone witnessed it, and if the story was passed along to someone else.

Maggie sat in front of me with Shay, her back straight as a poker, her wild mane of hair tamed into a bun at the base of her neck. Shay was subdued, shuffling, fidgety. I glanced down at my lap, which held a manila envelope Maggie had passed me – a piece of art left behind by Lucius DuFresne, who'd passed away over the weekend. There had also been a note on a piece of lined paper:

June has refused the heart. Have not told Shay.

If, on a long shot, we won this case – how would we break the news to Shay that we still could not give him what he so desperately wanted?

'All rise,' a U.S. marshal called.

Maggie glanced at me over her shoulder and offered a tight smile, and the entire courtroom got to its feet while Judge Haig entered.

It was so quiet that I could hear the tiny electronic gasps of the video equipment as the judge began to speak. 'This is a unique case in New Hampshire's history,' Haig said, 'and possibly a unique case in the federal court system. The Religious Land Use and Institutionalized Persons Act certainly protects the religious freedoms of a person confined to an institution such as Mr Bourne, but that doesn't mean that such a person can simply claim that any of his beliefs constitutes a true religion. For example, imagine what would happen if a death row inmate announced that by the tenets of his religion, he had to die of old age. Therefore, when balancing the religious rights of inmates against the compelling governmental interest of the state, this court is mindful of more than just the monetary cost, or even the security cost to other inmates.'

The judge folded his hands. 'That being said . . . we are not in the habit in this country of allowing the government to define what a church is, or vice versa. And that puts us at a standstill – unless we can develop a litmus test for what religion really is. So how do we go about doing *that*? Well, all we have to work with is history. Dr Fletcher posed similarities between Gnosticism and Mr Bourne's beliefs. However, Gnosticism is not a flourishing religion in today's world climate – it's not even an *existing* religion in today's world climate. Although I don't presume to be the expert on the history of Christianity that Dr Fletcher is, it seems to me a stretch to connect the belief system of an individual inmate in a New Hampshire state prison to a religious sect that's been dead for nearly two thousand years.'

Maggie's hand slipped back through the slatted rails that separated the first row of the gallery from the plaintiff's table. I snatched the folded note she held between her fingers. *WE'RE SCREWED*, she had written.

'Then again,' the judge continued, 'some of Mr Bourne's observations about spirituality and divinity seem awfully familiar. Mr Bourne believes in one God. Mr Bourne thinks salvation is linked to religious practice. Mr Bourne feels that part of the contract between man and God involves personal sacrifice. All of these are very familiar concepts to the average American who is practicing a mainstream religion.'

He cleared his throat. 'One of the reasons religion *doesn't* belong in a courtroom is because it's a deeply personal pursuit. Yet, ironically, something Mr Bourne said struck a chord with this court.'

Judge Haig turned to Shay. 'I am not a religious man. I have not attended a service for many years. But I do believe in God. My own practice of religion, you could say, is a nonpractice. I personally feel that it's just as worthy on a weekend to rake the lawn of an elderly neighbor or to climb a mountain and marvel at the beauty of this land we live in as it is to sing hosannas or go to Mass. In other words, I think every man finds his own church – and not all of them have four walls. But just because this is how I choose to fashion my faith doesn't mean that I'm ignorant about formal religion. In fact, some of the things I learned as a young man studying for his bar mitzvah resonate with me even now.'

My jaw dropped. Judge Haig was Jewish?

'There's a principle in Jewish mysticism called *tikkun olam*,' he said. 'It means, literally, world repair. The idea is that God created the world by containing divine light in vessels, some of which shattered and got scattered all over. It's the job of humanity to help God by finding and releasing those shards of light – through good deeds and acts. Every time we do, God becomes more perfect – and we become a little more like God.

'From what I understand, Jesus promised his believers entry into the Kingdom of Heaven – and urged them to prepare through love and charity. The bodhisattva in Buddhism promises to wait for liberation until all who suffer have been freed. And apparently, even those long-gone Gnostics thought that a spark of divinity was inside all of us. It seems to me that no matter what religion you subscribe to, acts of kindness are the stepping-stones to making the world a better place – because we become better people in it. And that sounds, to me, a bit like why Mr Bourne wants to donate his heart.'

Did it really matter whether you believed that Jesus spoke the words in the Bible or the words in the Gospel of Thomas? Did it matter whether you found God in a consecrated church or a penitentiary or even in yourself? Maybe not. Maybe it only mattered that you not judge someone else who chose a different path to find meaning in his life.

'I find under the Religious Land Use and Institutionalized Persons Act of 2000 that Shay Bourne has a valid and compelling religious belief that he must donate his organs at the time of his death,' Judge Haig pronounced. 'I further find that the State of New Hampshire's plan to execute Mr Bourne by lethal injection imposes a substantial burden on the ability to exercise his religious practices, and that they therefore must comply with an alternate means of execution, such as hanging, that will allow organ donation to be medically feasible. Court's adjourned, and I want to see counsel in my chambers.'

The gallery exploded in a riot of noise, as reporters tried to get to the attorneys before they left to meet with the judge. There were women sobbing and students punching their fists in the air, and in the back of the room, someone had begun to sing a psalm. Maggie reached over the bar to embrace me, and then quickly hugged Shay. 'I gotta run,' she said, and Shay and I were left staring at each other.

'Good,' he said. 'This is good.'

I nodded and reached out to him. I had never embraced Shay before, and it was a shock to me – how strong his heart beat against my own chest, how warm his skin was. 'You have to call her,' he said. 'You have to tell the girl.'

How was I supposed to explain that Claire Nealon didn't want his heart?

'I will,' I lied, the words staining his cheek like Judas's kiss.

Maggie

Wait until I told my mother that Judge Haig was not Catholic, like Alexander, but Jewish. No doubt it would inspire her to give me the speech again about how, with time and perseverance, I could be a judge, too. I had to admit, I liked his ruling – and not just because it had come out in favor of my client. His words had been thoughtful, unbiased, not at all what I expected.

'All right,' Judge Haig said, 'now that the cameras aren't on us, let's just cut the crap. We all know that this trial wasn't about religion, although you found a lovely legal coatrack to hang your complaint on, Ms Bloom.'

My mouth opened and closed, sputtering. So much for thoughtful and unbiased; Judge Haig's spirituality, apparently, was the kind that made itself present only when the right people were there to see it.

'Your Honor, I firmly believe in my client's religious freedoms —'

'I'm sure you do,' the judge interrupted. 'But get off your high horse so we can settle this business.' He turned to Gordon Greenleaf. 'Is the state really going to appeal this for a hundred and twenty dollars?'

'Probably not, Judge, but I'd have to check.'

'Then go make a phone call,' Judge Haig said, 'because there's a family out there who deserves to know what's going to happen, and when. Are we clear on that?'

'Yes, Judge,' we both parroted.

I left Gordon in the hallway, hunched over his cell phone, and headed downstairs to the holding cell where Shay was most likely still incarcerated. With each step, I moved a little more slowly. What did you say to the man whose imminent death you'd just set in motion?

He was lying on the metal bench in the cell, facing the wall. 'Shay,' I said, 'you okay?'

He rolled toward me and grinned. 'You did it.'

I swallowed. 'Yeah. I guess I did.' If I had gotten my client the verdict he wanted, why did I feel like I was going to be sick?

'Did you tell her yet?'

He was talking about June Nealon, or Claire Nealon – which meant that Father Michael had not had the guts to tell Shay the truth either, yet. I pulled up a chair and sat down outside the cell. 'I spoke to June this morning,' I said. 'She said Claire's not going to be using your heart.'

'But the doctor told me I was a match.'

'It's not that she *can't* use it, Shay,' I said quietly. 'It's that she doesn't *want* to.'

'I did everything you wanted!' Shay cried. 'I did what you asked!'

'I know,' I said. 'But again, this doesn't have to be the end. We can try to see what evidence still exists from the crime scene and—'

'I wasn't *talking* to you,' Shay said. 'And I don't want you to do anything for me. I don't want that evidence reviewed. How many times do I have to tell you?'

I nodded. 'I'm sorry. It's just . . . hard for me to be riding on the coat-tails of your death wish.'

Shay glanced at me. 'No one asked you to,' he said flatly.

He was right, wasn't he? Shay didn't ask me to take on his case; I'd swooped down like an avenging angel and convinced him that what I wanted to do could somehow help him do what he wanted to do. And I'd been right – I'd raised the profile of the nature of death penalty cases; I'd secured his right to be hanged. I just hadn't realized that winning would feel, well, quite so much like losing.

'The judge . . . he's made it possible for you to donate your organs . . . afterward. And even if Claire Nealon doesn't want them, there are thousands of people in this country who do.'

Shay sank onto the bunk. 'Just give it all away,' he murmured. 'It doesn't matter anymore.'

'I'm sorry, Shay. I wish I knew why she changed her mind.'

He closed his eyes. 'I wish you knew how to change it back.'

Michael

Priests get used to the business of death, but that doesn't make it any easier. Even now that the judge had ruled in favor of a hanging, that still meant there was a will to be written. A body to be disposed of.

As I stood in the prison waiting room, handing over my license so that I could visit Shay, I listened to the commotion outside. This was nothing new; the mob would grow at leaps and bounds through the date of Shay's execution. 'You don't understand,' a woman was pleading. 'I have to see him.'

'Take a number, sweetheart,' the officer said.

I looked out the open window, trying to see the woman's face. It was obscured by a black scarf; her dress reached from ankle to wrist. I burst through the front door and stood behind the line of correctional officers. 'Grace?'

She looked up, tears in her eyes. 'They won't let me in. I have to see him.'

I reached over the human barrier of guards and pulled her forward. 'She's with me.'

'She's not on Bourne's visitor list.'

'That's because,' I said, 'we're going to see the warden.'

I had no idea how to get someone who had not had a background check done into the prison, but I figured that rules would be relaxed for a death row prisoner. And if they weren't, I was willing to say what I had to to convince the warden.

In the end, Warden Coyne was more amenable than I expected.

He looked at Grace's driver's license, made a call to the state's attorney's office, and then offered me a deal. I couldn't take Grace into the tier, but he was willing to bring Shay out to an attorney-client conference room, as long as he remained handcuffed. 'I'm not going to let you do this again,' he warned, but that hardly mattered. We both knew that Shay didn't have time for that.

Grace's hands shook as she emptied her pockets to go through the metal detector. We followed the officer to the conference room in silence, but as soon as the door was closed and we were left alone, she started to speak. 'I wanted to come to the courthouse,' Grace said. 'I even drove there. I just couldn't get out of the car.' She faced me. 'What if he doesn't want to see me?'

'I don't know what frame of mind he'll be in,' I said honestly. 'He won his trial, but the mother of the heart recipient doesn't want him to be the donor anymore. I'm not sure if his attorney's told him that yet. If he refuses to see you, that might be why.'

Only a few minutes passed before two officers brought Shay into the room. He looked hopeful, his fists clenched tight. He saw my face, and then turned – expecting Maggie, most likely. He'd probably been told there were two visitors, and figured one of us had managed to change June's mind.

As he saw his sister, however, he froze. 'Gracie? Is that you?'

She took a step forward. 'Shay. I'm sorry. I'm so, so sorry.'

'Don't cry,' he whispered. He went to lift his hand to touch her, but he was handcuffed, and instead just shook his head. 'You grew up.'

'The last time I saw you I was only fifteen.'

He smiled ruefully. 'Yeah. I was fresh out of juvy jail, and you wanted nothing to do with your loser brother. I think your exact words were "Get the hell away from me."'

'That's because I didn't – I hadn't—' She was sobbing hard now. 'I don't want you to die.'

'I *have* to, Grace, to make things right . . . I'm okay with that.'

'Well, *I'm* not.' She looked up at him. 'I want to tell someone, Shay.'

He stared at her for a long moment. 'All right,' Shay said. 'But only one person, and I get to pick. And,' he added, 'I get to do this.' He reached for the tail of the veil wrapped around her face, which was level with his bound hands. Tugging, he unraveled it, until it fluttered to the ground between them.

Grace brought her hands up to cover her face. But Shay reached up as far as he could in his chains until Grace threaded her fingers with his. Her skin was pocked and puckered, a whirlpool in some places, too tight in others, a relief map of the topology of regret.

Shay ran his thumb over the spot where her eyebrow should have been, where her lip twisted, as if he could repaint her. The look on his face was so honest, so replete, that I felt like I was intruding. I had seen it before – I just couldn't place it.

And then it came to me. A Madonna. Shay was staring at his sister the same way Mary looked at Jesus in all the paintings, all the sculptures – a relationship carved out of not what they had, but what they'd been destined to lose.

June

I had never seen the woman who came into Claire's hospital room, but I'd never forget her. Her face was horribly disfigured – the kind that you're always telling your kids not to stare at in the grocery store, and yet, when push came to shove, you found yourself doing that very thing.

'I'm sorry,' I said quietly, standing up from the chair I'd pulled beside Claire's bed. 'I think you must have the wrong room.' Now that I had agreed to Claire's wishes and given up the heart – now that she was dying by degrees – I kept a vigil, 24/7. I didn't sleep, I didn't eat, because years from now, I knew I would miss those minutes.

'You're June Nealon?' the woman asked, and when I nodded, she took a step forward. 'My name is Grace. I'm Shay Bourne's sister.'

You know how when you're driving and skid on ice, or just avoid hitting the deer, you find yourself with your heart racing and your hands shaking and your blood gone to ice? That's what Grace's words did to me. 'Get out,' I said, my jaw clenched.

'Please. Just hear me out. I want to tell you why I . . . why I look this way.'

I glanced down at Claire, but who was I kidding? We could scream at the top of our lungs and not disturb her; she was in a medically induced haze. 'What makes you think I want to listen?'

She continued, as if I hadn't spoken at all. 'When I was thirteen, I was in a fire. So was my whole foster family. My foster father, he died.' She took a step forward. 'I ran in to try to get my foster father out. Shay was the one who came to save me.'

'Sorry, but I can't quite think of your brother as a hero.'

'When the police came, Shay told them he'd set the fire,' Grace said.

I folded my arms. She hadn't said anything yet that surprised me. I knew that Shay Bourne had been in and out of the foster care system. I knew that he'd been sent to juvenile prison. You could throw ten thousand more excuses for a sorry childhood on his shoulders, and in my opinion, it still wouldn't negate the fact that my husband, my baby, had been killed.

'The thing is,' Grace said, 'Shay lied.' She pushed her hand through her hair. 'I'm the one who set the fire.'

'My daughter is dying,' I said tightly. 'I'm sorry you had such a traumatic past. But right now, I have other things to focus on.'

Undaunted, Grace kept speaking. 'It would happen when my foster mom went to visit her sister. Her husband would come to my bedroom. I used to beg to leave my lights on at night. At first, it was because I was afraid of the dark; then later it was because I so badly wanted someone to see what was happening.' Her voice trailed off. 'So one day, I planned it. My foster mother was gone overnight, and Shay was – I don't know where, but not home. I guess I didn't think about the consequences until after I lit the match – so I ran in to try to wake my foster dad up. But someone dragged me back out – Shay. And as the sirens got closer I told him everything and he promised me he'd take care of it. I never thought he meant to take the blame – but he wanted to, because he hadn't been able to rescue me before.' Grace glanced up at me. 'I don't know what happened that day, with your husband, and your little girl, and my brother. But I bet, somehow, something went wrong. That Shay was trying to save her, the way he couldn't save me.'

'It's not the same,' I said. 'My husband would never have hurt Elizabeth like that.'

'My foster mother said that, too.' She met my gaze. 'How would you have felt if – when Elizabeth died – someone told you that you can't have her back, but that a part of her could still be some-where in the world? You may not know that part; you may not ever have contact with it – but you'd know it was out there, alive and well. Would you have wanted that?'

We were both standing on the same side of Claire's bed. Grace Bourne was almost exactly my height, my build. In spite of her scars, it felt like looking into a mirror. 'There's still a heart, June,' she said. 'And it's a good one.'

We pretend that we know our children, because it's easier than admitting the truth – from the minute that cord is cut, they are strangers. It's far easier to tell yourself your daughter is still a little girl than to see her in a bikini and realize she has the curves of a young woman; it's safer to say you are a good parent who has all the right conversations about drugs and sex than to acknowledge there are a thousand things she would never tell you.

How long ago had Claire decided that she couldn't fight any longer? Did she talk to a friend, a diary, Dudley, because I didn't listen? And had I done this before: ignored another daughter, because I was too afraid to hear what she had to say?

Grace Bourne's words kept circling around my mind: *My foster mother said that, too.*

No. Kurt would *never*.

But there were other images clouding my mind, like flags thrown on a grassy field: the pair of Elizabeth's panties that I found inside a couch cushion liner when she was too little to know how to work a zipper. The way he often needed to search for something in the bathroom – Tylenol, an Ace bandage – when Elizabeth was in the tub.

And I heard Elizabeth, every night, when I tucked her in. 'Leave the lights on,' she'd beg, just like Grace Bourne had.

I had thought it was a phase she'd outgrow, but Kurt said we couldn't let her give in to her fears. The compromise he suggested was to turn off the light – and lie down with her until she fell asleep.

What happens when I'm asleep? she'd asked me once. *Does everything stop?*

What if that had not been the dreamy question of a seven-year-old still figuring out this world, but a plea from a child who wanted to escape it?

I thought of Grace Bourne, hiding behind her scarves. I thought of how you can look right at a person and not see them.

I realized that I might never know what had really happened between them – neither Kurt nor Elizabeth could tell. And Shay Bourne – well, no matter what he saw, his fingerprints had still been on that gun. After last time, I did not know if I could ever bear to face him again.

She was better off dead, he'd said, and I'd run away from what he was trying to tell me.

I pictured Kurt and Elizabeth together in that coffin, his arms holding her tight, and suddenly I thought I was going to throw up.

'Mom,' Claire said, her voice thin and wispy. 'Are you okay?'

I put my hand on her cheek, where there was a faint flush induced by the medicine – her heart was not strong enough to put a bloom on her face. 'No, I'm not,' I admitted. 'I'm dying.'

She smiled a little. 'What a coincidence.'

But it wasn't funny. I was dying, by degrees. 'I have to tell you something,' I said, 'and you're going to hate me for it.' I reached for her hand and squeezed it tightly. 'I know it isn't fair. But you're the child, and I'm the parent, and I get to make the choice, even though the heart gets to beat in your chest.'

Her eyes filled with tears. 'But you said – you *promised*. Don't make me do this . . .'

'Claire, I cannot sit here and watch you die when I know that there's a heart waiting for you.'

'But not just any heart.' She was crying now, her head turned away from me. 'Did you think at all what it will be like for me, after?'

I brushed her hair off her forehead. 'It's all I think about, baby.'

'That's a lie,' Claire argued. 'All you ever think about is yourself, and what *you* want, and what *you've* lost. You know, you're not the only one who missed out on a real life.'

'That's exactly why I can't let you throw this one away.'

Slowly, Claire turned to face me.

'I don't want to be alive because of him.'

'Then stay alive because of *me*.' I drew in my breath and pulled my deepest secret free. 'See, I'm not as strong as you are, Claire. I don't think I can stand to be left behind again.'

She closed her eyes, and I thought she had drifted back into sleep, until she squeezed my hand. 'Okay,' she said. 'But I hope you realize I may hate you for the rest of my life.'

The rest of my life. Was there any other phrase with so much music in it? 'Oh, Claire,' I said tightly. 'That's going to be a long, long time.'

'God is dead: but considering the state Man is in,
there will perhaps be caves, for ages yet,
in which his shadow will be shown.'

— *FRIEDRICH NIETZSCHE, THE GAY SCIENCE*

Michael

When inmates tried to kill themselves, they'd use the vent. They would string coaxial cables from their television sets through the louvers, wrap a noose around their necks, and step off the metal bunk. For this reason, one week before Shay's execution, he was transferred to an observation cell. There was a camera monitoring his every move; an officer was stationed outside the door. It was a suicide watch, so that a prisoner could not kill himself before the state had its turn.

Shay hated it – it was all he talked about as I sat with him for eight hours a day. I'd read from the Bible, and from the Gospel of Thomas, and from *Sports Illustrated*. I'd tell him about the plans I'd made for the youth group to host a Fourth of July pie auction, a holiday that he would not be around to celebrate. He would act like he was listening, but then he'd address the officer standing outside. 'Don't you think I deserve some privacy?' he'd yell. 'If you only had a week left, would you want someone watching you every time you cried? Ate? Took a piss?'

Sometimes he seemed resigned to the fact that he was going to die – he'd ask me if I really thought there was a heaven, if you could catch stripers or rainbows or salmon there, if fish even *went* to heaven in the first place, if fish souls were just as good eating as the real kind. Other times he sobbed so hard that he made himself sick; he'd wipe his mouth on the sleeve of his jumpsuit and lie down on the bunk, staring up at the ceiling. The only thing that got him through those darker times was talking about Claire Nealon, whose mother had reclaimed Shay's heart. He had a grainy newspaper photo of Claire, and by now, he'd run his hands over it so often that the girl's pale face had become a blank white oval, features left to the imagination.

The scaffold had been built; throughout the prison you could smell the sap of the pine, taste the fine sawdust in the air. Although there had indeed already been a trapdoor in the chaplain's office, it proved too costly to decimate the cafeteria below it, which accommodated the drop. Instead, a sturdy wooden structure went up beside the injection chamber that had already been built. But when editorials in the *Concord Monitor* and the *Union Leader* criticized the barbarism of a public execution (they speculated that any paparazzi capable of crashing Madonna's wedding in a helicopter would also be able to get footage of the hanging), the warden scrambled to conceal the scaffold. On short order, their best arrangement was to purchase an old big-top tent from a family-run Vermont circus that was going out of business. The festive red and purple stripes took up most of the prison courtyard. You could see its spire from Route 93: *Come one, come all. The greatest show on earth.*

It was a strange thing, knowing that I was going to see Shay's death. Although I'd witnessed the passing of a dozen parishioners; although I'd stood beside the bed while they took their last breaths – this was different. It wasn't God who was cutting the thread of this life, but a court order. I stopped wearing my watch and kept time by Shay's life instead. There were seventy-two hours left, forty-eight, and then twenty-four. I stopped sleeping, like Shay, choosing instead to stay up with him around the clock.

Grace continued to visit once a day. She would only tell me that what had separated them before was a secret – something that had apparently been resolved after she visited June Nealon – and that she was making up for the time she'd lost with her brother. They spent hours with their heads bent together, trading memories, but Shay was adamant that he didn't want Grace at the execution – he did not want that to be her last memory of him.

Instead, Shay's designated witnesses would be me, Maggie, and Maggie's boss. When Grace came for her visit, I'd leave her alone with Shay. I would go to the staff cafeteria and grab a soda, or sit and read the newspaper. Sometimes I watched the news coverage of the upcoming execution – the American Medical Association had begun to protest outside the prison, with huge banners that read FIRST DO NO HARM. Those who still believed that Shay was, well, more than just a murderer began to light candles at night, thousands of them, spelling out a message that burned so brightly airplane pilots departing from Manchester could read it as they soared skyward: HAVE MERCY.

Mostly, I prayed. To God, to Shay, to anyone who was willing to listen, frankly. And I hoped – that God, at the last minute, would spare Shay. It was hard enough ministering to a death row inmate when I'd believed him to be guilty, but it was far worse to minister to an innocent man who had resigned himself to death. At night, I dreamed of train wrecks. No matter how loud I shouted for someone to throw the switch to the rail, no one understood what I was saying.

On the day before Shay's execution, when Grace arrived, I excused myself and wandered into the courtyard between buildings, along the massive perimeter of the circus tent. This time, however, the officers who usually stood guard at the front entrance were missing, and the flap that was usually laced shut was pinned open instead. I could hear voices inside:

. . . don't want to get too close to the edge . . .

. . . thirty seconds from the rear entrance to the steps . . .

. . . two of you out in front, three in back.

I poked my head in, expecting to be yanked away by an officer – but the small group inside was far too busy to even notice me. Warden Coyne stood on a wooden platform, along with six officers. One was slightly smaller than the rest, and wore handcuffs, ankle cuffs, and a waist chain. He was sagging backward, a deadweight in the other officers' hands.

The gallows itself was a massive metal upright with a crossbeam, set on a platform that had a set of double trapdoors. Below the trap was an open area where you'd be able to see the body drop. Off to both the left and right of the gallows were small rooms with a one-way mirror in the front, so that you could look out, but no one could look in. There was a ramp behind the gallows, and two white curtains that ran the entire length of the tent – one above the gallows, one below it. As I watched, two of the officers dragged the smaller one onto the gallows platform in front of the open curtain.

Warden Coyne pushed a button on his stopwatch. 'And . . . cut,' he said. 'That's seven minutes, fifty-eight seconds. Nicely done.'

The warden gestured to the wall. 'Those red phones are direct hookups to the governor's office and the attorney general – the commissioner will call to make sure there's been no stay of execution, no last-minute reprieve. If that's the case, then he'll come onto the platform and say so. When he exits, I come up and read the warrant of execution, blah blah blah, then I ask the inmate if he has any final words. As soon as he's finished, I walk off the platform. The minute I cross this taped yellow line, the upper curtain will close, and that's when you two secure the inmate. Now, I'm not going to close the curtains right now, but give it a try.'

They placed a white hood over the smaller officer's head and fitted the noose around his neck. It was made of rough rope, wrapped with leather; the loop wasn't made from a hangman's knot, but instead passed through a brass eyelet.

'We've got a drop of seven feet seven inches,' Warden Coyne explained as they finished up. 'That's the standard for a hundred-and-twenty-six-pound man. You can see the adjusting bracket above – that gold mark is where it should be lined up, at the eye bolt. During the actual event, you three – Hughes, Hutchins, and Greenwald – will be in the chamber to the right. You'll have been placed a few hours ahead of time, so that you aren't seen coming into the tent at all. You will each have a button in front of you.

As soon as I enter the control chamber and close the door, you will push that button. Only one of the three actually electromagnetically releases the trapdoor of the gallows; the other two are dummies. Which of the three buttons connects will be determined randomly by computer.'

One of the officers interrupted. 'What if the inmate can't stand up?'

'We have a collapse board outside his cell – modeled after the one used at Walla Walla in '94. If he can't walk, he'll be strapped onto it and wheeled up by gurney.'

They kept saying 'the inmate' as if they did not know who they were executing in twenty-four hours. I knew, though, that the reason they would not say Shay's name was that none of them were brave enough. That would make them accountable for murder – the very same crime for which they were hanging a man.

Warden Coyne turned to the other booth. 'How's that work for you?'

A door opened, and another man walked out. He put his hand on the mock prisoner's shoulder. 'I beg your pardon,' he said, and as soon as he spoke I recognized him. This was the British man who'd been at Maggie's apartment when I barged in to tell her Shay was innocent – Gallagher, that was his name. He took the noose and readjusted it around the smaller man's neck, but this time he tightened the knot directly below the left ear. 'You see where I've snugged the rope? Make sure it's here, not at the base of the skull. The force of the drop, combined with the position of the knot, is what's meant to fracture the cervical vertebrae and separate the spinal cord.'

Warden Coyne addressed the staff again. 'The court's ordered us to assume brain death based on the measured drop and the fact that the inmate has stopped breathing. Once the doctor gives us the signal, the lower curtains will close as well, and the body gets cut down immediately. It's important to remember that our job doesn't end with the drop.' He turned to the doctor. 'And then?'

'We'll intubate, to protect the heart and other organs. After that, I'll perform a brain perfusion scan to fully confirm brain death, and we'll remove the body from the premises.'

'After the criminal investigation unit comes in and clears the execution, the body will go to the medical examiner's staff – they'll have an unmarked white van behind the tent,' the warden said, 'and the special operations unit will transport the body back to the hospital, along with them.'

I noticed that the warden did not speak the doctor's name, either.

'The rest of the visitors will be exiting from the front of the tent,' Warden Coyne said, pointing to the opened flaps of the doorway and spotting me for the first time.

Everyone on the gallows platform stared at me. I met Christian Gallagher's gaze and he nodded imperceptibly. Warden Coyne squinted, and as he recognized me, he sighed. 'I can't let you in here, Father,' he said, but before the officers could escort me out, I had already slipped from the tent and back into the building where Shay was even now waiting to die.

That night, Shay was moved to the death tent. They had built a single cell there, one that would be manned round the clock. At first, it was just like any other cell . . . but two hours into his stay there, the temperature began to plummet. Shay kept shivering, no matter how many blankets were piled upon him.

'The thermostat says it's sixty-six degrees,' the officer said, smacking the bulb with his hand. 'It's May, for chrissake.'

'Well, does it *feel* like sixty-six degrees to you?' I asked. My toes were numb. There was an icicle hanging from the bottom rung of my stool. 'Can we get a heater? Another blanket?'

The temperature continued to drop. I put on my coat and zipped it tight. Shay's entire body was racked with tremors; his lips had started to turn blue. Frost swirled on the metal door of the cell, like a white feathered fern.

'It's ten degrees warmer outside this building,' the officer said. 'I don't get it.' He was blowing on his hands, a small exclamation of breath that hovered in the air. 'I could call maintenance . . .'

'Let me into the cell,' I ordered.

The officer blinked at me. 'I can't.'

'Why? I've been searched twice over. I'm not near any other inmates. And *you're* here. It's no different than a meeting in an attorney-client conference room, is it?'

'I could get fired for this . . .'

'I'll tell the warden it was my idea, and I'll be on my best behavior,' I said. 'I'm a priest. Would I lie to you?'

He shook his head and unlocked the cell with an enormous Folger Adam key. I heard the tumblers click into place as he secured me inside; as I entered Shay's six-by-six world. Shay glanced up at me, his teeth chattering.

'Move over,' I said, and sat down on the bunk beside him. I draped a blanket over us and waited until the heat from my body conducted through the slight space between us.

'Why . . . is it so . . . cold?' Shay whispered.

I shook my head. 'Try not to think about it.'

Try not to think about the fact that it is subzero in this tiny cell. Try not to think about the fact that it backs up to a gallows from which you will swing tomorrow. Try not to think about the sea of faces you will see when you stand up there, about what you will say when you are asked to, about your heart pounding so fast with fear that you cannot hear the words you speak. Try not to think about that same heart being cut from your chest, minutes later, when you are gone.

Earlier, Alma the nurse had come to offer Shay Valium. He'd declined – but now I wished I'd taken her up on his behalf.

After a few minutes, Shay stopped shaking so violently – he was down to an occasional tremor. 'I don't want to cry up there,' he admitted. 'I don't want to look weak.'

I turned to him. 'You've been on death row for eleven years. You've fought – and won – the right to die on your own terms.

Even if you had to *crawl* up there tomorrow, there's not a single person who'd think of you as weak.'

'Are they all still out there?'

By *they*, he meant the crowds. And they were – and were still coming, blocking the exits off 93 to get into Concord. In the end, and this *was* the end, it did not matter whether or not Shay was truly messianic, or just a good showman. It mattered that all of those people had someone to believe in.

Shay turned to me. 'I want you to do me a favor.'

'Anything.'

'I want you to watch over Grace.'

I had already assumed he'd ask that; an execution bound people together much like any other massive emotional moment – a birth, an armed robbery, a marriage, a divorce. I would be linked to the parties involved forever. 'I will.'

'And I want you to have all my things.'

I could not imagine what this entailed – his tools, maybe, from when he was a carpenter? 'I'd like that.' I pulled the blanket up a little higher. 'Shay, about your funeral.'

'It really doesn't matter.'

I had tried to get him a spot in the St Catherine's cemetery, but the committee in charge had vetoed it – they did not want the grave of a murderer resting beside their loved ones. Private plots and burials were thousands of dollars – thousands that neither Grace nor Maggie nor I had to spend. An inmate whose family did not make alternate plans would be buried in a tiny graveyard behind the prison, a headstone carved only with his correctional facility number, not his name.

'Three days,' Shay said, yawning.

'Three days?'

He smiled at me, and for the first time in hours, I actually felt warm to the core. 'That's when I'm coming back.'

At nine o'clock on the morning of Shay's execution, a tray was brought up from the kitchen. Sometime during the night, the frost had broken; and with it, the cement that had been poured for the base of the holding cell. Weeds from the courtyard sprouted in tufts and bunches; vines climbed up the metal wall of the cell door. Shay took off his shoes and socks and walked across the new grass barefoot, a big smile on his face.

I had moved back to my outside stool, so that the officer watching over Shay would not get into trouble, but the sergeant who arrived with the food was immediately wary. 'Who brought in the plants?'

'No one,' the officer said. 'They just sort of showed up overnight.'

The sergeant frowned. 'I'm going to tell the warden.'

'Yeah,' the officer said. 'Go on. I'm sure he's got nothing else to think about right now.'

At his sarcasm, Shay and I looked at each other and grinned. The sergeant left, and the officer handed the tray through the trap-door. Shay uncovered the items, one by one.

Mallomars. Corn dogs. Chicken nuggets.

Kettle corn and cotton candy, s'mores.

Curly fries, ice cream crowned with a halo of maraschino cherries. Fry bread sprinkled with powdered sugar. A huge blue Slurpee.

There was more than one man could ever eat. And it was all the sort of food you got at a country fair. The sort of food you remembered from your childhood.

If, unlike Shay, you'd had one.

'I worked on a farm for a while,' Shay said absently. 'I was putting up a timber-frame barn. One day, I watched the guy who ran it empty the whole sack of grain out into the middle of the pasture for his steers, instead of just a scoop. I thought that was so cool – like Christmas, for them! – until I saw the butcher's truck drive up. He was giving them all they could eat, because by then, it didn't matter.'

Shay rolled the French fry he'd been holding between his fingers, then set it back on the plate. 'You want some?'

I shook my head.

'Yeah,' he said softly. 'I guess I'm not so hungry, either.'

*   *   *

Shay's execution was scheduled for ten a.m. Although death penalty sentences used to be carried out at midnight, it felt so cloak-and-dagger that now they were staggered at all times of the day. The family of the inmate was allowed to visit up to three hours prior to the execution, although this was not an issue, since Shay had told Grace not to come. The attorney of record and the spiritual advisor were allowed to stay up to forty-five minutes prior to the execution.

After that, Shay would be alone, except for the officer guarding him.

After the breakfast tray was removed, Shay got diarrhea. The officer and I turned our backs to give him privacy, then pretended it had not happened. Shortly afterward, Maggie arrived. Her eyes were red, and she kept wiping at them with a crumpled Kleenex. 'I brought you something,' she said, and then she saw the cell, overrun with vegetation. 'What's this?'

'Global warming?' I said.

'Well. My gift's a little redundant.' Maggie emptied her pockets, full of grass, Queen Anne's lace, lady's slippers, Indian paintbrushes, buttercups.

She fed them to Shay through the metal mesh on the door. 'Thank you, Maggie.'

'For God's sake, don't *thank* me,' Maggie said. 'I wish this wasn't the way it ended, Shay.' She hesitated. 'What if I—'

'No.' Shay shook his head. 'It's almost over, and then you can go on to rescuing people who want to be rescued. I'm okay, really. I'm ready.'

Maggie opened her mouth to speak, but then pressed her lips together and shook her head. 'I'll stand where you can see me.'

Shay swallowed. 'Okay.'

'I can't stay. I need to make sure that Warden Coyne's talked to the hospital, so that everything happens like it's supposed to.'

Shay nodded. 'Maggie,' he said, 'promise me something?'

'Sure, Shay.'

He rested his head against the metal door. 'Don't forget me.'

'Not a chance,' Maggie said, and she pressed her lips against the metal door, as if she could kiss Shay good-bye.

Suddenly, we were alone, with a half hour stretching between us.

'How are you doing?' I asked.

'Um,' Shay said. 'Never better?'

'Right. Stupid question.' I shook my head. 'Do you want to talk? Pray? Be by yourself?'

'No,' Shay said quickly. 'Not that.'

'Is there anything I can do?'

'Yeah,' he said. 'Tell me about her again.'

I hesitated. 'She's at the playground,' I said, 'pumping her legs on a swing. When she gets to the top, and she's sure her sneakers have actually kicked a cloud, she jumps off because she thinks she can fly.'

'She's got long hair, and it's like a flag behind her,' Shay added.

'Fairy-tale hair. So blond it's nearly silver.'

'A fairy tale,' Shay repeated. 'A happy ending.'

'It is, for her. You're giving her a whole new life, Shay.'

'I'm saving her again. I'm saving her twice. Now with my heart, and once before she was ever born.' He looked directly at me. 'It wasn't just Elizabeth he could have hurt. She got in the way, when the gun went off . . . but the other . . . I had to do it.'

I glanced over my shoulder at the officer standing watch, but he had moved to a far corner and was speaking into his walkie-talkie. My words were thick, rubbery. 'Then you *did* commit capital murder.'

Shay shrugged. 'Some people,' he said simply, 'deserve to die.'

I stood, speechless, as the officer approached. 'Father, I'm really sorry,' he said, 'but it's time for you to leave.'

At that moment, the sound of bagpipes filled the tent, and an accompanying swell of voices. The people outside, maintaining their vigil, had begun to sing:

Amazing Grace, how sweet the sound . . .
That saved a wretch like me.
I once was lost, but now I'm found.
Was blind, but now I see.

I didn't know if Shay was guilty of murder, or innocent and misunderstood. I didn't know if he was the Messiah, or a savant who channeled texts he'd never read. I didn't know if we were making history, or only reliving it. But I did know what to do: I motioned Shay forward, closed my eyes, and made the sign of the cross on his forehead. 'Almighty God,' I murmured, 'look on this your servant, lying in great weakness, and comfort him with the promise of life everlasting, given in the resurrection of your Son Jesus Christ our Lord. Amen.'

I opened my eyes to find Shay smiling. 'See you around, Father,' he said.

Maggie

As soon as I left Shay's cell, I stumbled out of the circus tent – that's what this was, you know, a *circus* – and threw up on the grass in the courtyard.

'Hey,' a voice said, 'you all right?' I felt an arm steadying me, and I glanced into the dizzying sunlight to find Warden Coyne, looking just as unhappy to see me as I was to see him.

'Come on,' he said. 'Let's get you a glass of water.'

He led me through dark, dismal corridors – corridors far more suited to an execution, I thought, than the beautiful spring day outside, with its brilliant blue sky and tufted clouds. In the empty staff cafeteria, he pulled out a chair for me, then went to the cooler to get me something to drink. I finished the whole cup of water, and still could taste the bitterness in my throat.

'Sorry,' I said. 'Didn't mean to vomit on your parade.'

He sat down in a chair beside me. 'You know, Ms Bloom, there's a hell of a lot about me you don't know.'

'Nor do I want to,' I said, standing.

'For example,' Warden Coyne continued blithely, 'I don't really believe in the death penalty.'

I stared at him, snapped my mouth shut, and sank back into my chair.

'I used to, don't get me wrong. And I'll perform an execution if I have to, because it's part of my job. But that doesn't mean I condone it,' he said. 'Truth is, I've seen plenty of inmates for whom life in prison is just as well served. And I've seen inmates I *wish* would be killed – there are just some people you cannot find the good in. But who am I to decide if someone should be killed for murdering a child . . . instead of for murdering a drug addict during a deal that went bad . . . or even if we should be killing the inmate himself? I'm not smart enough to be able to say which life is worth more than the other. I don't know if anyone is.'

'If you know it's not fair, and you still do this, how do you sleep at night?'

Warden Coyne smiled sadly. 'I don't, Ms Bloom. The difference between you and me is that *you* expect me to be able to.' He got to his feet. 'I trust you know where you go from here?'

I was supposed to wait at the Public Information Office, along with Father Michael, so that we could be brought to the tent apart from the witnesses for the state and the victim. But somehow, I knew that wasn't what Warden Coyne had meant.

And even more surprising . . . I think he knew that I knew that.

The inside of the circus tent was painted with blue sky. Artificial clouds rose into the peaks, above the black iron of the gallows that had been constructed. I wondered if Shay would look at it and pretend that he was outside.

The tent itself was divided by a line of correctional officers, who kept the witnesses for both sides separated, like a human dam. We had been warned about our behavior in the letters from the Department of Corrections: any name-calling or inappropriate actions would result in us being hauled out of the tent. Beside me, Father Michael was praying a rosary. On my other side sat Rufus Urqhart, my boss.

I was shocked to see June Nealon sitting quietly in the front row across from us.

Somehow I'd assumed she'd be with Claire, especially given the fact that Claire would be getting ready for her heart transplant. When she'd called to tell me she wanted Shay's heart, I hadn't asked any questions – I hadn't wanted to jinx it. Now I wished I could go over to her and ask whether Claire was all right, if everything was on schedule – but I would run the risk of the officers thinking I was harassing her; and truth be told, I was afraid to hear her answer.

Somewhere behind that curtain, Christian was checking to make sure the rope and noose were exactly as they should be to ensure as humane a hanging as possible. I knew this was supposed to comfort me, but to be honest, I had never felt more alone in my life.

It was a hard thing, accepting to myself that I had befriended someone convicted of murder. Lawyers knew better than to become emotionally and personally involved with their clients – but that didn't mean it didn't happen.

At exactly ten o'clock, the curtains opened.

Shay seemed very small on the gallows platform. He wore a white T-shirt, orange scrub pants, and tennis shoes, and was flanked by two officers I'd never seen before. His arms were fastened behind him, and his legs were bound together with what looked like a strap of leather.

He was shaking like a leaf.

Commissioner Lynch walked onto the platform. 'There has been no stay of execution,' he announced.

I thought about Christian's hands checking the knot against Shay's neck. I knew the mercy of his touch; I was grateful that Shay's last physical contact with a human would be gentle.

The warden stepped onto the platform as Lynch exited, and he read the entire warrant aloud. The words slipped in and out of my mind:

. . . *Whereas on the sixth day of March, 1997, Isaiah Matthew Bourne was duly and legally convicted of two counts of the crime of capital murder . . .*

. . . *said court pronounced sentence upon Isaiah Matthew Bourne in accordance with said judgment fixing the time for the execution for ten a.m. on Friday, the twenty-third of May, 2008 . . .*

. . . *command you to execute the aforesaid judgment and sentence by hanging in a manner that produces brain death in said Isaiah Matthew Bourne . . .*

When the warden finished, he faced Shay. 'Inmate Bourne, do you have any final words?'

Shay squinted, until he found me in the front row. He kept his eyes on me for a long moment, and then drifted toward Father Michael. But then he turned to the side of the tent where the witnesses for the victim were gathered, and he smiled at June Nealon. 'I forgive you,' he said.

Immediately afterward, a curtain was drawn. It reached only to the floor of the gallows, and it was a translucent white. I didn't know if the warden had intended for us to see what was happening behind it, but we could, in macabre silhouette: the hood being placed over Shay's head, the noose being tightened against his neck, the two officers who'd secured him stepping backward.

'Good-bye,' I whispered.

Somewhere, a door slammed, and suddenly the trap was open and the body plummeted, one quick firecracker snap as the weight caught at the end of the rope. Shay slowly turned counterclockwise with the unlikely grace of a ballerina, an October leaf, a snowflake falling.

I felt Father Michael's hand on mine, conveying what there were not words to say. 'It's over,' he whispered.

I don't know what made me turn toward June Nealon, but I did. The woman sat with her back straight as a redwood, her hands folded so tightly in her lap that I could see the half-moons her own nails were cutting in her skin. Her eyes were tightly squeezed shut.

After all this, she hadn't even watched him die.

The lower curtain closed three minutes and ten seconds after Shay had been hanged. It was opaque, and we could not see what was happening behind it, although the fabric fluttered with movement and activity. The officers in the tent didn't let us linger, though – they hustled us out separate doors to the courtyard. We were led out of the prison gates and immediately inundated with the press. 'This is good,' Rufus said, pumped up with adrenaline. 'This is our moment.' I nodded, but my attention was focused on June. I could see her only briefly, a tiny crow of a woman ducking into a waiting car.

'Mr Urqhart,' a reporter said, as twenty microphones were held up to his face, a bouquet of black roses. 'Do you have any comment?'

I stepped back, watching Rufus in the limelight. I wished I could just vanish on the spot. I knew that Rufus didn't mean to use Shay as a pawn here, that he was only doing his job as the head of the ACLU – and yet, how did that make him different from Warden Coyne?

'Shay Bourne is dead,' Rufus said soberly. 'The first execution in this state in sixty-nine years . . . in the only first world country to still have death penalty legislation on the books.'

He looked out over the crowd. 'Some people say that the reason we have a death penalty in this country is because we need to punish certain inmates. It's said to be a deterrent – but in fact, murder rates are higher in death penalty jurisdictions than in those without it. It's said to be cheaper to execute a man than to keep him in prison for life – but in fact, when you factor in the cost of eleven years of appeals, paid for with public funds, it costs about a third more to execute a prisoner than to sentence him to life in prison. Some people say that the death penalty exists for the sake of the victims' family – that it offers closure, so that they can deal, finally and completely, with their grief. But does knowing that the death toll has risen above and beyond their family member really offer justice? And how do we explain the fact that a murder in a rural setting is more likely to lead to a death sentence than one that occurs in the city? Or that the murder of a white victim leads to the death penalty three and a half times more often than the murder of a black victim? Or that women are sentenced to death only two-thirds as often as men?'

Before I realized what I was doing, I had stepped into the tiny circle of space that the media had afforded to Rufus. 'Maggie,' he whispered, covering the mikes, 'I'm working this here.'

A reporter gave me my invitation. 'Hey, weren't you his lawyer?'

'Yes,' I said. 'Which I hope means I'm qualified to tell you what I'm going to. I work for the ACLU. I can spout out all the same statistics that Mr Urqhart just did. But you know what that speech leaves out? That I am truly sorry for June Nealon's loss, after all this time. And that today, *I* lost someone I cared about. Someone who'd made some serious mistakes – someone who was a hard nut to crack – but someone I'd made a place for in my life.'

'Maggie,' Rufus hissed, pulling at my sleeve. 'Save the true confessional for your diary.'

I ignored him. 'You know why I think we still execute people? Because, even if we don't want to say it out loud – for the really heinous crimes, we want to know that there's a really heinous punishment. Simple as that. We want to bring society closer together – huddle and circle our wagons – and that means getting rid of people we think are incapable of learning a moral lesson. I guess the question is: Who gets to identify those people? Who decides what crime is so awful that the only answer is death? And what if, God forbid, they get it wrong?'

The crowd was murmuring; the cameras were rolling. 'I don't have children. I can't say I'd feel the same way if one of them was killed. And I don't have the answers – believe me, if I did, I'd be a lot richer – but you know, I'm starting to think that's okay. Maybe instead of looking for answers, we ought to be asking some questions instead. Like: What's the lesson we're teaching here? What if it's different every time? What if justice isn't equal to due process? Because at the end of the day, this is what we're left with: a victim, who's become a file to be dealt with, instead of a little girl, or a husband. An inmate who doesn't want to know the name of a correctional officer's child because that makes the relationship too personal. A warden who carries out executions even if he doesn't think they should happen in principle. And an ACLU lawyer who's supposed to go to the office, close the case, and move on. What we're left with is death, with the

humanity removed from it.' I hesitated a moment. 'So you tell me
. . . did this execution really make you feel safer? Did it bring us all
closer together? Or did it drive us farther apart?'

I pushed past the cameras, whose heavy heads swung like bulls
to follow my path, and into the crowd, which carved a canyon
for me to walk through. And I cried.

God, I cried.

I turned on my windshield wipers on the way home, even though
it was not raining. But I was falling apart at the seams, and sobbing,
and I couldn't see; somehow I thought this would help. I had
upstaged my boss on what was arguably the most important legal
outcome for the New Hampshire ACLU in the past fifty years;
even worse – I didn't particularly care.

I would have liked to talk to Christian, but he was at the hospital
by now, supervising the harvest of Shay's heart and other organs.
He'd said he'd come over as soon as he could, as soon as he had
word that the transplant was going to be a success.

Which meant that I was going home to a house with a rabbit
in it, and not much else.

I turned the corner to my street and immediately saw the car
in my driveway. My mother was waiting for me at the front door.
I wanted to ask her why she was here, instead of at work. I wanted
to ask her how she'd known I'd need her.

But when she wordlessly held out a blanket that I usually kept
on the couch, one with fuzzy fleece inside, I stepped into it and
forgot all my questions. Instead, I buried my face against her neck.
'Oh, Mags,' she soothed. 'It's going to be all right.'

I shook my head. 'It was *awful*. Every time I blink, I can see
it, like it's still happening.' I drew in a shuddering breath. 'It's
stupid, isn't it? Up till the last minute, I was expecting a miracle.
Like in the courtroom. That he'd slip out of the noose, or – I don't
know – fly away or something.'

'Here, sit down,' my mother said, leading me into the kitchen. 'Real
life doesn't work that way. It's like you said, to the reporters—'

'You saw me?' I glanced up.

'On television. Every channel, Maggie. Even CNN.' Her face glowed. 'Four people already called me to say you were brilliant.'

I suddenly remembered sitting in my parents' kitchen when I was in college, unable to decide on a career. My mother had sat down, propped her elbows on the table. *What do you love to do?* she had asked.

Read, I'd told her. *And argue.*

She had smiled broadly. *Maggie, my love, you were meant to become a lawyer.*

I buried my face in my hands. 'I was an idiot. Rufus is going to fire me.'

'Why? Because you said what nobody has the guts to say? The hardest thing in the world is believing someone can change. It's always easier to go along with the way things are than to admit that you might have been wrong in the first place.'

She turned to me, holding out a steaming, fragrant bowl. I could smell rosemary, pepper, celery. 'I made you soup. From scratch.'

'*You* made me soup from scratch?'

My mother rolled her eyes. 'Okay, I *bought* soup someone else made from scratch.'

When I smiled a little, she touched my cheek. 'Maggie,' she said, 'eat.'

Later that afternoon, while my mother did the dishes and cleaned up in my kitchen, and with Oliver curled up at my side, I fell asleep on the living room couch. I dreamed that I was walking in the dark in my favorite Stuart Weitzman heels, but they were hurting me. I glanced down to discover I was not walking on grass, but on a ground that looked like tempered glass after it's been shattered, like the cracked, parched landscape of a desert. My heels kept getting stuck in the crevasses, and finally I had to stop to pull one free.

When I did, a clod of earth overturned, and beneath it was light, the purest, most liquid lava form of it. I kicked at another piece of the ground with my heel, and more beams spilled outward and upward. I poked holes, and rays shined up. I danced, and the world became illuminated, so bright that I had to shade my eyes; so bright that I could not keep them from filling with tears.

June

This, I had told Claire, the night before the surgery, is how they'll transplant the heart:

You'll be brought into the operating room and given general anesthesia.

Grape, she'd said. She liked it way better than bubble gum, although the root beer wasn't bad.

You'll be prepped and draped, I told her. Your sternum will be opened with a saw.

Won't that hurt?

Of course not, I said. You'll be fast asleep.

I knew the procedure as well as any cardiac resident; I'd studied it that carefully, and that long. *What comes next?* Claire had asked.

Sutures – stitches – get sewn into the aorta, the superior vena cava, and the inferior vena cava. Catheters are placed. Then you're put on the heart-lung machine.

What's that?

It works so you don't have to. It drains blue blood from the two cava, and returns red blood through the cannula in the aorta.

Cannula's a cool word. I like how it sounds on my tongue.

I skipped over the part about how her heart would be removed: the inferior and superior vena cava divided, then the aorta.

Keep going.

His heart (no need to say whose) is flushed with cardioplegia solution.

It sounds like something you use to wax a car.

Well, you'd better hope not. It's chock-full of nutrients and oxygen, and keeps the heart from beating as it warms up.

And after that?

Then the new heart goes to its new home, I had said, and I'd tapped her chest. First, the left atriums get sewn together. Then the inferior vena cava, then the superior vena cava, then the pulmonary artery, and finally, the aorta. When all the connections are set, the cross clamp on your aorta is removed, warm blood starts flowing into the coronaries, and . . .

Wait, let me guess: the heart starts beating.

Now, hours later, Claire beamed up at me from her hospital gurney. As the parent of a minor, I was allowed to accompany her to the OR, gowned and suited, while she was put under anesthesia. I sat down on the stool provided by a nurse, amid the gleaming instruments, the shining lights. I tried to pick out the familiar face of the surgeon from his kind eyes, above the mask.

'Mom,' Claire said, reaching for my hand.

'I'm right here.'

'I don't hate you.'

'I know, baby.'

The anesthesiologist fitted the mask to Claire's face. 'I want you to start counting for me, hon. Backward, from ten.'

'Ten,' Claire said, looking into my eyes. 'Nine. Eight.'

Her lids dropped, half-mast. 'Seven,' she said, but her lips went slack on the last syllable.

'You can give her a kiss if you want, Mom,' said a nurse.

I brushed my paper mask against the soft bow of Claire's cheek. 'Come back to me,' I whispered.

Michael

Three days after Shay's death, and two after his funeral, I returned to the prison cemetery. The headstones formed a small field, each one marked with a number. Shay's grave didn't have one yet; it was only a small raw plot of earth. And yet, it was the only one with a visitor. Sitting on the ground, her legs crossed, was Grace Bourne.

I waved as she got to her feet. 'Father,' she said. 'It's good to see you.'

'You, too.' I came closer, smiled.

'That was a nice service you did the other day.' She looked down at the ground. 'I know it didn't seem like I was listening, but I was.'

At Shay's funeral, I hadn't read from the Bible at all. I hadn't read from the Gospel of Thomas, either. I had created my own gospel, the good news about Shay Bourne, and spoke it from the heart to the few people who'd been present: Grace, Maggie, Alma the nurse.

June Nealon had not come; she was at the hospital with her daughter, who was recovering from the heart transplant. She'd sent a spray of lilies to lay on Shay's grave; they were still here, wilting.

Maggie had told me that Claire's doctor had been thrilled with the outcome of the operation, that the heart had started beating like a jackrabbit. Claire would be leaving the hospital by the end of the week. 'You heard about the transplant?' I said.

Grace nodded. 'I know that wherever he is, he's happy about

that.' She dusted off her skirt. 'Well, I was on my way out. I have
to get back to Maine for a seven o'clock shift.'

'I'll call you in a few days,' I said, and I meant it. I had promised Shay that I would look after Grace, but to be honest, I think
he wanted to be sure she'd be looking after me as well. Somehow,
Shay had known that without the Church, I'd need a family, too.

I sat down, in the same spot where Grace had been. I sighed,
leaned forward, and waited.

The problem was, I wasn't sure what I was waiting for. It had
been three days since Shay's death. He had told me he was coming
back – a resurrection – but he had also told me that he'd murdered
Kurt Nealon intentionally, and I couldn't hold the two thoughts
side by side in my mind.

I didn't know if I was supposed to be on the lookout for an
angel, like Mary Magdalene had seen, to tell me that Shay had
left this tomb. I didn't know if he'd mailed me a letter that I could
expect to receive later that afternoon. I was waiting, I suppose,
for a sign.

I heard footsteps and saw Grace hurrying toward me again. 'I
almost forgot! I'm supposed to give this to you.'

It was a large shoe box, wrapped with a rubber band. The green
cardboard had begun to peel away from the corners, and there
were spots that were watermarked. 'What is it?'

'My brother's things. The warden, he gave them to me. But there
was a note inside from Shay. He wanted you to have them. I would
have given it to you at the funeral, but the note said I was supposed
to give it to you *today*.'

'You should have these,' I said. 'You're his family.'

She looked up at me. 'So were you, Father.'

When she left, I sat back down beside Shay's grave. 'Is this it?'
I said aloud. 'Is this what I was supposed to wait for?'

Inside the box was a canvas roll of tools, and three packages
of Bazooka bubble gum.

He had one piece of gum, I heard Lucius say, *and there was enough
for all of us.*

The only other item inside was a small, flat, newspaper-wrapped package. The tape had peeled off years ago; the paper was yellowed with age. Folded in its embrace was a tattered photograph that made me catch my breath: I held in my hands the picture that had been stolen from my dorm when I was in college: my grandfather and I showing off our day's catch.

Why had he taken something so worthless to a stranger? I touched my thumb to my grandfather's face and suddenly recalled Shay talking about the grandfather he'd never had – the one he'd imagined from this photo. Had he swiped it because it was proof of what he'd missed in his life? Had he stared at it, wishing he was me?

I remembered something else: the photo had been stolen before I was picked for Shay's jury. I shook my head in disbelief. It was possible Shay had known it was me when he saw me sitting in the courtroom. It was possible he had recognized me again when I first came to him in prison. It was possible the joke had been on me all along.

I started to crumple up the newspaper that the photo had been wrapped in, but realized it wasn't newspaper at all. It was too thick for that, and not the right size. It was a page torn out of a book. *The Nag Hammadi Library*, it read across the top, in the tiniest of print. *The Gospel of Thomas*, first published 1977. I ran a fingertip along the familiar sayings. *Jesus said: Whoever finds the interpretation of these sayings will not experience death.*

Jesus said: The dead are not alive, and the living will not die.

Jesus said: Do not tell lies.

Jesus said.

And so had Shay, after having years to memorize this page.

Frustrated, I tore it into pieces and threw them on the ground.

I was angry at Shay; I was angry at myself. I buried my face in my hands, and then felt a wind stir. The confetti of words began to scatter.

I ran after them. As they caught against headstones, I trapped them with my hands. I stuffed them into my pockets. I untangled them from the weeds that grew at the edge of the cemetery. I chased one fragment all the way to the parking lot.

Sometimes we see what we want to, instead of what's in front of us. And sometimes, we don't see clearly at all. I took all of the bits I'd collected and dug a shallow bowl beneath the spray of lilies, covered them with a thin layer of soil. I imagined the yellowed paper dissolving in the rain, being absorbed by the earth, lying fallow under winter snow. I wondered what, next spring, would take root.

'There are only two ways to live your life.
One is as though nothing is a miracle.
The other is as though everything is a miracle.'

— *ALBERT EINSTEIN*

EPILOGUE
Claire

I have been someone different now for three weeks. It's not some-thing you can tell by looking at me; it's not even something I can tell by looking at myself in the mirror. The only way I can describe it, and it's weird, so get ready, is like waves: they just crash over me and suddenly, even if I'm surrounded by a dozen people, I'm lonely. Even if I'm doing everything I want to, I start to cry.

My mother says that emotion doesn't get transplanted along with the heart, that I have to stop referring to it as *his* and start calling it *mine*. But that's pretty hard to do, especially when you add up all the stuff I have to take just to keep my cells from recog-nizing this intruder in my chest, like that old horror movie with the woman who has an alien inside her. Colace, Dulcolax, pred-nisone, Zantac, enalapril, CellCept, Prograf, oxycodone, Keflex, magnesium oxide, nystatin, Valcyte. It's a cocktail to keep my body fooled; it's anyone's guess how long this ruse might continue.

The way I see it, either my body wins and I reject the heart — or I win.

And become who he used to be.

My mother says that I'm going to work through all this, and that's why I have to take Celexa (oh, right, forgot that one) and talk to a shrink twice a week. I nod and pretend to believe her. She's so happy right now, but it's the kind of happy that's like an ornament made of sugar: if you brush it the wrong way, it will go to pieces.

I'll tell you this much: it's so good to be home. And to not have

a lightning bolt zapping me from inside three or four times a day.
And to not pass out and wake up wondering what happened. And
to walk up the stairs – up*stairs*! – without having to stop halfway,
or be carried.

'Claire?' my mother calls. 'Are you awake?'

Today, we have a visitor coming. It's a woman I haven't met,
although apparently she's met me. She's the sister of the man who
gave me his heart; she came to the hospital when I was totally
out of it. I am *so* not looking forward to this. She'll probably break
down and cry (I would if I were her) and stare at me with an
eagle eye until she finds some shred of me that reminds her of
her brother, or at least convinces herself she has.

'I'm coming,' I say. I have been standing in front of the mirror
for the past twenty minutes, without a shirt on. The scar, which
is still healing, is the angriest red slash of a mouth. Every time I
look at it, I imagine the things it might be yelling.

I resettle the bandage that I'm not supposed to peel off but do
when my mother isn't there to see it. Then I shrug into a shirt
and glance down at Dudley. 'Hey, lazybones,' I say. 'Rise and shine.'

The thing is, my dog doesn't move.

I stand there, staring, even though I know what's happened.
My mother told me once, in her dump truck – load of fun facts
about cardiac patients, that when you do a transplant the nerve
that goes from the brain to the heart gets cut. Which means
that it takes people like me longer to respond to situations that
would normally freak us out. We need the adrenaline to kick
in first.

You can hear this and think, *Oh, how nice to stay calm.*

Or you can hear this and think, *Imagine what it would be like to
have a brand-new heart, and be so slow to feel.*

And then, boom, just like that it kicks in. I fall down to my
knees in front of the dog. I'm afraid to touch him. I have been
too close to death; I don't want to go there again.

By now the tears are here; they stream down my face and into
my mouth. Loss always tastes like salt. I bend down over my old,

sweet dog. 'Dudley,' I say. 'Come on.' But when I scoop him up – put my ear against his rib cage – he's cold, stiff, not breathing.

'No,' I whisper, and then I shout it so loud that my mother comes scrambling up the stairs like a storm.

She fills my doorway, wild-eyed. 'Claire? What's wrong?'

I shake my head; I can't speak. Because, in my arms, the dog twitches. His heart starts beating again, beneath my own two hands.

AUTHOR'S NOTE

For those wishing to learn more about the topics in this book, try these sites and texts, which were instrumental to me during this journey.

ABOUT THE DEATH PENALTY

Death Penalty Information Center: www.deathpenaltyinfo.org.

Death Row Support Project, PO Box 600, Liberty Mills, IN 46946. (Contact them if you want to write to a death row prisoner.)

Murder Victims' Families for Human Rights: www.mvfhr.org.

Murray, Robert W. *Life on Death Row*. Albert Publishing Co., 2004.

Prejean, Sister Helen. *Dead Man Walking*. New York: Vintage Books, 1993.

—— . *The Death of Innocents*. New York: Random House, 2005.

Rossi, Richard Michael. *Waiting to Die*. London: Vision Paperbacks, 2004.

Turow, Scott. *Ultimate Punishment*. New York: Picador, 2003.

ABOUT THE GNOSTIC GOSPELS

Pagels, Elaine. *Beyond Belief: The Secret Gospel of Thomas*. New York: Random House, 2003.

—— . *The Gnostic Gospels*. New York: Random House, 1979.

Robinson, James M., ed. *The Nag Hammadi Library*. Leiden, the Netherlands: E. J. Brill, 1978.